Also by
KAREN ROBARDS

Amanda Rose
Dark Torment
Loving Julia
Night Magic
Wild Orchids

Published by
WARNER BOOKS

KAREN ROBARDS

TO LOVE A MAN

WARNER BOOKS

A Time Warner Company

WARNER BOOKS EDITION

Cover design by Diane Luger
Cover illustration by Michael Raez
Hand lettering by Carl Dellacroce

Warner Books, Inc.
1271 Avenue of the Americas
New York, N.Y. 10020

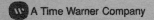 A Time Warner Company

Printed in the United States of America
First Printing: January, 1985
Reissued: March, 1994
10 9 8 7

To my son, Peter Douglas,
born August 30, 1983;
and, as always, to Doug

LISA Collins's slender body was huddled into a compact ball, her face just inches from the dirt floor as she pressed her nose and mouth hard into her bare, grimy arm. Smoke rose all around her, thick black smoke that rolled and curled and rammed oily fingers up her nose and down her throat. Choking, she coughed, desperately muffling the sound. Please God there was no one nearby to hear. If they heard her ... she shuddered. She had no illusion as to what her fate would be.

At least the screaming had stopped. Although she knew she shouldn't be, knew what the silence meant, Lisa was guiltily grateful for that. She had thought she would go mad, listening to the tortured cries of Ian and Mary Blass and their three children as they roasted to death inside the flaming inferno of what had once been their home. If she hadn't been outside when the soldiers came, making a quick, prebed visit to the shed that housed the farm's sanitary facilities, she would have been dead now, too. At the thought her body shook from head to toe. And she hadn't escaped yet, she knew. The killers were still here, all around her, putting the torch to everything, butchering animals as well as humans. The screams of pigs and cows had mingled with those of the Blasses. . . .

They were guerrillas, of course. For which side Lisa couldn't be sure. She had known of Rhodesia's civil war when she had asked for the assignment, but it had seemed like such a heaven-sent chance for escape that she had barely considered the possibility of danger. Besides, she had thought—naïvely, as was now abundantly clear—that her status as an American journalist would protect her. Well, as in so many other things in her life, she'd been wrong. Maybe dead wrong.

The smoke was getting worse every second that she lay there, coiling up under her protective arms to caress her face, doing its best to suffocate her. Lisa knew that she had to make a move, had to run for it while she was still capable of doing so, but the thought of leaving her hiding place, of venturing out into the open space of the yard, paralyzed her. She was mildly surprised to discover that, despite everything, she was not yet ready to die. . . .

On the other side of the thin wall, feet thudded to within inches of her head. Lisa stopped breathing as a man shouted something in an unintelligible language. Somewhere over her head she heard a dull *plonk*. Then, to her overwhelming relief, the footsteps ran on.

Lisa's heart was just regaining its normal rhythm when she became aware of an ominous crackling noise. Lifting her head, she looked around and saw that the whole back end of the shed was bathed in a hot orange glow. Fire! Tiny tongues of flame were licking at the roof, racing for the walls. She no longer had a choice: she had to run for it. Panic welled like vomit in her throat. She was scared—

scared to death. So scared she couldn't move—could she?

She could. Terror became her ally, forcing her cramped limbs to propel her in a low crawl toward the door. Her breath rasped painfully in her throat. Tears made scalding tracks down her face. She was going to die, she knew, right here on this isolated farm in southern Rhodesia. And she was only twenty-five! It wasn't fair! Oh, God, it wasn't fair!

The three feet to the door seemed like three miles. Lisa gagged on the smoke, her back muscles tensing in futile defense against the fire now raging directly above her. All around, small flaming pieces of wood dropped to the ground. Lisa knew that it was just a matter of a few minutes before the roof collapsed— and she would die. Did it hurt to die? she wondered. Of course it did. Think of how the Blasses had screamed. . . .

Her nails dug deep furrows in the dirt floor as she dragged herself forward. If she could just get outside she would live—at least for a little while. But when at last she reached the door she stopped, gasping for precious air as she lay on her stomach on the floor, her mind whirling in frightened circles. What awaited her beyond the door terrified her almost more than the crematorium she faced if she stayed.

"Into your hands, Lord," she whispered finally, and giving herself up to His protection she pushed the door. It moved easily. She opened it just enough so that she could see out. The night air, cool and sweet compared to what was in her lungs, flowed in through the crack, touching her face like a benediction. Lisa gulped it in, loving the pain of it as it chafed her raw throat. Air was wonderful, one part of her mind registered, as her eyes raced fearfully over the scene before her.

It was night, but it wasn't dark. Flames shooting out from the house and barn and various outbuildings illuminated the farmyard so that it was almost as light as day. Everywhere Lisa saw khaki-uniformed men, some standing gloating over the destruction they had wrought, some running through the yard brandishing flaming torches, some loading objects that had obviously been plundered from the farm onto trucks. None of them seemed particularly interested in the burning outhouse. Lisa took a deep, steadying breath. She had a chance, then. Just a chance.

Quick as a snake she was through the door, belly-crawling across the short, tough *takka* grass toward the line of trees that marked the end of the cleared ground. If she could just reach the jungle she could hide.... She might live! The thought, previously so impossible, was intoxicating. Lisa slithered across the ground faster than she had ever dreamed she could move, afraid to look anywhere but directly ahead. Rocks and sharp sticks tore through her jeans and short-sleeved T-shirt and ripped at her skin, but Lisa hardly felt the pain. Her whole consciousness was focused on making it across the arid patch of earth separating her from safety.

She had less than five yards to go when her clawing hand touched flesh ... cold flesh. Lisa looked to her left and froze. Sprawled just inches away was the body of a man—a man she had known. Cholly—that was his name. He'd been sent by Ian Blass to meet her at the small local airport and had driven her the sixteen miles out to the farm, talking volubly all the way. Was it only the day before? Impossible to believe. Now he was dead. Brutally murdered, his body awash in a pool of blood that was even now soaking into the ever-thirsty African soil, leaving behind obscene little clots that clung to his coffee-colored skin and the brown blades of grass.... His throat had been slit. The still-oozing gash stared up at the night sky like a wide, obscene grin where no grin should be. Lisa felt the gorge rise in her throat. Stomach convulsing, she vomited until there was nothing but clear liquid left inside her. Then, blindly, forgetting everything in the face of this newest horror, she lurched to her feet and ran stumbling toward the trees.

By some miracle she made it. But even then she didn't stop, didn't slow her headlong flight. She couldn't. Panic drove her on, plunging through the waist-high undergrowth, mindless of even the inch-long thorns of the lawyer vine that reached out to stab at her. Twice she tripped and fell headlong, but got up to run on. The only thought in her mind was that she had to escape... had to escape... had to—

"Jesus H. Christ, what in the hell is that?"

The savage exclamation brought her head swinging around. Soldiers! More than a dozen of them, standing in a loose cluster not three arms' lengths away. The pitch blackness of the jungle and her own terror had blinded her to their presence until this moment. Oh, God, to let her get so far and no farther was cruel....

Still, she tried. She ran desperately, leaping and twisting through the dense foliage. Behind her she could hear crashing footsteps as they chased her, and then the fast pant of a man's breathing. A flying tackle brought her down at last. Her body jarred deep into the prickly undergrowth, borne down by a man's hard weight. Slewing her head around in a wild attempt at self-defense, she saw the khaki sleeve of a uniform—and screamed. And screamed. And screamed. Until something slammed viciously into her jaw and the world went black.

Lisa dreamed that she was home again, a thoroughly spoiled teenager safe in her grandfather's big house on Chesapeake Bay. She was his pampered darling, his only surviving kin, and nothing in the world was too good for her. The best clothes, the best schools, a car—she had them all. But at nineteen she didn't want them. Or at least they weren't her top priority. Jeff was—Jeff Collins, the dreamily handsome, football-playing son of a state senator. She'd been out with him only twice, but she wanted him forever. And what Lisa wanted, Lisa got.

"What Lisa wanted, Lisa got." Even in her dream Lisa smiled humorlessly at that. She had gone after Jeff with the single-minded tenacity she'd inherited from her publishing-tycoon grandfather, and had wangled a proposal out of Jeff within six months. Their engagement was greeted with enthusiasm by both families. "An ideal match" was what everyone called it. Her own happiness was something Lisa took for granted. For people like herself, the "right" people, that was how life went. Things always worked out the way they were supposed to, and she expected no less than a "happily ever after."

And she had it. For nearly a year. Perhaps their marriage wasn't the shooting-stars-and-ringing-bells romance described in popular fiction, but it was good, solid, based on mutual trust and affection. Or so she told her girl friends. Privately, she began to wonder. Her sheltered upbringing had given her a very limited knowledge of sex—she'd been a virgin when she married, more from lack of opportunity (the best schools were always exclusively female) than any real moral convictions—but the little petting she had done on dates had shown her that physical contact with a man could be enjoyable. With Jeff, it wasn't. There was no getting around that. He didn't enjoy it either, although he tried very hard to hide his lack of enthusiasm. As time went on and things didn't improve, Lisa began to wonder sickly if the problem was *hers,* if perhaps she lacked whatever it was that turned men on. Certainly she didn't light any fires in Jeff, despite the fact that she was an exceptionally lovely girl—everyone said so. Her figure was good, tall and slender and rounded in all the right places. Her face had a delicate perfection of feature that could hardly be faulted. Her shoulder-blade-length ash-blond hair was always clean and shining, she wore only the faintest trace of makeup, in deference to Jeff's taste, to accentuate her tip-tilted green eyes, she smelled good, dressed well—so what was wrong?

She found out two days before her twentieth birthday—the same day she found out that she was pregnant. She had suspected her condition for several weeks, but hadn't wanted to say anything to Jeff until she was absolutely sure. On this particular morning, when the doctor confirmed that she was indeed expecting a child, Lisa canceled her planned lunch out and hurried home with her news, happier than she had been in a long time. To her pleased surprise, Jeff was home. His coat and hat were in the downstairs closet, and seeing them Lisa smiled joyously, anticipating his excitement when she told him that he was going to be a father. She walked up the stairs to their bedroom, still smiling. And sure enough Jeff was there. He was in their king-sized bed, quite naked, and with him was another man.

She would have divorced him then if it hadn't been for the baby, despite the fact that he cried and told her that this was the first time, that men really weren't his thing, that it would never happen again. He had begged her not to tell what she had seen, to give him another chance. Finally she had agreed—because of the baby.

It was the second biggest mistake of her life. She should have left him on the spot. As time went on it got harder and harder, because he was genuinely thrilled about her pregnancy and, after Jennifer was born, devoted to the child. Sweet little Jennifer adored her father from her first breath, and Lisa couldn't find it in her to take the child away. How do you explain to a toddler that Daddy loves other men better than he loves Mommy—because of course he did.

Lisa had been on the point of taking Jennifer and leaving despite everything when the most horrible chapter in the nightmare that had become her life began. Jennifer got leukemia. Not all the hundreds of thousands of dollars in Lisa's trust fund, nor all her grandfather's millions or his endless network of connections were able to save the most precious thing in Lisa's world. Numbly, she could do nothing but watch as her child wasted away, her anguish matched only by Jeff's. They died little by little together, the three of them, until at last it was over and Jennifer lay in a cold, dark grave. After that, Lisa collapsed. It was months before she could pass a day without crying, months before she could come to grips with the fact that her child was dead. Dead. Dead.

After a year she realized that she had to snap out

of it or be as dead as Jennifer. Her lifeline came in the form of a job on the *Annapolis Daily Star,* one of the many newspapers her grandfather owned. She hadn't asked for the job, didn't really want it, in fact, but her grandfather insisted. It was time she did some work for a change, he said, the concern in his eyes belying his gruff tone as he surveyed her too-slender figure and wan face. When Lisa tried to demur, he would have none of it. He needed some-one to cover local society events, he told her, and who better than his own granddaughter, who had been mingling with all the right people since her birth and had entrée into the best homes on equal terms? Lisa shrugged, and assented. The apathy that had shrouded her for months had left her incapable of defying her grandfather's iron will. So, reluctantly, she had started to attend the local luncheons and charity bazaars and hunt balls that had taken up so much of her time before Jennifer's birth. The only difference now was that she reported on who wore what, who said what, and who was with whom for the *Star.* To her surprise, Lisa found that she had quite a gift for writing. Soon she actually began to look forward to getting to work each day. She felt life begin to flow again in her body like sap rising in a tree. She renewed old acquaintances, forgotten in her anguish over Jennifer, and made new friends among the *Star's* staff and elsewhere. Finally she got to the point where she could once more con-template leaving Jeff. Only when she was free of him could she hope to achieve some measure of true happiness, she knew. But still she put it off, dreading her grandfather's reaction, Jeff's parents', their friends'.

When Grace Ballard, the *Star's* feature editor, casually mentioned over lunch one day that an old school friend of hers had married a Rhodesian farmer and was at that moment experiencing all the excitement and adventure of living in that country during its civil war, Lisa had felt only the faintest glimmer of interest. Until Grace had gone on to bemoan the fact that all the *Star*'s stringers in the area were too caught up covering the actual fighting to do the feature story she envisioned—something along the lines of "American Woman Raises Family Amid Bullets, Bombs." It was then that Lisa felt a premonitory quiver at the base of her spine. This was her chance, she realized, both to branch out into writing about something more substantial than weddings and dances, and, more important, to escape.

Speaking casually to hide her mounting excitement, Lisa had volunteered to travel to Rhodesia to get the story. Grace had been at first amused, and then, when she saw that Lisa was serious, horrified. John Landis, the *Star*'s managing editor, had flatly vetoed the idea. After all, he pointed out, Lisa had no real experience as a reporter, and Rhodesia in its current state of chaos was a place for only the most professional—and the hardiest. Finally Lisa was able to force an admission from him that the Blass farm was miles from the fighting, but Landis insisted that it made no difference: the idea was too outlandish, too dangerous, even to consider. But for once in her life, Lisa took advantage of her family connections to pull rank. She went straight from Landis's office to her grandfather and laid her request before him. He looked at her silently for what seemed like a long time, weighing the sudden, blazing life in the green eyes that only weeks ago had been as dull and lifeless as last night's embers, and at last gave his permission. Only as she was leaving his rosewood-paneled office at the back of his sprawling home did he tack on a brusque admonition for her to take care. Lisa nodded, smiling, but in truth she barely heard. That there could seriously be physical danger to her person she barely considered. She was far too elated about this plum that had dropped into her lap. It seemed like the answer to a prayer: the perfect way to make the break with her old life with no one the wiser until it was all over. And of course, as she prepared for the journey, she told no one that she wasn't planning to come back—at least not to Jeff or to the house they shared....

Lisa hurt all over. Pain brought her whimpering back to consciousness. Her skin felt as if it were on fire. Fire....she remembered fire. Was she burning, then? Had she passed out, only imagining that she had managed to escape from the shed? Had...Something sharp pricked her skin, and she flinched.

"Ouch!" she was surprised to hear herself say aloud, and opened her eyes. She was looking into a man's face, a tanned strong face with irregular features and a scar bisecting one cheek. It wasn't a handsome face—until one met the blue, blue eyes.

"So you're awake at last, sleeping beauty." The voice matched the face, very hard and male, with the unexpected overlay of a soft southern drawl. Lisa blinked, not taking her eyes from the man. At her bemused expression he smiled. One long-fingered brown hand came up and very gently smoothed the hair back from her forehead.

"Can you hear me?" he asked. Lisa nodded faintly, still staring. His teeth were slightly uneven, she noted, but they were very, very white in his dark face.

"Where am I?" she whispered. Her voice frightened her because it was so weak.

"You're safe," he said, not really answering, but it was the answer she wanted.

"Who are you?"

"My name's Sam. Sam Eastman. Who are you?"

"Lisa Collins." Her voice sounded as if it were coming from far away. Lisa began to wonder if perhaps she was imagining this whole conversation, if she had imagined the job, the fire, everything that had happened. If perhaps she had lost her mind in her grief over Jennifer's death...

"Are you real?" The suspicious question made him smile again.

"More real than you, I imagine, honey. Do you feel up to talking? Can you tell me if you have people somewhere near, somewhere we can take you?" He sounded kind and concerned. At his deliberate gentleness, Lisa felt hot tears begin to well in her eyes.

"I'm from Maryland," she whispered forlornly.

"Okay." The word was soothing. "Don't cry about it. You've been through a bad time, but you're going to be just fine. Now what you need is rest. I'm going to give you something to help you sleep. Okay?"

"Okay," Lisa echoed with a quavery attempt at a smile. In her present confused state she would have agreed with anything he suggested. It was strange, the effect he had on her. He made her feel safe, safe and protected....

Sam turned away to pick up something from the overturned box that served as a makeshift bedside table. Lisa's eyes never left his face as he turned back to her. Once again something pricked her arm. Groggily she realized that what had pulled her from her dreams had been the jab of a hypodermic needle. She continued to stare at him until the drug took effect and her eyes closed....

When Lisa woke again she became aware of several things at once. One, it was night. Two, she was in a large tent, its green canvas sides illuminated by a battery-powered lamp. Three, she was dressed only in a man's oversized shirt, and lay on an army-issue cot with a blanket over her protecting her from the night air. And four, she hurt.

She tried to sit up. Movement brought pain, but so did not moving. So Lisa persisted, struggling upright, holding herself there with her hands braced against the metal poles that formed the cot's sides. Out of the corner of her eye she caught sight of her arms, bare where the shirt sleeves were rolled up. Her once-smooth flesh was covered with deep scratches and red, angry-looking welts. With a small, incredulous sound, Lisa lifted one hand to touch the ugly marks on the opposite arm, and promptly lost her balance and fell back in the cot.

"Damn!" she swore out loud, not moving for a moment because of the pain that seemed to stab her in a hundred places at once. As soon as she said it, she felt better. It was good to know that at least her voice was back to normal.

"Is that any way for a lady to talk?" a gently mocking voice chided. Lisa looked up quickly as the tent flap parted to reveal a tall, broad-shouldered figure, stooped now as he entered through the opening, which was many inches too short for him. The sight of his khaki uniform made her eyes widen in instinctive fear, and then she looked up to meet the blue eyes and relaxed.

"Hello," she said, feeling ridiculously shy. She made no further attempt to sit up, but lay back in the cot, her blond hair fanned out over the utilitarian pillow and trailing over its side and down toward the floor. A faint, tentative smile of welcome curved her lips.

"Hello," Sam answered gravely, his eyes glinting as

they ran over her. "What was the naughty word in aid of?"

"Oh." Lisa remembered the marks on her arms almost as an afterthought. "I fell over. I was looking at my arms. They look awful—like somebody took a whip to them. What happened?"

"Do you remember running through the jungle?" Lisa nodded.

"Well, it's my guess that you tore up your arms then. You've also got some pretty nasty marks on your back—burns, I think. And bruises everywhere."

"The fire—the Blasses—how long ago was that?" she asked, her throat suddenly constricting.

"Four days." Sam's eyes were steady as they met hers. "We found you in the jungle—or, more properly, you found us—and we brought you back to camp with us. We—uh—went by the farm after we found you. If they were your folks, I'm sorry."

"They weren't." Lisa closed her eyes briefly, swallowing. "I hadn't known them long—less than two days. But they were so nice. . . ."

"Tough." His voice conveyed rough sympathy. Lisa opened her eyes. She didn't want to think about the Blasses. . . .

"Are you a doctor?"

Sam grimaced. "Hardly. I know a little elementary first aid. You pick things like that up, in this line of work."

"What line of work is that?" Lisa asked faintly, although she was afraid she already knew.

"I'm a soldier," he answered, as she had known he would.

"For—for which side?" Lisa hated to think that he might be on the same side as the animals who had attacked the farm.

"At the moment, the government's. But I'm flexible. My men and I are available to anyone who can meet our price."

"Your...price?" Lisa repeated blankly, not understanding. Then, not wanting to, she added hastily, "You're an American, too, aren't you?"

"That's right." His voice was expressionless. Abruptly he hunkered down beside her, his forehead corrugating in a frown as he took one of her arms in his hands.

"You've opened up some of these sores, moving around. Have you done yourself any other damage?"

He laid her arm carefully down beside her, then reached forward to draw the blanket down to her feet. Lisa shrank back instinctively. His eyes flickered to her face, grew thoughtful.

"It's all right, I won't hurt you," he said, rocking back a little on his heels. "But I need to check the burns on your back. You don't want them to get infected, do you?"

"N-no." Lisa met his gaze, held it for a moment, and felt like a fool. After all, the man had clearly been tending her injuries the whole time she'd been unconscious. It would be ridiculous to kick up a fuss at this late date. Besides, she instinctively felt that he was someone she could trust....

"I'm sorry," she murmured contritely. "I know you won't hurt me. It's just...just..."

"Just what?" he prompted when he saw she wasn't going to finish.

"Your uniform," Lisa answered in a rush, averting her head. "The soldiers at the farm...they wore uniforms like that. I'm sorry, I know you weren't one of them, but I can't help it if it makes me feel a little...sick."

Comprehension dawned in his face. He raised his

hand to cup her chin, turning her face toward him, studying it.

"I didn't realize..." he said reflectively. "That's why you ran like a scared little animal when you saw us. And you screamed like you'd gone crazy—I had to knock you out to shut you up."

"You—you hit me?" Lisa asked faintly, suddenly feeling uneasy. What did she know about this man, after all? He was a soldier, which in her opinion was merely a euphemism for a paid killer, and he hit women....

"I had to. You were screeching louder than a four-alarm fire. Another few minutes and the whole rebel army would have known our position." His voice was matter-of-fact. "Now would you mind turning over? I do have other things to do besides playing nursemaid to you."

Dumbly, Lisa complied, lying on her stomach with her face turned away from him. She felt color burn her cheeks as he slid the shirt up over her buttocks and back, stopping in the vicinity of her neck. She cringed at the realization that the whole rear of her body was left naked to his gaze....

He began to smooth a cooling cream into the sores on her back, his touch impersonal and yet oddly comforting. Gradually Lisa began to relax. Soldier or no, to her he'd been unfailingly kind....

"There," he said at last, pulling down the shirt so that she was decently covered and then drawing the blanket over her. Lisa turned so that she faced him, her cheeks still feeling faintly flushed. He noticed her heightened color and grinned, his eyes teasing.

"Hungry?"

Lisa nodded. Come to think of it, she was ravenous. It was possible that the disoriented feeling stealing over her was the result of not having eaten for days.

"I bet you are," he answered, his grin widening. He stood up, his head bowed in the too-small space. "We had pork and beans out of a can for supper. Fancy some?"

"I—I guess." If her voice was doubtful it was simply because she had never eaten pork and beans out of a can before and had no idea whether her stomach would tolerate it. But she was hungry enough at this point to try anything.

Sam was already crossing the rubber-sheeted floor to disappear through the tent flap. She heard him call, "Riley," and then caught just the murmur of his voice as he talked to the other man. In what seemed like seconds he was back, carrying a tin plate piled high with steaming food. Lisa looked at it, smelled the spicy aroma, and was doubtful. Then her stomach rumbled loudly. She flushed with embarrassed surprise, and Sam's lips quirked with humor. But he refrained from making any comment, for which Lisa was grateful.

"Here, let me help you," he said as she struggled into a sitting position. Before she quite realized what he was about, he put down the plate on the overturned box and straddled the end of the cot behind her, pulling her shoulders against him so that his body acted as a back rest. She allowed him to situate her as he wished, leaning back against his chest as trustingly as a child. By the time they were settled, his arms were around her waist and the plate of food rested on her lap.

"Can you manage?" he asked when she made no immediate move to eat, his breath stirring the soft hairs on the top of her head.

Lisa slanted a look back at him, was surprised to

find his face so near, and hurriedly glanced down at her plate.

"Yes, thank you," she murmured, feeling strangely breathless, and without more ado began to eat.

When the food was all gone she rested back against him contentedly, feeling replete. It seemed the most natural thing in the world for her to be held in his arms in such a way. Already she was feeling much better, strength flowing back into her limbs, her head clearing. She felt warm and comfortable—and secure. . . .

Her head was pillowed on the rock hardness of his shoulder, and she swiveled her face around so that she could look up at him.

"You're being very kind to me," she murmured, her eyes wandering curiously over his face. At such close range she could see the fine lines that fanned out from the corners of his blue eyes as well as the deep grooves bracketing his mouth. His skin, she saw, was the color and texture of leather, weathered by the sun and wind, with the jagged, whitened scar she had noticed before cutting across his left cheek. His hair was thick and black, with an apparent tendency to curl, and he wore it cut ruthlessly short. His nose had a bump on the bridge as if it had been broken once and improperly set, his mouth was long and hard with a faintly sensuous-looking lower lip, and his jaw was square and thickly covered with black bristles as if he hadn't shaved in several days. He looked both uncompromisingly masculine and thoroughly disreputable. Lisa was astonished at how totally safe he made her feel.

"Taking inventory?" he drawled, sounding amused. Lisa merely smiled dreamily in reply, allowing herself the luxury of nestling more fully into his arms. It was wonderful to have someone strong and male to hold her, someone who was more than able to protect and care for her. . . .

"Sam?" she murmured, suddenly feeling drowsy. After she said it her eyes flew guiltily back to his. She had not meant to say his name aloud, but merely to test it mentally. . . .

"Lisa," he responded with a shade of mockery, even as his arms tightened their grip on her.

"I must look a terrible mess." The words were said at random. She felt groggy, as if she were floating away on a cloud. Her eyelids were so heavy. . . . They fluttered down, then rose again.

"You look—fine." His voice was suddenly husky. "And now I'd better let you get some sleep. You're dead beat."

"Don't leave me," she protested, surfacing from the oblivion that threatened to claim her and clutching at the hand that still gripped her waist. But he got inexorably to his feet, lowering her gently back into the cot.

"I'll be nearby if you need anything," he said, his voice already sounding far away. Before he turned to leave the tent Lisa had fallen asleep.

Sometime during the night she began dreaming again, vivid, full-color dreams that seemed realer than life. At first they were pleasant, dreams of things she had seen and done as a child, but gradually they turned into nightmares. Finally she had a particularly horrible one about a fanged monster that was chasing her. She knew if it caught her it would kill and eat her. . . . Then fire started shooting from its mouth—red tongues of fire that reached for her, curling around her body, burning her. . . .

Lisa screamed. The sound was ear-shattering and dragged her, shaking, from her nightmare. She lay huddled beneath the blanket, trembling, for the moment not quite sure where she was. The thick darkness she was lost in lightened for an instant into charcoal gray, and she could just make out the outline of a man's broad form silhouetted in the open tent flap. She closed her eyes, not wanting to see it. Maybe it was just another specter from her nightmare. . . .

"Lisa?" The voice was low and familiar. Lisa opened her eyes to see a dark shape looming over her.

"Sam?" The identity of the owner of that voice burst on her like a revelation. Blindly she reached for him, feeling as if she would be safe only if he would hold her in his arms. He bent toward her, and her hands touched bare, muscled shoulders, slid around his neck, and clung, pulling him down with a strength she hadn't realized she possessed.

"Hold me, please, Sam," she whispered brokenly.

"What's wrong, honey?" Strange how that voice had grown so familiar to her in the short time she had known it. It was as if he was her dearest friend, someone known and trusted who could be depended on to keep her safe. . . .

"Oh, Sam, it was awful." The words were muttered shudderingly against his throat, her hands clutching him as if she would never let him go. He came down onto the cot with her, pulling aside the blanket to draw her fully against him. His arms came around her, pressing her to the long, hard length of him. Lisa's own arms stayed locked around his neck.

"Tell me about it," he murmured, his hands stroking her tumbled hair soothingly. She poured out the jumbled story of her nightmare while he held her, stroking her hair, her shoulders, her back. When she got to the part about the fire, she trembled and his grip tightened comfortingly. Lisa buried her face in the hollow of his neck when she finished, drawing a deep, shaking breath and closing her eyes. He said nothing, just continued to hold her, his hands never ceasing their gentle caresses.

After a few moments Lisa became aware of his chest hair tickling her nose. She moved protestingly, but the sensation didn't go away. So she put out her tongue to push it aside, only to encounter the warm, salty-tasting skin of his neck.

Unthinking, she followed her instinct, letting her tongue explore the throbbing hollow and find its way up the strong cord of his neck. Beneath her ear she could hear his heart begin to pound in slow, steady strokes. The sound excited her. Lisa opened her lips against his throat, kissing it. She felt his body tense.

"Lisa..." he said hoarsely, warningly. She kissed his throat again, passionately, refusing to think of anything except how right it felt....

"Love me," she whispered against his skin. "Please, Sam, love me."

Lisa heard the harsh indrawing of his breath with a little glow of satisfaction. It was intoxicating to realize that he wanted her, too....

"Lisa..." He seemed still inclined to argue, so Lisa did what all her senses were clamoring for her to do. She touched him, blind in the pitch darkness, one hand sliding down over his hair-roughened chest, sensuously stroking his flat, hard-muscled belly, coming to rest at the waistband of his pants. There it hesitated for an instant, then slid inside, worming its way across his tightening abdomen to surround the huge, granite monolith that burned and throbbed at her touch.

As her fingers closed on him he groaned, then groaned again, his hands coming up to catch her shoulders and flip her onto her back with such force that she was momentarily robbed of breath. Then he was on top of her, his body hard and heavy, his breath coming in fast, hard pants. His mouth fastened on hers with a greedy passion that seemed to want to devour her. Lisa's lips opened to him endlessly. Their tongues touched, warred, caressed. He kissed her hotly, and with fierce ardor she responded, wanting his possession more than she had ever wanted anything in her life. In the tiny part of her mind that was still capable of functioning, she realized dimly that this was what she needed, what she had been starved of for years: the hard, fierce lovemaking of a man....

His hands were unsteady as they undressed her, popping the buttons from her shirt in his haste. Lisa moaned as his fingers found her breasts, closing over the soft mounds in a grip that should have hurt but didn't. Then he was tugging at his pants and she was helping him, her mouth running greedily over his body, on fire for him. When he too was naked he pushed her back and she went willingly, her legs parting and her hands eager as she guided him to her. He thrust into her with hard urgency, and Lisa gasped with pleasure, thinking she would die of pure bliss. His answering growl inflamed her. She rose and fell with him as he moved in, then out, then in again, in a relentless, driving rhythm. Her head was thrown back, her mouth wide open as he took her, her nails digging mindlessly into his muscled back. There was no room in her head for anything except the wonder of her own need. Then his hands closed over her buttocks, lifting them so that he could thrust more deeply inside her, and his mouth clamped over hers with a harsh groan. Lisa could stand no more. Pleasure that had been denied for years burst gloriously inside her, and she cried out against his mouth. He felt her joy and responded with one final, savage thrust, holding himself inside her, shaking. Then it was over.

Lisa felt herself drifting off with his flesh still joined to hers and his body heavy and wet with sweat as he sprawled across her. Then, just before she gave in to the irresistible urge to sleep, she thought she heard him swear....

II

SAM was coldly furious with himself. He strode away from the tent without a backward glance, slapping irritably at the insects that swarmed to feast on his sweat-dampened bare back and shoulders. Only after he had covered quite a distance did he slow his pace and take a cigarette from the pack in his pants pocket. Flicking a match to life with his thumbnail, he was annoyed all over again to find that his hand was still not quite steady. Dammit to hell, anyway! He knew better! He was here on this flat, grassy plain to do a job, not to play stud to some man-crazy little hotpants. She could cause all kinds of complications if he let her. The only sane solution was to get rid of her, fast, before she disrupted his concentration or, worse, caused trouble with his men.

The question was, how? If he was half as unsentimental as he liked to think, he would simply turn around now, return to her tent, cut her throat, and have done with it. End of problem. But damn himself for a soft fool, he knew full well he couldn't do it. Cold-blooded murder of a beautiful young woman who had just eagerly bedded him was not his line.

He could send her away, of course. But where, and how? Salisbury, with its large, modern airport and jets that could whisk her out of the country, was the obvious where, but that posed additional problems. If she started babbling about her adventure, as she undoubtedly would, she could screw up his whole pitch. Besides, even if he was willing to take a chance that she might, if he asked, keep her mouth shut, how would he get her there? The small airfield nearby was now under the control of the guerrillas, which meant that he would have to send her to Salisbury by jeep. And that was impossible, too. To begin with, he needed every one of his men. They were a small group, specially selected by him for the job at hand, and all vital to its successful conclusion. He could not afford to send one of them careening off across the country as the chauffeur-cum-bodyguard of a stray young woman. Anyway, any move of that sort would be bound to attract a certain amount of attention, and that would be fatal. No, dammit, she would have to stay until the job was done, but he found that solution almost as unacceptable as the others.

A truly decent man would no doubt scrap the whole business rather than endanger a hair of that silvery-blond head, but he had known for years that decency wasn't one of his strong suits. He needed the money, that was the thing; a hundred thousand dollars was nothing to sneeze at. It would give him and Jay a big head start on the kind of life he had always wanted for them, would let them make a down payment on a ranch and stock it with cattle. There was no way he was going to kiss goodbye the chance of a good life for himself and his son just because some sexy little female had managed to get herself mixed up in a situation that might be the death of her. He had done more than anyone could reasonably expect by bringing her back to camp with him, when every vestige of common sense he possessed had urged him to leave her unconscious in the jungle. But some long-buried chivalrous instinct had surfaced, and to the slack-jawed amazement of his men he had picked her up and slung her into the back of the jeep. And, like all impulsive acts, this one was turning into a disaster of major proportions.

From the moment he had carried her into the tent and turned the beam of his flashlight on her, he'd known he had a problem. The red, oozing cuts and welts adorning her body hadn't been enough to disguise her long-limbed beauty. He had felt the first unwelcome stirrings of desire as he'd stripped her of her ruined clothing, and had had to force himself to forget that blondes had always been his weakness. He had reminded himself that she was hurt, and helpless, and that by picking her up in the jungle he had, however reluctantly, made himself responsible for her welfare. So he had continued to tend her hurts, reasoning that it would save trouble among the men if he was the only one to get near her. Somehow he'd managed to convince himself that he was in total control of his bodily urges, but then, of course, he'd had no way of knowing that the little witch would lure him into her bed on the pretext of a nightmare and then proceed to handle him in a way no red-blooded male could resist. The raging lust she had aroused had demanded instant satisfaction, and he had lost his head and taken what she had begged him to take. And God, it had felt good! Better than any sex he had had in years. Just remembering the feel of that soft, silky body writhing beneath his was enough to make his mouth go dry. Which was exactly why he mustn't remember, he told himself savagely. If anything was to be salvaged from this shambles, he would have to put her body out of his mind. From now on he would stay far from her. The job would be finished in less than three weeks, and then he would be back in the good old U.S.A. with enough money to buy any woman in the world.

The job, not the woman, was the important thing, Sam reminded himself, and it was one that only a crack bunch of commandos could pull off. Three months of painstaking effort had gone into assembling this squad, which numbered fifteen, plus himself. Another three months had been spent in training them. Soldiers who fight for money, mercenaries if you would, were the most professional of professionals. They had to be, because their lives depended on their skills. But it was on how well the group functioned as a team that the success of the job would hinge.

As the leader, Sam was well paid for his efforts, half in advance—fifty thousand cool smackers already safely tucked away in a U.S. bank—the other half when it was done. Plus expenses, of course, which had already been considerable. The men got less, amounts ranging from ten to fifty thousand dollars depending on what Sam felt their contribution was worth. And so far everything had gone like clockwork. They'd managed to get into the country without attracting attention, set up their base camp, and start the wheels grinding slowly into motion. Soon it would all be over. The only snag in the smoothly oiled plan was the woman....

Assassination wasn't really his bag, but the offer had been made at a time when he was desperate for money, and he had accepted. He allowed himself no regrets. A nameless group of backers was willing to pay, and pay well, to have Thomas Kimo, one of Rhodesia's foremost rebel leaders, killed in such a way that it would look as though supporters of a rival rebel leader had done the deed. The whys and wherefores of the proposed act had not been explained, but Sam had deduced that the murder was meant to cause an outbreak of infighting among the revolutionaries. While they were busy killing one another, Sam surmised, the ruling party would be consolidating its hold on the government. If he had guessed correctly, it was a good plan, and one that just might succeed. Not that he cared either way. Political convictions were the kiss of death for a professional soldier.

"Sam?" Frank Leads, his second in command and a good friend since they had seen combat together in 'Nam in 1964 and '65, had managed to come up on his left flank without his hearing a thing. Damn, he must be getting old! Too old to play this kind of game much longer. Thirty-nine this past month, and beginning to feel it . . .

"You okay?" Frank's question was guarded.

Sam grunted an affirmative reply, absorbing as much of Frank's typically bulldog expression as he could see through the darkness as his friend came to stand beside him. Frank was acting peculiarly. . . . There was no way he could know what had just happened with the woman—was there? Hell, he hoped not. Frank knew how he felt about women in general, and had many times heard his views on the folly of getting sex mixed up with business. The man would laugh his head off. . . .

"So what are you going to do about her?"

Sam's mouth twisted wryly. Frank did know.

Sam flashed his friend a derisive look and turned to start strolling back toward the camp.

"What did you use, radar?" The question was dry.

Sam punctuated it by taking a long drag on his cigarette.

Frank snorted, falling into step beside him. "Who needed it? You could hear her mewling like a scalded cat all over camp. You had to be either killing her or humping her, and somehow I didn't think you were killing her."

"Ummm." Sam was remembering the way she had cried out her pleasure at the end. The sound had sent him over the moon, but thinking back, he could see that it must have been damned loud. To his consternation, he felt hot blood creeping up over his cheeks. Christ, he was blushing! Like a high-school kid! Thank God for the darkness. If Frank saw his face turning red, he'd never live it down for the rest of his life.

"So what are you going to do about her?" Frank repeated his question patiently.

Sam grimaced. "Hell, what can I do? Nothing."

"What do you mean, nothing?" Frank exploded after a moment's stunned silence. "You can't do nothing. She could queer the whole thing!"

"What would you suggest?" Sam was getting sick of the whole topic. He felt like kicking himself for ever bringing her back with him in the first place, and as for what had happened later...

"We have to get rid of her. One way or another. If you're too squeamish—now—I'll do it."

"No!" Sam's refusal was sharp. "Dammit, I've just been all over this. She hasn't done anything to deserve killing, and there's no way to make sure she'll keep her mouth shut if we let her go. So, she stays." His voice went hard on the last three words.

After a moment's pregnant silence, Frank sighed heavily. "Somehow I had the feeling you were going to say that. All right, you're in charge here. I just hope to God you know what you're doing. But you realize she's going to cause trouble with the rest of the guys. Some of them can't so much as see a woman on the street without getting all het up."

"I know." Sam's reply was thoughtful. "She'll have to be kept out of their way—kept confined to her tent, maybe. Riley could sort of watch over her—he won't be affected."

Frank guffawed at this. Riley Bates's lack of interest in the opposite sex had been a standing joke for all the years they'd known him. Scuttlebutt had it that he'd stepped on a mine in Korea and had his vital equipment blown off. Maybe true, probably not, but either way the man was a hell of a soldier, and in a situation like this that was all that mattered.

"Good idea. But she'll have to leave the tent sometime—you know, call of nature and all that." Frank lowered his voice slightly, suddenly sounding embarrassed.

Sam grinned, his teeth a white flash in the darkness. He felt better knowing that he wasn't the only one to be reduced to blushing adolescence by the presence of a woman in their midst. "She can go—with Riley as escort," he said. "Do him good."

Both men chuckled at the irresistible picture this conjured up, and they were still grinning as they reached the camp. The small circle of tents was quiet. Frank yawned widely, clapped Sam on the back, and went off to bed. Sam made a quick tour of the camp, making sure that the men assigned to guard duty were awake and alert, then turned in.

Sunlight filtering through the open tent flap woke Lisa the next morning. She stretched, yawning, her eyes sleepily blinking open. Despite her various aches and pains, she felt as relaxed and contented as a cat in the sun. She hadn't felt this good in years, she marveled, not since before she had married Jeff. What was responsible for this delicious sense of well-being? What...?

Suddenly Lisa became aware that, beneath the blanket, she was completely naked. Her hand slid down disbelievingly to confirm the fact and encountered a faint stickiness on her abdomen and thighs. She blanched. Hazy memories of a hard, driving male body danced in her brain. Dear God, what had she done? She hadn't—please say she hadn't practically raped a total stranger. Snippets of her actions of the previous night played like first-run movies in her mind. Her paling face turned a bright tomato red. How could she have been so—so totally shameless? To beg him to make love to her, to touch him as she had done...!

Lisa closed her eyes, groaning. Whatever had possessed her? That she, usually so cool and reserved, could have behaved in such a way was crazy. And with such a man! A common soldier, for God's sake! But she knew, with a sinking sensation in the pit of her stomach, that it was true.

Lisa groaned again, pulling the blanket up over her head in an effort to keep out the world. What must he have thought, be thinking of her?

Finally a slow anger began to build. Maybe Sam wasn't as innocent in all this as she'd first thought. After all, he'd given her two injections that she knew of, and no telling how many more! Who knew what had been in them? Maybe he'd deliberately doped her up, hoping for that kind of reaction. Anyway, she hadn't been in her right mind last night, that much was certain, and he must have known it. Taking advantage of her in such a way was—was downright loathsome!

A soft footstep on the ground directly outside her

tent brought her head shooting out from beneath the blanket. Despite all her rationalizations, her face turned fiery crimson, and the hands clutching the blanket to her shoulders were unsteady. Any second now she expected to see that all-too-familiar shape step through the flap. But what did thrust through was only a head, and it was certainly not the arrogant black-haired one she was expecting. This one was balding on top, the glossy circle surrounded by a graying fringe, and the eyes that met hers were brown instead of the cobalt blue she remembered with such skin-tingling vividness.

"Who—who are you?" she asked faintly, suddenly feeling apprehensive. After all, embarrassing as she would find Sam's presence, he was at least a known quantity. This man was a stranger—and after her recent experiences she didn't feel overly trusting.

"Name's Riley Bates." He stepped inside as he answered. His tone could in no way be interpreted as friendly, but the familiar name allowed Lisa to relax. She had heard Sam call him last night, before . . .

"What do you want?" Keeping the blanket well up around her neck, she cautiously sat up. Her eyes went over Riley Bates assessingly. He was skinny and stooped and looked to be at least fifty years old. Like Sam, he was dressed in a khaki uniform.

"You hungry?" he asked brusquely. Lisa considered, then nodded. "I'll bring you something to eat."

While he was gone Lisa puzzled over his attitude. He was positively hostile—but why? To her knowledge, she hadn't done anything to offend him. Maybe he resented having to wait on her. Or maybe he just didn't like women.

Before she had arrived at an answer, Riley was back, carrying the same kind of tin plate she had eaten out of before. Unspeaking, he held it out to her. Lisa found herself in a quandary. To take the plate she would have to let go of the blanket, and that was clearly impossible. She bit her lip. Seeing her problem, Riley snorted and set down the plate on the overturned box along with a fork and a mug of what she hoped was coffee. Then, still without a word, he turned and left.

This time Lisa didn't bother to puzzle over his motive. The sight of food had set her stomach to rumbling, and she could feel her mouth watering hungrily. Quickly she stood up, wrapping the blanket around her body sarong-fashion, then sat down again on the cot and pulled the plate toward her.

The contents of the plate would have daunted a less eager stomach than Lisa's. There was a rubbery, whitish-looking mound that she tasted gingerly—scrambled eggs? If so, they were without doubt the worst she had ever eaten, and the sausages—she hoped—that went with them were just as bad. If she hadn't been absolutely starving she wouldn't even have attempted to get it down. But she had a sneaking suspicion that she would get nothing better, so she mastered her squeamishness as best she could and ate. The coffee at least was passable, hot and strong and liberally sugared.

"Them's for you."

Riley was back, carrying some limp-looking clothes. His attitude was, if anything, more surly than before. Lisa eyed him doubtfully as he threw the clothes down on the cot beside her.

"Thank you."

Riley snorted again. "Don't thank me, missy. This here's an army camp, and you can't run around it naked, no matter what you're used to. Fact is, you can't run around it at all. You're to stay in this tent, right inside, 'cept for a certain time of the day when

I'm with you. Otherwise, you ain't to step a foot outside. You got that?"

Lisa stared at him. She was to stay in the tent—he had to be kidding! Already it was stuffy in here, and she had a feeling that as the day wore on it would get positively unbearable. He couldn't be serious! Anyway, who the hell was Riley Bates? She couldn't believe he was the one who gave the orders.

"Where's Sam?" she asked coolly, lifting her chin. Despite the embarrassment the thought of seeing him again brought, he at least had been kind. And he had to have more authority than this little runt. . . .

"Sam's busy." Riley's reply was openly gloating. "He ain't got no more time for you. Besides, them orders came from *him*. He ain't a man to let his judgment be warped by a little slap and tickle."

Lisa stared at him with dumb shock, her cheeks slowly suffusing with crimson. From his words and tone, it was clear that he knew what had taken place between her and Sam the night before. Good Lord, had the conceited creature bragged to the whole camp about how easy she was? Her body burned from head to toe with embarrassment as she imagined Sam describing her behavior in intimate detail to a snickering circle of men. By the time she got through painting her mental picture, Lisa was more than willing to stay cooped up in the tent. In fact, wild horses couldn't have dragged her out!

"You understand?" Riley asked with a trace of satisfaction.

Lisa could only nod in reply. As he left the tent she covered her hot face with her hands, wishing that the ground would mercifully open up and swallow her.

The remainder of the two weeks she had planned to spend in Rhodesia passed in a blur of discomfort, inconvenience, and downright embarrassment. Only when the Tuesday of her scheduled departure from the country came and went with no mention of when—or if—she would be allowed to return to civilization did it begin to dawn on Lisa that she was in fact a prisoner. Diplomatically at first, and then more and more furiously as Riley ignored her as thoroughly as though he were stone deaf, Lisa demanded to be let go, or at the very least to be allowed to send a message to her family that she was safe. If her grandfather was aware of what had befallen the Blasses—and she was sure he would be by now, nearly two weeks after the event—he would be beside himself with grief. Because, to her knowledge, he had no way of knowing that she had not shared the Blass family's grisly fate.... The shock might even kill him. Despite his facade of vigor, he was an old man, and Lisa was all he had left in the world. But, for all the notice Riley took of her orders, entreaties, and even occasional attempts at outright bribery, she might as well have saved her breath. Clearly he intended to do absolutely nothing to help her. And he was her only link with authority—which was, in a word, Sam. Finally, seething, Lisa abandoned her efforts to persuade Riley to intercede on her behalf. It was hopeless, she knew.

During that time, humiliation was her constant companion. On the occasions when, under Riley's supervision, she left the tent, it was clear from the knowing smirks on the faces of the men she passed that her night with Sam was common knowledge. It was also clear that they considered her open to suggestions. She supposed she had Riley's constant guardianship to thank for the fact that their suggestions weren't followed up with action.

She saw Sam only at a distance. Just the sight of

his tall, broad-shouldered frame swaggering about the camp was enough to send her blood pressure shooting up. She was conscious of an almost overwhelming urge to injure him, and derived immense pleasure from conjuring up pictures of herself slapping his dark face until it stung.

One thing she'd been right about—the tent was hot. She sweltered during the long days, and her temper grew hotter as she did. The clothes that had been provided for her were no help. Her own underthings, laundered daily and made of nylon, were reasonably cool, but the cast-off military uniform she was forced to wear was not. For one thing, it was miles too big, so she had to fold up the sleeves and the pants legs into awkward rolls, and for another the material, designed for durability, was impossibly heavy. Finally she succumbed to temptation and ripped at the sleeves and legs until they tore right across. She was left with a very baggy pair of shorts that hit her at mid-thigh and a sleeveless shirt. The outfit was ragged, and she knew it must look ridiculous, but at least it let what little air survived in the tent reach her skin.

Riley was horrified when he saw what she had done, and expressed his disapproval volubly, refusing to take her outside dressed as she was. He ended his diatribe with a threat to go directly to Sam with the information that she was getting up to her whore's tricks again. Lisa, flicked on a raw spot, blew up.

"You can tell your precious Sam to go straight to hell," she spat in a low, shaking voice. "I don't give a damn what he, or you, or any of the rest of these animals around here, thinks. I totally despise you all!"

With that she burst into tears. Riley looked appalled, staring at her like she had suddenly grown two heads.

"Oh, get out!" Lisa sobbed furiously. After a moment's hesitation, he did.

The tears left almost as soon as Riley did. Lisa gulped, sniffled, and wiped her eyes. After all, what did she really have to cry about? She was alive, and reasonably safe and well cared for, and she was realistic enough to realize that her situation could have been immeasurably worse. Tension and physical discomfort were her only immediate problems, and they could be remedied. A long walk out in the fresh air would do it, or a warm, tingling shower. Lisa thought longingly of cooling spray washing down over her body, wetting her thoroughly, cleansing her. The only bath she had had for over two weeks had been a quick wash in a bowl, and she felt distinctly grubby. And her hair could use a wash....

On her daily excursions to the lime pit that served as the camp toilet, Lisa had glimpsed, not too far away, a small creek. Quite suddenly she made up her mind that she would have that walk and the bath, too. And if Riley, or Sam, or anyone else didn't like it, fantastic!

Gathering up her precious sliver of soap and the rough cotton towel, Lisa moved across to the tent flap and cautiously peered out. It was early afternoon, a time when the camp was usually almost deserted. Riley was around somewhere, she knew, but she didn't see him. This was probably the best chance she'd ever have to sneak away unseen. With luck, no one would ever know she'd flouted Sam's orders. Anyway, once she'd had her bath, she didn't much care if they did know!

Lisa ducked outside, blinking in the bright African sunlight, momentarily having to shade her eyes. It was good to feel the sun beating down on her head, to smell the fresh air, to see the beautiful cerulean sky and green-gold landscape so typical of this remote part of the world. Quickly she began to walk toward the creek, not slowing her pace until a bend in the path took her out of sight of the camp. She was surrounded by short, scrubby trees with deep green foliage and a charm uniquely their own. Brightly colored birds fluttered from branch to branch, their raucous cries filling the air. Butterflies with enormous, gaudy wings flitted all about her, and in the tall golden grass on either side of the trail she could hear little scurryings as small creatures went about their daily lives. The possibility of snakes being somewhere nearby caused her a moment's unease, but then she resolutely dismissed that quibble from her mind. She was going to enjoy her first taste of freedom for what seemed like months, and nothing short of a woman-eating alligator on the banks of the creek was going to send her back!

She passed the rough plank toilet and kept going, averting her nose from the strong smell of lime. There had been times over the past week when she would have given anything she possessed to see this place at times other than the measly one allotted to her, but, perversely, this afternoon her body was not interested. Lisa wondered at the contrariness of her own system, then forgot about it as the path ended at the edge of the creek.

To her eyes it was a beautiful creek, clear and shallow and sparkling in the sunlight. Lisa looked around, satisfied herself that she was alone, and quickly began shedding her clothes. An innate sense of modesty prompted her to leave on her peach-colored, nylon-and-lace bra and panties, which covered her as well as any of the swimsuits she possessed. And she was sensible enough to know that she needed her sneakers to protect her feet from whatever might lurk on the creek's bottom. Finally, she waded into the tepid water, which in the middle came no higher than her shoulders. Happily she dove beneath the surface, emerging to lather her hair and face and body with soap. It stung as she got it into her eyes, but she was too pleased with herself and the world in general to mind. At last she ducked under the water again to rinse away the soap, and when that was done she paddled joyfully about. She ended up floating on her back, her long hair trailing around her like pale seaweed. In that position she could enjoy an unimpeded view of the sky, and for a while she entertained herself by making pictures in the fleecy white clouds. It was only when a long shadow from a tree on the bank touched her face that she realized how quickly time had passed. Faint fingers of pink were beginning to streak the sky, and she could no longer see the sun. It must be nearly dusk. Lisa stood up, shaking her soaking hair back from her face, realizing with a sinking feeling that she had to get back. If she hadn't already been missed it would be a miracle, and the thought of a confrontation with Riley, or, a hundred times worse, Sam, was suddenly extremely unappealing. Quickly she waded to shore, twisting her hair into a rope and squeezing the water from it as she went. There was no time to lie on the bank and let the sun leisurely dry her underwear, as she had planned, and anyway the air was cooling rapidly. Lisa shivered as she kicked off her shoes, then unhooked her bra and stepped out of her panties, wringing them out and snatching up the towel to briskly rub herself dry. The marks on her arms were almost completely healed, she registered vaguely as she patted the moisture from them. Her back was, too, despite the fact that she had flatly refused Riley's reluctantly offered ministrations and insisted on tending her injuries herself. . . . Finally Lisa toweled her hair until it was just barely damp and turned to pick up her underwear. It was then, stooping and reaching, that she saw the two men.

They wore uniforms and they had been watching her. That much was clear at first glance. Lisa colored, snatching up the towel again and holding it in front of her in an effort to hide her body from their avid gazes. The fixed way they were staring at her, the glazed intensity in their eyes, their very silence terrified her. She began to back away slowly. One of the men, thick featured and heavily built, moved after her. He looked vaguely familiar. . . . The other man, younger and slimmer, moved too. They were stalking her.

Lisa's heart was pounding like a drum in her ears. She backed until she felt her foot touch the edge of the water, still clutching the towel before her like a shield. Desperately she glanced around, realizing that she had no place to run. The shallow creek offered no protection. Her only hope was that Riley had missed her and was even now nearby, looking for her. Taking a deep, shuddering breath, she opened her mouth to scream. To her horror, only a strangled squeak emerged from her suddenly dry throat. At the sound, the apish-looking older man smiled. His eyes were very small, a pale, watery blue. His hair was whitish. . . . Lisa stared at him with the same fascination she would have shown a cobra. Then, as he took another step toward her, she turned to run. Instantly they were upon her.

She could have screamed then. As soon as their hands closed on her body, clutching hurtfully at her naked shoulders and waist and arms, she felt the sound welling hysterically in her throat. But it never got a chance to come out. A sweaty palm clapped over her mouth, stifling any outcry. Lisa kicked and clawed and squirmed frantically as she was swung right up off her feet and carried some fifteen feet from the water's edge, where the tall grass swayed gently in a shaggy, golden carpet. Then she was borne toward the ground, still struggling with a strength born of terror, the salty-tasting hand still covering her mouth.

As she felt the grass prickle gently against her bare back, she braced her feet and lunged upward in a desperate bid for freedom.

"What's-a matter, babe? Ain't we handsome enough for you?" the white-haired man sneered breathlessly as she was thrust back down with ludicrous ease. Immediately he dropped on top of her, his weight knocking the breath from her lungs. Lisa's nails went with unerring instinct for his eyes.

"Grab her hands!" he bellowed, and the younger man hurried to comply, laughing as he dragged Lisa's arms over her head.

"No, no, no!" Her head thrashed frantically from side to side, unable to believe even then that this unthinkable thing, this rape, was really going to happen. Then, with desperate cunning, she forced her body to lie still as his khaki-clad legs forced themselves between hers. Maybe she could take him off guard. . . .

"That's better." He grunted approval of her apparent surrender, his hand moving to fumble with his zipper. Lisa's mouth was suddenly free and she opened it to scream. The sound was silenced by his mouth, fetid and slimy as it closed on hers, his tongue thrusting hotly between her teeth. His hands found her breasts, pinching roughly at the delicate pink nipples. Lisa thought despairingly that with his strangling of her scream she had lost her last chance. Still her body writhed in protest, her bare back and buttocks scraping painfully over the ground. Then, horribly, she felt the touch of his hot, throbbing maleness against her inner thigh.

She bit his tongue. The action was so simple, so obvious, that Lisa couldn't believe it hadn't occurred to her sooner. He screamed as her teeth met through the soft tissue, his hands coming up to close in a death grip around her throat. She didn't let go. With grim determination she kept her teeth buried in his tongue while his partner yanked at her hair and her victim howled and choked her. Her throat hurt horribly under the cruel grip. Lisa knew that he would soon crush her windpipe if she didn't release him. But she wasn't sure she could unlock her teeth even if she wanted to. Besides, she felt curiously detached from what was happening. Her eyes were wide open and glassy as she stared with dimming vision into the pain-contorted face above her. How long had it been since her starved lungs had managed to suck in any air? How long...

"Lutz!" The roar penetrated even Lisa's slipping consciousness.

"Holy shit, it's Eastman!" the younger man muttered.

Lisa felt the grip on her neck loosen fractionally and managed to roll her eyes in the direction from which the sound had come. It *was* Sam.... Her teeth unclenched of their own volition. The white-haired man rolled to one side, then stumbled to his feet, one hand clapped to his mouth. Lisa saw red rivulets of blood running beneath his hand to drip from his chin.... As she gulped in shuddering swallows of air she felt fiercely glad. She hoped that she'd severed his tongue....

Both men were on their feet now, facing Sam, their backs turned to her. Lisa wanted to stand up, too, but to her horror she found she couldn't move. Her useless limbs were racked with tremors, and she lay on the ground as naked and helpless as a newborn babe.

"Get back to camp."

The curt order, addressed to her attackers, came from Sam. His face was stony, his eyes hard as agates as he stared the two men down. He looked big, strong, and thoroughly dangerous standing there with his feet braced slightly apart and his arms crossed over his chest, and Lisa was devoutly thankful that his anger was not directed at her.

"She led us on," the younger man whined.

"Yeah, she stripped herself naked with us watching. What was we supposed to do?" the white-haired man added sullenly.

"I said get back to camp!" This time Sam's voice cracked like a bullwhip.

Lisa opened her mouth to deny what had been said. Not a sound would come out. She could only watch speechlessly as the two men slunk off toward camp, the older one still holding his mouth with one hand and fumbling with his zipper with the other.

Sam strolled toward her until he stood directly over her, his big body completely blocking out her view of the sky. He looked down at her distastefully, as if she were a piece of smelly garbage that he had found on his doorstep. Lisa realized with rising fury that he believed what those thugs had said. She could read nothing but contempt in Sam's blue eyes as they traveled slowly down her body, naked and bruised and sprawled limply in the grass.

"Get up." The command was harsh. Lisa blinked. She couldn't have moved if she had wanted to. Her muscles seemed to be paralyzed.

"Get up!" There was no doubt that he was furiously angry. It showed in the bite of his voice, the sapphire blaze of his eyes. Lisa licked her dry lips, closing her eyes.

The next thing she was aware of were his hands moving swiftly over her body. Her eyes flew open and she saw Sam kneeling beside her, rage still glittering in his eyes. He ran his fingers carefully along her narrow rib cage, then moved on to explore the smooth length of her arms and legs. Lisa shuddered away from his touch, moaning and wrapping her arms around her body in an age-old gesture of feminine protectiveness. Sam stopped what he was doing to stare down at her, his hands dropping to his sides.

"Are you hurt?" he asked sharply. Lisa's eyes were wild as she stared back at him; she could no longer distinguish friend from enemy.

"I said, are you hurt?" His voice was harsh. Lisa gulped in air, managing to shake her head in the negative. Her lips were trembling uncontrollably; words were beyond her now.

"Are you sure?" A muscle jumped convulsively at the corner of his mouth. His lips were clamped so tightly together that white lines radiated from their edges to the sides of his nose. He was obviously controlling himself with great effort. Lisa, shivering, was very much aware that some of that explosive temper was directed at her.

"I'm—sure." She forced out the words through chattering teeth. All she wanted to do was close her eyes and sleep, block out the whole terrifying ordeal.

"Played rougher than you liked, did they?" he bit

out. Lisa gasped, flinching as if he had struck her. He couldn't seriously believe that she had wanted what had happened, could he? Her eyes searched his face, looking in vain for some sign of softening.

"If you wanted it that badly, honey, all you had to do was let me know. We could have worked something out," he added, drawling.

As the import of that statement sunk in, a white-hot burst of rage lent sudden strength to Lisa's limbs. Gasping, abruptly sitting upright, her mouth contorting with fury, Lisa clenched her fist and swung it at him with instinctive violence. The blow connected squarely with the bridge of his nose, snapping his head back.

"Goddammit!" he yelped, his eyes widening with surprise and then narrowing with anger and pain. His hand came up to gingerly test his nose. "You little bitch, I ought to beat hell out of you for that!"

He glared at her; Lisa glared back just as angrily.

"Why don't you?" she dared him with breathless fury, too angry to consider the possible consequences. "You're big enough! So come on, bully, hit me! After all, you've done it before!"

She was so angry that she was shaking with it, too angry to take full heed of the fact that he could break her into little pieces with one hand if he chose—and at the moment he looked to be in the mood to do it.

"Don't tempt me," he snorted, some of the taut whiteness fading from around his mouth as he surveyed the picture she made, sprawled naked in the grass, her blond hair in wild disarray and her green eyes flashing defiance. His eyes darkened as they took in the silky texture of her skin, tawny pale against the golden-brown grass. Then he smiled tauntingly.

"You look right at home, naked." His words were as insulting as the look he passed over her. Lisa stuttered over a string of foul names for him, none of which quite made it out of her mouth.

"They attacked me, you pig! They were trying to rape me!" she finally managed to spit at him. Bloodlust shone from her eyes; she ached to kill him.

"Is that so?" That drawling voice was like gasoline to the already blazing fire of her anger. "Then tell me something, honey: if you're so innocent in all of this, what the hell were you doing out here in the first place? You're supposed to be confined to your tent, if I remember correctly. And where are your clothes? I don't see them lying around anywhere, looking as if they were torn from your struggling body! All the evidence backs up what Lutz and Brady said: you led them on. Granted, they may have gotten a little carried away, but the way I see it, that's more your fault than theirs!"

"You bastard!"

Lisa sprang to her feet, her fists clenching at her sides. Sam rose just as quickly; this time he was expecting her violence. As she lunged at him, he feinted, catching her by her hands, pulling her off balance. Then his shoulder made bruising contact with her soft stomach. Before she knew what was happening, he was hoisting her over his shoulder in a fireman's carry. Her head dangled helplessly, and her hair tangled down past his hips. Lisa struggled furiously, cursing as foully as she knew how, pounding his muscled back with her fists. The soft, taunting sound of his laughter flayed her like a many-thonged whip as he strode off with her.

"Last time you should have told me you like it rough. I would have obliged," he remarked conversationally to her bare, heaving backside.

Outraged, Lisa sank her sharp little teeth into his back, feeling them sink through the heavy cotton of his shirt and into his flesh with intense satisfaction. Sam yelped, then whacked her bottom so hard that she screamed.

"Behave," he said, the laughter suddenly, ominously absent from his voice. "Or I'll make you damned sorry."

The grimness of his tone convinced her as no amount of threats would have done that he meant what he said. Lisa was so furious that she could have chewed nails in half without a blink, but she had just enough sense left to know when to quit while she was ahead. Seething, she lay limply across his shoulder until a familiar landmark jolted her with the realization that they were almost there. God, he couldn't mean to walk through camp with her hanging naked over his shoulder—could he?

"Put me down!" she ordered imperiously. He continued to stride on as if he hadn't heard.

"Sam, put me down!" They had rounded the bend that brought them within sight of the camp.

"What's the matter? You were ready enough to let Lutz and Brady—and me—see you naked. Don't tell me a larger audience turns you off!"

"Dammit, they tried to rape me!" she cried, frustrated at his stubborn disbelief and furious at the same time.

"Oh, sure—just like I did that night in your tent, right?" Sam jeered, his voice biting. "Honey, you forget that I've seen you in action!"

His long legs continued to eat up the distance to the camp as he spoke. Lisa wriggled frantically, trying to throw herself to the ground, and was rewarded by another sharp slap on her rear.

"Sam, I swear I'm telling the truth!" she wailed in

a last, desperate effort to convince him. Then it was too late. He was carrying her through the camp, apparently oblivious to the hoots and catcalls of the gathered men. Lisa shut her eyes tightly, feeling humiliation wash over her entire body in a crimson wave. Then he stopped, and she looked up to find that instead of returning her to her own tent, he had brought her to his, for what purpose she didn't care to guess. He shouldered his way inside, dumped her unceremoniously on the floor, and turned to secure the tent flap, all without a word. As she struggled into a sitting position, face flushed and silver-blond hair curling wildly around her nakedness, Sam finished the task and swung back to stare down at her. Lisa quivered as she met the unrelenting diamond brilliance of his blue eyes.

"So they tried to rape you, huh?" he said gratingly. "You didn't want what happened out there at all! Honey, the only way you're going to convince me of that is to prove it to me!"

III

THOSE blue eyes fixed her like impaling shards of glass. Lisa's own eyes widened to huge emerald pools as, without a word, Sam began to unbutton his shirt. When at last he shrugged free of it and tossed it aside, Lisa's gaze traveled with a mixture of admiration and apprehension over the wide, bronzed shoulders and the flexing muscles of his arms and black-furred chest. A heavy leather holster strap crisscrossed his chest to hold a gleaming blue-black gun nestled just to the front of his left armpit. He unbuckled the strap, removing the whole deadly contraption and laying it carefully on the makeshift table. Then his hands moved to the buckle of his belt; he unfastened it with studied casualness. His eyes never left Lisa's mesmerized face as his fingers searched for and found the zipper of his pants.

Suddenly Lisa's shocked brain regained its ability to function. *Move!* it screamed, and she did, her mouth dry as she contemplated the test he clearly intended to administer. Hastily she scrambled to her feet, her hands shaking as she dragged the blanket from the cot and wrapped it securely around herself, tucking the ends into the hollow between her breasts. She couldn't, wouldn't, allow this to go any further;

not like this, as an experiment into the state of her sexual readiness, for God's sake! If she allowed it to happen, his taking of her body would be nothing but a barbaric act of domination, the age-old mastery of the female by the larger and stronger male. Why was she so horribly tempted?

Lisa bit her lower lip as she looked at Sam again and saw that he was now completely naked. Her hands came up to clutch the joined ends of the blanket covering her as he returned her look blandly, his mouth twisted into the merest suggestion of a sardonic smile. Of their own accord her eyes ran swiftly over his body, touching on the broad shoulders and widen muscled chest before following the beckoning trail of thick black hair downward past narrow hips and across a flat belly to long, powerful-looking legs. His upper body was deeply tanned, she saw with a curious little shiver, and so were the lower two-thirds of his legs. Which left quite a lot of pale skin in between ... All at once Lisa realized what she was doing. Horrified, she jerked her eyes away from him. Her face crimsoned.

"It's a little late to play at being shy," Sam taunted softly.

Lisa's eyes flew to his face. It was hard, implacable. Her eyes flickered away again. To tell the truth, she *was* shy, she thought unhappily. Jeff had had a thing about privacy, and the few times they had actually made love he had insisted on complete darkness. Lisa had never really gotten a good look at him without his clothes. Her knowledge of the appearance of the male body was pretty much limited to some sexy pictures she had seen once in a women's magazine she had taken unknowingly from a drugstore shelf. As she had flipped through the pages with idle curiosity, her shocked, fascinated gaze had been riveted by a layout of a bronzed, hairy, nude male. Almost instantly she had slammed the magazine shut, replacing it on the shelf with a guilty look around, hoping no one had seen her. But for months afterward her mind had returned at odd moments to re-create the disturbing image.... The embarrassing, unbelievable fact of the matter was that she had never really seen a naked man. Certainly not a man as blatantly, boldly naked as this one was, standing so casually before her with the increasing gloom of the tent's interior doing nothing to disguise his flagrant masculinity. He looked so tall, so strong, so very male, with his corded muscles and look of limitless strength, that Lisa was suddenly more aware of herself as a woman than she had ever been before in her life. And at the moment, his body was telling her in a way that was impossible to mistake that he wanted her....

"Come here, Lisa." The words were quiet. Sam's eyes glittered brightly blue as she looked up to meet them. Lisa swallowed, realizing with some distant part of her brain as she did so that her throat was beginning to ache quite badly. Then she took an instinctive step backward.

"You know you want to." There was a wealth of meaning in Sam's voice. Lisa mutely shook her head, backing another few paces. Her eyes never left his face. At her movement, his black-shadowed jaw clenched, and his mouth, beneath its faint smile, grew hard. Those blue eyes, as they watched her, seemed to freeze over.

"If you put me to the trouble of fetching you, you'll regret it." The threat was silky smooth, but it was unmistakably a threat. The smile had faded. Lisa felt the rhythm of her heartbeat increase as she faced the unwelcome fact that he could indeed make her regret it. With a sensation too complex to define, she realized that she was completely at his mercy.

"Look, this is silly. Either way, it's not going to prove a thing," she said jerkily, hoping to distract him from his purpose. She was very much afraid that if he touched her, she wouldn't be able to resist. . . .

"I said come here!" There was no question that he meant it, and meant her to obey. Still, Lisa tried once more.

"If you would . . ."

"Come here, damn you!"

Lisa looked at him mutinously. His blue eyes were as cold and glittery as glaciers. A muscle twitched warningly in his jaw. She realized that she had pushed him as far as he would be pushed; to defy him further could be hazardous.

"Oh, all right," she muttered ungraciously. Her head was high as she moved toward him. She didn't stop until she was close enough so that he could reach out and touch her.

"Now, would you please . . ." *Listen to reason* was what she meant to say. She found herself addressing her words to the pulse beating with heavy insistence at the base of his brown throat, because she was suddenly, ridiculously unable to look either higher or lower. Ruthlessly he cut her off.

"Drop the blanket."

This brought Lisa's eyes up to his in a hurry. To her dismay, she saw that they were frozen, a diamond-hard layer of ice lit at the backs by a leaping blue fire.

"N-no." Lisa, taken aback, uttered the negative instinctively. Then, as his eyes narrowed, she realized that she would have done better to be a shade more diplomatic in her reply. Still, she could not, would not, do as he said. It was time that she called a halt to this nonsense. He must be made to understand that she was not some little nobody whom he could order about and treat as he willed. Her green eyes met his bravely as she planned what she would say to make her position clear to him. Her hands clutched the blanket for dear life.

"Drop the blanket!"

The command cracked gunshot sharp. Startled, Lisa jumped about a foot in the air. Her hands nervelessly released their death grip on the blanket. It crumpled into an untidy heap at her feet. Stunned speechless by her unplanned capitulation, Lisa gaped down at her body. Her eyes then flew to Sam's face. She was made scaldingly aware of her nakedness and the effect it was having on the man studying her by the sudden flare of undisguised lust in the eyes that ran comprehensively over her. As Sam's gaze roamed with devastating thoroughness over every exposed inch of her skin, Lisa felt hot color creep into her cheeks. It was stupid and childish to feel so embarrassed, she knew. After all, the man had, by whatever quirk of fate, been her lover once already, and earlier this afternoon he had certainly seen all of her that there was to see. But she couldn't help it. This—this hard assessment of her body made her want to crawl into the nearest hole and hide. Still, she was damned if she would cower before him like some Victorian maiden. Squaring her shoulders, she faced him proudly, challenge showing in her eyes.

"You are totally wrong in what you're thinking, you know," she said with what she felt was creditable composure. "Believe it or not, I certainly did *not* entice those—those animals to attack me. I was simply taking a bath in the creek...."

Her voice trailed off, her bruised throat suddenly dry, when it became obvious that he wasn't listening. His eyes were fixed hungrily on the golden globes of her breasts. Even as she broke off he was lifting a hand to trail his fingertips over the soft curves.

"Beautiful," he murmured huskily. At his touch Lisa's turncoat body betrayed her, her small, strawberry-pink nipples standing up like soldiers suddenly called to attention. Taking a deep shaky breath, she struggled to go on with what she had been saying.

"They were trying to rape me," she got out distinctly, then reason fled as he cupped her breasts in his callused palms, running his thumbs lightly over the nipples. Lisa felt what was almost a physical pain deep in her belly. Her hands came up of their own accord to close around his strong wrists, attempting to still his maddening caresses. As she touched him he looked up in time to see her moisten her lower lip with the delicate pink tip of her tongue. He watched the tiny movement as if fascinated.

The passion that suddenly blazed in his eyes shook Lisa to the core. She closed her eyes in mute defense, then realized an instant later that she had made a tactical error. But by then it was too late. His mouth was on hers, hard and hot and compelling, kissing her with a fierceness that stopped her breath. Momentarily Lisa tried to resist, mentally scrambling for all the reasons why she should. It was worse than useless. Because, on the heels of more recent, shaming memories followed another one—the memory of a hard, thrusting body driving her wild....

She was lost. She knew it even before her lips parted helplessly beneath his, before her mouth opened to admit the conquering warrior that was his tongue. As his arms closed around her waist to pull her against his nakedness, her own arms slid convulsively around his neck, clinging to him, her fingers ruffling through the thick black hair at the nape of his neck. She returned the kiss wildly, on fire for him, loving the feel of his body hair rasping against her soft breasts and stomach and thighs, loving the steely muscles of his back and shoulders as her hands ran over them with blind urgency, loving the taste of his mouth, the drugging heat and man-smell of his body. He bent her ruthlessly back against his arm as he kissed her, his big male body in complete control of her smaller female one. And she loved it. The knowledge was utterly shaming, totally unbelievable, but true.

His hands were moving on her skin, handling her with a rough expertise that left Lisa gasping. He stroked her breasts, his touch feather light, lingering over each quivering nipple until it throbbed and pleaded for his touch. Then his hands moved lower, caressing her slim waist and flat stomach as if he had all the time in the world. Finally his fingers crept lower still to find the soft mound of hair between her thighs. He laid his hand flat against what was rapidly becoming the pulsating center of her being. Lisa stiffened instinctively. Sam paid no attention to her sudden stillness; his fingers began to explore, and gradually Lisa relaxed. What he was doing to her felt so good, so right, that she was soon melting in his arms, leaning heavily against him as his big body supported her weight, letting him do with her what he would. Her eyes were tightly shut. She didn't even hear the soft moaning sound rising from deep within her throat.

"Want me?" she heard him growl. Lisa had moved beyond reason, beyond shame, conscious only of the aching need he was deliberately arousing. Jerkily she nodded without opening her eyes.

"Say it," he ordered softly. Lisa hesitated, held back by some last dim flicker of pride. Then he lowered his mouth to nuzzle gently at one soft breast.

"Yes, oh yes..." She gasped.

"Yes, what?" His voice was a hoarse whisper. "Yes, you want me, or..."

His mouth suckled seductively at her breast. Lisa felt heat spiral crazily inside her. Her hands came up to clutch at his head, holding it in place. Her one fear was that he would stop.

"Yes, I want you." She surrendered without a struggle. She did want him, she thought hazily, so much....

Sam swung her up in his arms, holding her cradled against his chest. Lisa clung to him feverishly as he carried her the few paces to the cot. Her head was thrown back against his shoulder, her delicately flushed face tilted up to his. Her eyes were closed so that her lashes formed feathery dark crescents against her cheeks. Desire for him was melting her bones; her heart was pounding so fiercely that she thought she might die of it. Her whole body burned in anticipation.

He stopped, still holding her possessively against his chest. Lisa waited for him to lower her gently to the cot. Nothing happened. After a moment she opened her eyes, puzzled, to find him looking down at her with an odd, half-rueful expression. She didn't understand his look, but she certainly wasn't in the mood to puzzle it out. Murmuring soft encouragement to him, she shamelessly pressed her tingling breasts against the hard, hairy wall of his chest. She was impatient, more than impatient, to experience again the ecstasy of his lovemaking.... She pressed nibbling little kisses into the curve of his neck. Still he didn't move. Annoyed and faintly bewildered, she looked up at him questioningly. His eyes met hers. Then his mouth twisted mockingly, and he laughed.

Lisa froze. She was still staring up at him, her mouth slightly open, when she felt his arms drop away from her. Suddenly she was falling through space to land with a jarring thud on the cot. Stunned, she lay where he had dropped her. Her eyes blinked once or twice in shocked incomprehension as he turned away and unhurriedly began to dress.

"Sam . . . ?"

He had put on his shorts and was stepping into his pants, pulling them up over his muscular, hair-roughened thighs as Lisa watched with hungry bewilderment. He zipped them up, and was buckling his belt with careless hands when he finally looked up to meet her questioning gaze. Lisa was taken aback by the hostility she saw in those blue eyes.

"Honey, with a girl like you, the term *rape* doesn't even begin to apply," he said cruelly, then gathered up his shirt and gunbelt in one hand, swung on his heel, and strode from the tent.

Lisa felt as if she had suffered a crippling blow to her midsection. For long moments after he had gone, she lay huddled on the cot, feeling sick. It had taken her shocked brain only seconds to remember that Sam had deliberately set out to test her—to humiliate her. And, dear God, had he succeeded! Beyond anything he could have planned or imagined! She felt like crawling off and hiding under the nearest rock, never again to face the light of day. He had wanted her, she knew he had. She was not so innocent or naïve as to fail to understand the significance of the heat and throbbing strength of him. But he had kept a tight rein on his own appetites, while making her want him so much that she was willing to sacrifice pride, self-respect, everything in return for the physical satisfaction her body craved. He had made her beg for him, damn him to hell, and then he had laughed and turned away! The memory of every word, every touch, every sigh returned to haunt Lisa in all too vivid detail. She groaned, rolling onto her stomach to bury her face in the flat pillow. Her eyes were squeezed tightly shut as she fought to exclude the images that tormented her. He had aroused her with cool calculation, she told herself despairingly, and she would never get over it— never. She would hate him for the rest of her life. If only she could get out of her mind the picture of herself naked in his arms, clinging to him shamelessly as she pressed hot little kisses into the salty brownness of his neck!

After a while it occurred to her that she was still in Sam's tent, lying in his cot, as naked as the day she was born. If one thing was more certain than any other in this crazy world, it was that Sam would be sure to return. With a complete reversal of her earlier opinion of it, she longed for her own tent. The small green shelter seemed to offer a security that she desperately needed. She sat up abruptly, aiming to return to her tent before Sam returned to his. If he found her here, naked, he would probably assume that she was shamelessly waiting for him. . . . Lisa's face burned at the very idea. Detestable, arrogant beast! She swung her legs off the cot and stood up, determined to leave that very instant. Wildly she looked around for something to cover her nakedness. There was only the blanket. . . . Lisa's hell-bent desire to make herself scarce faltered momentarily at the picture of herself parading through the already-sure-to-be-snickering camp clad only in a blanket. But what other choice did she have? Anything was preferable to still being there when Sam returned.

The thought galvanized Lisa into action. She grabbed the blanket from the floor and wrapped it around herself in the same sarong style she had used earlier. What did it matter if the whole camp laughed and drew their own conclusions about what had happened inside Sam's tent? It was preferable by far to having to face Sam again right now.... Lisa headed purposefully toward the flap. A slight sound from just outside stopped her in her tracks. Someone was approaching the tent—and she had a shrewd idea of who that someone had to be. She froze, her face coloring ridiculously, her eyes glued to the tent flap. Her worst fears were confirmed when Sam entered, ducking his dark head as he stepped inside. Her clothes and shoes dangled from one strong brown hand.

He straightened, surveying her briefly as she stood there poised for flight. His mouth quirked, and then he reached out a hand to flick on the battery-powered lamp that stood on an overturned crate near him. The tent was immediately flooded with light. Lisa automatically put up a hand to shield her eyes, hating the brightness that would reveal to him every nuance of her expression. She thought she would want to die if he should guess how very sick of herself he had made her. Finally she realized that she would have to drop her protective hand. She did so, reluctantly, to find that Sam was watching her, his dark face inscrutable.

"Here," he said, tossing her clothes at her.

Lisa made no move to catch them, and they fell to the floor at her feet, surrounding her. Her eyes seemed glued to Sam's face. To her fury, she could feel hot pink color wash into her cheeks. Sam grinned hatefully. It was that grin that allowed Lisa to get a grip on herself. Her temper began to simmer, thankfully driving out the humiliation that threatened to make a bigger fool out of her than he had done already. Her eyes glittered like green glass as they met his. It was an effort to hold back the hot words that trembled on the tip of her tongue. But she knew that she would only amuse him if she let him know how much his particular brand of punishment had gotten under her skin. For the sake of her own self-respect, she had to show him that she was as unmoved by their late, unlamented encounter as he seemed to be.

"Thank you," Lisa said evenly, and was pardonably proud of herself for her coolness. Sam's eyes narrowed as they rested on her face. Whatever he had been expecting, she realized that she had surprised him with her calm.

"Get dressed," he ordered briefly.

Lisa looked at him with loathing. "Certainly." Her voice was icy cold. "If you'll leave, I'll be more than glad to."

Sam snorted. "Back to playing Little Miss Modesty, are we? I thought we'd already agreed that it's a little late for that."

It was all Lisa could do not to launch herself at that sneering face, her teeth and nails bared. But she had done that once already today, and the results had been something less than satisfactory. She could just imagine his delight if she were to give way to such an impulse. It would give him the excuse to humiliate her once again, and somehow Lisa had the feeling that humiliating her was something he enjoyed doing.

"You're right, of course," she answered as coolly as she could, hoping that he would not read in her eyes the bitter antagonism she felt.

Sam said nothing. Something flickered for just an

instant in those blue eyes, and then they were once again impenetrable as they watched her. Lisa refused to wonder what that fleeting expression meant. Instead, she bent with unconscious grace to pick up her clothes from where they lay on the floor. They were the ones she had been wearing earlier, she saw, and could only suppose that Sam had made the long trip back down to the creek to get them. She hoped with a touch of savagery that he wasn't expecting any thanks, because he certainly wasn't going to get them from her!

Lisa dropped the clothes on the cot, glancing at Sam out of the corner of one eye. He was standing just inside the tent, in the center where it was tall enough for him to remain upright. His arms were crossed over his chest, and an annoying little smile hovered around the corners of his mouth. He looked as if he was hoping that she would order him to turn around, or even leave, so that he could take great pleasure in refusing, thus proving to her once again that he was the indisputable boss. Lisa would be damned before she would give him that satisfaction. She lifted her chin, met his mocking look squarely, and dropped the blanket.

His eyes dropped the length of her body as if he couldn't help himself, and this time surprise and something else—sexual desire?—were plain in his face. Lisa felt an inward quiver of triumph as she stepped casually into her silky underpants. So the big, bad soldier was not as invulnerable as he liked to appear—that was something to be filed away for future reference. In the meantime, she deliberately took her time getting into the rest of her clothes. His face was once again unreadable, but Lisa knew that she had succeeded in disconcerting him. That knowledge went a long way toward soothing the humiliation he had inflicted earlier.

She clipped her bra around her waist and slid it deftly into position, adjusting the cups over her breasts until they fitted smoothly over the rounded flesh. Purposely she ran her hands over her breasts where they swelled into the flimsy, peach-colored garment, casting Sam a sidelong glance as she did so. His eyes were fastened on the barely concealed curves of her breasts. Smiling a little, Lisa allowed her hands to linger teasingly a moment, then slowly finished dressing. It was only as she was buttoning the last button of the raggedy, too-big shirt that she looked at Sam again. His eyes were opaque, his face schooled into his familiar expressionlessness. Not by so much as the flicker of an eyelid did he reveal that the sight of her body had disturbed him. But Lisa had seen the brief flare of hunger in his eyes, and it made her feel immeasurably better.

"Enjoy the show?" she asked nastily, with the sensation of getting a little more of her own back on him.

"Very nice," he drawled, his eyes resting on her face. "But then, I've seen more exciting stripteases at fifty-cents-a-head girlie joints. But, pardon me, yours was a dress-tease, wasn't it? That makes it a little more unique."

"Why, you...!" Lisa spluttered before she thought, furious at being compared to the type of woman who worked in a place such as he described. A satisfied smile curled his lips, and Lisa was brought up short, mentally kicking herself. Round two to him, she thought angrily.

"Honey, if I were you, I'd leave off the insults," he advised, dropping his arms so that they swung casually at his sides as he moved toward her. Lisa took an instinctive step backward. Sam's eyebrows rose in scornful inquiry as he merely crossed to the make-shift table in one corner of the tent and bent to look at one of the myriad papers strewn across its top. "Remember that old saying about people in glass houses? A hot little number like yourself is too vulnerable to start throwing dirty names around so freely."

Lisa's face flamed. Rage strangled all utterance, which was just as well, she reflected a moment later. By the time she had recovered the use of her voice, she had also recovered control of her temper.

"If you'll excuse me, I'll go back to my tent now," she said with icy politeness, her eyes shooting daggers at the broad back that faced her as he bent over his papers. Sam didn't turn.

"Uh-uh," he answered negligently just as she was stepping toward the tent flap. His attention never wavered from the papers before him.

The casual negative was like fuel on the fire of Lisa's bottled-up explosion.

"What do you mean, uh-uh?" she questioned carefully.

"Just what I said." He half-turned to face her, one hand resting on the small table. "You won't be going back to your tent."

Lisa gaped at him. "Why not?"

"Because I said so." He turned fully to face her, perching on the edge of the table and swinging one foot as he talked. Lisa wished fervently that it would break under his weight, sending him crashing to the floor.

"Would you mind elaborating on that a little?"

"Not at all." He sounded faintly amused. Lisa's soft mouth tightened ominously. "You are not going back to your tent because I can't chance a repeat of what happened down by the creek today. A man-hungry little tramp is a menace to the whole situation here. I've already had to discipline two of my men because of you, and they aren't feeling too kindly toward either of us as a result. I'm not going to make a habit of it."

Lisa's eyes blazed, but she managed to retain a grip on her slipping temper.

"If I'm not to go back to my tent, where do you suggest I go? Or are you saying that you're planning to send me home?" As this possibility occurred to her, Lisa's face brightened. She had not previously had the opportunity to discuss with Sam going home to the good old U.S., but Riley had given her to understand, when she'd asked, that she was stuck here in this godforsaken spot for the duration of whatever operation these brigands were planning. But maybe she'd made such a nuisance of herself that Sam had changed his mind.

"I'm saying, not suggesting, that you're going no-where at all." His eyes met her disappointed ones steadily. For a moment there, she had hoped. . . .

"What do you mean, nowhere?" Her voice was dull, sharpened by just an edge of resentment. Then, as a previously unthought-of possibility occurred to her, she snapped, "I'm certainly not staying in this tent with you!"

"Aren't you?" The grin in his voice made her want to hit him.

"No, I'm not!" All the light of battle had rushed back into her eyes. She faced him aggressively, her hands clenched at her sides.

"And I say you are." He was watching her with some amusement, but there was iron beneath his teasing look.

"If you think that I'm moving in here with you, so that you can—can get your rocks off whenever you feel the urge, you can just think again!" Her cheeks flamed with anger. Sam chuckled.

"Such language," he reproved with a grin, shaking his head in mock dismay. Then, as her eyes stabbed him, the grin faded from his face.

"You're overlooking one small but important detail, I think," he said coolly.

"What's that?"

"You don't run this show, pretty lady, I do."

This statement sent gushers of fire shooting through Lisa's veins. Just who the hell did he think he was, anyway, to order her around like some coolie, to expect her to become his live-in mistress just because he had decided that it would suit him to have ready access to a female body? He might be a man, and therefore bigger and stronger than she, and he might be temporarily in charge of this ragtag crew, but when it came right down to it he was nothing more than a hired soldier scrabbling around in the dirt after a few pennies! While she—she was the granddaughter of one of the wealthiest men in Maryland—possibly in the whole United States! And she felt that it was about time she made the distinction quite clear!

"Listen, mister, and listen good," she said through her teeth. Her green eyes were leaping in her whitened face as she stared him down. "I don't take orders from you! I don't know who the hell you think you are, and I don't particularly care, but I think it's time we got a few things straight. Before I got married, my name was Lisa Bennet—does that mean anything to you? Because if not, let me enlighten you! My grandfather is A. Herman Bennet—yes, that's right, A. Herman Bennet—and in case that still doesn't ring a bell, let me tell you that he's one of the richest men in the United States! He's probably got the whole U.S. Army out looking for me right now! And when they find me I sure as hell wouldn't want to be in your shoes! When I tell them how you've treated me, they'll probably shoot you on the spot!"

By the time Lisa finished this little speech, her breasts were heaving with exertion. Her eyes were fastened on his face with savage satisfaction, waiting for the change to come over it that her grandfather's name never failed to evoke. Usually she hated to use its authority on her own behalf, but she had reached the end of her rope. It was time he treated her with a little respect!

Maddeningly, Sam didn't appear particularly perturbed by his new knowledge of her identity. He was still sitting there in exactly the same way, his foot dangling casually, his blue eyes more speculative than worried as they rested on her heated face.

"So you're a spoiled little rich girl, are you?" he asked eventually, his tone expressing no more than idle interest. "I should have guessed. No normal adult woman would throw tantrums like a ten-year-old child. Your grandfather should have taken a belt to your butt when you were a kid, and you'd have grown out of that in a hurry. But since he didn't, and apparently your husband didn't—by the way, when you get back home, be sure to give the poor S.O.B. my sympathy—I just might rectify the omission. So I wouldn't press my luck, if I were you."

Lisa gaped at him. She was so enraged that she thought the top of her head might blow off any second. She opened her mouth, seeking words with which to annihilate him, then closed it again with a snap. There were no words that would do justice to the way she felt at the moment.

She eyed him silently for what seemed like a long time. He returned her look with interest. Her attempt to threaten him with the consequences of his actions had gone flat, like stale Coke. But maybe there was another way.... After all, he was here in Rhodesia because he was being paid. Perhaps she could pay him to leave—taking her with him, of course.

"All right, so you don't care who my grandfather is," she acknowledged in as reasonable a tone as she could muster. "But that doesn't alter the fact that he is very, very rich. And he loves me. What would you say if I told you that he would pay you whatever you ask—thirty thousand dollars, forty, you name the price—if you were to take me home safely—now?"

She dangled the carrot before him hopefully.

"I would say no, thank you," he said coolly. Lisa stared at him, aghast.

"Why not?" she demanded. "You don't want me here. I don't want to be here. You want money. I have money. So why not?"

"Because I don't choose to." He sounded as if he was beginning to lose patience.

"All right, you don't have to leave yourself, if you don't want to," she bargained desperately, seeing her best chance to get safely away from this whole horrible mess disintegrating before her eyes. "If you could just get somebody—Riley—to take me to the nearest airport, I'd see that you were paid, I swear it. And I'd be out of your hair."

"No." The single word was brutal. Sam stood up, shifting his attention back to his papers. It was clear that he considered the discussion closed.

"I won't stay here with you!" Lisa practically screamed the words at him. He said nothing. He didn't even appear to hear.

"You can't make me!"

At this he turned to look at her. The expression on his dark face was not nice.

"Ah, but I can," he said softly. "But I won't. I'll give you a choice instead. You can shut your damned mouth and do as you're told, or you can get the hell out of my camp and look after your own ass. It's up to you."

IV

LISA glared at him furiously, on the verge of telling him that nothing on this earth would give her greater pleasure than to leave his camp, and, not incidentally, himself, when a tiny niggle of common sense stilled her tongue. After all, they were in the middle of a vast nowhere with a guerrilla war being waged all around them. As a woman on her own, with absolutely no training or experience in survival under such conditions, she would be easy prey for the sometimes harsh climate, wild animals, and, worst of all, the brutish men who roamed the countryside in packs calling themselves soldiers. The land hereabouts was sparsely populated, she knew, and her chances of coming across a farm or dwelling where she might shelter were iffy at best. Even if she did, what was to stop the owner of the establishment that took her in from demanding the same price for her care that Sam was? And that was probably the best fate that she could expect. It was far more likely that she would fall prey to the same kind of animals who had attacked her earlier in the day. They would use and abuse her body for as long as it amused them, then probably kill her without a qualm. Lisa remembered the horror that had befallen the Blasses, and shuddered inwardly.

"You don't mean that," she said at last. Her tone had become noticeably milder.

"Don't I?" The blue eyes taunted her. "What misguided reason could you have for thinking that?"

"You wouldn't do a thing like that. You—you saved my life." She felt absurd saying that last after the way she had been screeching at him not three minutes ago, but she was suddenly terrified that he might be serious—that he might actually throw her out of his camp and leave her to fend for herself.

"More fool me," he murmured wryly. "As I said, you have a choice: you can live here in this tent with me, on any terms I care to dictate, or you can get out—now. I don't give a damn either way."

"That's blackmail," Lisa said slowly, but she knew she didn't really have a choice. Clearly, he meant what he said, and anything, even becoming his mistress, was better than being left on her own in a world gone mad.

"You're welcome to call it anything you like. Well?" He sounded impatient.

Lisa swallowed convulsively. "I'll—I'll stay."

"I thought you would." The words were cynical. "Don't bother to pretend you'll find it any great hardship to share my bed. We both know better. Don't we?"

Lisa didn't answer that. God, she hated him! Would he leave no shred of her pride intact? But she needed him, too. With a flash of insight, Lisa thought that she hated him most of all for that.

Lisa was so lost in her own thoughts that, when Sam straightened abruptly and took a step forward, she started. He gave her a derisive look.

"Don't worry, you're safe—for now," he said. "Come

on, let's go get chow. I'm starving, and after all the excitement you've had today, you must be too."

Whatever Lisa had been expecting, it had certainly been nothing as prosaic as that. She was conscious of a ridiculous sense of anticlimax as he headed for the flap. She started to follow him, then stopped. She couldn't bear to go out there and face them all—the two men who had attacked her and the others who had watched Sam carry her naked and struggling through the camp.

He had paused just inside the entrance, frowning as he looked back at her.

"Come on." He sounded impatient.

"I'm not hungry," she said, unaware that her face was flushed a bright pink.

Sam looked at her consideringly. "Yes, you are. You're just feeling embarrassed. Don't worry, I intend to make it very clear that you're now my woman. The men won't give you any trouble after that."

"I'm not your woman!" Lisa protested suffocatingly, hating the possessive male term.

"Yes, you are. As long as you're here in my camp, anyway. It's not precisely what I had planned, but it will serve as well as anything else to keep you out of trouble. Now come on. Let's go."

He turned and ducked out of the tent. Lisa, after a moment's unhappy hesitation, followed him.

The night was dark and clear, the sky a canopy of midnight-blue silk studded by hundreds of glittery silver stars. With the setting of the sun, the land came alive. Lisa could hear the cries of birds and mammals in the distance as they hunted or were hunted, killed or were killed. She shivered as she walked along beside Sam toward the small campfire in the center of the circle of tents. She was trapped in a primitive society, where only the strong could survive. And she was not particularly strong....

The men were seated on whatever perches they could find around the fire, rocks and overturned crates and even the ground. They were, for the most part, busy eating. Lisa hoped they would be so engrossed in their food that they would not notice her following meekly in Sam's wake. Her presence was bound to cause quite a lot of surprise and probably some lewd comments as well. Always before tonight, she had stayed hidden away in her tent, with Riley grudgingly bringing her her food.

Lisa's hopes of going unnoticed were in vain, as she had secretly known they would be. One by one the men looked up, saw her hovering nervously behind Sam's tall body, and suspended activity, staring. Sam appeared oblivious to the interested looks being cast their way and sauntered over to the camp-fire. Lisa trailed him, her eyes fastened on a spot midway between his shoulder blades so that she wouldn't accidentally meet the alternately worried, amused, or frankly lascivious looks that followed their progress. At least she could be thankful that the two who had attacked her were not present.

"She eatin'?" Riley inquired sourly as he ladled a particularly noxious-looking mixture of what appeared to be beef stew into a plate for Sam.

"Yes." The reply was laconic, but the look out of those blue eyes was not. Riley said nothing more, but filled a plate for Lisa. His expression was grimly disapproving as he handed it to her.

"Coffee?" Sam held out a tin cup filled to the brim with the brown liquid.

"Thank you." Lisa took the cup, carefully avoiding any contact with Sam's fingers.

"You want me to take her breakfast in the morn-

ing, or will she be eatin' with us from now on?"
Riley's tone said clearly that he resented Lisa's presence.

"She'll be eating with us from now on," Sam confirmed. The words were even, and his tone was mild
enough, but something in the gravelly voice silenced
Riley and sent the men's eyes flickering back down to
their plates. By the time Sam turned away from the
fire with Lisa following him, they all seemed to be
busily engaged in stuffing their faces. Despite herself, Lisa was impressed. These tough customers
must hold Sam in considerable respect. Which, when
she thought about it, she could certainly understand:
he was as big as a gorilla and as strong as an ox, and
had a disposition meaner than either!

Lisa almost cannoned into Sam's back when he
stopped, so engrossed was she in her own thoughts.
As it was, she had to frantically juggle the overfilled
plate she held in one hand and the sloshing coffee in
the other to keep from pouring them down the back
of Sam's shirt. Which she would not have minded
doing, except for the uncomfortable suspicion that
he wouldn't take too kindly to it.

When Sam turned to look at her, she had just
managed to save the major portion of her dinner
from ending up on the ground, and she was feeling
decidedly cross. His mouth twitched up in an invol-
untary half-grin as he read her expression. Setting
his cup on a nearby rock, he moved to take Lisa's
from her hand. She flashed him a venomous look
but allowed him to take the coffee. Sam indicated a
large, flat rock to his left with a jerk of his head.

"Sit," he said.

Lisa's eyes flared at the command, which sounded
for all the world as if it had been addressed to a dog.
But, bit by painful bit, she was gradually growing
wiser: she now knew better than to provoke Sam in

front of his men. So she sat on the rock, feeling as sulky as she looked. She only hoped that the stiffness of her movements adequately conveyed her dislike of his tone.

Sam handed her her coffee cup without a word, then effortlessly sank to the ground beside her, balancing his plate and cup seemingly without effort. Lisa watched him disgruntledly as he began to tuck into his food as if he didn't have a care in the world. Hateful man, she thought blackly.

Her stomach chose that moment to tell her loudly that it was ready for sustenance. She flushed, hoping that Sam hadn't heard, and picked up her fork to still the ravening organ. The stew, if that was indeed what it was, looked terrible and tasted no better, but she was growing used to camp food. The trick was to swallow it as quickly as possible, before her tastebuds had time to lodge a violent protest. This Lisa tried to do with her first mouthful, only to discover, as the sure-to-be-indigestible lump was halfway down her throat, that that same throat hurt abominably.

After a few more tries she gave up. Her throat hurt too badly to allow her to eat. Vividly she remembered the feel of her attacker's hands closing around her neck, cutting off her breath, squeezing the life from her. Another few minutes and she would have been dead....

Lisa took a sip of the scalding coffee, refusing to allow her mind to dwell on what might have been. The incident was over, and she had suffered no worse than a few bruises to her body—and, not incidentally, her pride. As she thought that, Lisa's eyes shifted to Sam. He had been responsible for most of the damage to her pride.

His black-haired head was on the level of her shoulder although he was sitting flat on the ground and she was elevated perhaps eighteen inches by the rock. Not for the first time she registered what a large man he was. . . . He was positioned slightly in front of her, and Lisa was able to watch him as he ate without his being aware that she was doing so. The flickering firelight painted his harshly carved features an orange bronze, accentuating their hard masculinity. For just an instant Lisa compared that uncompromising nose and jutting chin with what she remembered of Jeff's conventionally good-looking features. Jeff was undoubtedly the more handsome, but he lacked something that Lisa couldn't quite put her finger on, something that Sam possessed in abundance. Was it virility? Good, old-fashioned animal magnetism? Probably . . .

"Tell me something." Sam was looking at her over his shoulder. Lisa was embarrassed to have been caught staring at him. Hastily she took another sip of the hot coffee.

"What?"

"What the hell is A. Herman Bennet's granddaughter doing caught up in the middle of a civil war in Rhodesia?"

He sounded genuinely curious. Lisa shrugged.

"I work for a newspaper. They wanted someone to do a series of features on the effect the war was having on the lives of Americans living here. I volunteered." She grimaced. "It was supposed to be perfectly safe. I only planned to stay two weeks."

"Perfectly safe, huh?" He shook his head. "Whoever let you come over here has to be crazy. You're lucky you're still alive and in one piece. Didn't your grandfather try to stop you? Or your husband?"

Lisa shook her head.

"Why the hell not?" Sam's voice suddenly had a violent undertone.

Lisa looked at him, then looked away. She didn't feel like going into the whole, awful story—and it was none of his business anyway.

"They thought I needed to get away."

"To *Rhodesia?*" He sounded incredulous.

"Why not? The French Riviera is too crowded at this time of year." Her voice was flippant. Sam's face darkened.

"Anything for a kick, huh?" he muttered sarcastically, and turned back to his food. He swallowed a few more mouthfuls before casting her another assessing glance.

"How long have you been a journalist?"

"About a year."

"What did you do before that?"

He shot the questions at her as if he were conducting an inquisition. Lisa was taken aback.

"Why, nothing," she said with some truth. "Uh, I mean, I kept house. . . ."

"You and about five servants, I reckon." Contempt was plain in his voice. "I suppose you went to some fancy eastern college?"

"Bryn Mawr."

"What kind of classes did you take? What did you major in?"

"I—I took a lot of art history. I never declared a major. I was only there a year."

"You stopped going to school when you made a good marriage." It was a statement, not a question. Sam put scornful emphasis on "a good marriage." Lisa bristled.

"Yes, I did. What's it to you, anyway?"

Sam paid no attention to her growing annoyance. "So how long have you been married?"

"Six years, if it's any of your business."

"And last year you got bored, right? How did you

get the job on the newspaper without any kind of background in journalism? Wait, don't tell me." This came as Lisa tried to speak. "Let me guess: Granddaddy owns it. Right?"

"Yes."

"How convenient." He was openly sneering now. "No wonder the paper sent you over here. They were probably willing to do anything to get rid of you."

His derision flicked Lisa on a vulnerable spot. She knew full well that she never would have been hired by the paper if she hadn't been who she was, but she liked to think that since then she had proved herself to be a better than adequate writer, at the very least. Her eyes flashed angrily into his, and she got abruptly to her feet.

"What do you know about it, anyway?" she demanded in a low, furious voice, glaring down at the bronzed face lifted toward hers. "You . . ."

He reached up, seizing her wrist in a grip that hurt. "Sit down and shut up." His voice was low, but dangerous nonetheless.

Lisa was on the verge of throwing caution to the winds and telling him where he could go, when she happened to glance around and see the interested eyes of the men fastened on the little tableau she and Sam made. She sat down.

"I have one more question, and then we'll drop the subject: What did your husband think about you leaving him all alone to come over here?"

Lisa gave him a smoldering glare. "It was my decision. He doesn't try to tell me what to do."

Not for anything in the world would Lisa have told him the true state of her marriage. It was personal, private, and none of his damned business. Besides, he would doubtless want to know why her marriage hadn't worked out, and that was something she had never told anyone, not even her grandfather. She owed Jeff that much loyalty.

"Poor sod was probably as glad to get rid of you as the newspaper," Sam surmised brutally. "I bet you lead him a pretty dance. Tell me, do you cheat on him while you're at home, too, or do you confine your extracurricular activities to the times when you're conveniently out of the country?"

This was so unexpected, so grossly unfair, that Lisa gasped out loud. Then, not caring what he thought or what form his punishment might take, she jumped up and ran.

Sam didn't follow her. Lisa's steps finally slowed, then stopped altogether. Running away had been useless, a ridiculous waste of time and energy. Where could she go but to Sam's tent, to wait meekly for whatever form of retribution he chose to inflict on her? She was not stupid enough to fly heedlessly out into the bush. . . .

It was strange how much that last cutting remark of his had hurt. Funny, but she had never thought of that single, still slightly unreal night with him in terms of cheating on Jeff. Her marriage to Jeff had been dead for years, since before Jennifer had been born. If Jeff knew that she had made love with Sam, he wouldn't be hurt in the least. The only thing that might be even slightly dented was his pride, and she tended to doubt that. He'd been finding his own forms of amusement for years. . . . Why shouldn't she do the same? She would have done it long ago if it hadn't been for Jennifer.

Lisa pushed all thoughts of her daughter from her mind as she reluctantly headed for Sam's tent. What was past was past, and she had made a pact with herself to live only in the present and the future.

And her immediate future seemed likely to include a very unpleasant interview with Sam.

He had not yet returned to his tent, Lisa saw with relief as she entered. The lantern was still burning, and it very plainly revealed that the tent was empty. Lisa stood irresolutely in the middle of the floor, chewing nervously on a fingernail. Should she wait meekly for him to come in and chastise her, or should she return to her own tent and let him seek her out? She was tempted to go to her own tent, but the memory of Sam's ultimatum discouraged her. She was sure she had angered him already by making a scene in front of his men, and if he found her in her tent in defiance of his order he might very well carry through on his threat to cast her adrift and let her fend for herself. And that was too high a price to pay for a meaningless gesture of defiance.

Time passed, and still Sam didn't come. Lisa finally curled up in his cot, huddling miserably under the blanket. Her throat hurt, her stomach ached from lack of food, and she was growing increasingly apprehensive about what form Sam's anger might take.

She was determined to be awake when Sam finally returned to his tent. True, she couldn't stop him from taking her body, if that was what he planned, and she was about ninety-nine percent sure it was. If she was honest with herself she couldn't even deny that the idea wasn't exactly repulsive to her, either. But after everything he had said and done to her today, she was damned if she was going to make it easy for him. With grim relish she planned the words she would use to singe his arrogant ears.

It must have been about midnight when Lisa could no longer fight the compulsion to rest her eyes—just for a minute, she told herself. She let her lids drift closed, and was asleep almost instantly.

She awoke to the feel of hard arms curving around her body. Stretching sensuously against the solid shape that held her, she sighed and opened her eyes. It was dark. . . . It took her a few seconds to work out exactly where she was and whose arms enfolded her. Sam . . . Lisa knew, somewhere in the back of her mind, that she was angry with him, that she should be pushing him away instead of snuggling against him. But she was so sleepy, and the night air was so cold. . . .

Dreamily she realized that he was lifting her. Her arms curled automatically around his neck. He had taken off his shirt. . . . Her fingers stroked the iron muscles of his neck without conscious thought; her chilled little nose buried itself in the thick, curling hairs that covered his chest. He smelled so good, warm and faintly sweaty and all man. She pressed her lips against his chest, letting her tongue taste the saltiness of his skin.

He was carrying her. She didn't know where or why, but she certainly wasn't going to worry about it. It felt so good to be cradled in his arms. . . . Her toes curled in anticipation of what would happen when he finally put her down again.

He was lowering her onto a cot—whose cot?—that seemed to have sprung up on the opposite side of the tent from his. As the thin mattress took her weight, Sam's arms released their hold on her body, and he made a move as if to straighten. Lisa's arms clung protestingly around his neck. She didn't want him to go. . . . Why did he want to, anyway? This was surely what he had had in mind when he had asked— no, ordered—her to move in with him. Ahhh. Lisa smiled faintly as the solution to the puzzle presented itself. He had to finish undressing. . . . And then he would undress her, before... Her whole body tingled at the idea.

Her hands slid reluctantly down the front of his chest, her nails trailing through the crisp, slightly damp hairs. The curling strands rasped lightly against the sensitive pads of her fingers, and she gave in to a compulsion to tug on them. His breath sucked in in a satisfying little grunt.... Lisa had an uneasy suspicion that in the morning she would regret what she was doing, but at the moment she just didn't care. All she could think of was the melting warmth between her legs....

As her hands reluctantly released their grip, Sam straightened. Lisa could dimly make out the dark bulk of his big body as he moved a little away from her. With some small part of her consciousness she registered that he had apparently put out the lamp before awakening her....

She heard the clink of metal as he unfastened his belt, followed by the unmistakable sound of a zipper being lowered. Breathlessly she waited for him to remove his pants and return to her. He seemed to be taking forever.... Her eyes strained through the darkness. She could no longer make out exactly where he was.

"Sam?" His name was a husky whisper.

"God, you really are insatiable, aren't you?" he demanded tersely. Lisa heard the words with shock. Her breath caught in an audible gasp.

"Sorry, *Mrs.* Collins," he added when it became clear from the stricken quality of the silence that Lisa wasn't going to answer. His voice was harshly mocking. "You'll have to rock yourself to sleep tonight. I make it a rule never to shack up with married women."

V

LISA awoke the next morning almost in spite of herself. She surfaced groggily, her eyes blinking against the unwelcome fact that she was indeed facing another day. Her body felt as if it had been run over by a steamroller, and her spirits weren't in any better shape. Horrible, detestable man! was the first coherent thought to enter her brain. Then: God, my throat hurts!

One eye finally stayed open long enough to survey the interior of the tent. It was empty. Lisa felt a wave of relief so intense that all her muscles sagged with it. If there was one thing she could do without this morning, it was the knowing looks and snide remarks of a man who plainly considered her some kind of slut. That he might have some little justification for his belief, Lisa had to acknowledge, mentally reviewing her behavior since he had first laid eyes on her. To be absolutely fair, he was not to know that she didn't come on like a barracuda to every man she met. On the contrary... It was just something about *him*! And that was something that she certainly wasn't going to tell him.

If possible, Lisa felt even worse after making that humiliating admission to herself than she had upon awakening. Of all the men in the world—all the handsome, wealthy, respectable men in her social circle at home, all the intelligent, talented men at the paper where she worked, even the cute blond college boy who did odd jobs around her house—why in the world had her long-repressed sexuality chosen to batten on *him*? He was as hard-bitten as they came, tough and cynical and a male chauvinist pig to his toes. He wasn't even handsome, for God's sake! And she didn't like him—on his good days; at other times she actively hated him. But she craved the touch of his hands on her flesh like the Western world craved oil. She must be crazy! Which brought her thoughts back full circle. Horrible, detestable man!

Lisa sat up, not wanting to remember the events of the night before. She swallowed automatically, then winced in pained surprise. The inside of her throat felt as red and raw as hamburger. When she had tried to swallow, it had been pierced by a little stab of acute pain. Unwillingly she remembered the short, stubby hands of her attacker closing about her throat.... If Sam hadn't come when he had, the brute might have killed her. Lisa grimaced wryly. There was no *might* about it. He would have killed her, and by this time her body would have been picked clean of flesh by the carrion eaters of the jungle. There would have been nothing left but a skeleton.... Lisa shivered. Reluctantly she admitted that she owed Sam her life once again.

Pushing the tangled mass of her hair back from her face with one hand, Lisa sat up, swinging her legs over the side of the cot so that her bare feet touched the floor. Aside from her throat, the rest of her body seemed to be in reasonable shape. She was a little sore here and there, and probably had quite a few colorful bruises, but nothing that wouldn't heal in a couple of days. If nothing else, she thought wryly, this little—adventure—had certainly increased her tolerance of pain.

Lisa sat stiffly on the edge of the cot, not yet having summoned enough energy to stand up. She was still fully dressed except for her shoes, she registered idly, and remembered lying down on Sam's cot without doing anything more than kicking them off. Her attention shifted to his cot. It was still there, in the back right-hand corner of the tent. The little table littered with his papers was in the back left-hand corner. Her own cot was placed nearer the entrance, almost catty-corner to Sam's. A good four feet of space separated the two.... Apparently, from the presence of the extra cot, he had meant to let her sleep alone all along—with sleep being the operative word. If he truly had scruples about making love to married ladies, she was willing to bet that they had never troubled him before last night. She was quite, quite sure that he had said what he had merely to shame her....

A bronzed, strong hand parted the tent flap. Lisa started, her head swinging around to confront the intruder, her eyes wide with instinctive fright. Then she recognized the black curly hair and relaxed.

"Still in bed?" His voice was faintly amused. As he straightened and looked down at her, Lisa met those blue eyes. They were mocking.

"As you see." She meant the words to be coolly aloof, and was surprised at the dry croak that emerged from her throat.

Sam's eyes narrowed. He bent and took her chin in his hand before Lisa could move away, tilting her face up so that he could get a better look at her neck. He studied the slim column for a moment, unspeaking, but his darkening face spoke for him. Finally he brought his other hand up to stroke her throat, his touch surprisingly gentle. Lisa winced. Immediately he let her go.

"Your throat hurts." It was a statement, not a question. He was frowning heavily as he looked down at her.

"Yes." Her answer was faintly defiant.

"They really did play a little rougher than you had bargained on, didn't they?"

"Oh, for God's sake!" Lisa muttered angrily, closing her eyes and then opening them again to glare at him. To her surprise, he smiled at her. She was transfixed by what that slow smile did for his face.

"All right," he said, his tone placating. "I believe you about what happened down by the creek. I had a little—uh—talk with Lutz and Brady—the men who grabbed you—and they finally came clean."

"Did you send them away?" Lisa asked eagerly. It was good to know that Sam believed her, and it would be even better to know that the men who attacked her had left the camp.

Sam looked surprised. "I need them," he said, as if this explained everything.

"You mean that you're going to let them stay here, in this camp, after... after..." Her voice failed her.

"I told you, I need them." He sounded mildly impatient.

"But what if they... they...?" Her voice faltered, and she chewed anxiously on her lower lip without being aware that she was doing so.

"Try it again?" Sam finished for her. "Don't worry, they won't. I spent this morning putting the fear of God into them."

Lisa had to smile at that. "The fear of you, you mean."

Sam grinned. "You could put it that way."

"But I really would feel better if they weren't around. Can't you fire them, or whatever it is you do?" Her eyes, as she raised them to Sam's, were shadowed with remembered fear. He looked at her, his eyes running almost unwillingly over the tousled mass of ash-blond hair, the creamy skin of her face, which had been kissed to gold by the sun, the wide green eyes, and the soft, tremulous mouth. She looked femininely defenseless—which was a joke. She was about as helpless as a she-cat. Then Sam's gaze moved down to the livid black-and-yellow bruises that marred the long column of her throat, and he mentally corrected himself. She was out of her element in this man's world of war; for the moment, she needed his protection. But he was willing to bet a considerable sum that, on her own ground with her own female weapons, she was as devastating as a bazooka at twenty feet.

"I can't 'fire' them," he explained with more patience than he had shown previously. "We're here to do a job, and Lutz and Brady—however offensive they may have made themselves to you—are a vital part of this team. They are not expendable. None of my men are. I don't think you realize what a sacrifice it is for me to leave Riley hanging around the camp all day. I can't spare anyone else on your account."

Lisa was taken aback by this forthright speech. She had been so sure, now that he knew for certain that those animals had tried to rape her, that he would get rid of them. Apparently his "need" was more important than her safety. A measure of hostility showed in her eyes as she looked at him.

"I see," she said coolly.

"Good." The single word was brisk. "Now, if you'll stay put, I have some ointment that will make those bruises feel better. Hang on."

With that he turned and left the tent. Lisa stared after him, a mixture of anger and chagrin on her face. She was largely silent when he returned with the ointment, smoothed it impersonally into her throat, and went on about his business. It was only after he had left her again that Lisa realized she was suffering from a strong sense of injustice. He had admitted that she had been telling the truth all along. She had been right, he had been wrong. At the very least, she thought resentfully, he owed her an apology!

Lisa saw very little of Sam over the next three days. She shared his tent, and that was about all. He was gone from dawn to long after night had fallen. When he finally came in, he was so tired that he fell into bed with scarcely more than a grunt in her direction. Whatever the "job" he was engaged in involved, he was working hard at it. Lisa passed quite a bit of time speculating on what act or acts of skulduggery he and his men might be perpetrating. But when she had dropped a broad hint to Riley for information, he had told her meaningfully that he— or she—who knows least lives longest. Lisa took the hint, and forbore to ask any more questions.

Boredom was her primary complaint. There was absolutely nothing to do. Nothing to read, no television, no radio—at least none that played music— nothing. She managed to scrounge up a paper and pencil after much effort, and passed some hours attempting to set down what had befallen her in a fashion that the *Star* could use. If she could ever get it to them, which seemed more and more doubtful. But when she reread what she had written, she nearly cringed. In every other line was a mention of Sam. She tried leaving him out of it, but without describing how he had rescued and cared for her—

not to mention the other things he had done to and for her—she was left with a hole in her story big enough to drive a jeep through. And when she put him back in, the whole thing was too highly personal. Annoyed, she ripped her efforts into confetti and returned to glaring at inoffensive rocks. Grace and the *Star* would just have to live without her literary efforts—at least until she was home again.

There wasn't even anyone to talk to. Sam was gone all day, and so were the rest of the men—not that she objected to *that*—except Riley. And having a conversation with Riley was like pulling hens' teeth. He followed her around the camp like a surly little dog, uttering growls in response to her few conversational overtures. Lisa knew that only Sam's direct orders made him act as her bodyguard-cum-jailer; left to himself, he wouldn't give a damn if she was strung up by her toes and had the flesh peeled from her body millimeter by square millimeter. She finally decided that his demeanor was nothing personal: he disliked all women. But she sensed that he felt an extra dollop of resentment toward her. Clearly he considered it a waste of his time and talents to spend his days playing nursemaid to a woman who he thought was no better than she should be and had no business being where she was, in any case.

In desperation, Lisa took to cooking. There wasn't much that could be done with the canned goo Riley reluctantly described as C-rations, but she tried. From the dehydrated eggs she fashioned an elegant-looking omelet, and was so pleased with the effect that she offered to share it with Riley. He snorted, but took a bite, which he chewed silently for perhaps a second before spitting it on the ground. Lisa was a trifle daunted. When she tasted it herself, she had to admit that it was not exactly haute cuisine, but it was certainly better than the horrible scrambled eggs that were the staple of Riley's limited repertoire of menus. And if she cooked her own meals, at least she knew that everything that went into them was clean. Watching Riley's casual disregard for sanitation, she marveled that the men didn't come down with food poisoning at the very least. For a moment she considered cooking for Sam—and of course the other men—but then, with a toss of her head, she decided against it. She wasn't going to wait on him—them! But she continued to cook her own meals and doggedly ate most of what she prepared.

Living with Sam and yet not really living with him was bad for her disposition, Lisa acknowledged silently on the morning of the fourth day since he had blackmailed her into moving in with him. During that time he had made no move that could even remotely be classified as a pass; Lisa hated to admit it, but she was piqued. He undressed and dressed in front of her as casually as if he had been doing it for years. She ostentatiously averted her face, but she couldn't help the awareness of him that occasionally ran through her body like an electric shock. Since he was out of the tent so much, she had no need to worry about privacy for her own toilette. Not that she needed to worry about it in any case. She could have been a bundle of old rags for all the notice he took of her, she told herself waspishly. If she stripped stark naked in front of him she doubted that he would even notice, so intent was he on whatever work had brought him to Rhodesia. And if he did notice, she concluded with a darkling look in her eye, it would probably be only to tell her to get dressed before she caught a cold; he couldn't spare the time to nurse her.

Lisa's attitude toward Sam cooled until, if he had

been aware of anything except the task at hand, a single glance from her would have given him frostbite. He wasn't even conscious of her displeasure. Lisa knew this, and the knowledge made her long to slam something satisfyingly unyielding against his thick skull. At least then she would have his attention!

Early that afternoon, Lisa perched moodily on a rock near the perimeter of the camp while Riley squatted nearby. He was fiddling with the interior of a malfunctioning two-way radio and hadn't said a word for the past couple of hours. Lisa flashed him a resentful glance, then turned her attention back to watching the birds that wheeled and cried overhead. It was a beautiful, cloudless day in the middle of October, which was the start of Rhodesia's summer; the sun was hot and the sky was as blue as Sam's eyes. As soon as she made the comparison, Lisa was annoyed at herself. The color of the dratted man's eyes meant less than nothing to her, she told herself crossly. She had just used the simile because it was apt.

A jeep rattled into camp, causing her to turn her head with an expression of mingled interest and apprehension. When she recognized Sam as the driver of the vehicle, surprise took over. What was he doing back at the camp at this hour? she wondered bemusedly. He usually didn't return until long past dark. . . .

Riley had stood up at the approach of the jeep, and now as Sam brought it to a smooth halt some twenty feet away he walked toward it. Lisa hesitated a moment, then followed his example as Sam unwound his long body from the driver's seat and got out.

"Trouble?" Riley asked as he approached. Lisa was amused and also a little amazed to see him perk up like an alert terrier.

Sam shook his head reassuringly. "No," he said, his eyes flickering past Riley to touch on Lisa before moving back again. "You're needed now. I want you to decide where to set those charges."

Riley nodded as if he understood this incomprehensible statement perfectly. Then he jerked his head back toward Lisa.

"What about her?" he asked.

Sam looked at Lisa again. She returned his glance with a haughty tilt of her chin.

"I'll see to her—for this afternoon," he said, his attention totally focused on Lisa as she came to a halt just a few paces away. "After that, we'll see. You'll be needed from here on out." This last remark was addressed to Riley again.

The smaller man nodded once more. "Do you want me to take the jeep?"

Sam shook his head. "Take the spare. I may need this one."

"Okay." Riley loped off. Lisa was left alone with Sam.

"What was all that about?" Her tone was cool. One corner of Sam's mouth quirked upward in a tantalizing little smile.

"Isn't there a saying about curiosity killing...?" His voice trailed off as Lisa gave him an annoyed look.

"Oh, honestly," she said crossly. "I don't see why you're so mysterious. I don't give a damn what you're doing here. And even if I knew, there's certainly no one to tell!"

"Honey, believe me, the less you know, the better off you are," Sam said seriously. Then: "Besides, I never trust lady journalists. As soon as they know something and can tell it, they do."

Lisa didn't deign to reply to this, which she realized was designed to annoy her. Instead she favored Sam with an icy stare. Maddeningly, he chuckled.

"Not glad to see me?" he taunted.

Lisa snorted in a very unladylike way. "Not particularly."

Sam's grin widened. He took a step toward Lisa, his eyes twinkling in a way that would have made her heart beat faster—if she were still susceptible to his particular brand of charm, which she emphatically was not!

"I presume you have a reason for being here?" Lisa asked coolly, holding her ground. Sam stopped his teasing advance, folding his arms on his chest and regarding her quizzically.

"You presume right," he drawled. Then, as Lisa said nothing, waiting for him to expand on this theme, he reached down and withdrew a deadly-looking pistol from where it was tucked into his belt. Lisa's eyes widened to enormous green pools as she looked from the weapon to his face and back again.

"What . . . ?" she stuttered, alarm beginning to curl inside her. Perhaps he had decided that it would be easier all around to kill her. He was a soldier, after all; he must have killed dozens—no, hundreds. . . .

"Don't panic," he advised dryly, seeing the color drain from her cheeks. "You're perfectly safe. If I had wanted to get rid of you, I would have done it days ago. You're a nuisance, I admit, but I feel a kind of twisted responsibility for you now."

This hardly flattering speech had the effect of reassuring Lisa completely. Whatever else he might have done, Sam had never physically harmed her. In fact, he had saved her life more than once.

She acknowledged his remarks with an apologetic little half-smile. Sam accepted the implied apology with a nod, then turned his attention to the pistol once more.

"Have you ever used one of these?" he asked, weighing the weapon idly in his hand. Lisa stared at it, fascinated. Its gleaming black shape looked so horribly right in Sam's bronzed, totally masculine hand. . . .

"Of course not," she answered, still a little off balance by the continued presence of the gun. "When would I ever have had reason to use a gun?"

From her tone she might have been saying *snake*. Sam smiled.

"Pistol," he corrected absently. "Oh, I don't know. I had the idea that rich girls generally went fox hunting, or something."

"For heaven's sake, you don't *shoot* the fox!" Lisa stared at him, unsure if he was teasing. "Anyway, I hate guns. They should be banned."

"Is that right?" Sam looked amused.

Lisa stared at him coldly. If there was one political issue she felt strongly about, it was gun control. She felt that a lot more people would live to a ripe old age if the government would just step in and ban the deadly things.

"Yes," she said.

"Well, I'm sorry to make you go against your principles, ma'am, but you're going to have to learn to use one."

Lisa could feel her muscles tense in instinctive resistance. "Why?" she asked warily.

"Because I can't spare Riley any longer to wet-nurse you," he said, his eyes meeting hers squarely. "Because I can't watch after you myself. Because after today you're going to have to stay here in this camp all by yourself. And because I can't guarantee that some man won't come along and try to finish up where Lutz and Brady left off."

Lisa swallowed convulsively at the mention of her erstwhile attackers. Not until now, when she was faced with having to do without him, did Lisa realize how much she had come to depend on Riley's grudging presence. She had known that because Sam had told him to, he would keep her safe. . . . She remembered how she had felt in the jungle just after the attack on the Blasses, and how she had felt that day down by the creek when those two animals had stalked her—terrified and helpless. And she would be every bit as helpless here in this camp alone. . . .

"I'm—I'm afraid of guns," she said lamely at last. "I'm not sure that I could even shoot one."

Sam's eyes smiled at her. "That's why I'm here. To teach you. It's easy. Now, come over here and let me show you . . . ."

Reluctantly obedient, Lisa moved to stand beside him. Her head came to just a little above his muscled shoulder, she noticed abstractedly. She was fairly tall herself. He had to be at least six-feet-four. Beside him she felt almost tiny, and she was halfway ashamed to acknowledge that she liked the sensation.

"Are you listening to me?" Sam demanded with pardonable exasperation. Lisa started, then turned guilty eyes up to his face. He sighed, then patiently repeated what he had been saying.

Over and over again he showed her how the bullets went into the gun—pistol. Lisa watched, her expression doubtful. It was an automatic, she learned, which meant that the bullets went into a kind of cartridge and then the cartridge went into a hole in the gun's—pistol's—handle. After the cartridge had clicked into place, all you had to do was snap a sliding part of the gun's topside open and then closed again, and it was ready to shoot. It looked simple enough, Lisa thought, but when she gingerly tried to do it herself she pinched her thumb in the sliding panel. Sam laughed, and she glared at him furiously, sucking on the injured digit.

"You're doing very well," he praised soothingly, biting back a grin. "You probably won't have to do that, anyway. I'll clean it and keep it loaded for you—that's just in case you should have to reload."

"Are we finished?" Lisa asked hopefully. Her thumb still hurt, and she was sure that she would be better off throwing the stupid pistol at an attacker than trying to shoot him.

Sam shook his head, grinning.

"Uh-uh. Now that you know how to load—sort of—you need to learn to hit what you're aiming at. We're going to go target practicing."

Lisa looked up at him, aghast. It struck her that he was enjoying himself. The "me Tarzan, you Jane" mentality, she thought sourly.

"I'd really rather not..." she began. Sam silenced her with a chiding shake of his head.

"You're going," he said firmly.

Lisa looked at him, sighed, and gave up.

He herded her into the jeep and then got in himself. Lisa watched glumly as he inserted the key into the ignition and turned the motor over. Her last hope for a reprieve died as the engine fired. Fatalistically she clung to the side of the vehicle as it pitched and jerked across the bumpy plain, leaving two long lines of flattened grass in its wake. When at last Sam brought the jeep to a halt, she felt as if every tooth in her head was loose. Fixing him with a jaundiced eye, she saw that he was laughing again, his teeth cutting a sparkling white swath in his dark face. She glared at him feebly, wishing that her pitching stomach would realize the jolting ride was over.

"Come on, get out," he said unsympathetically, swinging himself out from behind the wheel. Lisa grimaced, but did as he said. She didn't seem to have much choice.

They walked a little way away from the jeep, then Sam left her standing while he went to pull some grass away from the shingled trunk of a large tree.

"That's your target," he said, coming back to her. Lisa didn't answer. Sam went through the whole routine of loading and unloading again, and made Lisa practice until she could do it without injuring herself. Finally he pronounced himself marginally satisfied.

"All right, let's see you shoot it." He was grinning.

Lisa looked down distastefully at the heavy metal weapon in her hand. "I don't want to." She made one last attempt to persuade him to see reason. The idea of actually shooting the thing ... What if it backfired? She would be blown to smithereens.

"Do it," he ordered, and came to stand behind her, his arms coming around her as he showed her the proper way to hold the pistol. Lisa felt the warmth of his body against her back, the solid strength of his muscles, and bit her lip. She had to force herself to concentrate on what he was saying. She refused, absolutely, to give in to this ridiculous weak-kneed feeling that made her want to lean back against him, letting his hard body bear her weight.

"Pay attention," Sam barked in her ear. Lisa jumped guiltily.

After that small lapse she did her best to listen to and absorb his instructions, squinting obediently down the length of their four arms as he helped her hold the pistol correctly. His arms, bared by sleeves rolled up above his elbow, looked bronzed and muscular and very strong next to her smooth, golden limbs. Crisp black hair covered his brown flesh, and Lisa shivered as it rasped against her soft skin. The feel of his large, callused hands wrapping her smaller ones made her remember....

"All right, now pull the trigger. Gently squeeeeze . . ."

Lisa automatically did as he said, then winced as the pistol spat in her hand. To her surprise, a twanging whine sounded instead of the deafening bang she had been braced for. Relieved, she would have lowered the pistol, but Sam's hands on hers made her continue to hold it stiffly out in front of her.

"Keep firing," he said encouragingly in her ear.

Lisa vaguely registered that the mouth of the pistol was still aimed at the hapless tree. Poor thing, she thought, then squeezed the trigger again. She shut her eyes so that she would not have to see the bullet tearing through the unoffending bark, and continued to fire with her eyes screwed tightly shut.

"You can ease up off the trigger. The gun's empty," Sam said wryly at last.

Lisa's eyes blinked open, and her fingers eased sheepishly off the trigger. To her relief, Sam stepped out from behind her and removed the pistol from her slackened grasp. Then he went to check the tree.

Relieved of the combined distractions of his nearness and the hated pistol, Lisa managed to recover a measure of her equilibrium.

"How'd I do?" she asked with some trepidation as he came striding back toward her.

He shook his head in disgust. "You can quit worrying. The tree doesn't have a mark on it."

"Oh." Lisa sighed with relief. Then, feeling as if she had disgraced herself, she added in a small voice, "Didn't I even hit it *once*?"

"Not once," he confirmed sparely. "Of course, it might help if you'd keep your eyes open. Come on, let's try it again."

Sam came around behind her again. This time his hands rested loosely on her shoulders as he left her to aim the pistol herself. Lisa would have interpreted his gesture as reassuring if she hadn't had a sneaking suspicion that he considered directly behind her the safest place to be.

The warmth and nearness of his body was a distraction, but Lisa did her best to ignore it. She pointed the pistol rather shakily at the tree, trying not to be conscious of the strength of his broad chest against her back and the muscles in the long, khaki-clad legs just brushing her own bare ones. The smell of him, made up of sweat and cigarettes and man, was intoxicating. Lisa felt perspiration bead her upper lip and immediately blamed it on the heat of the day. Although the spot where they stood was shaded by a clump of leafy teak trees, the sun beat hotly down all around, sending up heat in shimmering waves. It was that, and only that, that was causing her discomfort.

Grimly, Lisa pulled the trigger again, wanting only to get her mind off the reactions of her body. She felt like a murderer when a sickening thud came from the direction of the tree and a small piece of bark flew up in the air.

"Oh, no," she murmured, dismayed. The gun dropped slackly in front of her. Her hands continued to clutch it nervelessly.

"You hit it!" Sam sounded jubilant. "Good girl! Now do it again." His hands slid down to clasp her waist as he spoke. Lisa felt the length and strength of his fingers with a little shiver.

"I don't want to." Lisa looked at him over her

shoulder with unconscious appeal. She had to look up, way up, to meet his eyes. He frowned, but he didn't look angry. Those blue eyes seemed to be fixed on her mouth....

Lisa couldn't stop staring at him. She was so close she could see every line, every pore in his skin. She could see the faint black shadow that darkened his jaw, the jagged edges of the scar that should have lessened his appeal but didn't, the flaring of his nostrils, and every individual hair in his thick eyelashes. His black hair waved damply down over his forehead, and his blue eyes were alive and glittering with an emotion Lisa didn't attempt to define. His mouth was a hard, straight line that beckoned her excitingly....

Sam's hands tightened painfully on her waist. Lisa felt a long, tremulous wave of longing rack her body. Sam felt it, too. She could tell by the sudden flare of his eyes....

Slowly, moving as if she were hypnotized, Lisa turned in his hands, going up on her toes, one hand coming up to clutch his muscled shoulder for balance. She could no longer, for the life of her, resist the temptation of that hard mouth.

Her lips touched his softly at first, in a butterfly kiss that tantalized. Trembling, her mouth stroked his, pleading for response. Her eyes were closed tightly, seeking to shut out reality, to exclude everything except this compulsion she didn't have the strength to deny. She couldn't see his reaction to her boldness, but the suddenly harsh rasp of his breathing told her all she needed to know.

He stood motionless under her caress, making no move either to help or to hinder. Lisa trembled, moving closer to him so that the softness of her breasts brushed the hard wall of his chest. Her arms slid around his neck, clutching him; the pistol dangled forgotten from one hand. Her tongue slid out from between her lips to trace the unyielding outline of his mouth.

He stiffened. Lisa drew back her head, her green eyes opening languorously. Those blue eyes blazed down at her, as scorching as the African sun at midday. Still he didn't move. Lisa smiled at him sleepily; her breasts nuzzled into his chest of their own accord. His breath caught. Lisa could feel the momentary cessation of his breathing.

Then, "Hell, why not?" he muttered thickly, and his mouth came swooping down on hers.

VI

HE kissed her as if he were starving for the taste of her mouth. His lips and tongue alternately caressed and plundered, while his arms locked around her waist and back, holding her as if he would never let her go. Lisa met his ravening hunger with her own need, her arms wound about his neck, her head thrown back against his shoulder. She was shaking so badly that she doubted that her legs would support her if he released her. Not that there was any chance of that. She could feel his passion building like a raging inferno, searing her with its heat. He had taken over the kiss completely; she followed his lead with abandon. What she had done was totally shameless, she knew—and yet she was not ashamed. She wanted him too badly.

His mouth left the sweetness of her lips to slide hotly across her soft cheek to her ear. Lisa moaned softly as he nipped the tender lobe, his teeth punishing.

"Temptress," he murmured huskily, his breath warm against the shell-like structure. The word was meant to be accusing, Lisa knew, but somehow it came out sounding incredibly sexy. Her trembling increased until her limbs shook as if they were palsied.

He was totally supporting her weight, one large

hand cradling the back of her head as he tilted her so that his mouth could have easy access to the softness of her throat. Lisa closed her eyes against a momentary glimpse of blue sky, barely conscious of anything except the feel of Sam's hands and mouth and body.

His mouth was tracing its way down her neck, nibbling and sucking and licking at the soft column. Finally he reached the throbbing hollow; he rested there for a moment, his face pressed against her skin. She could feel the hardness of his jaw, the rasp of his unshaven chin, the moist heat of his open mouth as he nuzzled at her throat. Then one hand slid all the way around her back to cup her soft breast. The nipple hardened instantly, pressing into his palm through the thin layers of her shirt and bra. He took the importunate bud between his thumb and forefinger, gently rolling it back and forth. Lisa's knees buckled.

He let her sag to the ground, his arms supporting her until she was lying full length in the tall grass. Lisa's eyes flickered open in time to see a fleeting, rueful smile curve the hard mouth. She blinked, confused.

"I think you'd better give me that," he said, his voice slightly teasing despite the unmistakable passion that thickened his words.

"That" turned out to be the pistol, which she had forgotten all about. Sam removed it gently from her slackened hand. Lisa's eyes remained fixed on his face. Had she ever not thought him handsome? she wondered bemusedly. He was the most beautiful thing in the world to her now. Those rugged, uneven, intensely male features and that hard, brown, totally masculine body appealed to her in a way that she had never thought possible.

He was standing now, towering over her. Lisa watched hungrily as he unbuttoned his shirt with a quick economy of movement. When he shrugged out of it, letting it fall casually to the ground, her eyes slid desirously along the broad, bronzed shoulders to where they joined the strong neck, then moved down over the muscled, hair-matted chest bisected by the leather shoulder holster. His hands were at his belt, unfastening it, letting it dangle open while he first unbuttoned and then unzipped the khaki pants. Then he paused for a moment, hands resting negligently on his hips, a slow smile teasing his lips as he looked down at her fascinated face.

"Enjoying the show?" he asked softly, and Lisa vaguely remembered once saying something similar to him. Shamelessly she nodded. His smile widened, but something smoldered dangerously in his eyes. He had to sit to remove the heavy combat boots; his movements were slightly jerky as he slid out of his pants and shorts and unfastened his shoulder holster. Lisa smiled involuntarily when he cursed a particularly stubborn buckle. Then he was crawling toward her, naked, straddling her supine body while remaining on all fours.

"Now it's my turn," he threatened, and her smile died as her mouth went dry.

Sam hunkered back on his heels, still straddling her. His turgid flesh burned against the soft inner skin of her bare thigh where her shorts had ridden up. Lisa squirmed instinctively, but Sam held her effortlessly captive between his brown thighs. His hands went slowly, so slowly, to the buttons on her shirt. Lisa moved to help him, but her fingers were impossibly clumsy. He brushed them aside, unfastening the buttons himself. After each one was freed from its hole, he pressed a quick, seductive kiss into her yearning flesh. By the time he had her shirt open, Lisa was moaning audibly. She reached out for him, but he caught her hands, pinning them back against the hard ground. He held her that way, and she was forced to watch, helpless, as his eyes made a meal of her quivering body.

The flesh of her upper body was creamily pale against the faded khaki of her ragged cut-offs and opened shirt; her breast surged urgently against the silky peach cloth of the flimsy bra as they begged to be released from their confinement. Just above the belted waistline of her shorts, her navel enticed him. . . .

Sam's eyes feasted on the shape and texture of her. Lisa strained to free herself so that she could pull him closer, but he controlled her abortive movements easily. Her long, pale-gold hair formed a tangled halo around her head against the deeper gold of the long grass crushed beneath her; her eyes were a deep, gleaming green, half-closed and slanted like a cat's as they begged him. A lovely tawny-pink flush had crept into her high cheekbones; her mouth was as soft and luscious as the reddest rose.

Sam's heart began to slam against his rib cage in slow, painful thuds. His eyes darkened slumbrously. Lisa, watching these signs of his arousal with an excitement of her own, felt violent tremors snake out over her skin.

Her breath stopped as he bent his head to place his open mouth against her breast. His hot, moist breath burned through her bra to scorch her flesh; his tongue teased the nipple through the silky material. Her eyes closed helplessly; her head thrashed from side to side in tortured longing. She wanted him with a fierceness that shocked her. . . .

His mouth continued to torment her defenseless nipple; she gasped as his hand stroked down her flesh to explore her trembling navel with one hard finger, then continued on across her still-covered abdomen to press intimately between her thighs. She writhed as he touched her, pushing against his hand, helpless to end this torture.

"God," she heard him mutter. The word sounded strangled. Then his hands were tugging at her shorts, his fingers shaking as he fumbled with the knotted rope that served as her belt. She lifted her hips off the ground, aiding him as he dragged her shorts and panties and shoes off together. Then his big body was upon her, his weight crushing her into the ground as his hands thrust her bra out of the way of his marauding mouth.

"Now," she cried, moaning, her legs opening to him of their own volition. "Oh, now, Sam, please, now!"

He thrust into her urgently, his hardness impaling her soft flesh. She gasped, and moaned, and cried out his name as her legs wrapped themselves around his waist. Her hands clutched frantically at the thick, rough-silk hair that grew to his nape.

His arms clamped her to him with a bruising strength that would have hurt her if she had been aware of anything besides her body's desperate need; his groans mingled with her soft cries as he took her with him to the edge of ecstasy and beyond. Lisa's nails dug into his hard flesh; her body moved with his in a driving dance of passion.

"Yes, yes, *yes*!" she sobbed when at last he drove into her with a force that should have split her in two. He groaned an answer, his face buried in the sweet-smelling hollow of her neck, his body shuddering and throbbing deep inside her. Lisa surged against him, holding him tightly, moaning. Then, with a wonderful melting sensation more pleasurable than anything she had ever known, she quivered and went limp.

It could have been hours or only minutes before she came floating back to earth to feel the sun's rays beating into her skin. She opened her eyes to find that the patch of shade they had been lying in had shifted with the passage of time, so that she was now ruthlessly exposed to the full glare of the late-afternoon sun. For a long moment she stared down at her body, marveling at her new knowledge of the exquisite sensations of which it was capable. She had never dreamed that she could feel such passion. . . .

She flushed a little as it occurred to her how very wanton she must look, lying nearly naked in the middle of an open field with the glaring light of the African sun playing over her body. Groggily she sat up; her still-fastened bra formed a twisted line from armpit to armpit, and she pulled it down, straightening it with unsteady fingers. Her shirt, now crumpled and sweat stained, still hung loosely from her shoulders; she dragged it across her body. Then she looked around for Sam.

He lay sprawled on his stomach about two feet away. His face was buried in his folded arms, leaving only the back of his black head visible; his long legs were spread slightly apart. The shimmering sunlight gleamed off the dark bronze of his broad back. His buttocks were startlingly white against the rich mahogany of his back and legs. They were rounded and well muscled, and, as she knew from experience, hard to the touch. . . .

Lisa smiled a little as she looked at him. Whatever else he might be, he was a fantastic lover. Hesitant at first, she reached out a hand to touch him, letting her fingers trail over the hard muscles of his upper arm. She wanted him to look at her: she had to know if he felt as wonderful as she did. He didn't move. More confident now, she stroked his arm from shoulder to the wrist, her fingers finally coming to rest in the hair at his nape. Suddenly his hand shot out to capture hers, holding her wrist as he turned on his side, his free arm moving to prop up his head. He seemed sublimely unconcerned with his own nakedness.

His blue eyes raked over her, their expression impossible to read. With a little tingle of remembered excitement, she saw that a dark flush still mottled his cheeks. She felt a little shy as she remembered the things she had said and done in his arms, and was glad that the shirt shielded the most intimate parts of her body from his gaze. The slender length of her legs was left bare; they were shapely, tanned a light golden brown. His eyes surveyed them from the tips of her small toes to her thighs.

Suddenly he looked up, meeting her eyes. Lisa felt her cheeks grow warm as he studied her face, his eyes lingering on her mouth, which she was sure must still be red and swollen from his kisses. Rather tremulously, she smiled at him. He responded by carrying her hand to his mouth, pressing his lips against the inside of her wrist in a way that sent shivers zinging down to her toes.

"I have to hand it to you, honey," he drawled, kissing the ends of her fingers one by one. "You're the best goddamn lay I ever had."

For one incredulous instant, Lisa could not believe her ears. Then she stiffened in outrage, jerking her hand free of his hold. How could he...? she cried inwardly. How could he insult her so? He laughed at her stricken expression, a taunting sound denoting savage satisfaction. Then he rolled to his feet.

"What were you expecting, moonlight and flowers?" he jibed cruelly. Lisa winced. This couldn't be happening...it was a nightmare....She looked up at him, the pain showing in her eyes. He was standing there, still naked, looking down at her with his fists resting lightly on his hips and a nasty smile curling his mouth.

"I hate you," she whispered venomously. His smile widened, but his eyes were as hard as diamonds as they raked her where she crouched half-naked in the grass.

"Honey, I love the way you hate," he taunted. Lisa shut her eyes, wanting to block out the sight of this mocking savage who just minutes before had been her lover. She bit her lip to stem hot words of invective. She wanted to kill him—and she couldn't. She wanted to make him suffer—and she didn't have the power. She was helpless against the sadistic son of a bitch....

"You have grass in your hair," he said, his voice heavy with contempt, and bent to pick it out. Lisa jumped to her feet, knocking his hand aside. Then, before she thought, she slapped him full in his mocking face.

"Why, you..." he bit out, grabbing her wrist and holding it in a vise grip. Lisa should have been frightened, she knew, but she wasn't. She was too damned mad....

"You deserved that," she spat, her eyes blazing on his face. His hand tightened punishingly.

"For what?" he asked softly. "For taking what you've been dying to give me for days? You started this thing today, babe, not me. You were hotter than a bitch in heat, and if you're honest you'll admit it."

Lisa glared at him, hating him more than she had ever hated anyone in her life. If she could have willed him to drop dead on the spot, she would have. The horrible thing about it was, he was right. She had initiated their coupling, and she had been hot for him—but did he have to make it sound so—so impossibly nasty?

"Cat got your tongue?" he taunted. Lisa shook the tumbled mass of curls out of her eyes, her chin tilting up proudly.

"Would you please let go of my wrist?" she asked with icy politeness. "You're hurting."

"You slapped me," he reminded her softly. Lisa could see the dark red imprint of her fingers against his brown cheek. She hoped, with a viciousness that was usually foreign to her, that it hurt.

"You deserved it," she insisted stubbornly. He smiled, but his expression was not pleasant.

"I ought to slap you back."

"That's just the kind of thing you would do," Lisa answered with a contempt that matched his.

His eyes narrowed; he gave a sharp little tug on her wrist that sent her tumbling against him. He caught her, holding her an unwilling prisoner against his hard body. Lisa pushed furiously at his chest, but she might just as well have pushed at the Empire State Building: he didn't budge.

"You can pay me back in the way you're best at," he said softly.

Lisa glared at him; then, reading his intention in his eyes, she averted her face. He laughed unpleasantly; one arm continued to clamp her to him while his other hand came up to capture her unwilling chin. With ridiculous ease he turned her face up to his. Lisa knew what he meant to do, knew what direction his revenge would take, but she was powerless to prevent him. Against his strength she felt like a little child. He smiled down at her tauntingly, clearly reveling in her helplessness. Lisa stood rigidly as he slowly lowered his mouth to hers, her fists clenched against his chest, her every muscle stiff with outrage.

He kissed her roughly, hurting her, seeming to want to hurt her. Lisa suffered his prying invasion of her mouth because she could do nothing else. But when his hand slid up under her shirt and bra to close on her bare breast, she began to fight him, her small fists beating ineffectually against his chest, her legs kicking at his shins.

He laughed exultantly as her nipple hardened in instinctive reaction to his massaging palm. His mouth moved away from her bruised lips to ravage the silken cord of her neck.

"Come on, baby, beg me," he muttered outrageously against her skin. "You just might be able to talk me into giving it to you again...."

Lisa gasped. Rage and humiliation combined to give her an extra measure of strength as she fought to be free. He controlled her struggles easily. When at last she stood quietly in his hold, panting and subdued but still rigid with fury, his hands began a slow, insolent exploration of her body. He watched her as he stroked her most intimate places with a familiarity designed to be offensive. Lisa quivered with mortification; her eyes flashed disgust at him.

"I hate you," she whispered finally, as the fingers of one big hand searched for and found the secret recesses of her body. "No!"

This last startled cry came as his hands left their occupation to cup her buttocks, lifting her from the ground. Then they slid down to close on the backs of her upper thighs, parting her legs so that he stood braced between them. Off balance, her hands instinctively clutched at his shoulders. Before she had quite registered his intention, he thrust inside her. Then it was too late.

110

Lisa's rage strangled any passion she might have felt. She cursed him as he took her, her fists doubling to beat at whatever part of him she could reach.

After her first blow, he tilted her back away from him so that she could not reach his face, his hands clamped tightly around her waist. His possession was swift and brutal, a savage act of aggression. Lisa could do nothing but endure.

When at last he allowed her to slide limply down his body, Lisa was forced to lean against him for a moment before she could summon the strength to jerk away. He let her go. She moved a couple of paces from him; her eyes lighted on the pistol, which lay where he had dropped it in the tall grass.

Moving casually, she stepped toward it. When she was close enough, she dropped her pretense of nonchalance and swooped on it, snatching it up and turning to point it at him in one quick movement. Using both hands, she held it stiffly out before her in the way he had taught her; its mouth was pointed directly at his flat belly. Then she looked straight at him, smiling. Murder was in her eyes and in her heart.

VII

Surprise and something else flickered in Sam's eyes for just an instant as he eyed first the pistol and then her flushed face. Lisa glared back at him with a mixture of anger and triumph. At last she had the arrogant so-and-so where she wanted him. The tables were turned with a vengeance!

She had to admit that he did not look particularly worried. He was standing there with his fists resting lightly on his lean hips; the slight breeze ruffled his black hair and his head was cocked a little to one side like that of an inquisitive bull dog. Perspiration gleamed on his chest and shoulders; his body hair curled damply into little ringlets. He seemed totally unconcerned with his nakedness, and this annoyed Lisa.

"Don't move!" she warned, although he had given no indication that he planned to. Indeed, he looked as though he was prepared to stay where he was all day.

The pistol quivered in her grip. Biting her lip, Lisa steadied it. Already her arms were beginning to ache a little from holding it out so stiffly in front of her.

"Well, are you going to shoot me or not?" Sam demanded.

Lisa stiffened her arms again, pointing the mouth of the pistol squarely at his mid-section.

"Yes," she said positively. In truth, she was growing more reluctant to pull the trigger with each passing second. He deserved it, despicable creature that he was, but...

"It will make a hell of a mess, you know," he said unhelpfully. "That's a Colt .45, and at this range it will make a hole in my guts the size of a basketball. Might even split me clean in two."

Lisa felt her stomach begin to churn at this unlooked-for bit of information. She could just picture the grisly scene.... Blood would fly everywhere; Sam's body would be torn in half.... Her hands began to shake; the mouth of the pistol dipped. Hastily she jerked it up again, glaring aggressively at Sam.

"Go on, pull the trigger," he encouraged. The corners of his mouth were beginning to quirk suspiciously.

Lisa stiffened. If he dared to laugh at her, she *would* shoot him!

"You deserve it," she muttered angrily. She already knew that she wasn't going to be able to do it. Just the thought of that tall, strong body lying broken and bleeding on the ground, the life blown from it by her hand, was enough to make her sick. But Sam had no way of knowing that....

"But you can't do it, can you?" he answered dryly. "Honey, you couldn't even shoot a tree. You're not going to shoot me—and we both know it."

"Shut up!" she nearly shouted. What he had said was all too true, but if she was going to maintain her advantage, she had to convince him otherwise.

"If you move one step, I'll blow your balls off," she

113

said clearly. To her astonished rage, he laughed out loud.

"That's one thing I admire about you." He was openly grinning. Lisa felt her rage rising, along with a murderous urge to wipe that smirk from his face. "Your ladylike language under the most trying of circumstances. Bryn Mawr can be proud of you."

"Say one more word and I really will shoot you." She was glowering at him, angry color high in her cheeks. She *should* shoot him, for what he had done to her. It had been the most humiliating experience of her life, his brutal taking of her body without regard for her wishes. She should teach him a lesson...but she couldn't. Not this way. Besides, what would become of her if he died? At the thought, she almost stamped her foot in sheer frustration.

"No, you won't. And we both know it, don't we, Lisa?" He began to walk toward her, his movements slow and easy.

Lisa tightened her grip on the gun frantically. She wouldn't surrender so easily....

"Stay back!" she warned in a high, shaking voice. The pistol wobbled in her hold. Desperately she snapped it up, pointing it at him. To her fury, Sam kept coming.

"Give me the pistol, Lisa," he cajoled, his hand held out to receive it.

Lisa saw that he wasn't going to stop. She glared at him with impotent fury for a moment. He was so damned cock-sure that she wouldn't shoot, that she would just meekly hand over the pistol....For a moment Lisa seriously considered pulling the trigger, and to hell with the consequences. Then, with a sound midway between a sob and a growl, she hurled the pistol at him.

Sam caught it easily in one hand. Lisa ground her

teeth as she watched him pluck it out of the air as casually as if it were a baseball. At the very least she had hoped to leave him with a large bruise by which to remember this encounter.

He stopped, balancing the pistol in his hand. Lisa glared at him. He was close—close enough that he could reach out and grab her if he liked. Well, she wasn't afraid of him, and she wasn't moving an inch. Let him take whatever revenge he chose.

"Next time you hold a pistol on a man," he drawled infuriatingly, "make sure the safety's off. The effect is infinitely more threatening."

Grinning, he flicked the safety switch from off to on and back again. Lisa could have screamed with pure rage. No wonder he had been so casually confident!

"Now," he began. His words were interrupted by the unmistakable rattle of an approaching jeep. Instantly Sam stiffened; the teasing expression fled from his face, to be replaced by cold concentration. Lisa was frightened. Seen like this, she believed that he could kill....

"Someone's coming," he said unnecessarily. "Get back over in those trees and stay out of sight."

Even as he spoke, he was checking the chamber of the pistol. What he saw there appeared to satisfy him, because he clicked the compartment closed again, and, with a quick glance at Lisa to make sure that she was obeying him, he sprinted toward the jeep.

Lisa was already running for the trees, pausing only to scoop up those of her clothes that she could find. Panting, her heart beating like a hunted rabbit's, she reached the safety of the trees and cowered in their concealing shadow. Looking back at Sam, she saw that he was leaning over the jeep's side to pull a businesslike rifle from the rear seat. With his other hand he scooped up a belt stuffed with ammunition, slinging it over his shoulder. Quickly he checked the mechanisms of the rifle, then headed away from the jeep, moving fast.

Horrible memories of the night she had met him flickered through Lisa's brain like flashes from a movie. She was so frightened that her knees were shaking. If the approaching vehicle did indeed contain enemy soldiers, what would she and Sam do? They would both be killed.... Dazed, her eyes sought Sam again. He had dropped to one knee some little distance from the jeep; the rifle was held to his shoulder, its mouth pointed steadily in the direction of the sound that was growing ever closer. He was squinting purposefully down the long barrel; beside him on the ground, within easy reach, lay the pistol.

Just looking at him helped to steady Lisa's crumbling nerves. He was a cruel, calculating bastard, and she despised him, but she knew that he would protect her with his life if necessary. He himself had admitted that he felt responsible for her, and he was not a man to shirk his responsibilities at any cost. Even dressed as he was, in nothing but an ammunition belt, he looked tough and hard and capable of fighting off an army single-handedly if the need arose. Suddenly Lisa felt immeasurably calmer. As much as she hated to admit it, she knew she was in good hands.

Lisa made a quick inventory of the clothes she held in one hand. Whatever happened, she would be better prepared to face it fully dressed, she thought. Her panties were missing; they must still be out there in the field. She stepped into her shorts, tying the rope belt into a satisfyingly secure knot. Then she slid her feet into her sneakers and knelt to tie the

laces. Dressed, she felt better. Sam might be unconcerned with his own nudity, but she was not.

She pressed herself against the thick trunk of the
very tree she had been attempting to assassinate
earlier, and peered apprehensively around it. She
could see Sam where he knelt, rocklike, his body
almost hidden by the tall grass. Whoever was
approaching wouldn't see him until they were almost
upon him, and maybe not even then. If they spotted
anything it would be Sam's jeep, and they would
probably go over to investigate, giving Sam a chance
to take them totally by surprise.

As the jeep, for that was what it was, roared into
view, Sam's muscles tensed. Lisa could see them
bulge against the brown satin of his skin. . . . For just
a moment his hands tightened on the upraised rifle,
and she thought that he looked ready to fire on the
instant. But then, as the jeep came closer, he laid the
rifle down on the ground beside the pistol and stood
up. When the jeep rattled to a halt beside him, he
had put on his shorts and was very calmly stepping
into his pants.

Two men were in the jeep, and Lisa felt a wave of
relief as she recognized them as being from the
camp. They were both grinning broadly at Sam as he
zipped up his pants.

"Well, I see we didn't have any reason to be worried about you," one of them remarked jovially to
Sam. Lisa vaguely remembered that Sam had introduced him to her simply as Frank.

"No, you didn't," Sam responded, his tone dry. "As
you see, I'm alive and well."

"Yeah." Frank was grinning; from the knowing
tone of his voice, he had a very shrewd idea about
what had taken place in the field just prior to his
arrival. Lisa, staying out of sight among the trees

because she was too embarrassed to come out, felt her cheeks burning. She clapped her hands to them, hoping to dull their hectic color before anyone could see it.

Over by the jeep, Sam finished buckling his belt, picked up his shoulder holster, and strapped it on. Then he shrugged into his shirt.

"Hey, you forgot something!" Frank clambered from the jeep, walking over to a spot some little distance away from Sam and scooping something out of the tall grass. He was chuckling audibly, and Lisa had no trouble discerning the twitting note in his voice. An instant later, she saw its cause: as he held out the object he had retrieved, Lisa was horrified to recognize her own silky, peach-colored underpants dangling from his stubby fingers.

"Very funny." Sam took the undergarment from his henchman without any sign of embarrassment. Lisa, if she hadn't been feeling so thoroughly mortified, would have reluctantly had to admire his aplomb. As it was, all she could do was squirm with humiliation as he casually tucked her panties into his pocket.

"Now that you've assured yourselves that I'm not in any mortal danger, why don't you take off?" Sam made it clear that it was an order, not a request. "I think you've embarrassed the lady enough."

"Some lady!" The other man in the jeep spoke for the first time. Sam turned a suddenly furious frown on the man as he grinned at his own wit. Abashed, the man muttered something that sounded like an apology. Frank, meanwhile, had climbed back into the jeep.

"See you later," he said to Sam, turning the key in the ignition. Sam nodded curtly in answer as the engine roared to life, and then the jeep was bumping

118

away from him, headed back in the direction of the camp.

After it was out of sight, Sam strolled toward the trees where Lisa still hid. She watched him approach, wishing that the ground would open up and swallow her.

"You can come out now," he called dryly. Reluctantly, feeling a fool, Lisa stepped out into the sunshine. Sam surveyed her silently for a moment, then reached into his pants pocket.

"Here," he said, holding her panties out to her. Lisa felt as if her face were on fire. Knowing she must be turning beet red, she accepted the garment from him with a muttered word of thanks. He eyed her sardonically.

"Come on, let's go," he said, turning in the direction of the jeep. "And don't look so embarrassed. What you heard was just sour grapes. Every man jack of them would murder his grandmother to be in my place."

Speechless, Lisa followed him over to the jeep and obediently climbed inside. As they drove back to camp, she pondered this man who was stranger, enemy, and lover all at the same time. He had been brutal earlier in word and deed. When he had so ruthlessly taken her body she had wanted to kill him. Yet, when they had first made love out there in the grass, he had taught her body a lesson in passion that it had never thought to learn; and, later, he had been kind to try to alleviate her embarrassment.

When they reached the camp, he stopped the jeep and turned to her.

"Go on back to the tent," he said, his hands resting lightly on the top of the steering wheel as he regarded her broodingly. "I have some things to do. I'll see you later."

119

Lisa got out without argument. No sooner had her feet hit the ground than the jeep drove off.

After that, their relationship underwent a drastic change. Sam, disdaining her marksmanship and not being able to spare anyone to stay with her, started taking her with him whenever possible. Lisa was instructed to stay with the jeep, and this she obediently did. Sometimes she would take a blanket and curl up on the rear seat while he and his men did whatever they had come to do. She had learned better than to ask questions, and in truth she no longer cared. She only wished that they would finish the job in a hurry so that she could go home again.

Lisa no longer melted with passion at Sam's slightest touch. His crude words about her qualities as a "lay" had effectively stiffened her resistance. This rankled every time she thought of it; so did the knowing grins on the faces of the men as she accompanied Sam nearly everywhere he went. Perversely, now that she was determined to resist his lovemaking, he took her body every chance he got: at least once a day, sometimes more. If she feigned sleep when they were out late, he disregarded her pretended drowsiness, scooping her out of the rear seat and carrying her inside to his cot, where he would make passionate love to her until the walls of her self-control crumbled. Or sometimes, during the afternoon, he would take her wherever they happened to be. Once he even returned to the jeep while his men were out doing whatever it was they did in the jungle, climbed into the backseat of the jeep with her, and pulled her onto his lap. He proceeded to kiss her until she was limp and pliant in his arms, then took her with her straddling his lap as he sat upright on the car seat. At first Lisa had been terrified that someone would come and catch them in *flagrante delicto*, as it were.

But by the time Sam was finished with her, she wouldn't have cared if they had had a whole football stadium full of spectators.

Each time he took her, Lisa vowed that it would be the last. And each time she fought him until his rough caresses drove her beyond all reason. Then she went wild in his arms. Lisa found these episodes humiliating in the extreme, but Sam seemed to thrive on them. At any rate, his lovemaking showed no signs of diminishing.

Like the male chauvinist pig Lisa called him, now that she was in truth his "woman" Sam expected her to act like it. He would fling torn garments into her lap and expect her to mend them as she waited for him in the jeep. Back at the camp, she had the honor of making up his cot as well as her own. Doubtless he would have expected her to cook for him if he had had any confidence in the meals she continued to prepare for herself; as it was, after one hard glance at one of her more fanciful concoctions, he preferred to stick with Riley's efforts, apparently with the conviction that the devil he knew was better than the one he didn't. Lisa's temper simmered at his casual assumption that she would perform her "womanly" functions, but he had not pushed her to the point of an explosion—yet.

Lisa figured that she had been in the camp about three weeks. During that time, her life had settled down into a kind of routine. She felt oddly at home in this army encampment surrounded by hired killers, with all hell liable to break loose at any minute. Although she knew that their existence was precarious, she felt almost totally safe. She supposed, reluctantly, that her sense of security in the face of all the facts had something to do with Sam. His very presence inspired confidence. She was certain that he would get her out of this mess in one piece if there was any possible way to do it. And she was content to leave her deliverance to him. Not that she had any choice. He had made it perfectly clear that they would leave when the job he had come to do was completed, and not a moment sooner.

Sam, whether she hated him, as she did one day, or merely intensely disliked him, as she did the next, was beginning to seem like a fixture in her life. It was hard to imagine that she had known of his existence for less than a month. Soon—she hoped— she would be home again, and he would be out of her life for good. All of this would seem like a slightly fantastic dream—or a nightmare, depending on how one looked at it.

She no longer even tried to compose stories suitable for the *Star* on her adventures. They had become too many, and too varied—and too wound up with Sam. She could not write about what had befallen her without revealing some part of their relationship, and this she was determined not to do. She thought of Grace Ballard at the *Star,* of the ladies of Annapolis's upper crust who devoured the features she edited, of the titillation they would receive from ferreting out any hint of an intimate association between Lisa Bennet Collins and a hard-bitten mercenary soldier, of all things, and shuddered. The whispers, titters, and sidelong glances would be more than she could endure. And there was Jeff, who was still her legal husband after all, and her grandfather. They would be embarrassed as much as she was.

Lisa thought of her grandfather with a twinge of compunction. He would be frantically worried about her by now; she hoped he could somehow sense that she was all right. She was the only thing he cared about in the world, now that Jennifer was gone, and it would be extremely hard on him to imagine that something had happened to her, too.

Jeff might be superficially concerned about her disappearance, she acknowledged with a shrug, but he certainly wouldn't lose a lot of sleep over it. Over the past year they had existed like casual acquaintances, living in the same house and still legally married, but hardly seeing each other from one week to the next. Now that Jennifer, the glue that had held them together, was no longer a factor, Lisa had no doubt that he would agree to a divorce with very little argument. And she was now very, very sure that a divorce was what she wanted.

Jeff would never have married her in the first place, she judged, if it hadn't been for the pressure exerted on him by his family and her grandfather. Perhaps his family had some inkling of his secret, because they had certainly been eager to see him married to her, and then had been overjoyed when she produced Jennifer. Or maybe they had simply wanted him to marry her because she was A. Herman Bennet's granddaughter—his name alone made her the ideal prospect for a wife in the eyes of most of the boys she had dated. Little Miss Perfect, that's me, Lisa thought with a touch of bitter humor, then shrugged away all thoughts of the past.

She was sitting in the back of the jeep, her head thrown back against the top of the seat as she gazed up at the stars, a blanket huddled around her shoulders to ward off the night chill. The jeeps were parked in a small copse to shelter them from the view of any chance passersby—not that there were likely to be any in this remote place. The blowing branches above her head made strange patterns against the twinkly midnight-blue sky. Sam and the others had vanished into the thick jungle; they would return when they returned. The despised pistol was by her side. Its silencer had been removed so that she could use it to summon help if an emergency arose. A single shot was the signal they had agreed upon. Sam had decided, and she had whole-heartedly concurred, that if she actually tried to shoot someone, she would be putting herself and any chance bystanders in more danger than anyone who might be intent on doing her harm.

Just knowing that Sam was within earshot of her pistol made Lisa feel safe. Sitting there in the jeep, in the middle of the inhospitable African jungle, with fighting going on all across the country and the possibility of unfriendly soldiers appearing at any moment, she felt much as she had in the past when she had sat out after dark on the beach near her grandfather's house: warm and peaceful and slightly drowsy.

Sam had instructed her to stay awake while he was gone—after all, if she was asleep when an enemy closed in on her, she certainly wasn't going to be able to summon help, was she—and Lisa tried valiantly to obey. But tonight she was so tired.... It had been such a hot day, and she had spent most of it sitting in this damned jeep. Then they had returned to the camp for a quick dinner, and here they were again. Lisa was almost ready to tell Sam that she would prefer to remain at the camp alone while they went out on their little forays. Almost. But she had a sneaking suspicion that as soon as the little cavalcade of jeeps disappeared from her view, she would regret it: she would undoubtedly be scared out of her skull.

If she didn't do something, she would fall asleep, Lisa decided. Stretching, she unwound herself from the blanket and sat for a moment shivering in the cool air. Then she clambered over the side of the jeep. Surely it wouldn't do any harm to walk around a little; she would be sure to remain fairly close to the jeeps.

Crossing her arms over her chest for warmth, wishing now that she had brought the blanket with her, Lisa moved off a little way through the trees. The world about her was shrouded in a deep charcoal gray; outlines of trees and bushes stood out blackly like swaying ghosts. Lisa heard the scurrying of small animals in the undergrowth, and shivered again, but not from the cold. Then she heard a louder, more ominous crackling as something larger moved through the trees. She froze, her heart speeding up to pound deafeningly. She had horrible visions of a hungry tiger on the prowl.... Instinct warned her not to make a sound. Barely breathing, she shrank back against the nearest tree, her palms pressing flat against the rough bark. All at once it occurred to her that she had left the pistol in the jeep....

Lisa literally stopped breathing when the creature suddenly emerged from the trees not ten feet from where she stood. For one horrible moment she thought the looming shape must be a gorilla; then she recognized it as a man. This realization should have made her feel better. Strangely, it had the opposite effect. Her heart was beating in slow, irregular thuds against her chest; her mouth was dry. Something, some inner instinct, warned her that she was in danger. She didn't move so much as a hair.

The man stopped for just an instant, lifting his head to peer around like an animal testing the wind. Lisa closed her eyes, terrified that the faint light reflecting off them might make her visible in the dark. She opened them again when she heard him move. He was headed away from her, toward the jeeps, his movements stealthy.

Compelled by something she didn't understand, Lisa followed him at a safe distance, stopping when he stopped, taking care to make as little noise as possible. He seemed unaware of her presence.... As she had thought, he was headed for the jeeps. They were parked together, six of them, in a little cleared area surrounded by dense trees.

He seemed to know precisely where they were; he was still moving quietly, but surely, when he emerged into the clearing. Lisa stopped at the edge of the trees, sheltering in their shadow. The man crept around the first of the parked vehicles; his object seemed to be the jeep farthest from where she stood—Sam's jeep. The jeep she usually waited in.

Skirting around the edge of the trees, Lisa was able to keep the man in view. What could he want? To disable the jeeps? He didn't act like it; he had made no effort to do anything to any of them. To steal something, like an engine cart? Perhaps... Ducking, he reached Sam's jeep and moved swiftly alongside. Then suddenly he straightened. For a moment he stood motionless, staring at the inside of the jeep as if it was not what he expected to see. Then he swung around. Lisa was startled into taking a hasty step backward. A twig crackled under her foot. The small sound brought the man's eyes straight to her. Gulping, she met his gaze head-on. With a little frisson of shock she recognized him: it was the man who had attacked her that afternoon down by the creek, the man Sam had identified as Lutz. And with a sudden, horrible quiver of fear, she realized that he had returned to the jeeps in hopes of finding *her.*

They both stood frozen for an instant, staring at

each other through the silvery darkness. Then Lutz took a step toward her. Lisa whirled, ready to run into the jungle. There was no doubt in her mind that he meant to finish what he had started down by the creek that day....

"Lutz! What the hell are you doing here?"

Lisa nearly swooned with relief as Sam's voice sounded irately from the other side of the clearing. Lutz swung around at the sound, facing Sam.

"I—finished up."

"Your orders were to wait by the trail for the rest of us to join you."

As Sam spoke, the other men came silently up behind him. At his curt gesture, they headed for the jeeps. Sam himself was moving toward his own jeep.

"I—forgot."

"Don't forget again." Sam's voice was hard. As he reached the side of his jeep, looking vainly for her, Lisa thought she heard the harsh indrawing of his breathing. He swung around....

"Lisa?" he called, the necessary hush of his voice in no way mitigating its sharpness. Startled out of her momentary stupor, Lisa hurried toward him.

"I'm here, Sam," she answered breathlessly.

He waited for her; when she reached his side, he said nothing, but stood back to allow her to climb into the back of the jeep. To her surprise, he motioned to Frank to drive, and got into the back with her, letting Malloy, the other man who usually rode with them, sit in front for once.

"Are you all right?" Sam asked gruffly once the convoy was under way.

"Yes," Lisa answered quietly, touched by his obvious concern. Unobtrusively, she scooted a little closer to him on the seat. She found his hard warmth comforting after the scare she'd had.

"What were you doing out of the jeep? Lutz didn't...?"

"No." The word was soft.

Sam took a deep breath, releasing it in what sounded like a sigh. "After tomorrow, you won't have to worry about him anymore," he said, speaking low so that the two in the front seats couldn't hear him. "Tomorrow, we finish up, and then we go our separate ways. You should be home in a couple of days."

Lisa didn't reply to this. She had thought that she would feel jubilant when Sam at last told her that she would be going home, but she didn't: instead, she felt kind of—empty. She supposed it would take a little while for the news to sink in...

Sam too was silent the rest of the way back to the camp. But once they were alone in his tent, he made love to her with an intensity that seared them both.

The men stayed around the camp the next day, packing up the tents and loading the jeeps. By the time darkness fell, there was nothing left of the camp except a small circle of dead ashes and several patches of flattened grass where the tents had been. Even those signs, Sam told her, would disappear within days.

Lisa was sitting on her favorite flat rock, waiting for Sam to join her. At his direction, she had exchanged the raggedy shorts and shirt for one of his old uniforms—a whole one. His flak jacket rested on her shoulders. They would be on the move all night, he had told her, and it would get cold. When she had protested that he might need his coat himself, he had merely shrugged and said that he was a lot more used to difficult conditions than she was.

All day Lisa had sensed the tension that permeated the camp. This was it, their faces seemed to say; they were unusually quiet as they waited to finish the job they had come to Rhodesia to do. Lisa herself was as nervous as a cat. Whatever they were engaged in was dangerous, she knew. She was worried about the outcome—about her own safety and, as much as she hated to admit it, Sam's. Despite everything, she didn't like to think of him being hurt or killed.

When Sam came for her at last, she gaped at him through the deepening gloom. His face was as black as pitch.

"What on earth . . . !" She gasped.

He grinned, looking for all the world like a black-faced performer in an old-time minstrel show.

"Shoe polish," he explained laconically. "Makes you harder to spot at night. Want some?" He held out a small, flat can.

Lisa shuddered, shaking her head. Sam laughed and turned away, pocketing the shoe polish. But it wasn't long before he was back, herding her and his men into the jeeps. The mission was on.

They returned to the same spot they had used the night before. Again, Lisa was left with the jeeps while the men melted away into the jungle. This time, she was determined to stay with the vehicle and keep the pistol close at hand. Last night she had learned a valuable lesson.

She waited for what seemed like hours, her nervousness increasing with every passing minute. What if something went wrong and Sam never came back? What if . . . ? Resolutely she banished these horrible conjectures from her mind. Sam was a professional, he knew what he was doing, she comforted herself. But still . . . Her nagging doubts refused to be silenced.

Lisa had no idea what time it was when a slight sound brought her upright in the seat. Her eyes strained toward the direction from which it had come. Surely Lutz wouldn't be bold enough—or stupid enough—to try the same thing two nights running. Her hand closed over the pistol; a bullet was already in the chamber, so all she had to do was flick the safety off. This she did, her hand slightly unsteady. Then she turned back to peer into the woods in the direction of the noise.

She was just in time to see the night explode around her.

VIII

Sam was knocked flat on his belly by the force of the explosion. He lay there for a moment, stunned. Then his instincts, honed by years of being faced with potentially deadly situations, took over. Even before the sharp rat-a-tat of the machine guns began, he was on his feet, ducking and dodging through the dense jungle undergrowth. Bullets smacked into the ground and bushes and trees all around him. Severed foliage showered him like rain. Luckily, he seemed not to be hit—so far. At least he didn't feel anything. But then, he had known men to have an entire limb blown off and not know about it until they looked down and saw the bloody stump. Shock acted as a local anesthetic. However, he seemed to be in one piece, and as long as he was, he was going to run like hell. All around him he could hear hoarse curses accompanied by the crashing of the undergrowth as those of his men who had survived the explosion did the same thing.

What the hell had gone wrong? was the question that ran through his mind as he zigzagged at a dead run for the jeeps. What the bloody hell had gone wrong?

The damned explosives had blown too soon—that

was one thing. They'd barely had time to get ten feet away when the whole thing had gone up like a Chinese fireworks factory. The blast had sent them hurtling through the air like matchsticks in a tornado. When it was over, the charge that was supposed to have acted as a diversion while they got on with what they had been hired to do had killed four of his men. But the premature explosion wasn't the only thing. There had been soldiers waiting in ambush nearby, guns at the ready, clearly aware that some sort of attack would be launched from precisely that point, at precisely that time. Which meant that someone had talked—someone in his group, because they were the only ones who knew the details of the operation. But who? The question clawed at Sam's guts as he alternately pounded, rolled, and scrambled for the jeeps.

Now that he thought about it, the unexpected explosion had probably saved his life. Otherwise, he and the rest of the men would have walked right into the trap that was waiting for them. At least the enemy had been as taken by surprise as he and his men were. They had been flushed out of hiding before they'd been ready, and it was for this reason that he and most of his men were still alive—temporarily, at least.

Even as these thoughts ran through Sam's mind, another hideous possibility occurred to him. It was quite likely that another enemy military unit would be waiting at the jeeps. That would be the logical backup move on the part of the opposing commander, who seemed well versed in all the details of their operation and would surely know the location of the jeeps. Sam himself would make such a move. For an instant Sam pictured Lisa alone in his jeep, falling into the hands of men who would regard her as a sexual plaything for the entire company at best and a spy at worst, and winced. Then, deliberately, he blanked her image from his mind. This was no time to start getting sentimental. He needed every ounce of concentration he possessed just to survive.

They had to have the jeeps. That was the beginning and end of it. If they were to make the airstrip on time, to board the plane that would be waiting tonight to take them out of the country before all hell broke loose, they had to have the jeeps. Period.

Grunting, Sam jerked the M-16 from where it hung by its shoulder strap, checking the weapon quickly as he ran. Turning to fire at the unit closing in behind him would have been suicidal: if he stopped, he was as good as dead. But fighting for the jeeps was another story—they needed those jeeps to survive.

"Get ready to fire!" Sam yelled hoarsely in the direction of his men, hoping they weren't too far away to hear and understand. They were all seasoned fighters—they would realize the importance of the jeeps. He hoped.

Sam reached the edge of the clearing, ducking behind a large mopani tree and resting his back against it. Quickly he reconnoitered the clearing. Unbelievably, there seemed not to be any men lying in wait for them. You fool! Sam thought contemptuously of the opposing commander, then turned to fire several quick bursts at the enemy forces coming up behind them to cover his men's retreat.

All around him the men were hitting the clearing, some with rifles at the ready, the more stupid ones with their weapons still strapped to their backs.

"Let's get the hell out of here!" Sam roared at them, gesturing them into the jeeps. They didn't need any urging. The vehicles began to move out almost before the command had left his mouth.

Some of the men had to run to catch up and then leap precariously on board.

Sam saw his own jeep begin to roll, and ran toward it, still firing behind him at the soldiers who were almost at the edge of the clearing. Mike Harley, a young man who had been brought along on Frank's recommendation, was driving; he swung the vehicle in a wide arc to pick Sam up. Sam leaped on board, going over the side of the jeep in a low rolling dive. As he hit the rear seat, he felt his body crash against something soft and yielding. Lisa. Her breath expelled forcibly as he knocked the wind out of her. He straightened, catching just a glimpse of her white, frightened face before his hand was on her head, pushing it down below the level of the seat. Then he shoved her bodily down onto the floorboard.

"Get down and stay down!" he growled fiercely.

She said nothing, but crouched where he had pushed her, her eyes enormous in her pale face as she stared fearfully up at him. Sam spared her no more than a quick glance; then he was turning, kneeling on the seat, firing staccato bursts from his rifle. As the jeeps roared out of the clearing, with his the last in line, enemy soldiers began bursting through the trees, their machine guns blasting.

Sam felt the bullet that slammed into the left rear tire as if it had struck some vital part of his body. Cursing, he abandoned all attempts to provide cover fire for their retreat and concentrated on hanging on as the jeep veered wildly. On the floorboard, Lisa moaned and clutched at his leg; he could feel her nails digging through his pants into his calf. In the front, Harley fought valiantly to hold the jeep steady. For a moment there Sam thought he was going to be able to do it. Then another bullet slammed into the right rear tire. The jeep bucked like a rodeo bronc; its rear swung around in a crazy attempt to catch up to its front. There was a jolting lurch as they hit some sort of hole. As the jeep rolled over, with a kind of slow inevitability, Sam heard Lisa scream.

Miraculously, he was thrown clear; as soon as he hit the ground he was on his feet, crouching, moving, scrambling for his rifle, risking a scared glance back the way they had come. The enemy were closing on them, rifles spitting fire and death. God! He had to get out of there, fast. The thought had no sooner entered his mind than he was heading for the jungle. Then he saw Lisa. She was lying on her stomach in the dirt, her hands flung wide, her legs spread. She was not moving—she appeared not even to be breathing. As he dove toward her, Sam cursed himself for the thousandth time for not having left her lying in the jungle the first time he had ever laid eyes on her. She was going to be the death of him yet. But he could not bring himself to leave her.... She would be raped, tortured; a quick death would be the best she could hope for.

Cursing, sweating with fear, he ran quick hands over her body. She was breathing. All his haphazardly acquired medical knowledge screamed at him not to move her. He ignored it, scooping her up in his arms and flinging her over his shoulder, then heading at a dead run for the line of trees that offered a measure of safety. Several A.L.I.C.E. packs had been flung from the jeep and lay near the edge of the undergrowth. Instinctively, Sam scooped one up, hardly slowing his stride.

Bullets spat all around him as he leaped into the trees. Casting one more scared glance behind him, he saw that the soldiers had reached the overturned jeep. They stopped for just an instant, giving him valuable time; a single shot rang out. They'd done for Harley, poor kid, Sam thought, and said a brief prayer for the repose of his soul. All the while he was leaping through the undergrowth as fast as his legs would carry him.

They were coming after him; Sam could hear them as they reached the trees. Apparently they could hear him, too, because blasts of machine-gun fire began to pepper the area around him. Sam felt perspiration roll off his body in waves, more from fear than exertion. They were close behind him—too damned close. Lisa was a dead weight over his shoulder. Any professional soldier worth his salt would dump her on the spot. One thing they all learned early in their careers was that when the chips were down, you had to look out for number one. But, dammit, she was a goddamn girl! Cursing himself and her impartially, Sam knew he couldn't leave her.

Thorny branches tore at his face and clothes as he ran through the jungle. He could feel his skin tear in a dozen places; little trickles of blood ran down his face and neck. There was no pain—he was too scared.

Lisa's head thudded against the middle of his back. She was still not moving—he hoped she was merely unconscious. It was possible that one of the randomly fired bullets had caught her; she might be dead or dying even now. If so, there wasn't a thing in hell he could do about it. If he stopped, they were both dead.

Bullets whistled through the air around him; Christ, they were getting close. He prayed as he hadn't prayed since he was a kid....

"Ahhgg!" He couldn't prevent himself from crying out as a bullet smacked into his left shoulder blade. The force of the impact sent him sprawling; he fell heavily to his knees and one hand, the other going automatically behind him to clutch as close to the wound as he could reach. He felt blood pour over his hand; fiery knives seemed to be twisting viciously in his shoulder. Tears came to his eyes. God, that hurt! But he was still alive, though for how long was still a question. Behind him, the soldiers were getting closer with every heartbeat.

Lisa had been thrown a little way in front of him by his fall. He crawled over to her: she was breathing. Even as he bent over her, knowing that he would no longer be able to carry her but still not able to bring himself to leave her, she opened her eyes. They stared blankly up at him.

"Thank God!" he said, groaning. Then, taking her by the shoulder, he shook her roughly.

"Lisa," he hissed, desperation making his voice as cutting as icy whips. "You've got to get up! Do you hear me?"

She didn't move. He shook her again, beginning to despair. Christ, he couldn't carry her—but he couldn't leave her, either.

"Goddammit, did you hear me?" he demanded fiercely. "If you don't move your ass, I'm going to leave you behind. Do you understand?"

For a moment, sweating, he feared she wasn't able to understand. Then her hand came up to clutch at his shirt front. He breathed a heartfelt sigh of relief.

"No!" she whimpered.

He shook her again, but less forcefully. Bullets were singing in the air above their heads; the crashing sounds behind them told Sam that the enemy were getting dangerously close.

"Then crawl!" he ordered. "Come on, get up and crawl. We're going to have to hide!"

She blinked once, twice. Then slowly, too slowly

for Sam's taste, she got shakily up on her hands and knees. Sam was already looking desperately around them, his eyes seeking the best shelter. A pink-flowered chopinchuna bush thickly covered with a deep green hanging vine seemed to offer the best place to hide. Quickly he scooped leaves and mulch over the tell-tale blood from his wound, grabbed his rifle and the A.L.I.C.E. pack, then pushed Lisa toward the bush.

"Get under there!" He held aside the trailing vine so that she could crawl beneath the bush's sheltering branches. When she was safely hidden, Sam quickly found a small branch and brushed it over the ground they had disturbed. If this was going to work, they mustn't leave any sign. . . .

He threw the branch away and rolled under the bush himself, pulling the vine down so that it completely hid them—he hoped and prayed—from view. It was dark and cool inside, like a cave. . . .

Lisa was staring at him, her face white with shock and fear. He felt a twinge of impatient pity for her. Poor girl, she must be scared to death. Then he thought a trifle grimly that if it came down to it, he was scared to death himself.

"Sam," she whispered, her eyes fixed on him like those of a small, terrified animal. Whatever she had been going to say was lost as she saw for the first time the blood that covered his chest and shoulder like scarlet paint.

"You're bleeding!"

"Shut up," he said brutally, pushing her down so that she was lying on her belly in the thick leaves. "If you want to live to talk about it, don't make a sound. If they find us, we're dead meat!"

She shut up. Sam pushed her head down into the leaves, then rolled on top of her. It was an altruistic gesture, and a damned stupid one, Sam thought

138

grimly, but if the guys chasing them had any notion that they'd holed up, they were sure to pepper the area with bullets. He'd already taken one bullet—what were a few more? Then he grinned ironically to himself. The truth of the matter was, he couldn't stand the idea of this damned dumb helpless female getting shot. Chivalry was not dead.

Sam's wounded shoulder ached agonizingly. He thought longingly of the bottle of whiskey that was part of the A.L.I.C.E. pack's standard gear. What he would give for just one swallow... Then he ceased to think, ceased even to breathe. Soldiers were running past them; feet thudded into the ground just inches from where they lay hidden. Silently he readied his rifle. If they were discovered, he was prepared to roll away from Lisa and open fire. Beneath him, Sam felt Lisa jerk spasmodically. Swiftly he pressed her face into the dirt and leaves covering the ground. All it would take was one sound, a single whimper, and they would be discovered. And killed.

They lay there for what seemed like hours, listening to the soldiers beat the jungle in search of them, hearing them call back and forth in what Sam had identified as the Matabele dialect. Time and again they passed so close to the bush that Sam could have reached out a hand and caught one by the ankle. Beneath him, Lisa was shaking; long shudders of fear racked her body. Sam buried his face in the curve between her shoulder and neck, hoping to comfort her by his proximity. After all, she wasn't much more than a child—and she was a female. Considering that, he thought she was taking this whole ordeal marginally well.

Women, in his experience, were pretty, useless creatures with little or nothing between their ears. Oh, they were necessary—about twice a month. Other times, he could live quite happily without them. Beth, his ex-wife, had given him a distaste for the whole female sex. They'd been married only two years—and, God, he'd loved her, like the naïve young fool he'd been. He was willing to bet that during that time she'd bedded half his company. When he'd found out at last—tipped off by an embarrassed friend—he hadn't believed it at first. Until he'd confronted her with what he was sure were lies, and she'd laughed and admitted everything. Worse, she'd told him details—names and places and dates; he had stared at her dumbly, not wanting to believe. He hadn't even had the gumption to kick her out. He would have forgiven her—he still burned when he remembered that. But she hadn't wanted to be forgiven. She was glad he'd found out, she'd said: it would save her the trouble of telling him the score. He was boring, both in bed and out. She'd been crazy to marry him in the first place: he was nothing but a kid, and she wanted a man.

He hated to remember that he'd cried when she left. Twenty-three years old, a sergeant in the marines, and he'd cried like a baby. His only excuse was that after years of being shuttled from one foster home to another, of knowing that he belonged to no one and no one belonged to him, he had craved a family desperately. His wife and his baby son had been his whole world. Sam grimaced a little, wryly, as he thought back to the dumb kid he had been seventeen years ago. He had since learned that he was sufficient unto himself: he didn't need anybody, and he didn't want anyone but his kid needing him.

After Beth had left, he had volunteered for combat duty and been sent to Vietnam, where he had worked off his bitter rage by blowing away any gooks who were unfortunate enough to get in his way. He had taken a perverted kind of joy in killing—in watching bodies jerk as his bullets smacked into them, seeing blood and guts fly. It had helped him to exorcise his hatred....

He had come back to the States a different man, older and infinitely wiser. The first thing he'd done was retrieve his kid from Beth, who was tired of having a five-year-old hanging on her skirts anyway. She told him frankly, when he had come demanding his son, that she would be glad to get rid of the kid: he was cramping her style. Sam had come away feeling nothing but a cold contempt for her. She was no good, a tramp. He couldn't believe that he'd ever been in love with her.

There had been some rough times in the twelve years since, but he and Jay had managed to get by. A high-school dropout himself, he had insisted that Jay go to school every day, do his homework, and bring home good grades. Sam felt a surge of pride whenever he recalled that Jay would be graduating next May at the top of his class. The kid was smart, no doubt about it. And he would see to it that the boy went on to college, had opportunities that he himself had never had.

He had supported the two of them by hiring out as a mercenary, fighting in nearly every corner of the globe. Soldiering was all he knew, all he was equipped for. And the pay was good. Since he was out of the country so much, he had had to send Jay to a boarding school. But now—now he was getting tired of killing. All he wanted was a place to call home, maybe a few hundred acres of land, some stock, and peace. This job had been meant to assure that; even with only half the money, added to what he already had saved, it would give him a start—if they got out of here alive.

Beyond the bush, the jungle seemed quiet. Sam could no longer hear the soldiers crashing about. Maybe they'd gone—or maybe not. Maybe they were waiting, hoping the silence would lure them out.

Lisa was squirming uncomfortably beneath him. Very quietly, he eased off her, giving her shoulder a warning shake to tell her to be quiet. She turned to look at him; her face was streaked with dirt and leaves, and her blond hair tumbled into her eyes. Her hand, when she raised it to brush back her hair, was shaking slightly.

"Are they gone?" she whispered, the words barely audible.

"I don't know. I think so, but maybe not. We'll have to stay under here a little while longer. Are you hurt anywhere?" Sam's voice was as quiet as hers. His eyes swept her body, probing for injury. There was blood on the back of her jacket, but it was probably his. . . .

"N-no. I don't think so. Except my head hurts a little."

Sam eased the M-16 to the ground and ran his hand over her skull beneath the thick fall of her hair. There was a large bump at the back of her head; she winced when he touched it.

"You must have hit your head when the jeep rolled," he said softly. "I don't think it's serious."

She inclined her head in silent acknowledgment. Then, her eyes sweeping over his chest as he lay on his side facing her, she frowned.

"You're covered with blood. Are you shot?" She sounded both frightened and concerned.

Sam grimaced. "I caught a bullet in the back of my shoulder. I don't think it hit anything vital. I'll live."

"But you're bleeding so much. Shouldn't we bandage it or something?"

"Later. When we're someplace safer. For now we need to stay very quiet. They might not be gone."

Lisa shuddered visibly, then lay back down, hiding her face in her arms. Sam continued to lie on his side next to her, breathing in a long, steady rhythm as he fought to control the pain in a way he had learned from experience was roughly effective. Every ounce of his being was concentrated on listening to what went on beyond the confines of their makeshift shelter.

After about an hour of silence, Sam touched Lisa softly on the shoulder.

"I'm going to look around. You stay here and be quiet, no matter what."

Lisa lifted her head to look at him. Silently he handed her his pistol. Her hand shook as she took it.

"For God's sake, don't shoot me by mistake," he warned with grim humor. Then he was gone.

When he came back, she was sitting up. Her eyes met his fearfully as he crawled beneath the bush to join her. Unspeaking, he held out his hand for the pistol. She was only too glad to relinquish it.

"All clear—I think. Come on, let's get going."

"But—your shoulder. Shouldn't we do something for it? At least bandage it?" She frowned at him worriedly. What she could see of his face was white beneath the black camouflage that still streaked it; blood covered him from shoulder to waist in long smears. When he turned his back to her, she saw that the whole back of his shirt was dark with blood.

"Later," he said impatiently, as he had before. "Come on, I want to get out of here before they come back."

Lisa swallowed. She needed no more urging to crawl out after him.

Once outside, she got to her feet, then almost fell

down again. Her knees were shaky, and she was afraid they wouldn't support her weight. Sam saw her difficulty and frowned at her.

"Just stand there for a minute," he directed. "Take a couple of deep breaths. I know your head probably hurts like hell, and you're scared and wobbly, but we're going to have to walk out of here."

Looking at him, seeing his left arm hanging limply at his side, his paleness, and the blood that covered him, Lisa saw also that he was standing stiffly erect, his expression alert, his muscles tense. He looked ready for action—and he was hurt far worse than she. She felt a twinge of shame. All that ailed her were nerves and a slight headache. If he could walk out of here, then so could she. Straightening her spine, she nodded.

"I'm okay."

"Good." He knelt and reached back under the bush for the A.L.I.C.E. pack.

"Let's go."

He stood up, swinging the pack to the uninjured side of his back and hefting the rifle in his right hand. With a glance back over his shoulder at Lisa to make sure she was following, he headed out.

They walked for hours, until long after the sun had risen and the interior of the jungle had lightened to a filtered kind of brightness. It was hard going: the underbrush was thick and tough. Sometimes Sam had to use the knife he kept in his boot to hack a path for them. Sometimes he simply let his body forge an opening. Despite his wound, he seemed tireless. Lisa, trailing limply in his wake, was soon so exhausted that she wasn't even frightened. All she could think about was putting one foot in front of the other one more time.

The jungle teemed with life around them. Mosqui-

toes buzzed around their ears, lig
exposed inch of flesh, threatening to
Sam stopped and extracted a can of in
from the A.L.I.C.E. pack, spraying f
then himself. After that, it was a little
deep green canopy overhead allowed on an occasional sunbeam to slant through to the steamy forest
floor, piercing the virescent darkness with a sliver of
shimmering light. Vines as thick as Sam's waist twisted
down from huge teak, red syringa, and mopani
trees; birds and small animals were everywhere. Lisa
barely registered the cries of the birds and monkeys
overhead and the rustlings and flutterings as they
flew from one tree to another; she was equally
oblivious to the movement of the ground-level foliage as the denizens of the jungle scurried this way
and that. Sam told her over his shoulder that she
should be thankful that the larger jungle dwellers—
the lions and cheetahs—had apparently caught their
man smell and were staying out of the way. And Lisa
was, indeed, profoundly thankful, but that didn't
stop her from glancing nervously over her shoulder
every few minutes.

As the day wore on, the humidity combined with
the indescribable smell of the jungle made her feel
faintly nauseated. Hot and sweet, the smell was composed of decaying plants and animals. The moisture-
laden air made her hair curl damply around her
face. Sweat poured over her body. By the time Sam
finally stopped, she was swaying on her feet. With a
little groan, she dropped to her knees.

"We'll rest here for a while," he said tersely, sinking to the ground beside her and resting his right
side gingerly against a gnarled teak tree. With a stab
of compunction, Lisa remembered his wound. She

⸺een so caught up in her own misery that she
⸺d almost forgotten about it.

"Let me look at your shoulder," she roused herself
to say. Sam looked at her briefly, then shrugged his
acquiescence. Barely able to summon the energy to
move, Lisa crawled around behind him.

The back of his shirt was stiff and black with dried
blood, except for a small spot that was still moistly
red just above the jutting edge of his shoulder blade.

"Can you take off your shirt?" Lisa asked faintly.
She was hoping against hope that the wound wouldn't
look nearly so bad once the blood-soaked shirt was
out of the way.

Sam didn't reply but began to unbutton his shirt.
When it was unfastened, he rather gingerly started
to peel it off. The cloth was stuck to the wound. He
tugged at it gently for a moment, then when it didn't
budge Lisa heard him take a deep breath. With a
quick movement, he jerked the material free. As the
shirt dropped from his back, Sam's hand moved
around to the buckle of his shoulder holster. When
that too was off, his breath expelled in a low, whistling groan.

Lisa's own breath caught as she looked at his
shoulder. When he had pulled the shirt free of the
wound, it had started to bleed more freely again.
Thick red rivulets oozed from a black hole about the
size of a dime. The flesh around it was raised and
looked black and swollen beneath its covering of
blood. Blood, both fresh and dried, was smeared
thickly over the hard planes of his back. Staring, Lisa
felt sick.

"Well?" he grunted when she didn't say anything
immediately.

"It looks awful."

"It can't look any worse than it feels. It hurts like hell."

"I'm sorry." Lisa's voice expressed heartfelt sympathy. In truth, she couldn't imagine how he had managed to walk so far with such a dreadful-looking injury. Her respect for him, already considerable, went up a hundredfold. If she had had such a hole in her back, she was sure she would have died on the spot.

"Is it still bleeding?" He sounded only faintly interested.

Lisa swallowed before she answered, "A little."

"You'd better bandage it up, then. There should be first-aid supplies in the pack."

"Yes. All right."

Swallowing again, Lisa crawled around to where Sam had dropped the pack and, opening it, rummaged through the contents. After a moment she withdrew a small square black box marked with the universal symbol of a red cross.

"That's it." Sam confirmed what she had already deduced. Box in hand, she crawled back around behind him, positioning herself on her knees with her weight resting back on her heels. Then, opening the box, she stared blankly at its contents. She hadn't the faintest idea what to do next.

"What—what do you want me to do?"

Sam sighed. "There's a brown plastic bottle in there—see it?"

Lisa located the bottle and nodded. Then, remembering that he couldn't see her, she said, "Yes."

"It's antiseptic. Soak a pad in it and press it over the hole."

Obediently Lisa extracted gauze and a small pair of scissors from the box, cutting off enough gauze to form a small pad. She poured antiseptic onto the pad until it was soaking wet. Then, as she was about to press it to the wound, a thought occurred to her.

"Sam," she said faintly, staring at his back as if mesmerized. "What happened to the bullet?"

He snorted irritably. "What do you think happened to it? It's still in there."

Lisa closed her eyes briefly.

"Shouldn't—shouldn't we try to get it out?"

"With you performing emergency surgery? Not a chance. It'll just have to stay where it is until we get out of here."

"Will you be able to get about? To walk, I mean?"

"I'll have to, won't I?" He sounded increasingly exasperated. "Now, will you please get on with it?"

Lisa took a firm grip on her lower lip with her teeth, and leaned forward to press the pad to the wound. As the fiery liquid penetrated he stiffened; a little groan escaped through his clenched lips. Then suddenly he slumped limply against the tree. His name on her lips, Lisa rocked back on her heels. Her eyes were wide with alarm as she realized that he had passed out.

IX

S<small>AM</small>!"

He didn't move, didn't respond in any way. Lisa crawled around in front of him, praying that he had merely fainted. If something happened to Sam, what on earth would she do?

He was slumped against the rough gray bark of the tree trunk, his head lolling limply when she gently shook his uninjured shoulder. Beneath what remained of its greasy black covering, his face looked as white as death. But he seemed to be breathing normally, and with her hand pressed to his blood-streaked chest she could feel his heart beating in a steady rhythm. She started to call his name again, to try to shake him back to consciousness, then hesitated, sinking back on her heels. He had to be in considerable pain. There was no sense in waking him just to suffer while she did what she could for his wound.

Slowly Lisa crawled around behind him again, glad that they had gotten far away from the area where the enemy soldiers almost certainly still searched for them before Sam had passed out. With him unconscious, they were both helpless. Swallowing, she glanced askance at the fearsome-looking rifle lying in the leaves by Sam's leg. She would touch it only if absolutely necessary. Sam's lessons on the finer points of handling firearms had in no way lessened the horror she felt for the deadly things. If she had to use it, she would, to the best of her ability, but in the meantime she prayed that no one or nothing would stumble across them until Sam was able to protect them again.

Picking up the small gauze pad from where she had let it fall, she poured more antiseptic over it and then pressed it to the wound. She held it there until she judged the liquid had had time to penetrate the blackened hole, then took it away again. For a moment she sat staring rather helplessly at Sam's slumped back. He needed her, for once, and she hadn't the slightest notion what to do for him. The wound looked awful, she thought with an inward shudder. Blood still edged sluggishly from the jagged edges of the hole; the flesh around it had swelled and blackened until it resembled a small mountain. His entire left shoulder area was one huge bruise. With a sick feeling in the pit of her stomach, Lisa picked up the pad and began painstakingly to clean away the gore surrounding the wound. At the very least she could clean and bandage it for him. Working carefully to remove the dried blood that encrusted the hole, she was very much afraid that the wound was far more serious than Sam had let on.

When she had finished wiping the blood from the bronze silk of his back, Sam was still unconscious. Lisa began to worry more and more. If he didn't wake by the time she had his wound bandaged, then she would allow herself to panic, she thought. But in the meantime, she forced herself very calmly to make another pad from the diminishing roll of gauze, soak it in antiseptic, and tape it as well as she could over the wound with white surgical tape from the first-aid kit. With her small knowledge of nursing and the limited supplies at hand, it was the best she could do for him. She only hoped it was good enough.

When Sam's shoulder was at last bandaged to her satisfaction, she crawled around in front of him again. Using water from the canteen at his belt, which she managed to detach with some difficulty, she gently sponged away the streaks of dried blood on his arms and chest. Bathing the strong muscles now so helpless beneath her hands, Lisa was surprised by a sudden surge of something that was almost tenderness for him. Maternal instinct, she supposed wryly, but even that knowledge didn't make the strange feeling go away. With his eyes closed and his black head, usually so arrogant, resting limply against the tree, he looked younger, and very vulnerable. Lisa grimaced at herself, but her hands, as she reached up to wipe away the remnants of the greasy black camouflage that smeared his face, were almost absurdly gentle.

It was while she was slowly drawing the cool, wet gauze pad over his unshaven cheeks that his eyes flickered once, twice, then opened to regard her rather dazedly.

"What happened?" he asked after a moment. He sounded groggy, as if he wasn't quite sure where he was or who she was.

"You fainted," she replied matter-of-factly, continuing to draw the cool pad over his face. "You must have lost a lot of blood before we stopped."

He closed his eyes without answering. When he opened them again, perhaps a minute later, he seemed much more aware. Lisa finished wiping his face, then sank back on her heels, looking at him keenly.

"How long have I been out?" His voice was beginning to sound crisp again, but his face was still very pale beneath its sun bronze.

"Not long—maybe fifteen minutes."

"Did you get my shoulder bandaged?" Now he was starting to sound arrogant. Lisa, despite her exhaustion and worry, and their predicament, had to smile.

"Yes." He didn't like her smile, she could tell. He gave her a hard look from those glittery blue eyes, then to her surprise pushed himself away from the tree.

"What are you doing?" The question was torn from her. She could tell from the tensing of all his muscles when he moved that the action had caused him considerable pain.

"We've got to get a move on." He looked as if he was going to try to stand up at any minute. Lisa put out a hand to clutch his upper arm, unconsciously noting the steely strength of the muscles bunching beneath her hand as she sought to stay him.

"Don't be ridiculous!" She spoke sharply. "You need to stay still—to rest for a while! As I said, you must have lost a lot of blood, moving around like you have been all day. You can't mean to just go traipsing off into the wild blue yonder as if nothing's wrong!"

Sam looked at her steadily, his mouth a harsh, straight line.

"Honey, I don't think you quite understand the situation we're facing here," he said with weary patience. "Those men back there are still looking for us—never doubt it! And they probably have reinforcements in to help them by this time. If they find us—and they want us badly—they'll kill us. And by the time they get around to it, we'll probably be begging to die! Do you have any idea what fun they'd have torturing a woman? No, of course you don't! You probably think you could tell them who you are, and that you had nothing to do with what we had planned, and they'd let you go. Lisa, baby, those animals torture and kill just for fun! They'd love hearing you scream with pain...." He broke off, seeing her face pale at the graphic picture he had painted. Before, she hadn't really allowed herself to think about what would happen if they were caught.

"Anyway, we can't stop—not for anything—until we're safely out of the country," he finished in a milder tone.

Lisa sat for a moment, nervously chewing her lower lip. More than anything in the world she wanted to be out of this barbaric country....

"But you're hurt...." With his wound, she didn't see how they could go anywhere. If he fainted once, he would most likely do so again, unless he had time to rest and replenish his blood. And she certainly couldn't go anywhere without him. All at once Lisa realized that even if she could go on without him, she wouldn't want to. He needed her....

"I'll be a hell of a lot more hurt if those soldiers catch up to us—and so will you," he responded grimly. "Now come on."

He heaved himself to his feet on the last words. Lisa stayed on her knees a moment longer, looking worriedly up at him. The lines were very visible in his lean face as he stared harshly back. Finally capitulating to that commanding gaze, Lisa got to her feet without another word of protest.

"Could you hand me my shirt?" Sam gritted, leaning sideways against the tree for support and gesturing to where his shirt lay crumpled on the ground near where they had been sitting. Lisa took one look at the blood-soaked garment and shook her head.

"You can't mean to put that back on. I mean—look at it!"

Sam raised his eyes skyward.

"I sure can't go walking through the jungle like this." He indicated his bare torso with a gesture. "Unless I want to provide a meal for every insect known to man—plus some. Now, don't argue with me anymore. I'm getting damned tired of it. Just hand me my shirt."

"Why don't you wear this jacket instead?" She offered him the flak jacket that she had tied around her waist earlier when the heat had made wearing it more torture than protection.

"I damn well don't want to wear that jacket," he retorted, glaring angrily at her. The menacing effect was spoiled somewhat by the whiteness of his face and the obvious weakness that had him still leaning against the tree for support. "I want my shirt. Now, are you going to get it, or do I?"

From the uncompromising set of his mouth, Lisa knew better than to argue any further. Besides, it had occurred to her rather forcefully that they were wasting valuable time. If there really were enemy soldiers in pursuit, and if Sam was obstinately determined to press on despite his wound, then it served no purpose to stand around arguing with him—especially over something so trivial as a blood-stained shirt.

"Goddammit!" he roared when she made no immediate move.

Lisa, seeing that he meant to stoop to get his shirt himself and not wanting him to exert himself any more than he had to, bent and picked up the shirt. The cloth was already beginning to stiffen where the blood had dried on it.

"Give it here." His voice was milder but still noticeably

impatient as he reached for the garment. Lisa handed it over mutely. He pulled it on over his good arm, then tried to shrug it around his shoulders but stopped, wincing. Lisa, biting her lip, hurried over to help. Sam favored her with a long, hard look as she caught the edges of the shirt in both hands, but permitted her to ease the garment around his bandaged shoulder. She would have draped it around his left side like a cape, buttoning it up in front to hold it on, but Sam insisted that the shirt be put on properly.

"I'll need the use of my arm," he said. So Lisa, after one look at his whitening face, slipped the shirt back off and started over again, this time inserting his left arm first. Carefully she eased it around his shoulders and helped him get his right arm into the sleeve. Then, when the shirt was finally on, she came around in front of him and started to button it as she would have done for a child. The action was purely instinctive. She wasn't even thinking about what she was doing. It was only as she did up the last button and happened to look up into his face looming some inches above her that she saw his eyes fastened on her broodingly, an indecipherable expression in their depths.

"I'm not helpless, you know," he said, almost growling.

Immediately Lisa dropped her hands from where they had been resting lightly against his chest, and took a step back from him. She was more than a little embarrassed at the almost maternal concern she felt for him, which apparently he had sensed.

"Can you get the gear together?" he asked gruffly after a brief pause. He motioned toward the contents of the pack, which she had left strewn over the ground.

Silently, not looking at him, Lisa knelt and began to scoop things back into the pack. Sam bent to pick up his rifle and shoulder holster. Lisa, sneaking a glance up at him as he straightened, saw beads of perspiration break out along his forehead. His mouth was set in a tight line, as though to repress any small sounds of pain, as he stuck the pistol in his belt and handed Lisa the holster to be included with the other gear in the A.L.I.C.E. pack.

When the supplies were once again stowed securely in the combat pack, Lisa stood up. The bag dangled from one hand. It was heavy, but she was devoutly thankful for its presence. Without it, what would they have done? Then she made a wry face at herself. Sam was no doubt well versed in living off the land. He probably could have provided a three-course dinner for them at ten minutes' notice, if their need was great enough. One thing she had already learned about him: he was a man one could depend on in a crunch. . . .

"Give it to me," Sam said, breaking into her reverie, stretching out a hand for the combat pack. Lisa stared at him in disbelief, then gathered up the bag so that she was holding it rather awkwardly in both arms.

"I'll carry it," she said.

He looked impatient. "Give it to me."

"For God's sake!" Lisa was growing thoroughly exasperated. "Let me carry it! You just fainted, you idiot! You're wounded! You don't have to prove what a big, strong man you are to me—I already know it! But for once you're going to have to use a little sense. You're going to need every scrap of strength you possess just to stay on your feet and keep walking, much less carry this pack!"

Sam looked at her thoughtfully. Lisa felt her cheeks

take on faint color under the open speculation she saw in his gaze.

"You're awfully concerned about me," he observed finally.

Lisa bit her lower lip. Her motives were too uncertain to bear analysis—especially by Sam. She settled on the safest one.

"What would I do if something happened to you?" Her voice was only a shade defensive. Her eyes met his steadily. She was both relieved and sorry when the speculation died in his eyes.

"True," was all he said before turning his back and heading out through the trees.

Lisa stared after him for a moment. Then, swinging the heavy pack to her back as well as she could, she hurried to fall into step behind him. When he sensed her presence, he said, over his shoulder without turning, "If it gets too heavy for you, let me know."

Lisa made no reply.

As the day progressed, Lisa's respect for Sam, already unwillingly high, became something like awe. He moved doggedly onward, trampling through undergrowth so thick it appeared impassable, hacking a path for them both with the long, crooked knife he carried in his boot. Never at any time did he give any indication that he was in pain. But Lisa, having seen that dreadful hole in his shoulder, knew better. He had to be suffering agonies, to say nothing of feeling weak and light-headed from the loss of so much blood. Sheer strength of will had to be the only thing keeping him on his feet. Watching that broad back in the sweat-soaked, bloodstained shirt as it swung on ahead of her, seeing the paleness of his skin and the perspiration that had his black hair wringing wet and ran down between his shoulder blades in little rivers, Lisa was exasperated and moved at one and the same time. Crazy, too-proud man! Didn't he realize that he needed to rest—to stop? He wouldn't even let her help him! Seeing his face whiten as the day progressed, she had made the mistake of offering to let him lean on her as he walked. He hadn't even bothered with a verbal reply, just a blistering look that told her in no uncertain terms what he thought of her suggestion, and sent her stumbling back behind him again, where he no doubt thought she belonged.

Sometime during that interminable afternoon, it began to rain. Not a light, summer drizzle, but a full-fledged downpour. At first the thick jungle foliage protected them from the worst of it, but gradually they ran out of jungle. Walking through fields of tall, golden grass, nearly flattened now by the force of the rain, they were exposed to the full fury of the storm.

At first Lisa, exhausted almost to the point of mindlessness and so hot she felt like a steak on the grill, welcomed the cool drops that trickled down through the sheltering canopy of leaves to fall in a light patter on her head. But when that patter turned into a seemingly endless waterfall, and when there was no escape from it, she was soon more miserable physically than she had ever dreamed she could be. Water soaked her hair so that it dangled in dripping rats' tails down her back; it sluiced her face and drenched her clothes so that she was chilled to the bone. Even Sam's jacket—which he stubbornly refused to wear—was no protection. It was soon just as wet as the rest of her. From sweating profusely, she went to shivering so much that her teeth chattered. Her feet made little squelching sounds with each step. Helplessly she looked at Sam through the blinding downpour; he was moving steadily, already some little distance ahead of her. He had to be at least as wet as she was, and she knew that his shoulder must be hurting like hell. But he seemed oblivious to discomfort, and even to the rain that turned the grassy field into a quagmire beneath their feet. As he strode relentlessly on, she wanted to scream at him to stop, if only for a moment or two. Was he out to prove how macho he was—was that it? Lisa glared at his broad back in impotent outrage. She was dead tired—he had to be, too. It only made sense to stop for a rest. Surely their pursuers would have been halted by this storm. No sane human being would stay out in it any longer than absolutely necessary.

Finally she could stand it no more. A trio of huge, leafy baobab trees beckoned enticingly some thirty feet away, and she for one was going to take advantage of their shelter. If she didn't sit down soon, out of this miserable rain, she was afraid she would fall down.

"Sam!" she called, staggering toward the trees. "Sam, stop!"

Out of breath, wiping away the water that streamed down her face with both hands, she reached the trees and sank down beside one gnarled trunk, which was easily thirty feet in diameter, and leaned back against it. For a moment she feared that Sam had not heard, or, having heard, meant to go on, leaving her to her fate. Then, to her overwhelming relief, he turned, plodding toward her. When at last he stood towering over her, shielded from the worst of the rain by the spreading, interlocking branches overhead, she looked up at him with weary defiance. His face was paper white, marked with lines of exhaustion.

"What's the matter?" he asked, leaning one arm against the tree and letting it bear his weight.

"I have to rest a minute. Please." Lisa huddled at his feet and looked up at him appealingly. He made her feel incredibly small—and not just physically. He was the one who had been shot. That bullet hole in his shoulder should have laid him flat on his back, but he was carrying on without so much as a murmur of pain—even trying to make things easier for her, for God's sake. While she was perfectly whole, not hurt a bit, and yet she couldn't find the strength to move a muscle. It was humiliating, and didn't say a lot for her powers of endurance, but she couldn't help it. She had simply had all she could take. Nothing short of an atomic blast could have gotten her to move.

"Okay." Sam seemed to realize that she was really and truly at the end of her rope. "We'll take a breather. Ten minutes. No more."

With a sound that was midway between a sigh and a groan, he sank down beside her, his good shoulder propped against the tree next to her, one long leg drawn up close to his body while the other sprawled its length in the muck.

"How are you feeling?" Lisa asked after a moment, her concern for him growing appreciably as she looked over at him. He really did look awful, she thought with dismay. His head was resting limply back against the tree; his eyes were closed, and his mouth was a tight, bloodless line. His skin was more gray now than white; the scar on his cheek stood out in stark relief. At her words, his blue eyes flickered open to stare into hers. Uneasily Lisa saw that they seemed almost unnaturally bright.

"I have felt better," he admitted slowly. "But I don't think I'm in any immediate danger of dying. What about you?"

"I'm just tired, mostly," Lisa answered, striving for a light tone. "How does your shoulder feel?"

Sam favored her with a long, wry look. "How do you think it feels? It hurts like hell."

"I'm sorry," was all Lisa could think of to say. She felt hopelessly inadequate. "Is there anything I can do?"

"Since you're not a doctor or a magician, no."

After that unpromising answer, they lapsed into silence. Sam withdrew a package of sodden cigarettes and some matches from his pants pocket. As drops of rain blown toward them by the wind put out his first match, Sam cursed under his breath. He was more careful with the second, cupping his hand around it protectively and at last managing to light his cigarette. Taking a long drag from it, he offered it wordlessly to Lisa. She shook her head. He knew she didn't smoke. . . . Maybe he thought she needed something to calm her nerves. If a cigarette could do that, she thought wryly, she would gladly smoke a whole pack. But she was afraid her nerves were too far gone to be helped by a fix of nicotine. . . .

Her stomach growled loudly, reminding her that it hadn't been fed for almost twenty-four hours. With anyone except Sam, she would have been embarrassed by this uncouth evidence of her body's needs. But Sam was thoroughly familiar with every aspect of her person, including her dratted stomach's propensity for demanding food in a voice clearly meant to be heard.

"You're hungry." It was a statement, not a question, and it was both amused and resigned. Lisa glanced over at Sam to see a faint smile curving his pale lips.

"Yes."

"See those yellowish things hanging up there?" He pointed negligently above his head.

Lisa obediently looked up to see what appeared to be gourds nestled among the dark green leaves of the trees sheltering them.

"Yes."

"They're fruit, believe it or not. Quite good, in fact. If you can get one down, you can eat it."

Lisa looked from him to the fruit dangling tauntingly high out of reach.

"Very funny."

Sam grinned. "All right. If you don't feel up to climbing trees, there should be some packets of beef jerky in the pack. I guess you can eat one."

"Thanks very much. You're too kind." The glance Lisa cast at him was sour. She certainly wasn't in the mood to be teased! But she lost no time in rooting through the pack and extracting the beef jerky. There were two sticks of the spicy meat to a packet, and Lisa passed one to Sam. Despite his kidding around, she noticed with a little sniff, he fell upon his strip of beef just as eagerly as she did hers.

"Sam," she said in a small voice after her appetite was partly appeased.

"Hmmm?"

"What are we going to do?"

"After we eat? Keep walking."

"I mean—how are we going to get out of here? Where are we going?"

"I'd say we're a little to the west of Tuli right now—which is a town, in case you're not up on Rhodesia's geography. The South African border is probably about fifty miles to the south. We should be able to walk it in three, maybe four, days. Once we're across the border, we'll be safe."

"Oh." If possible, Lisa's voice was even smaller

than before. Fifty miles had always sounded like such a short distance—when she'd had a car. On foot, it could just as well have been halfway around the world.

"I'd steal us some sort of vehicle," Sam went on carelessly, as if stealing vehicles was the most natural thing in the world, "but they'll be expecting that. I bet they have roadblocks out everywhere."

"Who's they?" Lisa had meant to match his carelessness, but she succeeded only in sounding thoroughly scared.

"The guys chasing us."

"I know that." She threw him an exasperated look. "But who are they? What on earth did you do to them to make them want us so badly? If I'm going to lay down my life on the altar of some cause or another, I'd sure as hell like to know what it is!"

Sam sent her a sideways, considering look.

"You're better off not knowing. At least they can't get you to confess to anything you don't know—and you might live longer. If—and I say if, so don't look so scared—they should pick us up, they'll be after information ahead of anything else: Who hired us, and why."

"Well, who did?" she demanded impatiently. She was sick and tired of his patronizing attitude. Dyed-in-the-wool male chauvinist pig, she accused him inwardly for what must have been the hundredth time.

"I told you, you're better off not knowing."

"Oh, for God's sake!" Despite her tiredness, Lisa sat bolt upright, turning to glare at him. That the effect was somewhat spoiled by the sodden tails of hair hanging around her neck and the dirty streaks on her face, she neither knew nor cared.

"You really want to know?" Sam had shifted so

163

that he could look squarely into her eyes. Lisa thought, You're enjoying this, aren't you, you devil?

"Yes, I do!"

"Okay." His voice was suddenly expressionless. The teasing grin died. "You asked for it. Don't blame me if you don't like what you hear. The soldiers hunting us are rebels under the direction of Thomas Kimo— I presume you've heard of him?" Lisa nodded. "Apparently they got wind of what we came here to do. They were waiting. We walked into a trap."

"But what did you come here to do?" This was the crucial bit, Lisa knew. The part Sam didn't want to tell her.

Sam closed his eyes, resting his head back against the tree. Lisa, watching him as he leaned heavily against the trunk, his black hair glistening with water and curling in absurd little ringlets around his head, his face white as a corpse's, thought he looked indescribably weary. She bit her lip, on the verge of telling him that she didn't want to know after all, if it was going to bother him that much to tell her, when those blue eyes opened to fix on her steadily.

"We came here to kill Thomas Kimo." His voice was flat. Lisa's eyes widened on his tense face.

"Murder?" she squeaked.

"If you want to call it that. The actual term is, I believe, assassination."

His eyes met hers without expression. Lisa, staring into those fathomless blue depths, felt a chill that had nothing to do with the weather. It was suddenly being brought home to her with a vengeance that she knew absolutely nothing about this man, who he was, where he came from, what he did. All she knew was that he was fantastic in bed, and he could, on occasion, be kind. But he could also be brutal, and by his own admission he was fully prepared to commit cold-blooded murder. She shivered convulsively.

"But—why?" It was a shocked whisper.

"Because I needed the money," he said. His eyes never left her face. Lisa knew that the revulsion she was feeling must be clearly visible there, but she couldn't help it.

"You were going to kill a man—for money?"

"Yes, I was going to kill a man—for money. Now, are you satisfied?" His voice was suddenly vicious. Lisa recoiled.

Sam studied her for a moment, his eyes unreadable, then his brows snapped together to form a straight black line. Bracing his good arm against the tree, he pushed himself upright.

"Come on, let's go," he said harshly. He started walking again, striding briskly out into the rain, without even looking behind him to see if she followed.

Twilight had fallen. The rain was still coming down with no sign of letting up when they came across a small village. It was composed of about two dozen circular, thatched-roofed huts—called rondavels, Sam informed her brusquely—surrounding a much larger one, perhaps fifty feet in diameter. A wide, fairly deep-looking stream rushed nearby, its banks nearly flooded by the rain. Mopani and red syringa trees with their brilliantly colored, drenched flowers formed a sort of barrier between the plain and the village.

Sam stopped at the edge of the trees. Lisa nearly ran into his broad back.

"Why are you stopping?" All she could think of was the lovely shelter the huts would give them. Anything to get out of the rain...

"I want to make sure this place is as deserted as it looks. It probably is; most of the tribes that used to

165

live in villages like this were driven out by one side or the other in the war. But you never can tell."

"Sam—can we stay here overnight?" Lisa's eyes were unconsciously pleading as they met his. They had not exchanged more than half-a-dozen words since that unhappy conversation hours earlier. Now, Lisa was too tired and cold and wet to care if he was angry with her, or if he killed people for a living, or about anything else except their immediate situation. All she wanted to do was rest—preferably some-where dry.

"All right," he conceded slowly after studying her for a moment. "I doubt if anybody's going to be searching for us too hard until the rain lets up. You stay here while I go make sure we don't have any company."

Lisa felt her knees sag with relief. They were actually going to stop—to sleep. And eat. She thought longingly of the C-rations in Sam's pack. Suddenly they were as appealing as dinner at a five-star restaurant.

"Here." He took the smaller pistol—the one he usually wore in his shoulder holster—from where he had thrust it into his belt and handed it to her. "It's on safety. All you have to do is flick it off and pull the trigger."

Lisa took the pistol automatically, then stared down at it with loathing.

"I don't want it," she said with conviction, and tried to hand it back to him.

"Keep it," he advised sparely. "What would you do if I didn't come back—if you were stranded out here all by your lonesome? I admit, you're a lousy shot, but you just might be able to hit a bull elephant if you tried hard enough. Or, who knows, that pistol might just keep you from winding up as a boomslang's dinner."

Lisa shuddered at the picture this conjured up. A boomslang, as Sam had told her some days previously, was a large green tree snake three times as poisonous as the king cobra. Ever since he had described it to her, with loving detail, she had felt shivers run up and down her spine whenever she walked under overhanging branches. Grinning, he had said that it just dropped down on you, without any kind of warning. . . . Lisa was still shuddering as Sam moved off toward the huts, his .45 at the ready in his hand.

While he was gone, between glancing nervously around and shifting the pistol from hand to hand, Lisa did some serious thinking. All right, maybe Sam was a cold-blooded killer—but weren't all soldiers, really? What was the difference between murdering one enemy for money and murdering dozens on the battlefield? Was there a difference? So far, Sam had shown no disposition to harm her in any way—in fact, he'd been extremely kind and patient, under the circumstances. And he had saved her life more than once. She'd been unconscious after the jeep turned over, and she realized that Sam must have carried her to safety at considerable cost to himself. He had even been wounded while doing it. And without him, now, she would be as good as dead. For her own sake, if for no other reason, she would be well advised to save any moral judgments about him until they reached civilization. If they ever did.

"For God's sake, are you deaf? I've been calling you for five minutes!" Sam's voice hissing in her ear made Lisa jump a good two feet in the air. She came back to earth with a jolt to find him already heading back toward the village, his movements rather jerky.

With a small shake of her head to clear it, she followed him.

The hut he led her to was not the larger one as she had expected, but one of the smaller rondavels on the periphery of the village. Anyone looking for them would undoubtedly check the larger hut first, he explained when she asked him; by the time they got around to this particular hut, he and she would be long gone. He hoped.

Once inside the surprisingly sturdy structure, Sam pulled a flashlight from the A.L.I.C.E. pack, which he had taken from her and dropped to the floor. By its light, Lisa could see that the hut was no more than twelve feet across and perfectly round. The walls were made of mud and wattle and were as solid as brick. The roof was thatched, supported by interwoven, thin poles. The floor was of tightly packed dirt overlaid with a few dusty rushes. There were no windows, and the single small door was made from the same material as the walls. Sam had closed it behind them and bolted it with a large stripped branch wedged through woven loops at either side of the opening. The whole place smelled musty. As Sam pointed the flashlight upward, its beam arcing over walls and roof, Lisa screamed instinctively at the enormous spider that sat regarding them from its intricate web in the cone of the roof. Sam laughed unfeelingly at her choked-off cry.

"What's the matter?" he taunted, knowing perfectly well.

Lisa shuddered. "I hate spiders."

"You hate spiders, you hate guns, you hate soldiers— what the hell are you doing here? You should have stayed at home in Granddaddy's mansion where you belong."

Lisa was taken aback at the unexpected venom in

his voice. She stared at him, trying vainly to see his expression through the gloom. Even as she peered at him, the flashlight beam cut an arcing swath through the darkness as he used the flashlight to brush down the spider web.

"Thank you," she said in a subdued voice. He made no reply, but Lisa could almost feel his silent jeer.

Sam handed Lisa the flashlight. "Here, go find yourself a spot where there aren't any spiders and I'll open up our supper. Then we can grab a couple hours' sleep."

Lisa accepted the flashlight silently, turning to do as he'd directed. Then she remembered his wound, and her conscience smote her.

"I'll open up the cans. You go sit down. You must be exhausted."

Lisa could feel him staring at her through the darkness. She knew it was a measure of his tiredness that he did as she suggested.

Shining the flashlight on the contents, Lisa rummaged through the pack. There were a few cans of C-rations and a few more packets of the dried beef and other items—enough perhaps to last them a week if they ate sparingly. She extracted a can of pork and beans from the pack and then searched vainly for a can opener.

"What am I supposed to open this can with? My teeth?" she turned to demand irritably of Sam. Her eyes were accustomed to the darkness now, and she could see him sprawled on the floor nearby, his head resting back against the wall and his long legs bent slightly at the knees as they stretched in front of him. His eyes were closed; he appeared not to have heard her.

"Sam!" she demanded impatiently, raising her voice.

Still no reply, by word or gesture. With an exasperated snort, she crossed to lean over him.

"Sam!" Ordinarily she would have let him sleep— he must have been even more exhausted than she had realized to just drop off like that—but she was starving and he had to know some way of opening the blasted can.

"Sam!" He didn't move. She reached down to nudge his good shoulder. When she did so, to her horror, he slumped sideways to the floor. Quickly she dropped to her knees beside him, her heart in her throat. Clearly, he had passed out again. Her hands went over him frantically, checking to make sure he still breathed. As she pressed one hand against his wounded shoulder, her breath caught. The back of his shirt was soaking wet—and not just from the rain. This wet was sticky as well. . . . She pulled back her hand and stared down at the palm. Even through the darkness, she could see that it was black with blood.

X

LISA turned the flashlight on him. By its strong light she saw that his face was very pale, his lips almost bloodless. Holding her breath, she turned the beam on his back. As she had suspected, fresh blood soaked the whole left side of his rain-wet shirt. Lisa bit down on her lower lip so hard that she could taste blood as it seeped into her mouth. He must have been bleeding for hours.... Propping the flashlight on the ground to give herself some light to work by while still leaving her hands free, she began to unbutton Sam's shirt with fingers that shook. She had to try to bandage up that wound again. Left like this, he could bleed to death.

Sam came around almost as suddenly as he had fainted. One moment he was lying on his side on the dirt floor, his big body limp and still, and the next his eyes were flickering open and he was trying to heave himself into a sitting position.

"Stay still." Lisa's hands on his waist beseeched him. He looked up at her owlishly for just a moment, then groaned and subsided. Once she was sure he would not try again to get up, she resumed unbuttoning his shirt.

"God, did I faint again?" His voice was weak.

"Yes." Lisa continued to work his shirt buttons loose until the garment was open to the waist. With businesslike efficiency, she pulled the tails from his waistband, baring his chest. Then she gently began to ease his left arm, which was uppermost, out of its sleeve.

"I don't need your help to take off my shirt." His tone was almost hostile. Lisa glanced down at his face to find his eyes glittering up at her resentfully. It was a measure of his weakness, she realized, that he was making no physical attempt to stop her ministrations, instead making do with barbed words.

"Yes, you do," she replied with what patience she could muster. Had no one ever shown him any tenderness, taken care of him in any way? she wondered. Clearly he was not accustomed to needing or accepting help from anyone—not even when he was ill.

"No, I don't," he insisted stubbornly. His voice was stronger now, and he made a move as if to lever himself up on one elbow. Only Lisa's hand on the side of his neck kept him prone.

"Listen," she said between her teeth, her patience having suddenly deserted her. As she spoke she lowered her face so that it was just inches from his. "Your wound has opened up again and you're bleeding like a stuck pig. You must have known it! But like a stubborn, mule-headed fool you just had to keep going, didn't you? But now you're going to lie still and let me bandage that bullet wound up again, or I swear I'll—I'll take the butt end of that pistol to your head! Do you understand me?"

Lisa was almost spitting with temper by the time she had finished speaking. Sam said nothing, only stared at her bemusedly for a moment. Then, to her surprise and relief, a slight smile crooked the corners of his mouth.

"You're scaring me to death," he murmured mockingly. "You wouldn't really hit me over the head with something, would you?"

Lisa relaxed a little. Maybe he wasn't going to be difficult after all. But there was still a trace of belligerence in her voice as she answered.

"Yes, I would. So you'd better behave!"

"Yes, ma'am," he said meekly. Lisa gave him a stern look, suspecting him of making fun of her. His answering look was bland. With a disdainful sniff, she went back to easing his shirt off his injured shoulder. The bandage, she saw, was dangling by a single piece of tape, apparently a casualty of the rain. The white gauze was stained dark brown in places from blood. Dark crimson ooze crept from the wound to cover most of the left side of his back.

"How bad does it look?" he asked, sounding not terribly interested.

"Awful," she answered in a choked voice. She had no thought of sparing him the gory details. He would have to know the worst in order to tell her what to do for him. Surely he knew more about how to treat bullet wounds than she did. He certainly couldn't know less!

"What is 'awful'?" he questioned patiently, turning his head as if to see the wound for himself. It was impossible, of course, no matter how he craned his neck.

"It's all swollen, and there's a huge black and yellow bruise over the whole upper part of your shoulder and down almost to the middle of your back on the left. Plus the wound itself is bleeding—not too badly, but the blood looks kind of thick and it's coming in little spurts. It must hurt like crazy. Can you move your arm at all?"

Sam tried, and managed to move his left arm forward and then back. As he did, his face turned even whiter than before and he sucked in his breath sharply. Lisa, watching blood spurt with fresh enthusiasm from the hole in his back, cried out to him to stop. He did. His eyes closed, and sweat popped out along his forehead. For a moment, Lisa was afraid that he might have fainted again.

"Sam?"

"I'm okay."

It was obvious from the strained quality of his voice that he wasn't. Lisa looked down at him anxiously. He was such a big man, so muscular and strong, and yet he looked so helpless curled on his side, his face resting against the dusty rushes covering the floor.

"What should I do?" she asked humbly, hovering over him. "Do you want me to bandage it up again?"

"How steady are your hands?"

Lisa blinked down at him uncomprehendingly, then looked down at her long, slim fingers resting lightly against the bare skin at the back of his waist. They had been shaking earlier, when she had unbuttoned his shirt.

"Not—not too steady," she admitted. He made an impatient sound. His eyes were still closed, and he was as white as a marble statue.

"Then you'll have to do something to steady them. Look in the bottom of the pack. There should be a bottle of whiskey. Take a swig, and then pass it to me."

"Why?" Lisa asked faintly, horror in her face and in her voice. She was very much afraid that she already knew. . . .

"Because you're going to have to cut that bullet

out of me and then sew the hole up. There'll be a needle and thread in the pack, too."

Lisa was appalled.

"I—I can't," she stammered, sinking back on her heels and staring aghast at his broad back.

"You have to," he said. "My arm's stiffening up. By tomorrow I won't be able to use it at all. I can feel the damned thing in there, rubbing against the bone. Every time I move, it hurts like hell. It's got to come out, and you've got to do it. There's no one else."

"No..." Lisa said faintly.

Sam went on, his voice inexorable. "After you get the bullet out—it shouldn't be too hard to find, just follow the tunnel it made going in—I want you to pour disinfectant in the wound, then sew the edges together, just like you would a piece of cloth. Just be sure to soak everything you use, including the thread, in antiseptic first. I'd hate to end up with my shoulder infected—I'd be in worse shape than I'm in now. Got it?"

Lisa sat frozen, staring down at him. She couldn't do it.... The mere sight of blood had always been enough to make her sick to her stomach. And yet she had cleaned away the gore from that awful hole earlier, and then bandaged it up, without turning a hair,

"Sam, are you sure you want me to do this?" she asked finally, feeling numb. "What if I—hurt you?"

He rolled onto his stomach, cradling his head in his good arm. His face was turned away from her, but she thought she saw a faint, wry smile tilt his mouth.

"Don't worry, honey, there's nothing vital in the immediate vicinity—you couldn't kill me if you tried. And if you don't try, I'm not going to be able to move my arm at all, and then we'll have a hell of a time getting out of here. Go on, do like I said—get the whiskey. After that, I'll tell you what to do next."

Reluctantly obedient, Lisa crawled across to where she had left the combat pack earlier. Rummaging through it, she found a nearly full bottle of whiskey. Her hand shook as she pulled it out. The more she thought about what Sam wanted her to do, the more certain she felt that she couldn't do it.

Instead of trying to find what she would need right then, she dragged the combat pack with her as she crawled back to Sam's side. Looking at him as he lay on his stomach in the shadows, with only the flashlight she held in her hand to light a tiny area of his back, she felt a quiver of hope.

"I can't do it—there's not enough light. We'll have to at least wait until morning."

"There's some rope in the pack—string it up over one of those poles supporting the roof and tie the flashlight to the end. That should do it. I don't want to wait until morning—the sooner we get it done, the sooner we can be on our way."

"But, Sam..." Lisa started to protest, then gave it up. If he could so calmly contemplate her performing makeshift surgery on him, then he must think that it needed to be done. Because he knew as well as she did that it was going to cause him a lot of pain....

She had to weight the rope down with a rock before she could throw it over one of the poles, but at last she managed to get the light arranged as Sam had instructed. When finally she had the flashlight adjusted so that it hung about a foot above Sam's back, he turned his head to regard her handywork and gave her a thumbs-up sign. She herself was impressed with the efficient way the light illuminated his whole left-shoulder area. At least she would be able to see what she was doing—if she didn't faint right in the middle, that is.

"Now what?" she asked with trepidation when the light was adjusted to both her and Sam's satisfaction.

"Find the needle and thread it. You shouldn't need much—probably about a foot." He lay quietly while Lisa did as he told her. It took a little while, because her hands weren't quite steady as she guided the thread through the tiny needle's eye, but at last it was done.

"All right," she said.

"Don't forget to soak it in the antiseptic before you use it," he cautioned. She nodded silently. He continued, "Now get the knife out of my boot. You know where it is."

Lisa did indeed. She moved down his body to reach the knife he kept in a leather sheath inside his right boot. It was a wicked-looking thing, she thought as she held it in her hands, with a crooked blade and a razor-sharp point. Sam had told her previously that the Africans called it a kris.... She blanched as she contemplated using it to cut into Sam's hard brown flesh.

"I don't think I can do this." She gulped, crawling back up to sit beside him and staring down at the gleaming knife as if she had never seen it before.

"Yes, you can." She wished she felt as confident as he sounded, she thought nervously. Then he added, "You have to," and Lisa knew she had no choice.

Lisa stared at the knife a moment longer, then resolutely squared her shoulders. She had to. For herself and for Sam.

At Sam's instructions, she got out gauze and antiseptic and tape. Then there seemed nothing else to do.

"Ready?" Sam asked when it became obvious that

she was merely puttering for the sake of delaying the inevitable for as long as she could.

"I—guess." If she sounded doubtful, there was a very good reason: she felt doubtful.

"Okay. Take a swallow of whiskey and then pass it here. I think I might need it."

"Don't you dare get drunk on me," Lisa warned shrilly, assailed by a horrible vision of him crazy drunk and not able to help her should she need it.

"With you holding that knife? Not a chance," he said with a grimace. "Now come on. Get some whiskey down you. You're probably going to need it more than I will."

Lisa had never drunk raw liquor before in her life, but Sam was right—she needed a drink badly. She uncapped the bottle, put it to her lips, and swallowed a huge mouthful. It burned like liquid Drano all the way down. Coughing and spluttering, she gasped for air. But she had to admit, when her shocked system had settled down a little, that she did feel warmer—and, marginally, braver.

"Here." She passed the bottle to Sam, who took it in his good hand and tilted his head so that he could drink. As he guzzled, a quantity of amber liquid missed his mouth to pool on the floor beneath his head, but enough hit its target to faintly alarm Lisa.

"You promised you wouldn't get drunk," she reminded him reproachfully when at last he took the bottle from his lips.

He gave her a derisive look. "Honey, that little bit of whiskey barely gives me a buzz," he said scornfully. Lisa, looking down at the bottle which was now just about a fourth full, hoped he was right.

"Sam, are you sure you want to go through with this?" She gave him one last chance to change his mind.

"I'm sure," he said, handing the bottle back to her and closing his eyes. Then, as Lisa set the whiskey aside and leaned over him, the knife poised uncertainly, he flicked a look up at her.

"Think you can get my belt loose?" he asked unexpectedly, reaching down to undo the buckle as he spoke. Lisa's hands slid around his hard middle, brushing his aside, grappling with the buckle. In just a moment she had pulled the belt free.

"What do you want me to do with it?" she asked dubiously, visions of using the thick leather strap as some sort of a torniquet dancing in her brain.

"Give it to me," he directed. She did so. He very carefully folded the belt in half.

"What are you going to do with it?"

He slanted a look up at her. "You ever heard of biting the bullet?" To Lisa's horrified astonishment, he demonstrated putting the folded belt between his teeth. "This is the approximate equivalent."

Lisa made a small, strangled sound deep in her throat. She couldn't do it! She could not. . . . Sam must have read her sudden decision in her face, because he reached around and caught her hand in his. His skin enfolding hers felt very warm and hard. . . .

"It's all right," he said steadily. "I've been hurt a lot more than you're going to be able to do to me here. And you don't have a choice—you have to do it. Okay?"

Lisa looked down, met those blue eyes that were even now darkened with pain, and swallowed. Then she nodded, feebly.

"Good girl." He gave her hand a bracing squeeze, then released it. "Now let's get this over with."

He turned his head away from her, closing his eyes and putting the folded belt between his teeth.

Lisa just sat there staring at him. She couldn't just start digging the knife into his poor shoulder....

Finally he took the belt from between his teeth, and looked around at her. "Well?"

"I—don't know what to do."

He sighed, and repeated the instructions he had given her one more time. He made her say them back to him, and when at last he was satisfied that she knew what to do, he put the belt back between his teeth and lay waiting.

Lisa poured antiseptic liberally over her hands and the knife as Sam had instructed. Then there was nothing left to do but begin to cut. She risked a quick glance up at Sam's face. It was tense, with all his muscles tightened in expectation of the pain she had no choice but to inflict on him. His white teeth bit into the leather belt, and his fists were clenched. Looking at him, registering him as the man she had slept with and argued with and depended on for the last few weeks, she felt butterflies in her stomach. Resolutely she tore her eyes away from his face, dropping them to his shoulder instead, willing herself to think of him as something inanimate, like the frog she had once dissected in biology class.

It worked. After a few minutes her stomach settled down. Then she began.

By the time the knife was imbedded about two inches into Sam's shoulder, Lisa was biting her lower lip so hard that blood was filling her mouth. More blood, thick scarlet waves of it, rolled from the deepening hole in Sam's shoulder. Lisa made no effort to wipe it away, and soon it was everywhere, on her hands, the knife, smeared across Sam's back and the back of his pants. As she probed ever deeper, Sam made one sudden, abortive movement, which he controlled almost at once. Lisa flicked a quick, anguished glance at his face. It was white and clammy, with beads of perspiration rolling down his forehead and across his cheeks. His eyes were clenched as tightly shut as his fists; his teeth had bitten almost halfway through the doubled leather of the belt. Lisa felt tears spring to her eyes. She blinked them away, but immediately they were replaced by more until they ran down her face unchecked. She tried to tell herself that she didn't mind hurting him, and deliberately thought back over all the times he had humiliated her. He deserved to hurt a little—but even as Lisa tried to convince herself of that, she knew it was a waste of time. Whatever he was, whatever he had done, she could not bear to see him suffer. She realized with a sense of shock that she would gladly have borne the pain of this impromptu operation herself, to spare him. It was illogical, crazy really, considering that she had spent most of the time she'd known him hating his guts, but it was the way she felt. Lisa was conscious of a sinking feeling in the pit of her stomach as she was forced to entertain the suspicion that she had perhaps grown fonder of him than it was wise to be.

Her tears practically blinded her, but it made no difference, because she couldn't see into the wound anyway with all the blood welling from it. She had to rely on her sense of touch alone as she probed, slowly and carefully, deeper into his shoulder. She was just beginning to despair when the tip of the knife struck something with a small, metallic-sounding chink.

"I think I've found it," she said to herself as much as to Sam. The thankfulness in her voice made the words sound like a prayer. Sam, of course, didn't reply, but she thought his facial muscles relaxed slightly.

Working as quickly as she could, remembering Sam's instructions, Lisa poured antiseptic over long tweezers from the first-aid kit and worked them down into the bloody path carved out by the knife. Cautiously nudging aside sections of skin and muscle, she reached the bullet with the tweezers in an amazingly short period of time, especially considering how long it had taken her to locate it in the first place. Then it took merely a couple of seconds to grasp the bullet between the ends of the tweezers and lift it from the wound. Staring down at the blood-covered bit of metal, she felt so relieved that she wanted to sing.

"I've got it, Sam, I've got it!" she said joyfully.

He winced when she poured antiseptic directly into the open wound, and winced again when she started to close the jagged edges with careful, though inexpert, stitches. But she felt that some of the tenseness had left his muscles, and knew that he was as glad to have this ordeal over as she was.

By the time she had finished cleaning the blood from his back and covering the wound with sterile gauze, she felt as limp and wrung out as a used dishrag. Blinking, she sat back on her heels, wiping her hands on Sam's shirt and looking down at him. He lay sprawled on his stomach, his eyes closed, his skin paper white except where it was streaked by blood or perspiration. Lisa gently removed the nearly bitten-through belt from between his teeth. Then, wetting a small square of gauze, she began to wipe his face.

"Are you okay?" she asked huskily after a moment, when he had made no gesture acknowledging her action. He didn't answer; Lisa chewed her lower lip anxiously, fearing that he had fainted again. Which she could certainly understand, she thought. She was amazed that he had been able to endure as long as he had. Picturing Jeff in similar circumstances, Lisa knew that he would have been screaming with pain and fear from the very first instant the bullet had entered his flesh.

Then, to her overwhelming relief, Sam's clenched fists slowly straightened out, and his eyes opened.

"I'm okay," he said on a long, indrawn breath. "You did a good job, Dr. Collins. I'm proud of you—and you can be proud of yourself."

"Th-thank you." Ridiculously, her voice was wobbly. Sam heard the quivery note, and laboriously turned over onto his uninjured side. To her dismay, he pushed himself into a sitting position, propping his right shoulder back against the wall, ignoring her hands outstretched to stop him.

"Sam, you shouldn't..."

"You've been crying," he interrupted. The words sounded like an accusation.

Lisa brought up her fists and rubbed self-consciously at her still-damp eyes, feeling for all the world like she was about ten years old. So she had been crying— it didn't mean anything, she told herself defiantly. She had been known to cry over sad movies, hurt pets, books, anything and everything. It certainly didn't mean what it sounded like he was trying to make it mean—that she was beginning to feel a kind of affection for him! She sniffled inelegantly, trying to control the tears that were once again threatening to burst forth.

"Haven't you?" he persisted softly, making no move to touch her but eating her with those impossible eyes.

"So what?" Her rude reply was defensive. She didn't want him probing any closer—although she refused to admit why even to herself.

"Why, Lisa?"

He was going to worry the subject to death, she could tell. At all costs, Lisa wanted to keep him from guessing about the absurd soft spot she seemed to have uncovered for him. He would undoubtedly laugh and mock her. And she—she was too uncertain of her feelings where he was concerned to let him catch a glimpse of the unwelcome tenderness she had just discovered she felt for him.

"I always cry when I'm under stress," she said in a gruff little voice. Then, trying to change the subject, she added, "Shouldn't you be lying down?"

Sam ignored this last, as she should have known he would. He tilted his head back against the wall, his eyes fixed on her consideringly. Lisa felt color begin to heat her cheeks as she endured that searching perusal.

"You've been under stress of one sort or another ever since I met you," he said slowly. "And I've never seen you cry before. Why not admit it, Lisa? You were crying because you didn't like hurting me."

Lisa said nothing. Of their own volition her lashes dropped to shield her eyes from his probing gaze. Drat the man anyway, she thought irritably. Was he bound and determined to embarrass her?

"Weren't you?" he persisted.

Lisa's lower lip quivered with humiliation. If he made fun of her, she would want to die....

"So what if I was?" she demanded belligerently, her eyes flashing open to meet his head-on. To her surprise, his lips parted in one of those devastatingly sweet smiles that never failed to rock her to her core.

"So I like the idea," he said softly, his eyes suddenly warm as they moved over her pink face. "Come here, honey."

He reached for her with his good arm as he spoke. Without knowing quite how it came about, Lisa found herself cuddled against his uninjured side, her face buried in the warm curve between his neck and shoulder. His arm was like a steel band around her back as he held her against him.

"I hated hurting you," she confided shakily into the strong cords of his neck. He pressed her comfortingly closer.

"Not long ago you gave me the impression that you would willingly have slit my throat," he said with just the suspicion of a teasing smile in his voice. "What made you change your mind?"

This was what Lisa had been expecting. She stiffened, trying to pull away from him. Injured or not, he was still infinitely stronger than she was, and he held her with seeming ease.

"Don't you make fun of me!" she said in a high, shaking voice.

Immediately he held her a little away from him, looking down into her face. They were outside the small circle of light cast by the dangling flashlight, and it was difficult to read his expression clearly through the shadows.

"I wasn't making fun of you, honey." Oddly enough, he sounded sincere. "I was just wondering what brought on the change."

"I don't know. I don't want to talk about it."

Sam studied her for a few moments longer, then pulled her back against his side.

"Okay," he said agreeably. "We won't talk about it—at least not now." He was murmuring his words into the ear closest to him, his lips nudging aside the soft hair covering it so that his breath softly caressed the tender skin. Despite herself, Lisa felt her head droop onto his broad shoulder. With a tiny sigh, she relaxed against him. She was so tired. . . .

"Hey, don't go to sleep on me," he said after a few minutes' silence.

Lisa murmured drowsily in reply. Sam shook her gently with the arm that curved around her waist. Reluctantly Lisa looked up at him, her eyes big pools of sleepiness. Sam studied her small flushed face for a moment without speaking, then his hand moved up to tilt up her chin. Before Lisa realized what he was about, he leaned over to plant a soft, butterfly kiss on her mouth. Her lips trembled at his touch.

"You're cold," he said with a quick frown, thankfully misinterpreting her shiver. "You need to get out of those wet clothes before you catch pneumonia."

In truth, Lisa hadn't spared a thought for her clothes. They were merely damp now, instead of soaking wet as they had been earlier. But now that she thought about it, she realized that they were uncomfortably clammy against her skin. This time, when she shivered it was genuinely from the cold.

"I will if you will," she said, straightening away from him and looking over at the still-wet pants that clung to his muscular hips and thighs as closely as a second skin.

"Deal," he answered lightly, but his tone was belied by the odd little light that shone in his blue eyes.

Looking at him, Lisa had the oddest sensation, like her heart was trying to do a somersault in her chest. To give her thoughts a new direction, she began hurriedly to unbutton her shirt. After living with him as she had, she felt no shyness about undressing in front of him. Sam had already seen, and more than seen, every single millimeter of her body.

He leaned forward and began to unlace his boots, but then had to lean back again with a groan. Lisa, looking up to see the spasm that crossed his face, was immediately beside him, glaring at him.

"I told you not to move," she scolded in a tone used by fond but exasperated mothers. "You should try listening."

Sam returned her look. He was very pale, and his skin was drawn, but the ghost of a grin hovered around his mouth.

"Sorry," he murmured. Lisa gave him one more monitory look, then scooted down to do the job herself.

She removed his boots one at a time, trying not to jar him as she worked them from his feet. When the boots were finally off, she peeled off his socks, thinking what nice feet he had. They were large and brown and strong-looking—dependable feet, she thought, then was immediately disgusted with herself for giving in to such foolishness. Whoever heard of dependable feet? Again she had to caution herself against growing too attached to him: once they were back home again, they would be going their separate ways.

When his feet were bare, she unfastened his pants, her actions totally natural, without embarrassment. His eyes never left her as she slid his zipper down; she had no way of knowing that he was thinking what a pretty picture she made with her silver-gilt hair forming a curling halo around her small, flushed face and her lower lip caught characteristically between her teeth as she concentrated on her task. Her shirt was open to the waist and only her flimsy bra hid her soft breasts from his gaze. She looked up then and caught his eyes on her, and smiled.

"Can you lift yourself up?" She had to repeat the question twice before he understood.

Sam did as she asked, and she slid his pants and shorts down past his hips, then pulled them all the way off with little difficulty. Sam remembered that she was no novice at undressing men, then banished the thought from his head. It made no difference to him, in any case. . . .

Naked, he still looked very much the man in charge, Lisa thought, not even realizing that her eyes were moving over his long body until she noticed the goosebumps ridging the flesh of his arms and legs.

"You'll freeze, sitting around like that," she said with swift concern.

"There's a blanket tied to the bottom of the pack. We can share it."

Lisa remembered seeing the blanket, tightly rolled and bound with nylon cords, when she had rummaged through the pack earlier. Quickly she fetched it, shaking it out and draping it over Sam's shoulders. He drew it around him, shivering convulsively.

"Come on, it'll be warmer if we share."

Sam's words brought home to her again how cold she really was. Lisa hastily shed the rest of her clothes, then stood before him, naked and shivering, her arms wrapped around herself for warmth.

"Hand me the rifle and switch off the flashlight. We need to save the batteries," Sam directed. Lisa did as he told her. He put the rifle carefully within reach, then opened one side of the blanket in an inviting gesture that Lisa could just barely make out through the darkness.

"Come here, honey." His voice was a low, soft drawl. Lisa, obediently crawling in beside him, thought how much she had grown to like the sound of it.

Sam's arm curled warmly about her waist, and she snuggled against his side, wanting to warm herself and at the same time warm him. The blanket, a thick, tightly woven wool with a plastic underside, kept out most of the chilly night air, but it was Sam's body heat that gradually stopped her shivers. When at last she felt warm, she stretched her arm outside the blanket and groped for the pack, which she had had the forethought to leave within reach.

"What are you doing?" Sam sounded as if he was on the verge of sleep. Lisa felt guilty about having disturbed him after all he had been through that night, but she was starving.

"I'm hungry," she whispered in explanation, searching through the pack for another packet of the beef jerky.

"Oh, God, I should have guessed." He sighed. But when Lisa held a strip of the dried beef to his lips, he displayed no hesitation in taking a healthy bite. Snuggling against him, Lisa alternately took a bite and then fed him one, knowing that he was perfectly capable of feeding himself but wanting to pamper him a little. Surprisingly, he didn't object. She excused her action inwardly by reminding herself that he had saved her life on more than one occasion—so why should she feel self-conscious about taking care of him for a change?

They talked very little as they huddled together naked under the blanket, Sam's arm still securely wrapping Lisa's waist and Lisa feeding him bites of their impromptu meal. But their bodies, pressed intimately together, conversed in a language all their own. There was nothing sexual about their closeness. Instead it was as if they were old and intimate friends, or lovers of long standing.

When they had finished eating, Sam carefully lowered Lisa with him to the floor, the blanket protecting them both from the dirt beneath and the cold air above them. He lay on his uninjured side; Lisa was turned on her side, too, with her naked back pressed up against his chest. His head was pillowed on one of the less unyielding corners of the pack, while his good arm served as Lisa's pillow. Before they were settled comfortably, Sam's other arm was draped gingerly around her waist, and her small, chilled feet had carved a niche between his thighs.

"Your feet are like blocks of ice," he grumbled in her ear. But when Lisa would have removed them, his thighs tightened punishingly and he nipped her ear with his teeth.

"Did I say I didn't like it?" he murmured. Then, before Lisa could reply, his suddenly deepened breathing told her that he had dropped off to sleep with the suddenness of exhaustion.

XI

LISA awoke with the vague feeling that something was wrong. She lay unmoving for a moment, still in the same position in which she had fallen asleep. The interior of the rondavel had lightened to a gloomy gray—apparently she had slept straight through the night and into the morning. Outside, she could hear the rain still beating relentlessly against the thatched roof and sides of the hut. It sounded as if it would never stop.

Sam's arm still curved around her waist, holding her tightly against him. Pressed close to the naked skin of her back and buttocks, she could feel the heat and hardness of his body. The mat of hair on his chest and belly and thighs provided a soft, sometimes prickly cushion between them. His breathing was loud in her ear, but almost too shallow and fast to denote a deep sleep. For a moment Lisa allowed a smile to touch her lips, thinking that he was awake and wanting her. Apparently his injury was not severe enough to interfere with his most basic natural instincts.

Then Lisa's eyes widened and the smile fled from her lips as she felt a long tremor rack his body. He continued to shiver violently against her, and Lisa realized that this was the sensation that had brought her from sleep. Moving with difficulty because of the tightness of his grip on her, Lisa wiggled around so that she was facing him. He still held her clamped against his body, but his eyes were closed and she knew that he hadn't the slightest awareness of what he was doing. She didn't even have to work a hand free and place it against his forehead to ascertain that he was burning up with fever. The scorching heat of his body as he pressed her ever closer told her that.

"Sam!" His name came out before she could catch it. It would do absolutely no good to wake him up, she realized with the thinking part of her brain, but the emotional part of her needed the reassurance of his awareness. When he made no sign to indicate that he had heard her, she was frightened. Dear God, they were alone in a hostile wilderness under the most primitive of conditions, and he was clearly very ill. What in the name of all that was holy was she to do?

Reason temporarily fled; she tried shaking him, desperately wanting him to open his eyes, to somehow acknowledge her presence. At least if he was conscious, she rationalized, he could tell her what to do for him. But he remained oblivious to her efforts. Lisa could have cried. She had never felt so helpless, so inadequate. Was she totally useless? she railed at herself. Couldn't she—just this once—be strong and capable for both of them instead of automatically turning to him for guidance and support?

Another long shudder rippled over Sam's body. His hold on her tightened again. Lisa realized that he was clutching her so painfully close in an effort to share her body heat. This time his teeth chattered loudly with the force of his chill. The ominous sound spurred Lisa to action. She was on her own; there was no one to help her or give advice—and Sam needed her desperately. For once in her life, she had to come through.

It was hard work prying his arms from around her. His left arm trailed limply across her shoulder, but his right one curved beneath her to grip her with steely strength. Finally she managed to free herself and rolled quickly away from him. Then she sat up, looking at him with a worried frown puckering her brow while the cool dampness of the air snaked over her body like icy fingers.

Sam moaned a protest at her desertion, pulling the blanket more closely around him and huddling into it. His knees curled up against his chest. The blackness of his hair and the two-day growth of beard obscuring his hard jaw made an alarming contrast with the pasty gray whiteness of his face. His skin was perfectly dry, without a drop of perspiration in evidence. Biting her lip, Lisa crawled closer to lay her hand first against his forehead and then against his cheeks. His skin felt as if it were on fire.

Dread held her immobile for a moment. Then she forced herself to think. His fever was clearly very high, and she was the only one who could bring it down. She had to restore him to something approximating his normal good health—for both their sakes.

Her first order of business had to be to check his wound, she decided. Maybe her amateur operation was somehow responsible for the state he was in. But last night, after it was over, he had seemed perfectly all right—or at least as all right as it was possible to be under such circumstances. And surely infection couldn't have set in this fast. Could it? She didn't know. Her grasp of first-aid and nursing principles was minimal at best.

She was shivering, feeling gooseflesh break out everywhere on her naked body, her nipples hardening painfully from the cold. In a moment she would get dressed, but first she had to see. . . .

Carefully she pulled the blanket from around his wounded shoulder, which thankfully was uppermost. Blood had seeped through the bandage, staining it, but that was only to be expected. Anyway, there didn't appear to be much. . . . Working gently, she loosened a long strip of surgical tape so that she could pull away the gauze pad. It came free with some difficulty, because of the dried blood gluing it to the wound. Sam moaned and muttered something as she tugged, his hand coming up to push hers away. Lisa caught his hand in both hers, pressing her cheek against the hot palm for just an instant before returning it firmly to his side. As she touched him, she winced from the burning dryness of his skin. His fever had to be brought down soon or the consequences could be too awful to contemplate. It was even possible that he could die. . . . Lisa was both surprised and a little alarmed at the sick feeling that accompanied the thought, and the overwhelming sense of impending loss. She had not dreamed she could feel such pain again for anyone—not since Jennifer. . . .

To her unknowledgeable eye, the wound looked all right. Her white-thread stitches were bloodstained in places and were crookedly inexpert, but they seemed to be holding. Just a little blood had seeped from the pulled-together edges of the hole to form a dark crust over the wound. The flesh around it was still swollen and severely bruised, but the wound itself wasn't infected. At least she didn't think so. With the hazy memory of some mystery novel to guide her, Lisa leaned over to sniff at the wound. She had read that one could identify gangrene by its sickly sweet odor. But, no matter how hard she sniffed, she could smell nothing but the tang of antiseptic overlaid by the musky scent of man. Relieved, she taped the bandage in place again, then got rather unsteadily to her feet.

Her clothes were filthy, stiff with dirt and rain, but at least they were dry. She accorded their unappetizing appearance a token shrug before pulling them on. She had more urgent matters to occupy her thoughts than wishing uselessly for clean clothes—anyway, she was getting used to feeling like a refugee from a pig sty. She didn't think she had felt clean from head to toe since her long-ago bath in the creek near the camp.

Dressed, she felt marginally warmer. It was gloomy inside the windowless hut, and she thought that perhaps the absence of light might be contributing to Sam's chill. But there was nothing she could do about it.

Her only source of supplies was the combat pack. Crouching on the floor, she dumped its contents out into the dirt. Besides the first aid kit there were several cans of C-rations, two packages of the dried beef jerky they had eaten last night, cigarettes, matches, a lighter, maps, a compass, collapsible cups, a cooking pot and eating utensils, and a variety of miscellany.

Lisa looked from the collection of objects at her feet to Sam. He rubbed his head pitifully against the blanket, seemingly searching for a nonexistent pillow. Lisa pondered for a moment, then began to stuff his discarded clothes into the empty pack. It made a lumpy but serviceable pillow; when she put it under Sam's head, he snuggled into it gratefully.

Sam needed medicine to bring down his fever, Lisa knew. She frowned over the contents of the first-aid kit. Most of the pills and ointments it contained were unfamiliar to her, and their labels—long medical names for the most part—were useless in helping her to identify the purposes for which they were intended. About the only thing she recognized was a bottle of aspirin. Thankfully, she fished it out. Aspirin was good for bringing down a fever—at least she thought it was.

In the bottle, though, the tablets were useless. She had to get him to swallow a couple. Shaking the canteen, she discovered that there was only a little water left—barely enough to help Sam down the aspirin. After those few swallows were gone, she didn't know what they would do. Then, listening to the rain beating down against the roof and sides of the hut, she shook her head at herself. Lack of water seemed destined to be the least of their problems.

Crossing to kneel beside Sam, she pondered how best to force the aspirin down his throat, and had just concluded that it would be impossible to get an unconscious man to swallow anything, when he rolled onto his side. Then, to her relief, his eyes blinked open.

"Water," he said with a groan, running his tongue over his parched-looking lips. His blue eyes were glazed with fever; he seemed unaware of her presence.

Lisa's first impulse was to hold the canteen to his lips, but then she realized that if she gave him the water first he would have none left to wash the aspirin down with. She would have to get him to swallow the tablets first.

"Water," he repeated in a pleading croak that wrung her heart.

"In a minute," she promised soothingly, moving so that his head was cradled in her lap. Carefully she lifted it so that it rested higher against her breasts, holding him so that he could swallow without choking. "First I want you to take some medicine. Can you swallow these aspirin for me?"

Almost unconsciously, she was speaking to him as she would have to a sick child. His eyes closed; for a moment she was afraid that he might have drifted off again. But then his eyes flickered open and seemed to focus on her.

"Sam?" she whispered hopefully.

His brow puckered, and he moved his head against her restlessly.

"Beth?" he muttered.

Lisa felt her heart contract at the unfamiliar female name. Who was Beth? she wondered as she forced the aspirin between his lips, then quickly held the canteen to his mouth, tilting water down his throat so that he was forced to swallow. Girl friend, sister, daughter—or wife? With a shock Lisa realized that she didn't even know if he was married. Until now, it hadn't seemed to matter. But as she thought about it, it seemed more than likely that he had a wife and several children. He was a devastatingly attractive man—and he could be very charming when he chose to be. It was almost inconceivable that he could have reached his present age—late thirties? forty? she didn't know that either—without having been snapped up by some eager female. Picturing him with a wife—a plump little homebody with a ready smile and an affinity for the kitchen—and a couple of kids sent a queer little pang shafting through her. Absently smoothing his hair, she realized that, in some strange way, she had begun to consider Sam as hers—her property. Which was ridiculous!

Suddenly becoming aware that she still had his head cradled to her breasts, and that his blue eyes were fastened on her and gave the appearance at least of being aware, she quickly lowered his head to rest on the makeshift pillow.

"Sam?" she queried again, but this time her tone was brisk.

"Water," was his reply, uttered in a dry, pleading voice. "Please, water."

Clearly, he was out of his head. Lisa felt a hard knot of worry lodge in her throat as she took the cooking pot out into the rain to catch more water.

Sam was delirious all day. Lisa sat beside him, sponging his hot body with the cool rain water when he fretfully threw off the blanket, climbing into the pallet beside him and gathering him in her arms when he switched to shivering with chills. Lisa imagined bitterly that he supposed she was the absent Beth. Her jealousy of this woman—whoever she was, whatever she meant to Sam—grew like a weed in a flower garden, despite her refusal to acknowledge it for what it was. Mechanically she fed him aspirin and sips of water. When he woke up, saying bluntly that he had to pee, she even helped him with that. And all the time she felt—unreasonably, she knew—as if he'd dealt her body a blow that went straight through to her heart.

Finally his shivering fits became so violent that she felt she had to risk starting a fire. Judiciously she gathered some of the reeds from the floor into a pile—just enough to make a small fire. She didn't want to burn the hut down. She built the tiny blaze as close to Sam as she dared, praying that there was enough ventilation in the hut that the smoke wouldn't do them any harm. She was afraid to open the door for air. Anything—man or beast—could be outside. Although she tried not to think about it, it was quite possible that the soldiers searching for them could be in the vicinity. She certainly didn't want to draw them to the hut by the flickering, unmistakable beacon of a fire.

She left Sam only to eat or to relieve herself. With a vague recollection of "feed a fever, starve a cold," she tried feeding Sam, but the C-ration version of pork and beans obviously didn't agree with him. He obediently swallowed a couple of mouthfuls in response to her repeated proddings of his lips with a spoon, but no sooner had it gone down than it came back up. After that, she decided to limit his menu to water and aspirin.

By the time night fell, Lisa was beginning to despair. Sam was certainly no better; it was even possible that he was getting worse. She didn't know enough to judge.

Long tremors racked his body at closer and closer intervals. When that happened, his teeth chattered as loudly as busy typewriter keys. Not knowing what else to do for him, Lisa finally undressed and slid in naked beside him, her arms wrapping around his waist as she pulled him close in an attempt to warm him. He was muttering incoherently, making small restless movements with his arms and legs, and Lisa was afraid that he would injure his wounded shoulder. To keep him still, she turned and lay flat on her back, then drew his head down so that it was pillowed on her breasts. Curling her arms around his head, she stroked his hair, his bristly cheek, the back of his neck, whatever she could reach. Instinctively she began to croon to him, murmuring senseless cajolery, finally beginning to hum a lullaby into his hair. It was one she had often sung to Jennifer—but she wasn't thinking of Jennifer now. After a few minutes she was rewarded when Sam quieted. But she continued to sing to him until at last she had sung them both to sleep.

It must have been very early when she awoke, because the hut was just starting to change from pitch blackness to a lighter gray. She ached all over, she thought, carefully stretching her cramped limbs, moving stealthily so as not to disturb Sam. He still lay in the same position in which he had fallen asleep, his face nuzzling into the warm valley between her breasts and his right arm curled around her waist. He felt very big and solid lying against her. She thought it was absurd that she, so slight compared with his strength, should be in the position of protecting and caring for him. However much she had fought with him, and hated him, he had been a rock for her to lean on ever since he had first found her in the jungle. He had bullied her, yes, and made her mad enough that she could willingly have brained him more than once, but always she had known, somewhere in the recesses of her mind, that however much he might torment her himself, he would permit no one else to do so. He would protect her with every atom of his considerable strength, she knew. Now the tables were turned, however, and it was up to her to look after him.

His skin didn't feel quite so hot, she thought, making a feather-light inspection of his face with her fingertips. Maybe he was getting better. Even as she thought it, she felt his arm tighten around her. Then he opened his eyes.

That was nothing unusual. Many times the day before he had stared straight at her and not recognized her—but at least he had not called her Beth again. Lisa thought with a wry twist to her mouth that she should be thankful for small favors. But this time, as his eyes traveled over the soft roundness of a breast that was directly in his line of vision, lingering there for just an instant before moving up to her face, she could swear that he was fully aware....

"Lisa?" he asked in a husky voice.

Lisa's eyes widened. Her arms tightened convulsively around his head, and she hugged him to her. She could have wept with relief.

"Oh, Sam, thank God!" Her response was heartfelt. "I've been so worried about you!"

Suddenly aware that she was tenderly caressing his face and hair, she dropped her hands self-consciously to her sides.

"Don't stop," he murmured, his lips warm against her skin. "Please." Shy but obedient, Lisa resumed her gentle stroking of his hair. He sighed, resting against her with his eyes closed.

"How do you feel?" she asked after a little while. He nuzzled his face deeper into the satiny skin between her breasts before replying.

"Dead tired—and my shoulder's sore as hell. Did you get the bullet out? I can't seem to remember...."

"Yes. But that was night before last. You've been so sick...."

"The fever." He sounded resigned as he continued to lie against her with his eyes closed.

Lisa's finger feathered his bristly cheek as she realized that he was indeed, as he had said, dead tired. Then something about what he had said made her hands pause briefly before resuming their soothing task.

"It was a fever—yes. How did you know? You were out of your head...."

"I've had it before." She thought he was going to leave it there, but after a moment he continued, "It's something I picked up in 'Nam. It comes back every once in a while. I haven't had an attack in—oh, three years. I thought maybe this time it was gone for good."

"What is it?" Lisa was worried that he had to suffer like that periodically. Surely, with modern medicine, anything could be cured. . . .

"At the V.A. hospital they gave it some long, fancy name I never can remember. Generally it's called jungle fever. They can't cure it," he said, anticipating her next question. "But it's not life-threatening or anything. I manage to live with it without too much problem. Usually I feel an attack coming on, but this time I didn't. And, God, what a hell of a time for it!"

"Do you think they're still looking for us?" Her voice caught in her throat.

Sam's eyes opened, and he slanted a considering look up at her. For an instant he hesitated, as though debating whether to tell her the truth.

"Most likely," he said at last. Lisa was both glad and sorry that he had chosen not to lie to her; she had known the answer in her bones anyway. "But they won't get a lot done in this downpour. The ground's like quicksand and their jeeps will get mired up if they get off the roads. I think we're pretty safe here—at least until the rain stops."

Closing her eyes, Lisa said a silent prayer of thanks for the deluge she had been cursing just minutes before.

"The fever—does it always come and go like that? So fast?" She spoke almost at random, wanting to distract her thoughts from the mental image of soldiers bursting in on them, guns at the ready.

"The worst of it." He paused, then went on reluctantly, "But I'll probably go off a couple of times today—not as bad as yesterday, but the fever takes a while to run down. Then I'm generally weak as a kitten for another day or two."

Lisa met his eyes worriedly. If he was going to "go off" again, she had better find out what to do for him.

"Do you have some medicine with you that you usually take? I've been giving you aspirin because I didn't know what the rest of the pills in the first-aid kit were."

"Aspirin's as good as anything. There's really not much that helps with this thing. Except time. It always goes away by itself in a few days."

His arm slid from around her waist, and his hand came up to cup her breast in a warm, intimate gesture. The blanket was around his shoulders, which brought it down to the middle of her rib cage. Lisa was suddenly overwhelmingly aware of her nakedness—and his. To her embarrassment, a little tingle of wanting ran clear down to her toes.

"Did anyone ever tell you that you have beautiful tits?" he murmured against her skin, his fingers gently stroking a soft peak. Lisa felt herself color hotly, although she knew it was silly to do so.

"Did they?" he persisted, shooting her an indecipherable look. His fingers continued with their distracting task.

"No," she admitted truthfully, wriggling a little as she tried to get free. Despite his illness and his injury, he held her easily.

"Not even your husband—what's his name?" His voice was very low; he shot her that odd look again.

"Jeff. And, no, he didn't." As if Jeff would tell her that her breasts were beautiful—or had ever even thought so.

"He must be crazy—or blind." Sam was probing—oh, so casually—for information. Lisa felt her heart speed up; she was afraid he could hear it pounding under his ear. He almost sounded jealous—which was wishful thinking on her part, Lisa admitted with an inward grimace. Then the thought occurred to her: Why should she wish him to be jealous?

"Are you hungry?" She was determined to banish her wayward thoughts before they were irrevocably set on paths that were better avoided. Sam rested against her silently for a moment, and Lisa feared that he was not going to allow the subject to drop. Then he removed his hand from her breast, and looked up at her again with those soul-destroying blue eyes.

"Yeah. But I've got a problem that's a little more urgent—I've got to go to the bathroom."

"Oh." After caring for him as she had, Lisa knew that it was ridiculous to feel embarrassed—but she did. After all, ministering to the needs of a man who was out of his head with fever was a very different matter from helping a man who was very much awake and aware. A man she found far too attractive for her peace of mind.

"If you'll let me up, I'll—I'll get the pan."

"Is that what you've been doing?" he asked with a grimace of distaste. "No, thanks. I think I can manage to walk outside."

"I doubt if you can even stand up," Lisa protested, appalled at the idea of him standing and walking— and probably falling—after the debilitating events of the last few days.

"Really, I don't mind—about the pan." Lisa said this in a diffident tone, in case—as unlikely as it seemed—he was embarrassed about having her attend to his needs.

"Well, I do," he answered firmly.

Then, before Lisa could argue with him further, he rolled off her and got rather shakily to his feet. He was obviously very weak and swayed alarmingly as he stood towering next to her. Immediately she ran around to prop herself under his good arm. To her surprise, he accepted her help—as far as the door. From there he insisted on going on by himself. Taking a single look at his grimly determined face, Lisa didn't argue. She was in a fever of worry, until, after about ten minutes of nail biting, he came back around the corner of the hut, his hand braced against the surprisingly solid wall for support. For just an instant she registered the sheer physical splendor of his naked body before hurrying forward to help him. He shrugged away from her touch, clearly intending to walk the few feet into the hut under his own steam. She paced herself anxiously beside him, trying not to feel hurt at his rejection of her assistance. But once inside, with the door shut and bolted behind them, he seemed only too glad to let her help him ease back down onto the blanket.

"You got wet," she accused as he lay back, exhausted. Small droplets sparkled in his hair and a few more rolled waywardly down his face and chest.

"That overhang is damned narrow," he said, grunting.

Lisa, clucking like an anxious hen, pulled his shirt out of the combat pack and used it to wipe him dry.

"Now, what about that food?" He sounded weaker. Lisa was afraid that his little journey out into the rain had done him no good at all. Silently, she went to open a can.

Lisa had to help him eat. When he had swallowed several mouthfuls, he began to shiver and pushed the food away.

"I'm cold," he said, and his shivers grew more violent.

Lisa set the food aside and came under the blanket with him, cradling him in her arms as tremors shook him. She hadn't bothered to undress, but his head twisted restlessly against the roughness of her shirt until at last she unbuttoned it and pulled his head down onto her breasts. Then at last he lay quietly. Lisa thought he was either asleep or unconscious. She was surprised when he looked up at her, his hands clutching her waist beneath her opened shirt.

"Sing to me," he muttered. "That song you were singing last night. I like it."

Fighting a wave of fierce tenderness for him that seemed determined to engulf her despite her best efforts, Lisa began to hum the Brahms lullaby that had been Jennifer's favorite. Gradually she added words; after a while he sighed heavily and seemed to sleep.

He lapsed in and out of sleep for most of that day. Awake or asleep, he wanted her near him, his hands clutching her close with an almost desperate strength. It didn't seem to matter whether he was burning with fever or shaking with chills—either way, he clung to her as if he was afraid that she would vanish if he relaxed his grip.

He talked a great deal, most of it incomprehensible to Lisa. From the few words she could understand, she thought he imagined himself caught up in some long-distant war. Once or twice he called again for Beth, sounding so unhappy that the pain she felt was overlaid with pity for him. Beth was a very lucky woman, Lisa thought bleakly, and tried not to let herself be too moved by the way Sam seemed desperately to want her own presence. It was more than likely that he thought she was the absent Beth.

But at least once, when she tried to wriggle free of his grip, he knew precisely who she was. As she pried gently at his imprisoning hands, those blue eyes opened and looked directly into hers. She held her breath, not knowing if he was rambling or coherent.

"Don't leave me," he muttered. "Lisa, don't leave me. Let me hold you. You're so warm, and soft.... Please don't leave me."

He was begging—begging her, Lisa, not to leave him. Lisa smiled shakily down at him, feeling a tremendous warmth steal over her.

"I won't leave you," *darling*, she almost added, but managed to bite back the word in time. Her arms curled around the back of his head, her fingers stroking the rough silk of his hair as she held him.

"Promise?" he demanded, his eyes still fixed on her. He seemed to know what he was saying....

"I promise," she affirmed softly. This seemed to satisfy him, for he sighed deeply and closed his eyes.

The next day he was much better, never once lapsing into delirium. He no longer kept Lisa chained to his side, and she managed to feed and wash herself and help him do the same. Toward afternoon, he once again made the trip outside, but when he came back in he didn't return at once to his pallet. Instead he chose to sit up, his uninjured shoulder propped against the wall. He was naked, as he had been for the last three days, but it seemed not to concern him in the least. His eyes were fastened on her, but she wasn't sure if he really saw her. He seemed to be thinking deeply about something.

"Here," she said after he had sat there for perhaps five minutes, apparently oblivious to the chill bumps that were breaking out in ridges along his arms and legs. Scooping the blanket from the floor, she wrapped it around him. He accepted her gesture without a word, but when she would have moved away he caught her by the wrist, pulling at her. Hunkering down beside him, she looked at him with a question in her eyes. He regarded her with a brooding look of his own.

"Thank you for taking care of me," he said finally. "I owe you one."

Lisa returned his look with cooling eyes. Whatever she wanted from him—and she was not even sure that she wanted anything—it certainly wasn't gratitude.

"I owed you," she countered brusquely. "Now we're even." And she pulled her wrist away and stood up.

By the time another twenty-four hours had passed, he was so much better that his healing shoulder wound caused him more discomfort than the remnants of the fever. It was still raining, but the torrent was beginning to slacken. In another day or so they would have to move on, whether or not Sam was well enough to go. Lisa thought of the miles they would have to trudge to safety with danger and possible death lurking all around, and felt dread run along her veins like droplets of ice. Biting her lip resolutely, she did her best to banish it, although it refused to disappear completely. Still, she told herself that she would face whatever happened when it happened. In the meantime, she had to concentrate all her energy on getting Sam well again.

He had put on his shorts and pants, the first time he had gotten dressed since he had become ill. The clothes made him seem almost like a stranger. Lisa felt faintly ill at ease, cooped up in such close quarters with him. To pass the time, they took to playing tic-tac-toe and hangman in the dirt floor. Sam was clearly superior at tic-tac-toe—he played with a devilish strategy she couldn't quite get the knack of—but she beat him five times out of six at hangman. After all, words, as she informed him with a superior grin, were her stock in trade.

They talked, but not about anything important. Sprawled on their stomachs in the dirt like two kids, not caring that they were getting filthy, they kidded and played like children barely out of nursery school. When Sam finally won at hangman—on "incendiary," as in "bomb," for God's sake!—he practically crowed with triumph. Lisa laughed at him, accusing him teasingly of cheating because he had put too many spaces in the game. Watching him as he grinned at her, his black hair falling carelessly over his forehead and his blue eyes sparkling, she wondered once again how she had ever thought he wasn't handsome. Unshaven, dirty, still pale and weak with fever, he was so good-looking that he stopped her breath. His raffish, rakish look, accentuated by that broad, bare chest and the faint scar bisecting his cheek, only added to his wicked attraction. Lisa was conscious of a sudden, almost irresistible impulse to kiss him....

"Tell me something," she said casually, her eyes on the new game they were just starting.

"Ummm?" he answered absently, clearly engrossed in trying to figure out what an eight-letter word with a g in the middle could be.

"Who's Beth?"

XII

S<small>AM</small> felt all his muscles tighten warily.

"How did you hear about Beth?" If Frank, the only person in whom he'd ever confided, had told her about Beth, he'd wring his damned neck for him if ever he saw him again. That part of his life was behind him forever. He saw no point in remembering it.

Lisa's green eyes met his. "You called for her. When you were delirious."

"Oh." Inwardly, Sam was cursing himself. He remembered dreaming that he was back in 'Nam, in the days after he'd first been sent into combat. He'd been wounded, his face blown to hell, temporarily blinded—although he hadn't known it was temporary at the time—by a grenade that had come out of nowhere while he was sleeping. All through that awful time he'd called repeatedly for Beth, had even had the chaplain write to her and tell her what had happened to him, for God's sake. She hadn't even bothered to reply, as he should have known she wouldn't. Especially since the chaplain had included the news that he had been blinded. Beth would want no part of a man who wasn't whole.

"Who is she?" Lisa persisted.

Sam looked at her, as she lay on her belly on the floor, her chin propped up in both hands, her lovely hair curling wildly around her perfect face. God, she was beautiful, he thought irrelevantly. Then a wry smile curved his lips. Her emerald eyes were fastened on him for all the world like she was a kid waiting for a bedtime story.

"She—was—my wife." Gracing Beth with the title of "wife" was doing her too much honor, Sam thought. She'd never been his wife, not even at the beginning when he'd loved her as madly as only a young boy can love. She'd been more like his live-in whore, sleeping with him and letting him feed and clothe her while she waited for something better to come along.

"You're married?" Lisa's voice sounded odd, almost hoarse. He slanted an inquiring look at her while he jerked his head in the negative.

"I *was* married," he corrected. Then, seeing her exasperated look, he amplified that a little. "We got a divorce."

"Why?"

Sam's eyes narrowed. He hated talking to anyone about his past. It was like giving them a little piece of himself, something they could use to bind him to them. He especially hated talking to women about his past. In fact, he never had. His fiasco with Beth had turned him off females for every purpose but one for the rest of his life. He wanted no part of the faithless creatures.

"If you don't want to talk about it, I understand."

Her hasty disclaimer, oddly enough, had the effect of making him want to talk about it for almost the first time in his life. Something about this girl, young and spoiled and quick-tempered though she was, made him feel like he could confide in her. The ghost of a grin twitched up one corner of his mouth. One thing he sure couldn't accuse her of was having mercenary designs on his earnings. Compared to what she was no doubt used to, even the money he would get for this job—the half that failure entitled him to seemed like an enormous sum to him—would be a drop in the bucket to her.

"I don't mind," he answered, surprised that he really didn't. "What do you want to know?"

Lisa looked up at him, her face very pale and earnest. Sam felt like grinning again. Dressed as she was, with those absurd, too-big fatigues swamping the delectable curves of her body, her face clean of even the smallest scrap of makeup, and those huge, jewellike eyes fixed eagerly on his face, she looked ridiculously young. Younger than Jay. Maybe fifteen . . .

"How long have you been divorced? What went wrong? Did you—do you—have any children?"

Sam shot her a wry look and closed his eyes briefly in mock dismay.

"You want to know all about it, huh?" he murmured, and had to muffle a chuckle at her sudden self-conscious look. He felt suddenly very lighthearted, despite his pain and their predicament and the damned depressing rain and everything else. "Care to tell me why you're so interested?"

She immediately looked defensive. "I just thought it would give us something to talk about," she said repressively, transferring her eyes back down to the game scratched in the dirt.

Sam studied the top of that blond head for a moment. She was looking at the game as if her life depended on solving it.

"I've been divorced for nearly fifteen years. She decided I didn't suit her requirements. And, yes, I have a son. His name's Jay—Jason, really—and he's seventeen. Almost as old as you," he added with a sardonic look.

"I'm twenty-five." She looked up as she said it.

Sam cocked an eyebrow at her mockingly. The sure sign of the young, he thought, was that they were always so defensive about their age, or lack of it.

"And you—unlike me—are married." It came out flatly. He hadn't meant to say it, and certainly not in that tone. Hearing himself, he thought that he sounded almost jealous. Which was the stupidest thing he had ever thought of! He hadn't been jealous of a woman in years. Beth had cured him of that forever with her shenanigans—or so he had always thought.

"We're separated," Lisa answered, her eyes flickering down for just an instant. Then they came back up to meet his. "But we were talking about you. What went wrong with your marriage?"

Sam sighed and maneuvered himself up so that he was sitting cross-legged, his hands resting lightly on his thighs.

"I told you. She decided I didn't suit her requirements."

"Why not?"

"Do you really want to hear all this? It's pretty boring."

"Yes. Please."

The wistful note in her voice did it. Sam grimaced, more at himself than at her, and began.

"She was two years older than me, for one thing, and she'd been around. I was only twenty when I asked her to marry me, and I was as young and dumb as they come. She was working as a waitress in a bar near base—I was in the marines then—and, like the credulous fool I was, I thought I would take her away from all that. What I didn't know was that she didn't want to be taken too far away from it, thank you very much. She wanted respectability, and money for clothes and things, but she also wanted to have a good time. When she found somebody who could give her a better time than I could, she left me. And that was that."

"How long were you married?" The question was quiet.

Sam looked at her suspiciously, afraid from her tone that she might be feeling sorry for him. The very thought made the back of his neck burn. But she seemed to be absorbed in studying the game....

"Two years."

"And you never married again?"

"No." It was said with conviction, and earned him a slanting look from her green eyes.

"What about your son? Jay, you said his name was? Does he live with your w—with Beth?

Sam gave a rude snort of laughter. "Not hardly. She decided when he was about five that she didn't want him hanging around, cramping her style. We haven't either one of us heard from her for the last ten years. Which suits me just fine, although sometimes I think that Jay regrets it. Most kids kind of want a mother. I tell him that he's better off without her—which is true, believe me—but still I think he hankers after her every once in a while. With me gone so much."

Sam was surprised at himself. He had never discussed his worries about Jay's unspoken feelings for his mother with anyone before. But it had bothered him for years—although he had never admitted it even to himself—that Jay might somehow blame him for separating him from his mother. If there was one human being in the world he loved, it was his kid; he didn't know how he'd take it if Jay started hating him over Beth.

"Where is he now? With your family?" Lisa asked, her eyes compassionate as they moved over his face. Sam recognized the compassion, but was surprised to find that he didn't really mind it after all. In fact, he kind of liked it—coming from her.

"He's in school. Boarding school. He stays there during the year while I'm out of the country, and then I try to keep summers and holidays free and we spend them together."

"What about your parents? Are they living?"

"I have no idea," he answered shortly.

"What do you mean, you have no idea?" She reared back her head to look at him questioningly. "How can you not know if your parents are..."

"I never knew my parents," he cut in, tracing patterns in the dirt with his forefinger. He had never talked about this with anyone; it hurt almost more than Beth's defection had. At least he was over Beth, had been for years. He didn't think he'd ever get over the shame and pain of knowing that his parents had just abandoned him like a stray puppy they'd found and had no use for.

"Who brought you up? There had to be someone." Her voice was soft, and looking up Sam saw that her eyes were soft, too.

"The state of North Carolina very kindly made itself responsible for me when I was about two years old. Before that, I suppose I lived with one or the other of my parents. I don't remember, and nobody ever bothered to enlighten me. Not that it makes any difference. From the time I was two, I was shifted from one foster home to another. About the time I started feeling secure somewhere, something would happen, the woman would get pregnant or have to go back to work or something, and they'd move me somewhere else. Finally I got so I wouldn't let myself like any of them, because it hurt too much when they took me away."

"Poor little boy," Lisa said softly, and her hand came out to pat the hard muscles of his thigh comfortingly. Sam looked down at those pale slender fingers for a moment, then covered them with his hand. Her skin was so soft. . . . She twisted her hand in his grasp so that her fingers were entwined with his.

"Don't feel too sorry for me," he warned with a faint grin, even while he retained his grip on her hand. "By the time I was ten years old, I was the closest thing to a hoodlum Greenville ever had. I cut school every chance I got, drank, smoked, and was so wild in general that most of the good people who took me in soon threw me out again. Finally, I learned to hot-wire cars." His lips twitched as Lisa looked up at him, wide-eyed. He was willing to bet that the closest she'd ever gotten before to the kind of people who did things like that was the television set in her living room. "You might say that was what got me into the marines."

"Hot-wiring cars?" She blinked with incomprehension.

Sam chuckled. "Yup. I hot-wired one too many, and got caught. Not that we meant to actually steal it, just drive it around until we got tired or it ran out of gas. But the sheriff didn't see it that way. My buddies got off with probation. Because I was driving, they gave me a choice—the service or two years in prison. I joined the marines, but sometimes, especially in boot camp, I wished I'd opted for prison instead. I kept thinking, how much worse could it be?"

"You're making that up!" Lisa accused, sitting up to study his face intently. Her hand was still holding his, and she made no move to free it. Sam stroked her fingers with the blunt fingertips of his free hand, absently noting how dark and coarse his skin looked next to the creamy pale gold of hers.

"What part? About cutting school, or drinking, or hot-wiring cars, or..." He was teasing her. Clearly, she'd never been exposed to the kind of life he'd led. She'd always been sheltered, cared for, and protected.

"About almost being sent to prison. Aren't you?"

"Nope. It's the truth, I swear to God."

"But how old were you?"

"Seventeen. I had to lie about my age to get the marines to take me."

"But what about school? You couldn't already have graduated!"

"I never did graduate. I was in the eleventh grade when that happened, and I never went back. Later, while I was in 'Nam, I took up reading, and sort of educated myself. Unlike some people," this was accompanied by a teasing look, "I didn't have a doting granddaddy to send me to college."

"And then you married Beth," Lisa said softly.

Sam could tell that she was struggling to envision the kind of life he had led, which must sound as foreign to her as her pampered existence did to him.

"That was three years later. My enlistment was almost up, and she persuaded me to reenlist. Then she married me. After she made sure that she'd have a steady source of income."

"You must have loved her very much." The words were almost a whisper.

Sam looked over at her wryly. "Oh, I did—at the time. But she soon cured me of that. If it wasn't for

Jay being her son, she'd never even cross my mind now."

"But you called for her—when you were sick."

Sam's mouth tightened. "Whenever I get that fever, I imagine I'm back in 'Nam, where I was the first time I got it. My mind just goes back. I guess I called for Beth because I wanted her—then. Anymore, I probably wouldn't recognize her if she crossed the street in front of me. I saw her for what she was years ago. If I hadn't taken Jay, he probably would have ended up the way I did—going from one foster home to another until he got into trouble so deep he couldn't get out. Beth sure didn't want him."

"What's he like, your son?"

Sam's face softened. "He's about my height, but he's thinner. Hell, he's just a kid, he'll put on meat as he gets older. And he's better-looking than I ever was. Same coloring, basically, dark hair, blue eyes, although his hair's straight. And he's smart. Honor roll all through high school, and next year he's going to college. He hasn't decided where, yet, but he can take his pick. He's got the brains, and I can afford it."

"Do you make that much money, doing what you do?" The question was impolite, Lisa knew, but she couldn't help it. It just popped out. As a profession, soldiering had never struck her as being particularly well paid.

"I make enough. Sometimes more than others. But I've made some investments over the years that have paid off, and with the money from this job as a nest egg, I can afford to send Jay through college, wherever he wants to go, with enough left over to do something I've been wanting to do for a long time."

"And that is?"

Sam shrugged. His grin was lopsided, as if he was

embarrassed to admit to something as human as having a lifelong dream.

"Buy a ranch. Oh, not outright, but I have enough to make a good-sized down payment and stock it with cattle. Jay and I have it all picked out. It's called the Circle C, in Montana."

"It sounds wonderful." Lisa was thinking that it did indeed sound wonderful. And it occurred to her, with heart-shaking knowledge, that she would give a lot for the privilege of sharing that ranch with Sam and his son. Which was ridiculous, she knew, but...

Sam leaned back against the wall, stretching his long legs out in front of him. He grimaced, twitching his injured shoulder. Lisa was beside him at once, their discussion forgotten for the moment.

"Are you in pain?" she asked anxiously, scanning his face for signs of suffering.

He grinned. "To tell the truth, the damned thing itches. I don't suppose you can do anything about that, can you? Because..." His voice trailed off as Lisa inserted a hand beneath his shirt, which was stiff from the rainwater she had washed it in but at least was reasonably clean. Careful not to jar the healing wound, she began very delicately to scratch the skin around the edges of the bandage. He arched his back under her ministrations, his eyes closed. Lisa thought that he looked for all the world like a big, battle-scarred, hardened tom cat getting his first taste of loving care.

"Don't stop," he begged when she withdrew her hand at last.

"I don't want to spoil you," she answered pertly, giving his bristly cheek a consoling pat. He caught her hand, pressing it down against the sandpaper flesh of his jaw.

"I wouldn't mind," he assured her. "You can spoil me anytime."

"Shouldn't you be resting? You're supposed to be recouping your strength. After all, when the rain stops, we'll have to start walking again." She looked at him severely as she spoke.

"Uh-uh. You're not getting out of it that easy. You made me tell you all my deep, dark secrets. Now I want to hear yours. You can start by telling me about what's-his-name—Jeff." Sam was surprised at the acerbity of his own voice as he said her husband's name.

Lisa shrugged, then moved so that she leaned on the wall next to him. He caught her hand again; her fingers curled warmly around his. Their linked hands rested lightly on the reed-covered dirt between them.

"There's not much to tell. We've been married six years, but we were only really happy the first one. At least, I was. I don't think Jeff was, even then. Like your Beth, he had other interests." Lisa forbore to describe the exact nature of the "other interests." It could make no possible difference to Sam what sex Jeff's lovers were, and she still owed a measure of loyalty to Jeff.

"Why did you marry him?"

"Because he was perfect—the perfect Prince Charming that every girl dreams about. He was handsome and well educated and rich—and he was willing to live close to my grandfather. That was very important, at the time. I didn't ever want to live too far away from Amos."

"You call your grandfather Amos? I thought his name was Herman."

Lisa smiled whimsically. "Herman's a family name. I almost got stuck with it myself, as my middle name, instead of Ruth. Amos is my grandfather's first name.

And he hates it. That's why I call him that. I'm one of the few people he lets get away with it."

"Brat," Sam remarked without rancor.

Lisa nodded. "Yes, that's true. Or at least it was. I'm not so sure anymore."

"Well, go on. What happened with you and—Jeff?" For the life of him, he couldn't control the sneer that came through on that name. It was such an upright, respectable name, to go with an upright, respectable, perfect guy, if Lisa's description was accurate.

"What went wrong, do you mean? I told you. He had other interests, and I found out."

"Five years ago. And yet you're still married to him. Why? Does he have money?"

Lisa sent him a reproachful look. "All women aren't like Beth, Sam. I didn't marry Jeff for his money, and I wouldn't stay married to him for his money. Although, yes, his family is quite wealthy. But so is mine. There's nothing he can give me that I can't get for myself."

For some reason, that remark made Sam feel a sinking sensation in the pit of his stomach, as if he'd just hit a huge dip while riding a roller coaster. If she was blithely unconcerned about the millions that must make the guy "quite wealthy" to her, what would she think about his bank account, which was pitiful in comparison? There was no way he could compete.... What was he thinking of? Sam caught himself up sharply. He didn't want to compete. Once back in the United States, the girl sitting next to him in his cast-off combat fatigues would be so far above his touch that they wouldn't even be in the same stratosphere. Not that he would want to have anything to do with her anyway. When they got back to the United States, he would go his way and she would go hers. Separate. Which was the way he wanted it, he told himself, and the way she undoubtedly did too.

"I don't suppose a dedicated career woman like yourself had any time for having kids?" he asked, the sneer coming out stronger than he'd meant it to. To his surprise, she looked stricken. Her mouth shook, and her eyes shone with suspicious moisture. She didn't answer.

"You do have kids?" he asked slowly, probing, knowing that her devastated look had to mean something. Maybe she did have kids—they couldn't be much more than babies, with her as young as she was—and she'd left them to go traipsing off to Rhodesia. Maybe that stricken look was guilt.

Still she didn't answer. Her eyes closed, the long curling black lashes resting like feathers against the paleness of her cheeks.

"Lisa?" he asked, puzzled, and tightened his grip on her hand. Whatever she had done or not done, she obviously felt like hell about it now. Her hand clung to his like a monkey holding on to a palm tree for dear life in a hurricane.

Her eyes opened. They were awash with unshed tears. She looked at him steadily.

"I had a daughter," she said tonelessly. "Jennifer. She died last year."

Sam felt as if he'd been punched in the gut. She looked so hurt, so sad, with tears swimming in her eyes and her lips trembling as she tried to be brave and not cry. Her very forlornness touched his heart like nothing had in years. Suddenly it occurred to him that, despite her money and social position and doting grandfather, she might actually be as lost and lonely as he was. His hand tightened on hers, tugging, and he pulled her into his arms, cradling her head against his shoulder, holding her tightly and

222

rocking her back and forth as if she were a hurt child.

"Tell me about it, honey," he whispered in her ear, tenderly smoothing away the hair from around her averted face.

Hands clutching his shirt, her voice barely audible at times as she spoke with her head buried in his shoulder, she obeyed. Words spilled out, faster and faster, as she relived the torment of Jennifer's death, sharing it with him, intent on easing her own pain as she shifted some of the burden of it to his broad shoulders. He held her as she talked and cried, murmuring soothing words to her, not understanding more than one word in three but knowing that it would do her good to get it all out. He felt a tenderness for her that he'd never felt for any woman, not even Beth. She was so little and helpless in his arms, clinging to him and sobbing her heart out, that he suddenly knew that he would ask nothing more of life than to be allowed to stand between her and the world, protecting her from all sadness and harm. As he held her, and rocked her while she cried, he felt a fierce possessiveness toward her. This is mine, his heart shouted, and while his head immediately disputed that, reminding him of all the reasons why she wasn't his, and could never be his, his heart would not be convinced. Which meant that he was now in a peck of trouble.

Finally she quit talking and just cried, gasping and sobbing into his neck for a long time. He continued to hold her, stroking her hair and back, murmuring to her, pressing an occasional light kiss to the top of her bent head. It seemed like she cried for hours, but Sam didn't mind. He thought that he could ask for no greater boon than the privilege of holding her while she cried.

At last the heartrending sobs stopped, and she sniffled and gulped for a while before exhaustion left her resting quietly against his shoulder. Sam's good arm tightened around her, telling her silently that she was very welcome to stay where she was for as long as she liked.

"I'm sorry," Lisa muttered eventually, pulling a little away from him but keeping her head bent so that he could not see the mess her tears had made of her face. "I—I've never broken down like that before. I don't think I've ever told anyone most of what I just told you."

Sam wrapped his fingers around the silken length of her hair, tugging at it gently so that her head was tilted back and he could see her face. Her eyes were red-rimmed and swollen; tears had traced dirty paths down her cheeks. Her mouth was very red and a little blurry-looking. Sam thought that he had never seen a woman look more pathetic and, at the same time, more beautiful.

"I'm sorry," she said again, trying to smile. The trembling of her lips wrung his heart.

"Don't be," he said huskily. "You can cry on my shoulder anytime. Believe me, I'm honored."

Lisa felt her heart stop beating as he smiled that breathtaking slow smile.

"I love you," she said, shaken to the core.

His eyes froze on her face, widened. His hand dropped from her hair to rest loosely at his side.

"What did you say?" His voice was hoarse. A bright blue flame seemed to leap to life at the back of his eyes.

"I said I love you," Lisa repeated, more clearly this time, knowing as she said it that it was true. When it had happened, or how, she didn't know. She knew only that it had, that she loved him more than she had ever loved anything in her life, that she wanted him and needed him. . . .

"You shouldn't say things like that if you don't mean them." God, he was tempted, so sorely tempted, to take her words at face value, to sweep her up in his arms and never let her go. He wanted her with a fierce hunger that had little to do with physical passion. He wanted her heart and mind and soul as well as her body, forever and ever.

"I do mean it," she said steadily, and then smiled at him again, her green eyes still misty from her recent tears. "I love you, Sam Eastman. So why don't you do something about it, instead of sitting there staring at me like I've grown horns or something?"

"Christ," he murmured, closing his eyes briefly.

Then he was reaching for her, hauling her to him, his arms closing convulsively around her. Lisa lifted her face wordlessly, her arms coming up to encircle his neck, her lips parting as she shamelessly invited his possession.

"Kiss me," she was driven to say, as he studied her up-tilted face like a buyer suspicious of being taken for a ride. "Please, Sam, kiss me. . . ."

His mouth swooping down on hers muffled the last word. He kissed her as if he were starving, as if he meant to make up for all the years that they had not shared. Lisa responded with joyful abandon, answering his caresses with her own, feeling as if she had truly come alive for the first time in her life. I love him, she told herself over and over, as if she was afraid that this was a dream from which she might awaken at any moment. Love him, love him!

With little regard for his wound, Sam lowered her to the floor, pressing her down into the dirt and reeds as he kissed her with hot possession. Lisa felt with happy triumph the tremor that racked his long limbs. His body was telling her that he loved her, even if he had not yet put the thought into words.

His hands were on the buttons of her shirt, but his left one was still not capable of dealing with the intricacies of such items. She helped him, then unbuttoned his shirt, running her hands over his darkfurred chest with sensual enjoyment as he rested on his side next to her. The muscles of his chest felt hard and sleek, the curling hairs soft yet surprisingly wiry. . . . She stroked down to his belly, her finger slipping beneath the waistband of his pants to tease his navel. At her playfulness, he groaned.

"Witch," he called her as her fingers darted away again. As punishment, his good hand slid down the back of her pants, cupping first the soft buttocks and then sliding intimately between her legs. As his fingers stroked her soft inner thighs, she wriggled with pleasure, then moaned when he took his hand away.

"I want you like hell," she whispered daringly into his ear, her tongue darting out to brand the tender lobe.

Despite his arousal, Sam had to grin. "Remind me, later, to have a talk with you about your language. It leaves something to be desired, for a lady."

"And is that what you want? A lady?" She was deliberately provoking him with words and touch, and his response was all she could have desired. Hot red blood rushed into his high cheekbones, and his eyes darkened to blue smoke. His hands, as he pulled her back against him, were shaking.

"Not at the moment, no," he admitted hoarsely, and then his mouth was on hers, silencing her in the most effective way known to man since the beginning of time.

They undressed each other with trembling hands, Lisa helping him with the parts he could not man-

age, until they were both lying naked in the dirt.
Their bodies were on fire for each other, their hands
both beseeching and promising at the same time as
they explored each other's bodies as if they had
never seen them before, as if this were the first time
for both of them. Lisa wanted him to hurry, to
possess her body before she died of the exquisite
agony he was inflicting on her, but Sam was determined to take his time. His hands and mouth left no
part of her body untouched, as if he was intent upon
staking his claim. Finally Lisa was writhing mindlessly
beneath him, her hands clutching at his body in
wordless demand. When Sam could control himself
no longer, he almost roughly thrust his hard thigh
between her legs, forcing them apart. Lisa surged
upward to meet him, but still he held off.

"Say it," he ordered hoarsely. "I want to hear you
say it."

"What?" Lisa blinked up at him in bewilderment.
All she could think of was how much she wanted
him....

"Tell me you love me. I want to hear it."

"I love you," Lisa repeated obligingly. "Love you,
love you, love...Oh!"

He took her then, as she was saying the words,
possessing her with a savage tenderness that was like
nothing she had ever known before. He took her to
heaven and back, and she felt as if she were dying in
his arms.

When at last it was over, Lisa lay quietly beside
him, cradled close against his long hard body as he
lay on his side. Sam brushed a gentle kiss across her
cheek, and Lisa smiled dreamily in response. She
was memorizing his face, her eyes and fingers ex-
ploring the hard angles and satiny smooth skin
roughened by nearly a week's growth of bristly black

beard. He looked like a ruffian, she thought, with that beard and the scar and his black hair growing longer to curl beguilingly around his ears and over his forehead. Those blue eyes were smiling at her, and she thought that she had never seen anything more heart-stoppingly beautiful in her life.

"I hope you're planning on a hasty divorce," he drawled as she touched his hard mouth with a wondering finger. "Because as soon as we get home, you're going to marry me."

XIII

FOR a moment Lisa just stared into that dark face, her eyes gradually widening. As he looked gravely back at her, smiling just a little, she at last allowed herself to believe what she had heard.

"Oh, Sam, do you mean it?" she squealed, sitting bolt upright and staring down at him in delight.

His eyes moved over her with lazy ownership, touching on the excited eyes glittering down at him like emeralds with the sun shining through them, the soft, just-kissed redness of her mouth, the lovely line of her neck and shoulders, the beguiling uplift of her breasts, her small waist and flat stomach....

"Sam!" Lisa interrupted his slow inspection with impatience. He looked up again to find her regarding him with a mixture of irritation, amusement, and what he desperately hoped was love.

"Did my ears deceive me, or did you just ask me to marry you?" she demanded, half-laughing.

"I don't think I asked," he said meticulously. "I think I just made a simple statement of fact. You can't go around telling men you love them, and not expect to marry them."

The words and voice held a teasing note, but the eyes did not. They watched her with a hunger that

229

made her pulse speed up so that it pounded in her ears like a trip hammer. God, just looking at him was joy enough to last her for the rest of her days. . . .

"That's not what I'd call a proposal," she grumbled, keeping an eye on him so that, if he should take her teasing seriously, she could shout "yes!" before he changed his mind.

"It's the best you're going to get from me," he said with pretended indifference laced with a touch of humor. When she continued to eye him speculatively, wondering if she could coax him into a few pretty speeches before she accepted, he cocked an eyebrow at her inquiringly. "Well?"

Those blue eyes twinkling at her, but holding just a touch of uncertainty in their depths, were her undoing. She abandoned all thoughts of prolonging her decision just for the joy of baiting him, and threw herself against him, her arms going around his neck, hugging it tightly. She forgot all about his wound until she felt him wince.

"I'm sorry," she said at once, drawing back. His arm around her refused to let her go. Instead, it drew her closely against him. Lisa felt the impact of his big naked body pressed intimately against her smaller, softer one all the way down to her toes. He felt it, too. She could tell by the sudden smoldering in his eyes and the stiffening of all his muscles.

"I'm all right," he answered huskily. "Or at least I will be as soon as you say yes. I refuse to make love to a woman who won't have me for a husband."

She drew back her head so that she could see his face as she gave him her answer. Her eyes smiled into his. His face softened, and his eyes smiled back warmly.

"Yes," she whispered. The smile in his eyes widened and spread to include his hard mouth.

"That's a good girl," he said approvingly, then captured her mouth with his. He kissed her with exultant ownership, clearly bent on impressing on her that he was now the man in possession. Lisa kissed him back with abandon, her arms twining around his head to hold him closer, her fingers tangling in the thick strands of his black hair. To her surprise, and faint amusement, she found that she loved his atavistic display of male dominance.

She murmured adoring phrases into his ears as he took her, which seemed to drive him wild. She could feel his heart hammering against his ribs, taste and smell the perspiration that rolled from his body onto hers, and hear his rasping breath as he made love to her with a driving need tempered with care for her pleasure. Finally, at the end, when he had driven her almost out of her mind with rapture, he said the words she had been dying to hear.

"I love you, Lisa," he said, groaning, stilling her for an instant as she rode astride him. His big hands nearly spanned her hips, his fingers digging into the skin of her lower back, his flesh imbedded deeply inside her. His breathing was impeded as he looked up at her; his eyes glazed with passion as they met her equally dazed ones, then moved comprehensively over her body. "Christ, I love you."

"Sam . . ." She gasped, wanting to be even closer to him than she was at that moment, wanting to absorb him into her body and never let him go. She reached for him, but his hands on her hips started her in motion again, and she forgot everything except the wonder of her own mounting enchantment.

Later, he held her against him as he smoked one of his few remaining cigarettes. Lisa curled happily against his side, warm beneath the blanket he had dragged over them, her fingers idly twisting the hairs on his chest into tiny curls.

"I'm not going to let you take it back, you know," he said with a faint grin, but his eyes were serious as they looked down at her. "You promised, and you're going to marry me. And you're going to stay married to me for the rest of our lives, and you're never going to so much as look sideways at another man. Understand?"

"No time off for good behavior?" she teased, giving the curl she was making a tiny yank. His hand came down to capture hers and free the imprisoned hair.

"None at all," he confirmed sparely, giving her an admonishing look.

Lisa made a face at him. "I can see you're going to make a very possessive husband," she murmured provokingly.

"Damn right," he answered, his jaw tightening. He slanted her a hard look.

"Well, if you really feel that strongly about it, I guess I can tell all my lovers that I'm no longer available."

"You'd better," he said, growling. "I think if I saw another man so much as lay a hand on you, I'd kill him. And I've never felt like that about a woman in my life."

Lisa knew the admission had cost him something, so she pressed a rewarding kiss into the thick mat of hair on his chest.

"Sam," she said softly, wanting to clear up any misconceptions he might still be harboring about her. "Except for Jeff, there's never been anybody but you in my life. I've never slept with anybody else, I've never wanted anybody else. And Jeff..."

But he didn't let her finish.

"Is that the truth?" His voice was incredulous. When she looked up, his eyes were, too.

"I swear it."

He was quiet for a minute. She looked up again to find that he was smiling. The faintly smug expression on his face made her smile, too. He liked the thought of that, she could tell.

"And here I was thinking that you turned on like that for all the guys," he said, mocking both himself and her.

"No. Only you."

"Only me." He lingered over it, savoring the thought like a child who has just been given a shiny new present. Then he added, teasing but with an underlying note of warning, "And it better stay that way."

"Yes, Sam," she answered with proper meekness.

He grinned at her, looking suddenly very young and carefree. "Now, that sounded very nice and wifely," he approved. "If you can just keep that up, I might be able to stop myself from beating you three times a week."

Lisa punched him in the ribs for that. He yelped, clutching his side, laughing.

"Can't you take a joke?" he complained, and then she demonstrated very clearly that she could not, of that sort, anyway.

The rest of the day was spent like that, making love and lighthearted banter and playful war. Lisa had never been so happy in her life. This man was what she had been searching for for years, what she wanted and needed and absolutely had to have. He was as necessary to her now as water, or food, or any other basic of life. She loved him with a completeness that hurt.

Even mundane acts such as bathing and eating and changing his bandage took on a new glow because he loved her. She felt foolish smiling all the time, but she couldn't help herself. Sam was equally happy, she could tell. He laughed and played and joked like a teenage boy in the throes of his first love.

When at last it was time to sleep, Lisa was still wrapped in a warm glow. She felt as if the world had suddenly righted itself, as if nothing could ever go wrong for her again. Even the dangers of their present situation held no terrors for her now; she had complete and utter confidence in Sam. He would get them out of this crazy country, and they would go home and marry. . . . On that delectable thought, she fell asleep.

It was morning when Lisa awoke. She could tell because of the characteristic light grayness of the interior of the hut. For just a moment she lay still, basking in Sam's presence and the knowledge that he loved her, not even minding the unyielding hardness of the ground beneath her as she listened to his breathing. It was slow and regular—and almost unnaturally loud. Frowning, Lisa lifted a quick hand to lay it softly against his brow. Had the fever come back? she wondered. No, his skin was no warmer than it should have been. It was something else. . . . Then, with a curious sinking feeling, she realized that the absence of background noise was what was making his breathing sound so much louder than usual. Sometime during the night, the rain had stopped.

"Sam!" She nudged him. His arm tightened automatically around her to prevent her from moving away.

"Hmmm?"

"Wake up! The rain has stopped!"

This brought him instantly awake. He lay for a moment with his eyes open, listening to the silence.

"We've got to get going, then," he said unemotionally at last.

"Yes." Lisa was moving away from him. He let her go, sitting up and rubbing his face. He was naked, his bare chest looking very virile as it rose in a muscular V shape from the blanket covering his lap. Lisa, already splashing water on her face and then getting dressed, felt a quick surge of pride. He was every inch a man, hard, strong, reliable, handsome, tough as boot leather when the occasion demanded it yet capable of infinite tenderness—and every scrumptious inch of him was hers. She smiled at the thought.

"You look like the proverbial cat that swallowed the canary," he observed as he got to his feet and reached for his pants. "Care to let me in on the joke?"

"You are the joke," Lisa replied impishly, her eyes sparkling as they moved over him.

He zipped up his pants and then stood for a moment, barefoot, fists resting lightly on his hips as he looked her over from head to toe.

"Getting cocky already, are you?" he said at last. Only the slight twitch at the corners of his mouth told her that he was not serious. "Watch yourself, woman, or I'll take my hand to your backside."

Lisa grinned at him. "I'd like that," she said, laughing shamelessly. He laughed, too.

"You're asking for trouble," he threatened, sitting cross-legged on the ground to pull on his boots. He moved his left arm with some degree of difficulty, but still he managed. "When we get home again, remind me to give it to you."

"Yes, sir." Lisa saluted smartly, hoping to provoke him into grabbing for her, but he only grinned.

He was still dressing when she went outside for a quick visit to their makeshift toilet. Out of necessity, they had designated one of the other huts as the bathroom, to provide both protection from the rain and a modicum of privacy. As Lisa headed toward it, she marveled at the sun-washed freshness of the morning. The world positively sparkled around her. Moisture still clung in thousands of tiny droplets to the grass, which seemed to have turned a lush green overnight. The trees fringing the camp, cleansed of their customary coating of dust, were also newly green. Sweet scents of grass and fruit and the gorgeous red flowers of the syringa trees filled the air. Brilliantly colored birds fluttered about, calling raucously to one another, their chatter overlaying the deep gurgle of the nearby stream. An inquisitive baby gnu poked its head through the scrub brush near the perimeter of the village, and Lisa knew that a herd of its fellows must be nearby. The rain had temporarily turned the barren scrubland surrounding them into a verdant paradise. Lisa soaked it all in, amazed at the change.

When she had finished in the makeshift bathroom and was heading back to the hut she shared with Sam, she thought there was something different in the air. She could sense it, like an animal. She stopped walking and looked slowly around her, cocking her head and frowning as she tried to figure out what had changed. Was there a lion or cheetah in the vicinity? was the first thought that crossed her mind, as she noticed that the birds had quietened and the gnu was gone. Heart in her throat, she looked toward the trees, but nothing seemed out of the ordinary. The morning was still almost unbelievably beautiful.

"Abetusdisti-koweba!" The shouted words, which she had heard before on the night when the guerrillas had come out of the jungle to blow up her world and

the Blasses', meant "white devils," Lisa knew. She whirled toward the direction whence the shout had come, and stood petrified as she saw an African soldier, garbed in khaki with the typical white head-dress under his cap, advancing on her, rifle at the ready and an evil grin on his dark face. A little beyond him, Lisa saw that a motorboat had pulled up to the bank of the stream without her hearing it. Two of its four occupants were approaching her; their guns were pointed squarely at her midsection. The third man was making for the first of the huts, presumably intending to search the village. The fourth stayed at the controls of the boat. Its engine was still running.

Lisa didn't move, didn't make a sound. She sensed that if she did so, they would kill her on the spot. Which, she thought through a mind hazy with fear, might be preferable to what they had in mind. Horrible visions of rape and torture preceding her inevitable murder flashed through her brain. Still, she could not bring herself to do something that would make them kill her any sooner than they meant to. She thought of Sam, and one part of her mind seized on that tiny ray of hope and clung to it. Any minute now, he would miss her, if he hadn't already. If he saw what was happening before being surprised by that one guerrilla—if he didn't come walking blindly into this situation before he knew that it existed—they might have a chance. Lisa thought of the four men Sam would be facing, each as heavily armed as he was, but strong and healthy and well fed, and felt that small flicker of hope die. The odds were impossible; she might as well face it.

"Lisa, when I give the word, I want you to drop to the ground. Cover your head and don't look up. Understand?"

She didn't dare look in the direction of Sam's voice, which came from some little way behind her and which was too soft to be heard by the approaching guerrillas. She could only suppose that he had somehow seen what was happening, gotten out of the hut without being seen, and circled around through the trees. Clearly, the guerrillas had no idea that he was nearby; their continued approach, slow but not particularly wary, told her that.

With a tiny, just-perceptible nod, she acknowledged Sam's instructions. Then she stood tensely, wondering when the word he had warned her of would come, and what he would do.

The two guerrillas were very close to her now, less than twelve feet away. Lisa was so frightened she could hardly breathe; her throat was so dry she couldn't swallow. Her knees were shaking like Jell-O, and she could only hope that they would support her until Sam was ready. Part of her mind, clear and steady and alert, was focused on the situation, and continued to observe it quite clearly; another part was a jumbled mass of terror, sending up prayers for her own safety and for Sam's.

As Lisa made no move to attack or escape, or scream for help, the approaching men relaxed fractionally. Their rifles were still pointed at her, but they were talking to one another, and their eyes had ceased to dart warily from side to side.

"Now, Lisa!" Sam's shout made her start, prepared for it though she was. Even as she was obediently throwing herself to the ground, her arms coming up to protect her head, she saw the whites of the guerrillas' eyes as Sam caught them by surprise, saw their mouths drop open with sudden alarm, and saw, too, as they jerked their rifles up, fingers tightening on the triggers. Then she covered her head, sobbing, praying, screaming as a staccato burst of gunfire roared from behind her. More gunfire answered; a man screamed in mortal agony. Forgetting Sam's instructions in her anxiety for him, she looked up. The two guerrillas lay on the ground in front of her, one so close she could have reached out a hand to touch him. They were clearly dead, or dying. The feet of the man nearest her were kicking convulsively in what were obviously his death throes. Blood poured from the part of his head that was still attached to his body; the top of it had been blown clean off. Gray brain matter mixed with bits of bone and blood spattered the ground as far as five feet away.

Lisa felt her stomach heave, but she had no time now to spare for her body's squeamishness. Where was Sam? Looking beyond the two corpses, she saw him running, then throwing himself to the ground and rolling as one guerrilla emerged from a hut and the other leaped from the boat, both with rifles firing. He seemed unhurt, she noted thankfully, watching as he dived into the safety of the trees, positioning himself so that a tree trunk shielded him from the hail of gunfire as he fired volley after volley at the guerrillas, who were trying to inch up on him while remaining under cover as much as possible. None of the three men seemed to spare the slightest thought for Lisa's presence; she might have been as much out of the picture as the two dead men before her.

The guerrilla who had stayed with the boat was darting from hut to hut on Sam's left, trying to circle around behind him. Lisa could see quite clearly what he was up to, but she thought that Sam was taken up with the man who was approaching him from the right; anyway, most of Sam's gunfire seemed to be heading that way—maybe he just feared hitting her if he shot at the boatman who was between Sam and herself. She thought about shouting to warn Sam, then immediately thought better of it. She had no desire to draw the guerrilla's attention to herself. He could deal with her in a matter of seconds. But still, she had to do something. She couldn't just lie help-less on the ground with her head in her hands while those murderers did their best to kill Sam!

Keeping a cautious eye on the man nearest her, Lisa began to crawl toward the rifle of one of the dead men, which lay just a few feet away. He had been shooting when he'd gone down; the rifle would still be ready to fire. All she would have to do was point it and pull the trigger. At this range—perhaps twenty-five feet—how could she miss? Sam had told her once that if one just continued to hold down the trigger, any automatic rifle would keep shooting until it ran out of bullets. That was an automatic rifle—she could tell from the cartridge. Silently Lisa blessed Sam for his lessons in marksmanship. She had hated them at the time, but they might save his life today.

The guerrilla was closer by the time Lisa reached the rifle. She lay looking from it to him for a mo-ment, suddenly suffering severe qualms about what she was about to do. If she missed—and she very well might, she thought, remembering the untouched target tree—he would undoubtedly kill her. Maybe she would do better to stay quietly out of the way and leave the fighting to Sam.

The decision was made for her perhaps three minutes later. There was a sharp burst of gunfire, followed by a hoarse cry that she recognized as Sam's. The guerrilla closest to her was immediately on the move, headed in a circular, crouching run toward the trees where Sam had taken cover. Without even thinking about it, Lisa snatched up the fallen guerrilla's rifle, put it to her shoulder, caught the running man in her sights, and pulled the trigger. The gun roared in her ear so loudly that it seemed to fill the world; it kicked back against her shoulder with the force of a locomotive. For one horrible instant, as the guerrilla whirled around and seemed to be moving in her direction, she thought that she had missed and he was coming to kill her. Then he fell to his stomach on the ground; blood gushed in a bright red stream from his mouth.

As suddenly as the shooting had begun, it was over. An eerie silence pervaded the village. Lisa could do nothing but stare at the still form of the man she had killed while a ringing sound went off over and over again in her ears; she hoped vaguely that she wasn't permanently deafened from shooting that wretched gun. Sam emerged from the trees, moving quickly toward her with his pistol drawn, taking the precaution of stopping to assure himself that the man she had shot was really dead. Lisa saw all this, but it didn't really register. She felt as if she were watching through a thick pane of plate glass.

"Are you okay?" Sam had dropped to his knees beside her, removing the rifle from her slackened grasp. Lisa's tongue came out to wet her lips; she nodded. Sam rolled her over, scooping her up into his arms and holding her tightly against him. Lisa, shaking, her arms going around his neck to lock behind his head in a strangle hold, saw fresh blood pouring from a wound in his neck.

"You're hurt!" The sight of his blood—bright red like a child's poster paint—running down the side of his neck to stain his shirt brought her out of the trance of fear that had held her in its grasp.

"It's nothing. Just a graze." His hands closed over

her arms and he pulled her a little away from him so that he could see her face. His own face was white and drawn, and Lisa couldn't tell if it was from pain from his wound or if it was from fear for her.

"You stupid little bitch, you scared me to death!" he said gratingly after his eyes raked her thoroughly from head to toe, searching for and not finding any signs of injury. "When I heard that gun go off, I nearly had a heart attack! I thought the bastard had decided to kill you before he came after me! Then I saw you with that damned gun—you, who couldn't even shoot a fucking tree!—and I couldn't believe it! Don't you know, if you'd missed, he would have blown your head off?"

"I'm sorry," she said in a small voice.

Sam shook his head, closing his eyes momentarily. Then he pulled her back against him again. "Don't ever do anything like that again," he admonished, his voice muffled as he pressed his mouth to her hair. "Next time trouble starts, you stay the hell out of it! How do you think I'd feel if something happened to you? I'd want to blow my own head off!"

Lisa was gradually recovering from her fright, and she felt faintly indignant that he should scold her for what she had done. After all, she had been trying to save his life....

"I got him," she pointed out with immense dignity, pulling back her head so that she could see his face.

He met her eyes, disbelief in his. Then a reluctant grin split his face. "Christ!" he said, dropping a hard kiss on her mouth. "You're something else, you know that? Yes, you got him! That was damned good shooting, honey, but please, if you love me, don't ever do anything like that again. I don't think my system can stand the shock."

"You must be getting old," Lisa muttered disdainfully,

and Sam grinned again. Then he stood up, pulling her to her feet with him.

"Come on, we've got to get out of here before somebody else comes nosing around. The boat makes everything a lot easier: we should be out of the country by nightfall."

As he spoke he was pulling Lisa after him into their hut; together they snatched up the gear, cramming it into the A.L.I.C.E. pack as best they could. Then Sam hurried her toward the boat, which had drifted several feet away from the bank. They waded in after it, and Sam reached it first, hauling himself and the gear aboard and then reaching down a hand to help Lisa up. When she was safely aboard, Sam started the engine, then reversed until they were far enough away from the shore so that he could turn her prow around. It was just a matter of a few minutes before they were headed downstream.

Lisa cast one quick look back at the village as the boat rounded a bend. From that distance, she could see nothing except the thatched, cone-shaped roofs silhouetted against a background of trees. It was a scene of peaceful serenity; she found it hard to believe that just a short time before, four men had lost their lives there—one of them at her hands.

"Don't think about it," Sam advised quietly, seeing where she looked and correctly divining what was on her mind. "You did what you had to do." Then his eyes softened on her white face. "In case I forgot to say it earlier in all the excitement: Thanks. You probably did save my life. When that bullet winged me, I took my eyes off your friend for a minute. At the rate he was moving, it's very possible that he might have managed to get around behind me before I located him again."

Lisa felt a rush of warmth at Sam's words. She

smiled at him, wondering if he was telling the truth or if he had said that merely to make her feel better about having killed a man. Whatever his motive, she did feel better. She would have shot down a whole army without a qualm, to keep them from hurting Sam.

"I love you," she said. His eyes turned toward her again; she saw that they were smiling. She was fascinated by the way the sunlight seemed to sparkle off the blue of his eyes. With his raggedy, bloodstained clothes and week's growth of bristly black beard, he looked like the roughest kind of roughneck. She loved him so much that it hurt.

"You tell me that at the damnedest times," he complained, a groove deepening in his hard cheek as he half-smiled at her. "Come here, honey." He held out his hand to her.

Lisa, who had been sitting on the vinyl-covered seat that ran around the rear half of the boat, almost flew to where he stood at the controls. He folded her against him, his mouth coming down to brush her lips before bestowing a harder, longer kiss. All the while he kept his eyes trained on the water in front of them. When he returned his full attention to the boat, Lisa still stood beside him, her head resting contentedly against the hard sinew of his shoulder, her arms linked loosely around his waist. She had no doubt that Sam would bring them out of this safely. She knew that she could, and did, trust him with her life.

"Oh, your neck!" she exclaimed after a while, suddenly remembering that he had been shot again.

He smiled down at her, dropping a quick kiss on the tip of her small nose. "I told you—it's just a graze," he said. "I've done worse to myself shaving. It's already quit bleeding."

Lisa had to look for herself, just to make sure, but she found that he was quite right: the wound was barely deeper than a scratch, and the blood that earlier had welled so brightly had now dried. Still, Lisa shuddered to think what would have happened if that bullet had hit just a couple of millimeters to the right. It would have gone clean through his neck. . . .

"It didn't happen," he said quietly, once again seeming to read her mind. "A lot of things could have gone wrong back there," this was accompanied by a reproachful look at Lisa, "but they didn't. So let's forget about it, okay? If my calculations are correct, we should be in South Africa in time for supper."

"Really?" If he had meant to distract her, Sam succeeded admirably. Now that she no longer had to be worried about the parting from him that she had thought was inevitable, she longed to be safely back in civilization. She thought of food, a hot bath, and a real bed with longing. And Sam would share it all. . . . The thought made her smile.

As the day wore on, Lisa grew increasingly nervous. It had occurred to her that the dead men in the village might have been discovered by their comrades and that the chase might be on with a vengeance. She half-expected at any moment to hear boats roaring up the river behind them. But nothing happened. Hours passed, while the sun beat down and the water glinted and birdsongs filled the air.

The stream they had started out on had joined a river, probably a tributary of the Limpopo, Sam told her. If it was the river he thought it was, it bisected the southern tip of the country before joining the waterway that formed the border between Rhodesia and South Africa. Once they reached that point, they would be safe. They would continue on down the river, taking care to stay on the South African side, until they reached the South African town of Messina. After that, it would be relatively simple to arrange transportation back to the United States.

Lisa, sitting in the bottom of the boat and leaning against Sam's muscular leg, listened to his voice without really registering the words. It was enough to be close to him, to know that he was alive and pretty much in one piece and that he loved her. Her earlier nervousness was beginning to seem absurd. They were so close now—what could happen?

But she knew when she felt his leg stiffen, even before she heard the urgent note in his voice.

"For God's sake, stay down," he hissed, and she felt a sudden surge of power beneath her as he gunned the boat.

"What . . . ?" she asked, struggling to see despite his order. His hand on the top of her head pushed her down again. Looking fearfully up at him, she could see that he was as tense as a tiger on the prowl.

"There are a couple of jeeps running alongside the river," he said between his teeth. "They probably don't know a thing in hell about us. But just in case they do, I don't want you to do a thing but keep down and cover up your head. Understand?"

"Yes."

"That's what you said the last time," he muttered. "But this time, so help me . . ."

He never finished.

"Stay down!" he said again, sharply, crouching himself as the boat shot through the gently rolling water. Lisa risked a quick look over the side before she obediently lay down flat in the bottom of the boat. What she saw scared her clear to her toes. Instead of a couple of jeeps, as Sam had so casually

said, there must have been half a dozen—at least
three on either side of the river. Even as she looked,
they slammed to a halt and soldiers leaped out. She
was lying down before they opened fire, but it was
clear what was happening: the soldiers were shooting at the boat. Situated in the middle of the open
river as they were, she and Sam were sitting ducks.

XIV

Six weeks later, Lisa sat in a semicomfortable chair in Sam's hospital room in Annapolis, Maryland. It was a nice room, as hospital rooms go, its walls painted a cheery yellow instead of the usual dirty white and with deep blue carpeting on the floor. Saint Mary's was a small, private hospital that cost the earth, and it treated its patients with as much deference as their various illnesses and injuries allowed. As a former marine, Sam could have gone to the naval hospital in nearby Bethesda, but Lisa had preferred to pay for his room and treatment at Saint Mary's. Sam had been conscious for only brief periods since that horrible afternoon when four bullets had torn into his body, leaving him bleeding like a sieve, so he had not been consulted. The decision had been strictly Lisa's.

Amos was so glad to see her alive and well that he had asked very few questions about this brawny stranger whose side she had refused to leave, except for such necessities as eating and sleeping, since the South African river patrol had pulled the two of them out of the half-submerged remains of their small, bullet-riddled motorboat. Lisa had had only a minor bullet wound to the arm; it was almost healed now and seldom bothered her. Sam was in much worse shape: he'd caught a bullet in the forehead just above his left temple, but fortunately it had bounced off his skull without doing too much damage; a bullet in the chest, which had punctured his left lung; and two bullets in his right thigh, one of which had broken the thick femur bone.

It was a miracle that he hadn't bled to death before the river patrol had arrived and rushed him to the nearest hospital. And getting him safely back to the United States had almost required another miracle. Lisa knew that only her stubborn refusal to leave him, which had resulted in Amos's pulling a multitude of strings, had gotten him out of South Africa with a minimum of questions asked. To the South Africans she had said that he was a journalist like herself, caught up in the fighting through no fault of his own. After one long look at Sam, who exuded toughness even while lying unconscious in a hospital bed, they had been clearly skeptical. But once they found out who she was, and had gotten in touch with Amos through embassy contacts, they had not quite liked to question her word. So Sam, still unconscious in a portable hospital bed, had been allowed to leave the country with Lisa in the small private jet that Amos had sent for them.

All she had told Amos was that Sam had saved her life more than once and that she owed him. Amos understood that—he never could bear to owe anybody anything. Lisa would have told him the truth, would have said that Sam was the man she loved and was going to marry, except for two circumstances: one, she had discovered that it was a touch awkward to describe one man as one's fiancé while still being legally married to another; and, two, she was not quite sure of Sam's feelings about announcing their plans to all and sundry. Maybe he would want to tell his son first, or ... Well, she would wait for him to get well enough to face the world with her. The doctors had assured her that it would be only a matter of time before he was himself again.

Since returning, she had quietly set the wheels in motion for a divorce. She had not yet broken the news to Amos, preferring to wait and tell him everything at once, but Jeff had been very decent about the whole thing. In fact, now that she no longer thought of him as her husband, Lisa had discovered that Jeff could be a very good friend. He was the only one in whom she had confided, and while he had lifted his eyebrows at the thought of her marrying a professional soldier, he had also been quick to offer his best wishes for her happiness. Like herself, he preferred to wait and present Amos and his own family with the divorce as a fait accompli; that way, there would be little anyone could do about it.

Sam's son, Jay, had been tracked down by one of Amos's secretaries, and he had spent nearly as much time at the hospital as Lisa had. He was staying with her and Amos (she had moved back into her grandfather's house, saying that it was nearer to the hospital, which it was; Amos had made no comment). At seventeen, Jay was a gangly version of Sam himself. For this alone Lisa would have loved him, but he was a very likable teenager, polite and well mannered, and clearly devoted to Sam behind the budding machismo that forbade him to say so. He had accepted Lisa's explanation of how Sam had found her in the jungle and saved her life with much admiration for his father but with few questions. She liked to think that the two of them were on the way to becoming fast friends.

At the moment, Lisa was occupied in staring out the blue-curtained window at the gray waters of Chesapeake Bay. It was the middle of December, so the bright regatta that sailed the bay in summer was absent. Only scudding whitecaps and the occasional far-distant fishing vessel disturbed the rolling waters. Heavy, dark clouds hung low over the surface of the waves, threatening snow later in the day.

It was cold, and Lisa was dressed in a finely tailored jade-green wool skirt suit that she had always liked because it brought out the green of her eyes. A silk blouse with a high, ruffled collar in a paler shade of green and simple brown leather pumps completed her outfit. One of the first things she had done upon getting home was visit the hairdresser, so her blond hair hung in a simple yet sophisticated style around her shoulders, its deep waves caught up on one side by a jade clasp. Her hands were freshly manicured, the nails buffed and shaped into ten perfect ovals and polished a delicate rose. She knew she looked a far different creature from the ragtag female Sam had hauled out of the jungle, and she was eager to hear Sam's reaction to her changed appearance. To tell the truth, she was dying to bowl him over. But it might be days or even weeks before he was really aware of his surroundings, so she would just have to be patient. At least the doctors seemed certain that he would recover, and that was the main thing.

Except for a brief phone call to Grace at the *Star* to let her know that she had made it back to the United States in one piece after all, Lisa had had no contact with anyone from the paper. She suspected that Amos had had something to do with that. Grace, upset by Mary Blass's death but too much of a reporter not to think of the scoop Lisa could write for them—an eyewitness account of a massacre of an entire family, no less!—had almost pleaded with her to do the story. Lisa had said no as tactfully as she could, but Grace was persistent by nature and profession. Lisa knew the other woman well enough to know that she would never have let the matter rest unless pressure was brought to bear. And Amos was the only one with the will as well as the authority to apply the necessary pressure. He had been horrified at her carefully edited account of what had happened at the Blass farm and afterward, horrified to think that his granddaughter had been exposed to such horror, had lived with such fear. Seeing the remembered horror and fear reflected in Lisa's eyes, he had hugged her—an unusually emotional gesture for him—and told her to put it out of her mind. And he apparently meant to see to it that she did. At any rate, after that one phone call to Grace, no one at the *Star* had tried to get in touch with her. And Lisa did not contact them again. Aside from all the other considerations, it had occurred to Lisa that explaining just what Sam and his men had been doing in Rhodesia might prove a little sticky. She wasn't positive, but Lisa suspected that there was some sort of law against what Sam had been up to. She thought it might even be illegal to be a mercenary. It would be best all around to keep the story out of the newspapers, she decided, and was thankful that the power that went hand in hand with Amos's money permitted him to do that.

Sighing, she turned her attention from the view out the window to the man in the hospital bed behind her. His eyes were closed, and a small white bandage adorned his forehead where the bullet had struck just above his temple. His hair, which had been trimmed but was still longer than he usually wore it, looked very black against the crisp white pillow. His skin was still deeply bronzed. He was clean-shaven, thanks to the nurses who performed that chore for him daily, and his lean, hard jaw looked aggressive even in sleep. His wide shoulders were left bare by the blanket that came up only as far as his armpits. The outline of his powerful physique could be seen clearly through the bedclothes, and it had provoked more than one admiring glance from the younger nurses. An intravenous needle was taped to his left arm, its cord extending like a long, slender umbilical to the I.V. unit beside the bed. His right leg was in traction, strung up above the bed by a contraption that looked like a triangular pulley. It, too, was covered by the white blanket.

Lisa's face softened as she came to stand beside the bed, her hand going automatically to smooth away the curls that fell over his forehead. He murmured something, moving restlessly, and Lisa wondered if he was in pain. They had been giving him drugs to control it, but they wore off from time to time and the doctors were afraid to give him too much; they didn't want him to leave the hospital an addict.

From the time the last bullet had crashed into his chest, leaving him unconscious and, Lisa had feared, possibly dying on the floor of the boat, she had never been sure that he was aware of her presence. Oh, he had opened his eyes and looked at her, but Lisa couldn't tell if he recognized her. But she liked to think so—at least, this time, he had not called for Beth.

"How is he?" Jay spoke from the door, his voice hushed.

Lisa looked up to smile at him, and saw her grandfather following him into the room. Her smile widened to include them both. Amos must have brought Jay over....

"Still the same," she answered cheerfully. She had stopped whispering in Sam's presence weeks ago. He would wake up when his body was ready, the doctors had told her, and until then there was no need to worry about disturbing him.

"I told the boy he wouldn't be awake," Amos said testily, "but he insisted on coming by just to make sure. I told him you'd let us know if there's any change."

Lisa nodded. "Yes, I will, but I'm sure Jay wanted to see for himself. After all, Sam is his father."

"Yeah," Jay agreed, coming around the end of the bed to stand beside Lisa and look down at Sam's recumbent form with a slight frown on his face. "If I was in here, he'd be here every day, I know. He's that kind of guy."

This was the closest Jay had ever gotten to putting into words the deep love he and Sam shared, and it clearly embarrassed him. Lisa hid a smile as she watched dark color creep up over his cheeks. He was very sensitive about his status as an adult male, and he wasn't yet old enough to confess to feeling any softer emotions without being afraid of seeming unmanly. He was a scant eight years younger than herself, but Lisa, looking at him as he stood towering beside her, his hands jammed deep into the pockets of his corduroy car coat and his long legs clad in the inevitable jeans, felt aeons older.

"What are you two going to do this afternoon?" she asked, knowing that Amos enjoyed being with the boy and that the two of them spent much time together while she was sitting with Sam.

Amos grinned. Lisa thought with pride how very well he looked for seventy-two. His body was still strong and erect, although he wasn't much taller than she was herself—tallness wasn't a characteristic of the Bennets, although, Lisa amended with a quick look at Sam's considerable length, it might be in the future. Amos's iron-gray hair might be a little thin on top, but he had all his own teeth and was almost never sick. Today, dressed as he always was in a conservative business suit topped by a camel-colored cashmere overcoat, he could easily have passed for sixty.

"Oh, we thought we might drive down to D.C., maybe take in a show." From Amos's shifty-eyed reply, Lisa inferred that he and Jay really had quite different intentions. Probably they were going Christmas shopping, she guessed, remembering that there were less than two weeks remaining until the holiday. She had some shopping to do herself; she'd been so wrapped up with Sam that she had not yet bought a single present. Maybe this weekend . . .

"That sounds nice." She went along with Amos's explanation without so much as the bat of an eyelash to reveal that she saw clear through him. He had always liked to do his shopping in secret, pretending that Christmas was the last thing on his mind until the big day itself, when she would come downstairs to find enormous piles of presents. Lisa smiled, remembering. Amos had always spoiled her rotten.

"Well, maybe now that the boy here has seen for himself that his dad is still in one piece, we can get on with it. Eh, boy?"

"Okay." Jay had quickly gotten used to Amos's irascible manner, and his only response to this testy speech was a tolerant grin. "I'll come by again later, Lisa, and stay with him for a couple of hours while you go home and rest."

"Thanks, Jay." Lisa smiled at him gratefully as he moved back around the bed to join Amos by the door. He looked so much like Sam that he pulled her heartstrings, but even if he hadn't, she thought, he was a fine boy. Sam could be proud, she told herself. He had done a hell of a job raising his son.

"Why you two think the man needs somebody with him constantly when he doesn't even know where he is is beyond me," Amos grumbled, as he had done frequently since Lisa had returned and had taken to spending nearly every hour of the day in Sam's room. He gestured at the traction unit. "You got him by the leg; he's not going anywhere."

"I want somebody to be here in case he wakes up," Lisa said stubbornly. Amos shook his head at her, then shepherded Jay out the door.

"That's awful nice of you," observed a faint but familiar voice.

Lisa whirled, her eyes widening as she met Sam's blue ones—wide awake and plainly aware.

"Sam!" she exclaimed joyfully, moving to bend over him.

"Lisa," he mocked, but he smiled at her. She returned his smile with a delighted one of her own.

"How long have you been awake?" she asked, wondering why he hadn't spoken to his son.

"Long enough. I would have said something sooner, but I didn't feel up to tackling that formidable old gentleman who was growling at you and Jay."

"That was Amos," Lisa explained, still smiling foolishly down at him.

Sam grimaced. "I figured it was." Then his voice changed. "Don't I get a kiss?" he asked plaintively.

Lisa's eyes softened, and she bent down to press her lips against his mouth. When his lips hardened and he would have deepened the kiss, she straightened away from him.

"What's the matter?" He was frowning. Lisa ran a teasing finger across his lower lip; he caught it between his teeth, nipping it sharply before releasing it.

"Ouch!" Lisa shook her finger at him admonishingly. "That hurt!"

"Changed your mind?" he asked, so casually that she didn't immediately understand what he was getting at.

"About what?" She stared down at him, puzzled.

"Marrying me."

"No way. Were you hoping?" Her words were teasing, but her eyes were tender as they met his. He had been afraid she had changed her mind, she realized, seeing his quick look of relief before he grinned at her.

"Just a little," he said, and then his hand moved to catch hers and squeeze it warmly. The I.V. bottle swung precariously with his movement, and Sam shot it a look of distaste.

"I feel like a trussed chicken," he complained, glaring at his leg, which was suspended from the ceiling, to the I.V. unit that dripped liquid steadily down into his arm. "I hope this place doesn't catch on fire. I don't think I can move."

Lisa grinned in appreciation of the picture this conjured up. "Oh, I don't think you have much to worry about," she said lightly. "The nurses wouldn't forget about *you*."

"Got the hots for me, have they?" he asked complacently. Lisa had to laugh at him, and he grinned back. "In that case, you better kiss me again to remind me who I belong to. Just in case one of them tries to run off with me."

Lisa giggled, and complied. This time Sam's hand came up to cradle the back of her head, holding her in place until she had been very thoroughly kissed.

"That's better," he said when he let her go at last. Lisa's cheeks were flushed rosy from his kiss, and her lips were red and faintly swollen. He looked at her for a long moment, smiling slightly, and then he lifted her hand to his lips and pressed his mouth to the back of it.

"You're beautiful," he said huskily, his mouth still warm against her hand. His eyes moved over her from her shining blond head to as far down the jade suit as he could see, and his lips pursed in a soundless whistle. "Quite the fox."

Lisa stared down at him. "Fox?" she repeated, nonplussed.

Sam grinned, turning her hand over and pressing the palm against his hard cheek. "That's what Jay calls girls who knock him off his feet," he explained.

"Oh." Lisa laughed. "Thank you, kind sir. I think."

Sam pressed another kiss into the palm of her hand, and then his eyes wandered around the room.

"I think you'd better fill me in on what's been going on. I've already concluded that we're safely back home, but I'd like to hear exactly how it came about. The last clear thing I remember is being in that damned boat while those soldiers took potshots at us. After that, everything is pretty much a blur."

"You . . ." Lisa began obediently, only to break off as a white-garbed nurse, one of the older ones who wouldn't swoon over Robert Redford if she found him naked at her feet, bustled into the room, then stopped short as she realized that her patient was conscious at last.

"You should have called us, Mrs. Collins," the woman said reproachfully, approaching around the foot of the bed. Lisa withdrew her hand from Sam's rather self-consciously.

"I didn't think," Lisa said, feeling guilty. Sam cast her a mocking look.

"I think I took Mrs. Collins by surprise." Sam's mouth had a wry twist to it, and he put a faint, but to Lisa unmistakable, emphasis on her married name. Lisa knew he didn't like being reminded that she was married to another man, but she couldn't do a thing about it. Whether he liked it or not, that *was* her name. For the time being, at least.

"You shouldn't be tiring yourself out by talking," the nurse said severely to Sam. "You've been very seriously injured, and you need to rest. How long has he been awake?" This question was directed almost accusingly at Lisa. Stammering, she answered. The woman sniffed.

"I'm sorry, Mrs. Collins, but I'm going to have to ask you to leave. Dr. Peters asked to be notified *immediately* when Mr. Eastman woke up, and I really don't think he should be tiring himself out with visitors until Dr. Peters has seen him and given the okay."

Lisa and Sam stared wryly at each other. His hand moved out to capture hers again, telling her wordlessly that he did not want her to go, but to Lisa what the nurse had said made sense. Sam had been very ill; for the first several days it had been touch and go whether he would even recover. It would be silly to jeopardize his health at this point. . . .

"She's right; I must go, Sam," Lisa said softly. "I'll be back later tonight—if Dr. Peters says it's all right."

Sam frowned at her, then nodded reluctantly. But

when Lisa would have moved away, his hand tightened on hers and he refused to release her.

"Excuse us for a moment, would you?" he said to the nurse. She looked first surprised, then disapproving, but went out and left them alone.

"*She* doesn't have the hots for me," Sam muttered darkly when the woman had gone. Lisa had to giggle at the idea. He grinned back at her, his blue eyes caressing her face.

"Kiss me," he directed huskily.

Lisa shook her head at him. "What would the nurse say?"

"To hell with her. Kiss me."

"Then I really have to go," Lisa warned, then bent to kiss him.

It must have been another ten minutes before she got out of that room.

It was late the next afternoon before Sam was allowed to have visitors again. Jay and Amos went on in while Lisa stayed in the hospital corridor for a few minutes talking to Dr. Peters. Sam was much better, the doctor told her, but still very weak. He needed plenty of rest, and since he was unlikely to lose consciousness now that he had finally regained it, he had to be kept as quiet as possible. Which meant that visitors would be strictly limited, for the next few days, at least. If all went well, Sam should be ready to be released within a month. After that, he could expect to spend another couple of months quietly convalescing.

When Lisa walked into the room, it was to find Amos standing silently and a touch awkwardly at the foot of the bed while Jay stood closer to his father and pumped his hand in a vigorous handshake. Jay was grinning from ear to ear, while Sam was grinning back with the kind of wry twist to his mouth that fathers have when they realize that their sons think they are now too old for any less-manly display of affection.

Lisa was just in time to hear Sam growl at Jay, "What the hell are you doing out of school?" Jay's grin widened, if possible; he finally let go of Sam's hand, to Lisa's secret relief.

"If you go around doing dumb things like getting shot up, you can't expect me to stay in school," the boy retorted. "Somebody's got to keep an eye on you."

"Oh, is that right?" This squabble between father and son was not meant to be taken seriously, Lisa knew. They were both grinning affectionately at each other. "The day I need a smart-ass kid to keep an eye on me is far distant, let me tell you."

"You could have fooled me," Jay muttered unrepentantly, eyeing Sam from his bandaged head to his suspended foot. Sam fixed him with a steely eye.

"Now that you've seen that I'm alive, you can get yourself straight back to school. Like tomorrow."

"It's just three days till break!"

Lisa judged that it was time to intervene, and moved around the side of the bed to stand beside Jay, drawing Amos with her. Sam's eyes softened as they met hers; admiration showed plainly in them for just an instant as they ran over her slender body in the rust-colored silk dress. He acknowledged Amos with a nod.

"Jay's going to stay with us until his school starts again after Christmas," Lisa told him. "He can go back after break." Then, changing the subject hastily, as Sam seemed inclined to argue, she added, gesturing at Amos, "Sam, I don't think you've met my grandfather."

"Mr. Bennet." Sam held out his hand. The older man took it and shook it briefly.

"Major Eastman."

Lisa looked at Amos in surprise, while Sam's eyes narrowed. Only Jay looked unperturbed.

"Amos..." Lisa turned to her grandfather questioningly.

Sam silenced her with a gesture and said to Amos, "You've been checking up on me."

Amos shrugged unrepentantly. "You couldn't expect me not to. She is my only granddaughter."

"I see your point," Sam conceded, while Lisa stared from one to the other of them, her bewilderment coupled with growing indignation.

"I can look after myself," she said admonishingly to Amos, who looked unconvinced. Then, to Sam, she added accusingly, "You never told me you were a major."

"It never came up."

"He was promoted through the ranks in Vietnam when all his unit's officers were killed," Jay rushed in, fairly bursting with pride as he recounted Sam's exploits. "They made him a major when he captured an enemy position almost single-handed. He's got all kinds of medals: the silver star and—"

"Shut up, Jay." Sam scowled at his son. Jay looked affronted, but he obediently fell silent.

"I want to thank you for saving my granddaughter's life," Amos said formally to Sam. "She tells me you did it more than once."

Sam shrugged. "No thanks are necessary. It was my pleasure." He sent a faint smile glimmering in Lisa's direction. "Besides, she more than repaid me. Did she tell you how she saved my life?" Seeing that both Amos and Jay looked blank, he added under his breath, "I didn't think so."

"Lisa..." Amos and Jay spoke at once, turning to look at her with identical expressions of astonishment.

"It didn't come up," she repeated Sam's words defensively.

Sam's mouth tightened; he muttered, for her ears alone, "I can see a lot of things didn't come up," while she pacified Amos and Jay with a promise to tell them all about it later.

When the nurse came in to shoo them away, Sam caught Lisa's hand.

"Excuse Lisa for a moment, won't you," he said pleasantly to Amos and Jay. "I want to talk to her."

They looked surprised, then speculative as they observed Sam's hand holding Lisa's, but Jay left at once. Amos went out more slowly, and only after Lisa's jerky nod told him that she had no objection to being left alone with Sam.

"You neglected to tell them any number of things, didn't you?" Sam asked when they were alone. His eyes were hard as they met hers. Lisa felt guilty, which was ridiculous. She hadn't done anything wrong!

"If you mean that I didn't tell them that we're— that I'm—that we're going to get married," she began, sounding defensive in spite of herself.

Sam inclined his head ironically. "That is what I meant, yes," he murmured sarcastically.

Lisa glared at him. "I thought you might want to tell Jay first," she snapped. "After all, it would be a little awkward for me to walk up to him and say, 'Oh, by the way, I hope you like the idea of having me for a stepmother, because I'm going to marry your father'!"

Sam thought about that for a moment. "Sure that's the only reason you haven't told them?"

"Of course!" She was still glaring at him. Sam's eyes lost some of their hard gleam as he looked at her, with her eyes bright and her cheeks flushed with temper. Her soft mouth was set mutinously.

"Now you look like the Lisa I remember," he said softly. "At first, you were always mad at me. I couldn't get over how beautiful you were, with your eyes spitting fire at me and your hair looking like a squirrel might have built a nest in it and your face dirty more often than not. I was going crazy for you.... But yesterday and today, in your fancy clothes and with makeup on your face and your hair all fixed up, I've hardly recognized you."

The glare died out of Lisa's eyes, to be replaced by tenderness as she met Sam's wry gaze. This situation was as strange to him as it was to her, she realized. He was as uncertain as she was herself.

She sat down carefully on the edge of the bed, uncaring that the nurse might walk in at any minute, and bent to kiss him. When he let her go, she rested her cheek alongside his.

"I haven't changed," she whispered in his ear. "It's just the clothes, Sam. I still want to marry you more than anything in the world."

He pressed his lips into the curve of her neck, nuzzling aside the high collar to move his mouth hotly against her skin.

"Lisa..." he said huskily, only to be interrupted by the militant entrance of the nurse. At the sound of the door being opened, Lisa jumped away from him as if she had been shot. Sam's mouth compressed at her instinctive movement.

"I'll have to ask you to leave, Mrs. Collins," the nurse said firmly, her professional training masking any surprise she might have felt at seeing a supposedly married woman in her patient's arms. "Mr. Eastman needs his rest."

"Yes—all right." She smoothed her dress self-consciously before looking at Sam. "I'll see you tomorrow, Sam. Can I bring you anything? Magazines, or . . ."

"No, thanks," Sam said politely. "Jay knows my taste in reading material better than you do. I'll have him bring me something."

Lisa nodded jerkily and turned to go. As she opened the door, Sam called after her.

"Yes?" She turned back to look at him. The hospital bed was still elevated to a semisitting position, as it had been ever since she had entered the room, and Sam was bare to the waist. He looked very dark and virile against the white sheets; if it hadn't been for the bandages on his chest and forehead, and the I.V. unit still strapped to his arm, she would have thought he looked disgustingly healthy.

"I think you were right about that matter we were just discussing," he said, face and voice expressionless. "Let's keep it to ourselves for the time being, okay?"

Lisa stared at him. Those blue eyes were as fathomless as the ocean.

"If that's what you want," she said slowly after a moment.

"It is."

"All right." Then, with the nurse frowning at her, Lisa left the room. As she walked down the corridor to join Amos and Jay, Lisa was conscious of the most ridiculous urge to cry.

Sam made great progress over the next few days, and Dr. Peters, pronouncing himself delighted with him, said that if all went well, Sam might even be permitted to go home before Christmas. Lisa fully intended Sam to convalesce in her grandfather's house, under her own eye, but persuading Sam took some doing. Finally he gave in, simply because Dr.

Peters told him that unless he agreed to stay within commuting distance of the hospital and have someone available to look after him, he would not release him for another month. Privately, the doctor told Lisa that Sam would have trouble getting around for a long time, that he would have to use crutches for weeks or months and would probably have a limp for the rest of his life. This information made no difference to Lisa, although she was sorry for Sam; he wasn't going to like the idea at all, she knew. But Dr. Peters had decided to say nothing of this to Sam for a while yet. He didn't want worry to retard his truly remarkable recovery.

Sam's attitude to Lisa was hard to define. He was glad to see her, she knew. His eyes lit up unmistakably when she came through the door on her daily visits to his room. He teased her, and laughed at her, and even kissed her, but he never once told her he loved her or referred to the fact that they were engaged to be married. When Lisa tried to broach the subject, he would smilingly refuse to discuss it. They would talk about it again when he was out of the hospital, he said, and would say nothing else.

Dr. Peters finally agreed that Sam could be released from the hospital on Christmas Eve. When the big day arrived, Lisa and Jay went to the hospital to bring him home. Amos stayed behind; it was freezing outside, and the cold hurt his old bones, he said.

When they reached Sam's room, he was fully dressed and sitting on the side of the bed. His leg had been taken out of traction the day before; it was now enveloped in a white plaster cast that extended from the top of his thigh to his foot. Only his toes had not been wrapped in plaster, and they were covered by a thick white athletic sock. He was dressed in tan corduroy pants slit up the side to accommodate the cast, a tan-and-blue plaid flannel shirt, and a sheep-skin jacket. The clothes were Sam's own and had been procured from where they had been left in storage.

When Sam saw them, he grinned, and, waving away both Lisa's and Jay's outstretched hands, he swung himself to his feet, positioning a crutch firmly under each arm.

"I'm getting pretty good at this," he said, taking an experimental few steps. He maneuvered the crutches expertly, and Lisa could only shake her head at him. Was there anything he did not do well?

"Come on, let's go," Sam said, heading out into the corridor through the door Lisa had left open. Lisa hurried after him, wanting to stay close by in case—just in case—Mr. Expert should require some assis-tance after all. Jay grabbed the case containing Sam's things and followed.

As they waited for the elevator, Dr. Peters came walking down the corridor. He greeted Lisa and Jay pleasantly and congratulated Sam on how well he was managing his crutches. Sam laughed and shook the doctor's hand, thanking him for putting him back together again.

"You should set yourself up as a rival for the six-million-dollar man," Dr. Peters told him, grin-ning. "With what it cost to get you back in one piece, I'm set for life."

Sam groaned. "I'll probably suffer a relapse when I get the bill."

Dr. Peters looked surprised. "Oh, it's all been taken care of. Mrs. Collins . . ."

The elevator arrived, interrupting him. Lisa prac-tically dragged Sam onto it, waving a pseudocheerful goodbye to the doctor. Sam was silent all the way down, but when they were walking through the lobby toward where Lisa had parked the car just outside the door, and Jay had gone on ahead to unlock the car, Sam growled through one side of his mouth, "I want that bill as soon as we get to your grandfather's house. I pay my own bills, understand?"

Looking sideways at him, Lisa saw that he was blazingly angry.

XV

Jay's presence kept Sam from saying more. But during the drive to the house, which took about twenty minutes, Lisa was conscious of his anger smoldering beneath the cheerful front he assumed for Jay's benefit. Lisa was driving. In deference to Sam's cast, she had chosen a big Lincoln, which was one of five cars owned by her grandfather. Sam sat beside her, his leg stretched out stiffly before him. Jay rode in the back, his arms draped over the leather upholstery of the front seat as he leaned forward, talking excitedly all the while.

When Lisa pulled in between the stone posts that guarded the drive leading to the house, she could sense Sam's stiffening. He said nothing as she drove up the driveway, which was flanked on each side by a row of denuded oak trees. The house itself was a three-story dwelling built of rough-faceted stone with a gabled roof and wings extending back on either side of the main part of the dwelling. It was a beautiful house, set like an unpolished jewel amid the forty landscaped acres that made up the estate, and it had been the Bennet family home for nearly half a century. Maybe at one time the family had been large and had needed every one of its twenty-two rooms. For herself and her grandfather, so much space seemed almost obscene. Lisa, casting a sideways look at Sam as he absorbed the magnificence she had always taken for granted, could see that he felt much the same.

"Isn't it great? What do you think?" Jay demanded excitedly of Sam as Lisa drove on around the house to the six-car garage that had been converted from a stable at the rear.

"Great," Sam agreed. Lisa hoped that Jay hadn't caught the biting edge to his voice.

As Lisa stopped the car in front of the garage, not bothering to pull in, the middle-aged man who was husband to the housekeeper and cared for the cars as well as doing odd jobs around the place appeared.

"The old family retainer, I take it?" Sam observed snidely to Lisa. She sent him a burning look, then opened the door and got out of the car. On the other side, Jay had already slid out the rear door and was helping Sam with his crutches. Plainly, her presence was unnecessary, but she walked around to that side of the car anyway.

"Want me to put the car up now, Mrs. Collins?" Henry Dobson asked, coming to join the little group that centered on Sam, who was standing on his own now, the crutches positioned securely under his arms. Sam's eyes went swiftly to the speaker, their expression unreadable.

"Thank you, Henry. The keys are in the ignition," Lisa said politely. To Sam she added, "This is Henry Dobson. He's been helping to take care of us for years, and I don't know what we'd do without him— or his wife, who's our housekeeper. Henry, as you've probably guessed, this is Major Eastman."

"Nice to meet you, Major," Henry said, nodding.

"I've heard a lot about you from your boy here. Good kid, he is."

"Thank you." Sam's reply was brief. His eyes were hooded as he watched Henry get into the car and start to maneuver it into the garage. Then, with Lisa leading the way, the three of them started for the house, moving slowly in deference to Sam's crutches.

Once inside the house, they were met in the entrance hall by Mary Dobson, Henry's plump, gray-haired wife. Lisa introduced her to Sam, then assured her that they could manage fine on their own, and the woman went on about her work. When Lisa turned back to Sam, his eyes were moving inscrutably over the green-flecked terrazzo floor, overlaid in the center with an obviously genuine green-and-blue oriental carpet, to the pale solid ash of the carved paneling and the elegant little tables and mirrors with which the hall was furnished.

"Come on, Dad," Jay said impatiently, leading the way toward one of three doors set under the huge walnut staircase that curved up from either side of the hall to a second-floor landing. "Lisa put you on the ground floor so you wouldn't have to worry about getting up and down the stairs with your crutches. My room's just across the hall. Wait until you see it. It's..."

"Great. I know." Sam's voice was dry.

Lisa sent him a quick, anxious look as he followed Jay through the door into the hall that led into the right wing of the house. The hall bisected the four bedrooms that made up the lower part of the wing, leaving two bedrooms on each side. The bedrooms to the right had been converted into a suite consisting of a bedroom, a sitting room, and a private bathroom. It was to this that Jay led Sam.

"Think you can stand it?" the boy asked proudly,

dumping Sam's case down in the middle of the sitting room and hurrying to throw open the doors to the connecting bath and bedroom so that Sam could revel in the full glory of the space that had been allotted to him. Sam's eyes moved swiftly over the elegant rooms, furnished in Early American style in shades of rust and brown and gold.

"I think so," he answered, his eyes coming to rest on Lisa. Their expression was unreadable, but she knew that the sight of her home had done nothing to appease his earlier anger.

"You must be hungry," she said nervously, operating on the principle that a well-fed man was easier to handle. "Lunch should be ready...."

"Great! I'm starved!" came enthusiastically from Jay, who had flung himself on the gold-plaid couch. "Dad, wait until you taste Mary's cooking! She makes the best hamburgers."

"You go along. I think I'll wait until dinner," Sam said evenly, smiling briefly at his son before his eyes returned to fix on Lisa. She squirmed beneath that diamond-hard gaze, feeling a lot like a butterfly on a pin.

"You sure?" Jay asked, getting to his feet and looking from his father to Lisa as though realizing for the first time that everything might not be perfect between them.

"I'm sure. You go on and eat." Dismissal was plain in his tone. Jay looked quickly at Lisa, who smiled at him as naturally as she could. Reassured, he left the room to find Mary and lunch.

"Close the door," Sam ordered softly.

Lisa didn't even think about the irony of being told what to do in her own home. Swallowing, she went to close the door, then returned to the center of the room, her hands clasped nervously in front of her.

Sam said nothing, just watched her with a brooding look in his eyes.

"Look, I'm sorry about the hospital bill," Lisa burst out at last, unable to stand that silent inspection another instant. "I didn't think. I just didn't want you to have to worry about it, while you weren't well. . . ." Her voice trailed off.

Sam's mouth twisted up at one corner. "Tell the truth, Lisa," he said evenly. "You just didn't think I had the money to pay it. Right?"

Lisa looked miserably at the brown-carpeted floor. The thought had crossed her mind, she had to admit—but not to him.

"Well?" he barked, and she jumped at something in his tone.

"That wasn't it at all," she defended herself stoutly, her eyes coming up to meet him with a bravado she was far from feeling.

"Liar."

That one soft word brought hot color stinging into Lisa's cheeks. She bit her lip, then quickly released it as she realized how telling the gesture was. Sam hadn't missed it, she could tell from the tightening of his jaw.

"All right, so I thought you might not have the money," she admitted boldly, deciding that it was useless to lie. Anyway, might it not be better to get the whole silly thing out in the open once and for all? She had more money than he did, and it was too bad if he didn't like it, but that was the way it was. He would have to learn to accept it, and then they could work from there. "What's so terrible about that? Money doesn't mean much. Look at it this way: if you were rich and I was . . ." she nearly said "poor," but caught herself in time, "not, wouldn't you want to share what you had with me? Everything I have is yours, Sam. You can have anything you want. You never have to ask."

As soon as the words were out of her mouth, she knew she had said the wrong thing. His eyebrows snapped together to form a single, devilish black line over eyes that had frosted over. His mouth was clamped so tightly together that it looked bloodless, and a muscle twitched warningly at the side of his jaw.

"Let's get one thing perfectly clear," he said through his teeth. He was still standing, leaning heavily on his crutches, separated from her by the width of the carpet. Lisa wished he would sit down, knowing that it must be costing him a lot to remain on his feet for so long, but not quite having the nerve to tell him to do so while he was in his present mood. "I pay my own way, understand? I've never taken charity in my life and I'm not starting now!"

"Sam, it's not charity," Lisa practically wailed. "I love you: how can it be charity if I love you?"

If she had thought to soften him up with her words, it didn't work. If anything, he looked even angrier.

"I want that hospital bill, and I want it tonight," he bit off. "And if you ever—ever—do anything like that again, I'll walk out. Is that clear? When—if—you marry me, you're going to have to live on what I can give you. As far as I'm concerned, there's no other way, and that's something you'd better think hard about. To begin with, I don't have a house like this, and I never will have. And I'm damned if I'm living here," he added in a furious aside, as if she would ever dream of asking him to! Then, his eyes flicking contemptuously over the fluffy blue-fox jacket that just reached her hips, the toning silver-gray silk blouse and charcoal wool slacks beneath it, right down to the gray suede boots and matching handbag she was clutching nervously in front of her, he said coldly, "You're a very expensive dolly, honey. I'm not sure I can afford you."

Lisa stared at him for a long moment, anger at his infuriating attitude and fear that he might actually be thinking about forgetting the whole thing battling for supremacy inside her. Fear won out. If she lost Sam, she didn't know what she would do. She would be more alone than she had ever been in her life.

"Please sit down," she said at last, her voice calm but her eyes pleading. "You know you're not supposed to stand for long periods on those crutches."

"To hell with the crutches!" He glared at her explosively. "Didn't you hear one single, solitary word I said?"

Lisa grimaced. "How could I help it? You're not exactly whispering, you know. I've said I'm sorry about the hospital bill. What else can I say? It won't happen again, all right? Now, would you please sit down?"

Sam looked more enraged than ever. "And you think that's all there is to it? You say you're sorry and I forget all about it? Until the next time? Like hell! We're going to get this straight once and for all: if you're going to marry me, you're going to have to live in the kind of house I can give you, wear the kind of clothes I can buy, do your own damned housework—"

"I understand," Lisa interrupted calmly. "And I agree. All right? Do you want me to sign a contract or something? And would you please *sit down!*"

"No, I damned well won't sit down," Sam retorted, glaring at her.

"Now you're being childish," Lisa said, her eyes beginning to spark in their turn. "Do you want to know what I think? I think you're just trying to find a way of wriggling out of marrying me. You knew I had a lot of money all along, and it never bothered you before. Why make such a big thing of it now? I tell you, it doesn't matter. We'll work it out. And if you don't sit down, you're going to fall down!"

"Don't call me childish and don't tell me to sit down!" he roared, moving toward her with as much angry determination as his crutches would allow him. "I'm not some damned tame dog for you to order around. I..."

As he swung around the back of the couch toward her, Lisa saw a brown lamp cord hook the end of one of his crutches.

"Sam, look out!" It was too late. He was off balance, then falling, turning the air blue with his curses as he hit the floor with a resounding thud, pulling the lamp off the table to crash down beside him. Lisa was at his side almost instantly, kneeling, her hands shaking as she touched him. He lay on his back like a turtle on its shell, his eyes closed, a grimace twisting his face. A steady stream of curses fell from his lips.

"Are you hurt?" Lisa's hands were moving anxiously over his cast. It seemed to be in one piece. He opened his eyes, glaring at her. She glared back at him just as fiercely.

"I told you to sit down!" she snapped.

He looked furious, but then, to her surprise, his lips twitched. "You did, didn't you?" He was grinning crookedly at her. Lisa stared at him dumbly, taken aback by the sudden laughter that twinkled in his eyes. "Next time, remind me to listen."

"You're not hurt, are you?" A smile was hovering on her own lips as she scanned him from head to toe. He had propped himself up on one elbow, and he looked very long and wide lying there on the brown carpet, his white cast thrust out stiffly before him.

"No, no thanks to that thrice-damned lamp!" He gave the offending lamp a vicious prod with the end of a crutch. It rolled, and its whole back side fell off. He looked at it for a moment, then started laughing. Lisa, looking from his face to the lamp and back, joined in.

"Laugh at me, will you, my girl?" he growled at her through bursts of merriment. "I'll teach you to show some respect!"

He grabbed for her, pulling her down against his chest. Lisa lay on that wide expanse, giggling helplessly while he made threatening noises against the silky skin of her throat.

"What's going on in here? We could hear you in the kitchen!"

They hadn't heard Jay enter, but there he was, leaning over the back of the couch and looking disapproving as he watched them wallowing on the floor behind it.

Lisa pulled away from Sam and sat up, smoothing her clothes and hair. She looked from Sam, who was making no move to get up and still had the remnants of a grin hovering around his mouth, to Jay, who was looking more and more bewildered.

"Oh, nothing much. Your father was just asking me to marry him," she said airily, then grinned as she watched identical dumbfounded expressions appear on both hard male faces.

"You're kidding," Jay said finally, looking as if he didn't believe a word of it.

Lisa shook her head. "No."

"You really asked her to marry you?" Jay looked to Sam for confirmation.

Sam grinned. "I guess I did—if she says so. Far be it from me to call a lady a liar."

Lisa sent him a killing look.

"Well, what did she say?" Jay demanded, impatient with all their fooling around.

Sam looked at Lisa, his eyes holding a question.

"She said yes," Lisa told Jay, but she could feel the sudden relaxation in the long body that lay stretched out behind her.

"That's great!" Jay yelled, coming excitedly around the couch. "Really great! Congratulations, Lisa! I knew he really liked you, of course, but—marriage! Are you sure you know what you're doing?" This was directed at Sam, along with a worried frown. Then he added hastily to Lisa, "No offense, but he doesn't usually do this kind of thing. You don't suppose it's the drugs or anything, do you?"

"Thanks a lot," Lisa muttered, making a face at Jay. Sam roared with laughter.

"It probably was," he told his son, recovering. "But it's too late now: I'm committed. Just think how embarrassing it would be for Lisa if I were to back out."

"Yeah." Jay appeared to take this seriously. Lisa, indignant, opened her mouth to defend herself, but Jay had another thought. "You'll be my stepmother, won't you?" He grinned cheekily at Lisa. "Think I should start calling you Mom?"

"'Lisa' will do," Sam said dryly. "She's not all that much older than you."

"She's not, is she?" Jay pondered that for a moment. "Do you think you two will have kids?"

Sam shot Lisa a teasing look. She could feel her face turning red.

"We'll talk about it later," he told his son firmly,

sitting up at last. "Come here and give me a hand up."

Jay obediently came around in front of Sam and, taking hold of his outstetched hand, hauled him to his feet. Lisa got up in the meantime, and stood next to the two of them, self-consciously brushing down her clothes.

"What were you doing down on the floor, anyway?" Jay asked, looking from one to the other as Sam moved around to the front of the couch and collapsed on the upholstered seat. "It seems like a funny place to propose."

"Your father tripped," Lisa said, frowning at Sam repressively as he chuckled.

"Your lunch is probably getting cold," Sam said to Jay, giving Lisa a quick, gleaming look.

The boy shrugged. "I finished it before I came."

Sam lifted an eyebrow at him. "Then..."

"Oh, I get it, you two want to be alone, right? Okay, I'm going. By the way, is this a secret? Can I tell anybody?"

Sam looked at Lisa. She smiled at him.

"Tell whoever you want," she said to Jay. "It's not a secret."

And Sam returned her smile with a slow, charming one of his own as Jay went out.

Amos took the news well, considering everything. At the very least, he seemed resigned. He wasn't senile yet, he told Lisa in the privacy of his study, and he'd known for a long time that things weren't working out between her and Jeff. If she was sure Sam was what she wanted, he wouldn't stand in her way.

"You're going to have trouble managing him, though," he said warningly to Lisa as she was about to leave him to go to bed. "He's used to giving orders, not taking them. I can't see you wrapping him around your little finger like you do the rest of us."

Lisa turned back from the door, smiling at her grandfather. "I don't care. I love him," she said softly.

"Then grab him, girl," Amos answered, his voice gruff and his eyes suspiciously bright as he looked at her. "If you think he'll make you happy, grab him. Your happiness is more important to me than anything in the world."

"I know. I love you, too, Amos," Lisa said, coming back across the room to kiss his leathery cheek. He hugged her briefly, then sent her off to bed with a watery chuckle and a pinch on the chin.

Christmas Day dawned cold and clear and very bright. During the afternoon, a few fat flakes of snow fell, not sticking to the ground but adding to the atmosphere. They stuffed themselves on turkey and all the trimmings, expertly prepared by Mary Dobson, then spent the remainder of the day lazing around the roaring fire in the huge fireplace that took up one wall of the living room. Amos and Jay played chess, while Sam and Lisa sat side by side on one of the overstuffed couches that flanked the fireplace and murmured to each other. From time to time Sam toyed with the gift Lisa had given him. It was a pocketknife containing everything from scissors to a corkscrew to a can opener, and he seemed very pleased with it. Lisa had agonized over what to get him for some time, instinctively knowing better than to buy him anything too expensive. Sam's gift to her, purchased through Jay, was a lovely porcelain figurine of an eighteenth-century girl. It was exquisitely detailed, and she loved it.

Lisa, after kissing Sam and Amos good-night and

being assured that Jay would render Sam any assistance necessary in getting to bed (Sam had flatly rejected the services of the male nurse she had hired for him, and, after one quick look at that stony countenance, Lisa had told the man to go), went to bed early. It had been a long day, and she was tired. She still slept in the lovely, old-fashioned bedroom that had been hers since childhood, partly out of deference to Amos's sensibilities and partly because Sam, with his injuries, needed to sleep undisturbed. Sam himself was not terribly thrilled with this arrangement, but he accepted it with grim good humor. As Lisa told him, as soon as her divorce was final—perhaps another three months, according to her lawyer—and they were married, they would be sleeping together for the rest of their lives. It wouldn't hurt them to spend what little time she had left under Amos's roof honoring an old man's prejudices.

Her room was furnished in stately Queen Anne, with a huge, elaborately canopied and draped bed set against the far wall. The bed was flanked by two long windows that looked out over the grounds and afforded an occasional glimpse of the bay. A gold velvet chaise-longue cut diagonally across the wide-planked floor and one corner of the fringed oriental carpet. The whole room was decorated in shades of green and silver with touches of gold. It was a beautiful room, and Lisa loved it. She had chosen its furnishings and decorations herself.

It didn't take her long to prepare for bed. She took a bath in the connecting green-and-silver bathroom, then came through to her bedroom, brushed her hair, creamed her face, and slid into her nightgown. This last was a deceptively simple affair of silvery gray silk and lace that was a handful of nothing until she put it on. Then it took on the shape of her body, leaving very little unrevealed without being at all revealing. The neckline, edged with lace and descending from spaghetti straps, was demure. The skirt was long, covering her to her ankles. It was the shimmery, clinging quality of the silk itself that made the garment worth every penny of the quite exorbitant price she had paid for it. Lisa smiled at her reflection in the mirror, wishing Sam could see her like this. He would be staggered, she knew. Remembering the rough, dirty khaki uniform she had worn nearly ever since she had known him, she was dying to show him just how feminine and seductive she could be in her own clothes. For a moment she was tempted to sneak downstairs and join him in his bedroom. Then she thought of his injuries, and Amos, and sighed. He would have plenty of time to be entranced by her after they were married. In the meantime, she could go to bed alone. She had been sleeping alone for almost the past two months, during the whole time Sam had been in the hospital, so why was it so difficult for her tonight? Then she thought of Sam in the room directly below hers, and grimaced at herself. While he had been in the hospital, he had definitely been unavailable. Now he was close, just a staircase away, and she knew he would welcome her with open arms. Lisa thought of that long, hard body sprawled between the sheets, and felt her mouth go dry. She wanted him with an intensity she had never dreamed she could feel. When she had been married to Jeff, they had often gone for months at a time without so much as exchanging a halfhearted kiss, and it had bothered her not at all. In fact, she had begun to think that she had a low sex drive, as she had read some people did. But since she had met Sam, her body had gone crazy. It craved the touch and smell and taste of him so much that it was like a physical pain inside her. She was addicted to him, she realized with a half-rueful smile, like a junkie to a drug. If she didn't get a steady fix, she suffered withdrawal pangs.

Lisa hesitated a moment longer, then climbed into bed, turning out the light and subsiding with an irritable thump against the pillows. She would not go sneaking downstairs to him like some sort of sex-crazed adolescent. She was an adult woman, in total control of her senses, and she could wait....

It must have been around midnight, and she had been dozing fitfully for the past hour, when she heard a series of muffled thumps in the hallway that led past her door. What on earth...? she thought, sitting up and reaching to flick on the bedside lamp. Had the plumbing gone crazy, or was the house being burglarized, or...

Her doorknob turned, and Lisa stared at it with disbelief. Then the door itself swung open before she could so much as open her mouth to scream. Her eyes huge, she looked fearfully at the tall apparition that stood on her threshold—and immediately relaxed.

"How did you get up here?" she demanded, looking at his cast and crutches and thinking of the tall, curving staircase.

Sam grinned, levering himself over the threshold and closing the door behind him.

"Don't ask," he advised her. "Believe me, it wasn't very dignified."

"You could have broken your neck!"

"I was careful," he assured her, moving toward the bed. His eyes slid over her, widening appreciatively on the lovely picture she made, sitting bolt upright with the bedclothes down around her waist. Her silver-gold hair was wildly tousled, and her face, innocent of makeup, was delicately flushed. The paler silver of that unbelievable nightgown emphasized every luscious curve of her body. He grinned faintly as he realized that her nipples were erect and pressing against the silk. Scold or not, she was glad to see him. . . .

"You idiot, you shouldn't be climbing stairs! If you fell, you'd be back in the hospital for months! If it didn't kill you outright! You need a keeper!"

He was standing beside the bed now, grinning at her, looking devilishly handsome with his black hair curling around his ears and over his forehead and those blue eyes sparkling roguishly down at her. He was dressed only in a white toweling robe that was tied at the waist and reached to just above his knees. Beneath it, she knew, he was naked. She could see the crisp curling hairs and hard muscles of his chest where the lapels of the robe parted; his skin against the white terrycloth was deeply brown. A faint bluish black shadow darkened his jaw, and deep grooves slashed his cheeks as he smiled. She wanted to bash him over the head for his foolishness and pull him into her arms at one and the same time. She frowned crossly at him.

"Don't be mad at me," he said coaxingly. "I brought you a present."

Balancing on one crutch, he reached a hand into the pocket of his robe and withdrew a small, gaily wrapped parcel. Lisa, staring at it, felt her heart speed up. She knew instinctively what was inside.

He gave her the package, then sat down on the edge of the bed beside her and watched her with a smile in his eyes as she unwrapped it with unsteady fingers. As she had suspected, it was a ring: a beautiful square-cut emerald flanked with diamonds. It was the most gorgeous piece of jewelry she had ever seen, and she looked from it to him with delight.

"Well, aren't you going to put it on?" he asked with a broad grin. Her amazed reaction pleased him enormously.

"You do it," she said, holding out both the box and her left hand to him.

He took the ring from the box, took her hand in his, and gently slid the ring onto her finger. Then he lifted her hand to his mouth and pressed a lingering kiss to its back. His eyes, looking at her over her hand at his mouth, said a thousand things she knew he would never put into words. She smiled tremulously back at him.

"It must have cost you the earth." The words had been hovering around the back of her mind, but when she heard them come out of her mouth Lisa could have kicked herself. That was the worst thing she could have said—especially when she loved the ring and the man so much that she wanted to die and he was sensitive about their relative financial positions anyway.

He lowered her hand from his mouth, his movement deliberate, and stared at her. Lisa looked back at him with trepidation. She had spoiled it—that lovely, lovely moment—with her big mouth. She couldn't even find the words to try to mend it. All she could do was stare at him wide-eyed.

"Do you always ask your suitors how much their presents cost?" he asked presently, with a distinct edge to his voice. Lisa was galvanized into speech.

"Oh, Sam, I'm sorry," she said miserably, clutching his hand. "I didn't mean it—I just don't want you to feel that you have to buy me expensive presents. I don't need them. . . ."

"I think you'd better shut your mouth before you

get into real trouble," he said quite gently, giving her chin an admonitory tap. "Believe me, I can afford the ring. The question is, do you like it?"

Relief that he was going to let her off so easily made her response especially fervent.

"I love it!"

He smiled crookedly at her. "Just the ring?"

It took Lisa a moment to catch on to that. When she did, she flung herself against him, her arms closing tightly around his neck and her mouth burying itself somewhere behind his ear.

"You too. Of course, you too!"

The force of her impetuous action nearly sent both of them tumbling over the edge of the bed to the floor. Sam managed to save them at what was almost the last minute. His arms closed tightly around Lisa's waist, and he returned her hug with interest, his face buried in her hair. After a moment he twisted around, maneuvering his cast with some difficulty, and lowered her back down onto the mattress. His eyes gleamed brightly blue as he leaned over her.

"Show me."

The words and the look that accompanied them were unmistakably lascivious. Lisa smiled bewitchingly up at him, her hands coming up to slide seductively along his broad shoulders in their terrycloth covering.

"What did you have in mind?" she whispered, her hands slipping beneath his robe to trail over his hair-covered chest, her nails delicately torturing his hard muscles.

He told her. And showed her. His hands and mouth were unbelievably erotic as they explored her body, leaving no part of her unclaimed. At his direction, she did the same to him, feeling a hot, sweet satisfaction as she elicited groan after groan from his hard mouth. Her nightgown and his robe had long since been discarded; naked, their bodies writhed together, burning where they touched, on fire with a passion that threatened to consume them in its flames. Still Sam withheld the final hard glory of his possession until Lisa was sobbing with desire against his shoulder, wanting him so badly that she was going out of her mind. When he could control his own need no longer, he took her. Her little cry of ecstasy was muffled by his mouth. His body worshipped hers, feeding it and being fed from it in turn. By the time it was over, Lisa felt as if she had been drowned in a red-hot lava sea.

It was nearly dawn before they fell asleep in each other's arms. Lisa, with no thought of sending him back to his own bed, barely had enough strength left to pull the blankets over them before curling against his chest and falling into a deep, dreamless sleep.

XVI

A brief knock brought Lisa blinking from sleep. She lay still for a moment, not sure exactly what had awakened her. Sunlight poured in through the windows, bathing her bedroom in a cheery golden glow. A delicious warmth rested against her back. Close to her ear she could hear a man's steady breathing, and a hard arm curled possessively around her waist. Sam. Lisa smiled, stretching luxuriously as she remembered what had taken place between them the night before, and turned in his arms, meaning to kiss him awake.

"Lisa!"

The muffled summons, accompanied by an impatient knock on her bedroom door, brought her bolt upright. Beside her she could feel Sam stiffen suddenly, and she knew that he had heard it, too. Before she could answer, the door swung open. A handsome, moderately tall young man with a shock of tobacco-brown hair stood regarding them from the doorway, surprise plain on his face.

Lisa gaped at him, as surprised as he was, completely forgetting that she was naked and that, sitting up as she was, he had an excellent view of her bare body to the waist. Beside her, Sam levered himself into a sitting position against the pillows, thrusting the sheet into her hands and indicating that she should cover herself. Blushing, she did.

"Who the hell are you?" Sam growled at the intruder, looking menacing. Which was no small feat, Lisa thought hysterically, when one was caught naked in bed with another man's wife—by the other man!

"I'm Jeff Collins," her legal husband answered, crossing his arms over his chest and leaning negligently against the doorjamb. To Lisa's annoyance, she saw that he was starting to look amused. "You, I take it, are Eastman."

Sam's eyes narrowed. Before he could reply, Lisa hastily intervened.

"Did you want me for something, Jeff?" Which was a stupid question, she knew. Obviously he did, or he would not be standing in her bedroom door grinning at her.

"I brought you your Christmas present," he said, straightening and thrusting his hands into the pockets of his impeccably tailored tan slacks. "Sorry to be so early, but I thought you'd be up: you usually are, by this time. And I'm going out of town on business after lunch, so it was now or never."

"That's all right," Lisa said, feeling a fool as she clutched the sheet to her, miserably aware of Sam's hard eyes moving from her face to Jeff's. "You're right, I'm usually up. But this morning..." Her voice trailed off. It was glaringly obvious what had kept her in bed this morning. How could anyone possibly overlook six feet four inches of belligerent male?

"I can see that you got tied up this morning," Jeff said with admirable gravity, only the twinkle lurking in his eyes revealing that he was laughing at the predicament she was in. "I'm sorry I intruded. I never expected..." His voice trailed off, too, as he met Sam's distinctly unfriendly eyes.

"No, of course you didn't," Lisa prattled, hardly aware of what she was saying but knowing that she had to get Jeff out of there before Sam decided to react to the situation. "If you'd wait for me in the sitting room, I'll be right there. I just have to get something on." As soon as she said it, she felt herself blushing furiously again. Jeff grinned, saluted her mockingly, and turned away. As he walked down the hall toward the door that opened into her sitting room, he called back over his shoulder, "Oh, by the way, nice meeting you, Eastman."

Sam did not reply. Lisa clambered out of bed, retrieved her nightgown from where it had wound up on the floor nearby, and pulled it over her head with hands that were not quite steady. Then she went to close the bedroom door. Sam didn't miss a move she made.

"What the hell is he doing here?" he said with a growl as she picked up her robe from the chaise-longue and slipped her arms into the sleeves.

"You heard him: he came to give me my Christmas present." Lisa was as flustered as she had ever been in her life. Why, oh why, had she never told Sam the exact nature of her relationship with Jeff? From his deepening scowl, she knew she was going to have to do a lot of explaining before they recaptured the mood of the night before.

"Why the hell is he giving you a Christmas present?" Sam demanded harshly. "Doesn't the fool know you're divorcing him? Or did you 'forget' to tell him?"

"Of course he knows I'm divorcing him," Lisa

answered indignantly, her hands busy tying the belt of the gray satin robe. "But we're still friends. Oh, Sam, I'll explain it all to you in a few minutes. But first let me get rid of Jeff."

Sam looked at her, still frowning heavily. "All right," he conceded finally. "Go get rid of him. But if you're not back here inside ten minutes, I'll take great pleasure in getting rid of him myself."

Lisa was back in eight minutes exactly. Sam was seated on the edge of the bed, smoking a cigarette, the toweling robe he had worn the night before belted around his muscular waist. He looked up as she came in. His eyes were a hard, glittering cobalt.

"Well?" he drawled, when she had shut the door but hadn't immediately said anything.

Lisa sighed, then came to kneel in front of him, looking earnestly up into his stony face. In that position, she told him about Jeff.

He was silent for so long after she had finished that she began to get worried. His face told her nothing. It was totally expressionless.

"Sam?" she queried softly, when she could stand his silence no longer.

"So he's the only man you've ever slept with—besides me?" he asked ruminatively.

"Yes."

"No wonder you were hot as a firecracker," he said, his eyes bitter. "And to think I thought it was me! You would have been like that for any man: you didn't want me—you just wanted sex!"

Lisa stared up at him, barely able to believe what she was hearing.

"That's disgusting," she hissed, jumping to her feet and glaring at him furiously. "Sam, if all I wanted was sex, there have been dozens of men I could have slept with! They just didn't turn me on! You did—do—though God knows why! Do you think you're the only man who's ever tried to get me into bed? Don't be ridiculous! If all I wanted was sex, I could have had plenty!"

"You should have tried it," he said ironically. "You might have liked it."

Lisa had to control a strong impulse to slap his stubborn face until he saw stars.

"Do you realize how very insulting you're being?" she asked at last, her voice deliberately even. "What is between us is special, and it has been from the beginning, and you know it. Your problem is that you're afraid to trust me, afraid to trust what's happened to us, because you might get hurt! I never thought you were a coward, Sam!"

He didn't say anything to that, but he didn't much like it, Lisa could tell from the sudden narrowing of his eyes.

"What do you want me to do, Sam?" Her voice was softly provocative. "Prove to you that you're special? I could go out and sleep with another man—or two men, or six men—then come back and compare. Is that what you want?"

Sam's jaw tightened until white lines appeared around his mouth.

"I'd want to kill every one of them," he admitted, the taut lines around his mouth adding veracity to his words. "And then I'd probably start on you." His blue eyes gleamed at her. Lisa felt her anger begin to die.

"Then what do you suggest, Sam? I've told you I love you. What do you want me to do to prove it?"

He looked at her for a long moment, his eyes slowly losing that frightening glitter. Then he smiled at her, his mouth rueful, and Lisa knew with an overwhelming sense of relief that it was going to be all right.

"I guess I'll have to take your word for it," he said dryly. "It's too late now for anything else. You're mine, and I'll be damned if I'll give you a chance to change your mind. If you want sex, you'll have to make do with me."

Lisa glared at him, torn between anger and laughter. The latter won out.

"I'll force myself," she said with mock seriousness. "But you'd better not fall down on the job. Because if you do, you'll have to take the consequences!"

"No, you'll have to take the consequences," he said with a growl, reaching for her and pulling her down on his knee. "If I ever see you even look at another man, I'll paddle that luscious little bottom of yours until you can't sit for a year. And then I'll make love to you until you're so exhausted you can't look at anything but me."

"Threats, Sam?" Lisa murmured into his ear, where her tongue was making a teasing foray.

"No," he answered, bending her back over his arm and pressing his mouth to her satin-covered breast. "Promises."

It was past noon before they got downstairs that day.

In the week following, everything seemed fine between them—outwardly, at least. But Lisa, her love making her extrasensitive to Sam's moods, thought she detected a certain wariness in him that had not been there before, a tendency silently to question her motives where once he had been ready to accept her actions at face value. When he brought her to the point of crying out for his possession while they were making love, she could sense a kind of cynicism in him before he complied with a controlled savagery that he had never previously displayed. She suspected that he still harbored nagging doubts about the sincerity of her love for him, and she could have kicked herself for not having told him about Jeff from the beginning. The whole thing was silly in the extreme, she knew, and if she had not been so crazily in love with Sam she would have giggled endlessly at the idea that he thought she wanted him only for his body or his prowess in bed. Under the circumstances, however, she had never felt less like laughing. But she feared to bring the subject out into the open, feared that any overt action on her part might precipitate a confrontation that she could very conceivably lose. And if she lost Sam now, she thought, she would want to die. She loved him in a way she had never thought to love anyone.

Ever since the night he had come to her room, Lisa had spent her nights in his bed. She told herself it was simply to keep him from making that risky journey up the stairs again, but secretly she knew it was because she feared to give him too much time alone, time to decide he didn't want her enough to face all the difficulties that loving her entailed. She tried to be circumspect about her behavior, leaving him before anyone else was awake and creeping downstairs after they had all gone to bed, but she had the feeling that every member of the household from Amos to Jay to the most anonymous part-time housemaid knew that she and Sam were lovers. In that day and age, when women took lovers more easily than they bid a hand at bridge, it was ridiculous to feel uncomfortable about openly sleeping with a man to whom she was engaged, she knew. But knowing it and being able to help it were two different things.

She drove Sam to Saint Mary's every afternoon for the physical therapy that had made it necessary for him to stay near the hospital in the first place. Without it, Dr. Peters had warned, he might never recover complete use of his leg. Sam told her that he would be quite happy to have Jay drive him in, or even Henry Dobson; there was no need for her to make the trip each day, then hang about for two hours while he did the repetitious exercises that had been set for him. To this, Lisa replied that she was happy to do it, and that was the absolute truth. She valued every minute with Sam as a chance to reinforce the love he felt for her; she wanted him to need her as she knew she needed him. Only then would she feel secure in his love. As it was, she had the horrible suspicion that she stood to lose more in their relationship than he did, and the idea scared hell out of her.

Every New Year's Eve since Lisa could remember—excepting only the one sixteen years ago, which had fallen a mere three days after her parents had been killed in a car crash—Amos had held a huge party in the ballroom that took up the entire second floor of the main wing of the house. Lisa had always handled most of the planning and acted as her grandfather's hostess. Her marriage to Jeff had not interfered with this arrangement since they had lived less than five miles away, but she had missed the previous year because she had still been sunk in despair over Jennifer's death. But Amos had taken it for granted that this year Lisa would take up the reins of the party again, and Lisa saw no reason to decline. In fact, she had always enjoyed doing it. Amos used the occasion to observe the people who managed his companies in a less formal setting than that provided by most of his offices, and more than once he had launched the career of a young politician in whom he believed by introducing him to moneyed influentials. There was always an interesting mix of guests and usually several unexpected happenings. Most people, Lisa included, enjoyed themselves tremendously.

Sam was not overenthusiastic about the party, especially when Lisa told him that he would be expected to wear a tuxedo, but he agreed to come and be introduced to her friends, relatives, and acquaintances. Jay opted for a pizza and a football game instead. Lisa had the feeling that Sam's inclination was to join his son, but out of deference to her feelings he didn't say so. For which she was glad. She was dying to show him off. She had a feeling that dressed in a tuxedo he would be spectacular.

On the night of the party, Lisa made one last check on the arrangements, then turned everything over to Mary Dobson's capable hands. She would supervise the food and drinks, while Lisa, as hostess, concentrated on putting everyone at ease and making sure that no one was left without someone to talk to. The band that had been hired for the evening was already warming up by the time she hurried to her room to dress, and, looking out a front window, she saw the caterer's van arrive. She was late, she realized, and would have to make haste getting dressed.

She opted for a shower instead of a bath, lingering under the lukewarm spray just long enough to soap and rinse her body. After toweling herself dry, she applied afterbath powder and then perfume in her favorite scent before shrugging into a light robe. Doing her makeup took less than ten minutes; she kept it light, using a variation of the look she used for day, the only difference being the silvery-green powder she dusted over her eyelids and the faint gold shimmer she applied to her cheeks and lips on top of the warm dusky rose color she ordinarily used. A flick of black mascara, a whisk of transparent powder, and she was finished.

Although Lisa knew that most of the women who would be coming to the party had spent the afternoon at the hairdressers', having elaborate coiffures created for them by experts, she had chosen to arrange her hair herself, in the interests of saving time. The style she had selected to wear was deceptively simple: a chignon secured at the nape by a diamond clasp that allowed enticing tendrils of silvery-blond hair to escape and curl around her face.

Her dress was an unrelieved black silk-jersey sheath with an overlay of smoky chiffon pleats shot through with glimmering touches of silver. It descended from one shoulder, where it was secured with a diamond brooch, in a dark cloud to the floor, whispering around her feet and shimmering with every movement. Looking at her reflection in the mirror, Lisa knew that the garment suited her perfectly, enhancing her slenderness to the point of fragility and providing a startling contrast with the creamy paleness of her skin. Pear-shaped diamond eardrops and Sam's ring were her only jewelry. Her eyes, wide with excitement and slightly tip-tilted above exquisitely molded cheekbones, and the matching emerald on her hand provided her only touches of color.

When she was satisfied with her appearance, she walked downstairs to find Sam, careful not to trip in the high-heeled silver sandals that added three inches to her height. She was afraid that Sam might have found the attractions of the football game too much to resist and she might have to prod him into getting dressed. But she need not have worried. When she walked into the sitting room adjoining his bedroom, he was, it was true, watching the football game with Jay. But while Jay, dressed casually in jeans and a sweater, sprawled on the couch, Sam stood beside it, fully dressed except for his tie, which hung loose around his neck. They were both so caught up in what was happening on the screen that they didn't hear her come in, and Lisa had a few minutes' leisure to study Sam. He looked, as she had suspected he would, spectacular. In the severe black coat and pants and pleated white shirt of his formal clothes, he exuded raw male attraction. Against the starkness of his clothes, his skin looked very bronzed, and his harshly carved features had an appeal that made the word *handsome* seem inadequate. His hair had been neatly brushed, for once, but the curl had apparently been impossible to subdue entirely; it framed his head like rippling black sable to curl over the collar of his shirt in back. His height and powerful physique gave him an aura of power that was in no way lessened by the white cast revealed by a slit in the satin stripe of the pants, or the crutches he needed to stay on his feet. He looked superb, every hard male inch of him. Just the sight of him sent a surge of heat through Lisa so intense that she thought her bones might be melting.

"Did you see that block?" Jay demanded excitedly of Sam, half-turning on the couch as he did so. Immediately he caught sight of Lisa. "Oh, hi, Lisa," he added. Then his eyes widened as they swept over her. "Boy, you look great!"

"Thank you." Lisa was laughing as Sam turned to look at her, a sheepish smile on his face.

"I just thought I'd watch for a minute," he explained guiltily. "Am I late?"

Lisa shook her head. "I came down early to see if I could help you with anything. Like tying your tie."

Sam grinned. "You must be a mind reader. I decided a few minutes ago that it is impossible for a man on crutches to tie his own tie. I thought I was going to have to ask Jay, but I don't know how good he is at things like that. He's just barely past the stage of learning to tie his shoelaces."

"Ha ha," came the response from the couch. Sam and Lisa both grinned at Jay, who was once again absorbed in the football game.

Sam turned his back on the television and hobbled toward Lisa. As he approached, his eyes swept her from head to toe. As Jay's had earlier, they widened appreciatively.

"Wow!" He grinned, stopping in front of her, his wide shoulders blocking her view of the rest of the room. "The kid's right, for once: you do look great." Jay, caught up in the action on the screen, merely grunted scornfully in reaction to that dig. Lisa giggled as Sam added for her ears alone, "Good enough to eat."

"Thank you." She smiled up at him, her rosy nails tracing a teasing path up the pleats at the front of his shirt. "So do you."

Sam gave her an exaggerated leer. "Remind me to remind you of that later," he murmured wickedly.

Lisa twinkled up at him. "You won't have to remind me," she promised, her voice a tantalizing whisper.

Sam grinned and bent to kiss her, his mouth hard against her own. Lisa, breathing in the faint, tangy scent of aftershave, felt her stomach muscles tighten.

Her hand slid around behind his strong neck, her nails digging into the sinews there.

"I hope you guys aren't going to be mushy like this all the time." Jay's disgusted voice broke apart what had promised to become a fairly heated exchange. Sam grinned ruefully down at her as Lisa reluctantly pulled her mouth away from his.

"Isn't it past your bedtime?" Sam threw with mock irritation over his shoulder at Jay. The boy didn't even bother to honor this piece of heresy with a reply.

"Let me tie your tie." Lisa's lips were twitching at this banter between father and son. Their relationship warmed her to her toes. They loved each other with a slightly embarrassed, seldom expressed love that was totally masculine and outside anything she had ever experienced.

Sam smiled warmly down at her while she dealt efficiently with his tie, arranging it into a neat bow at his neck. This was a service she had performed many times for Amos, whose fingers were stiffened from a mild form of arthritis, and occasionally, in the early days of their marriage, for Jeff. Which last piece of information she had no intention of divulging to Sam. She suspected that he could, if provoked, be a very jealous lover indeed.

"There." She patted the side of his cheek when she had finished, loving the feel of the slightly rough texture of his jaw against the soft skin of her fingers. He caught her hand, holding it against his face while he pressed an intimate little kiss into her palm.

"Thank you," he said huskily. Lisa felt her breath stop momentarily at something in those blue eyes. If ever a man's heart could be said to have shown in his eyes, Sam's did then. Lisa smiled up at him mistily.

"Are you two going to stand there staring at each other all night?" Jay demanded, sounding disgusted again. Sam lowered Lisa's hand from his mouth while still retaining his grip on it.

"Watch yourself, pal, or I'll sell you to the next Arab who offers," Sam warned over his shoulder. Jay hooted. Lisa, laughing, pulled Sam from the room.

The party was a great success, as Lisa had known it would be. She circulated from group to group, keeping Sam at her side as much as possible so that he wouldn't feel too lost in a gathering where he knew only her and Amos. She was pleased with the impression he made on the male and female guests alike. The men seemed to respond instinctively to his natural air of authority, bred, she supposed, from his years in the military, while the women positively drooled over the long hard body in the elegant evening clothes. She was conscious of being on the receiving end of more than one distinctly envious look from other females who would have given their all if Sam had so much as crooked his little finger. And, being human, she enjoyed it immensely. To his credit, Sam appeared oblivious to the very obvious attempts of some of the women guests to attract his interest. The most they ever got from him in response was a polite smile.

To those who asked after Jeff's whereabouts, Lisa briefly said that he was out of town on business. She did not feel that so large a gathering was the place to announce that she and Jeff were getting a divorce, or that she was planning to marry the man at her side. She introduced Sam by his name only, feeling that no explanation of the exact nature of their relationship was called for. Speculation was rife among the female guests particularly, she knew, but she had no intention of satisfying their curiosity, and so far none of them had quite gotten up the nerve to ask her outright who Sam was.

At exactly one hour before midnight, the dancing started. Lisa, with an apologetic little murmur to Sam, left him sitting in a chair talking to another gentleman who could not or would not dance and went to do her duty as hostess. As she whirled about the room in the arms of one man after another (Amos refused to have disco played or danced at his parties, so the dances were mainly waltzes and fox-trots), Lisa could feel Sam's eyes on her. When she glanced over at him after freeing herself from one man who had imbibed too much champagne and had, in consequence, held her far too closely and with too much obvious enjoyment, she was amused to see his eyes narrowed and a faintly grim set to his hard mouth. She flashed a twinkling, naughty smile at him, to which, after a moment, he reluctantly responded. But all the same, it gave her a little thrill to realize that he felt so possessive about her. The notion was strangely appealing, chauvinistic or not.

After the next dance, she resolved to go sit with Sam for a while and perhaps explore the fascinating possibility of his feeling jealous. After he admitted it, which she imagined might take some doing, she would assure him that he was by far the most attractive man in the room, and possibly set about proving it. Which could get extremely enjoyable, she thought, with another of those naughty smiles.

"Lisa, darling, you look like the cat who's been in the cream," a slightly nasal female voice purred from behind her.

Lisa turned, smiling, to see Elise Sutton, a slender bottle blonde of about thirty who wore a red dress slit to her navel, too much makeup, and was in the process of divorcing her fourth husband. Lisa had known Elise for years, since they had both competed for Jeff. Lisa recognized the feline expression on the other woman's face from experience. It said that Lisa once again had her claws into a man Elise fancied.

"Maybe I have," she parried with a mocking tilt of her head.

"I'd say, definitely." Elise was smiling that charming, social smile she always assumed when talking with other women and which was as false as the color of her hair. "That's some toy you got for Christmas. Mind telling me where you found him? He looks to be just my type."

Lisa smiled as falsely as Elise. "On the very highest shelf in the toy store," she answered solemnly. "And, sorry, Elise, but he was the only one of that kind there."

Elise shrugged, the movement elegant. "Oh, well, then you'll just have to let me know when you get tired of playing with him. I'd like to play with him awhile myself."

Lisa's smile came again. "Oh, I'll certainly let you know when I get tired of him," Lisa promised mendaciously, thinking: Too bad you won't be holding your breath, you cat.

Elise smiled again, but this time it had a teasing, taunting quality and was directed at a point directly above and beyond Lisa's head.

"I knew you would. After all, we always shared our—toys—didn't we, darling?" she purred. Then, casting another of those provocative smiles over Lisa's head, she drifted away.

Lisa already had a sinking suspicion that amounted to a certainty about whom Elise had been smiling at so seductively. Turning, she saw that her suspicion was right.

"Making plans to pass me on to your friends already, Lisa?" Sam's mouth was smiling, but his eyes had a hard, icy gleam to them that frightened her. "You should have told me I was starting to bore you: I'm sure I could have come up with a few more new tricks. After all, it would be a shame if your Christmas toy didn't even last past New Year's, wouldn't it?"

"Oh, Sam, don't be silly," Lisa murmured miserably. "You must know it was just—just party talk. I didn't mean it—and neither, probably, did Elise."

"I don't like being the subject of 'party talk,'" Sam bit off, still smiling that frightening smile. "In fact, I don't much like this party. If you'll excuse me, I think I'll take my leave." He made a mocking little bow that underlined the ironic politeness of his last words.

"Sam!" Lisa practically wailed as he swung away from her. Her voice attracted several speculative looks from the people standing around them, and Lisa bit her lip as she hurried after Sam, who was already more than halfway across the room.

She caught up to him on the stairs, which he usually took with extreme care. This time he was paying scant heed to his crutches, swinging down the steps two at a time with apparent disregard for the ease with which he could break his neck.

"Sam!" Lisa hurried down the stairs after him, horrified at the hard recklessness of his actions. "For goodness' sake, be careful!"

Sam maneuvered down the rest of the stairs without more than a glittering glance at her as she hovered helplessly beside him, her hands outstretched in a futile gesture to catch him if he should start to fall. Which she had about as much hope of doing as a butterfly had of toppling Mount Rushmore, she thought.

"What's the matter, Lisa?" he taunted when he reached the bottom of the steps, barely pausing before swinging along the entrance hall toward the door leading to the right wing. "Afraid your toy might get broken before you've quite finished playing with it?"

"Oh, Sam, you're being ridiculous!" Lisa was hurrying along beside him, practically having to run to keep up. "Would you please stop and listen to me for a minute? It was only a joke!"

"I don't like being the butt of your jokes." He did stop, abruptly, but Lisa knew that it was not because she had asked him to. His voice was vicious as he stood glaring at her, towering head and shoulders above her, leaning slightly toward her as he balanced on his crutches. They were still in the entrance hall, where anybody coming down the stairs or from the kitchen could have overheard what they were saying. At the moment, Lisa didn't particularly care. "I don't like being called a toy, either," Sam added, snarling.

"You're deliberately misunderstanding a perfectly innocent conversation!" Lisa snapped, beginning to get angry in her turn. "That's just the way Elise always talks about men. I think she thinks she's being sophisticated."

"I'm not deliberately misunderstanding anything," Sam said gratingly. "I watched you tonight, playing with every man in the room, leading them on, playing with me! And I think your friend hit the nail on the head. That's exactly what I am to you: a toy to be played with until you get tired of playing, then thrown into a corner somewhere while you go looking for a new one! Well, I don't like being used that way, my little rich-bitch darling. And I won't be! You can go buy yourself a new stud, honey, because I just quit playing!"

Lisa gasped in outrage at his insults. Before she thought, her hand came up to make stinging contact with his hard cheek. He sucked in his breath sharply, his hand flying to cover the spot that was rapidly beginning to suffuse with blood. The rest of his face was white with rage, while those blue eyes glittered furiously down at her.

"How dare you talk that way to me!" she said, hissing, her eyes as angry as his. "Who the bloody hell do you think you are, anyway? I don't have to put up with this kind of abuse from you! We're not married yet, you know!"

"No, we're not, are we?" he said slowly, his eyes dueling with hers. "Thank God for small mercies!"

Lisa's temper hit the flash point at that.

"If you feel that way about it, you swine, you can take your damned ring and stuff it!" she shouted, pulling at the offending piece of jewelry until it slid off her finger, then flinging it at his face. He put up a hand to catch it automatically, but his crutches impeded him and it struck his hard cheekbone, the stone catching in his flesh and tearing it slightly so that a little drop of bright red blood welled up. "I wouldn't marry you now if you got down on your knees and begged me!"

"That's just the way I feel myself," he said, turning on his heel and swinging away. He made no move to retrieve the ring; it lay on the floor, the stones flashing green and white under the light from the chandelier. Lisa stared from it to the door that was already slamming behind Sam. As she stood there unmoving, her eyes as bright as the discarded emerald in her pale face, horns began to blow in the ballroom above, and dozens of excited voices yelled at once, "Happy New Year!"

XVII

Bʏ the time Lisa got up the next morning, both Sam and Jay were gone. Mary told her stolidly that Major Eastman had phoned for a cab to take them to the airport soon after six o'clock. It was now after nine. Lisa, absorbing Mary's words slowly, felt almost sick to her stomach as the awful truth sank in. Sam wasn't going to treat this as a lovers' quarrel. He had actually accepted her hasty words of the night before and considered their engagement broken. He wasn't going to marry her—not even if she got down on her knees and begged! Remembering the words she had flung at him the night before, Lisa shuddered. To a man as proud as Sam, they must have stung like blows from a whip. How could she have said such a thing? When Mary expressionlessly handed her the emerald ring that she had thrown so furiously at Sam, saying that she had found it on the floor when she was sweeping up after the party, Lisa felt the hard knot of pain that was cramping her stomach begin to dissolve. She barely managed to make it to the privacy of her bedroom before bursting into tears.

By the time she had cried herself out, Lisa's emotions began to change. For one thing, she had recalled the very nasty things that Sam had said to her the night before, and the unreasonable way he had refused to listen to any explanation of what was really a perfectly innocuous conversation. She was certainly not the only one at fault in their quarrel; he owed her an apology every bit as much as, and perhaps more than, she owed him one! And he could just be the one to eat humble pie for a change! She was sure that when his temper cooled and he had time to reflect on the things he had said to her, he would realize that he had goaded her into breaking their engagement and would beg her pardon like the imminently fair man she knew him to be. In the meantime, there was no point in upsetting herself. Sam would soon realize the absurdity of the situation and come back to her. Of course he would!

Amos, when she confided this belief to him, seemed unconvinced. At first Lisa told him merely that she and Sam had quarreled, without going into details, but the habit of relying on her grandfather's advice was too strong to break. Hesitantly at first, and then with words tumbling out of her mouth one over another like a waterfall, she told him the whole miserable story, not leaving out even Sam's touchiness on the subject of her wealth and his lack of it.

"I guessed that was the problem," Amos said when Lisa confessed this last. "I could tell he didn't like the whole setup here. I don't blame him. I wouldn't like it myself, if I were in his shoes."

"But that's silly!" Lisa protested, chewing on her lip as she stared across the study at Amos. "I don't care that he isn't rich. So why should he make such a big deal out of it?"

"Because he's a man, and he's got a man's pride," Amos said bluntly. "I'd feel the same way myself. A man wants to provide for his woman, to give her things, to spoil her a little. There's nothing he can give you that you haven't already got, and probably a lot better than he can provide. He knows it—and it bothers him. Only natural."

"Not to me," Lisa muttered resentfully, sinking deeper into the comfortable armchair and looking pensively into the fire that blazed and crackled on the hearth. Then, rousing herself from her reverie, Lisa asked, "What would you do if you were me?"

"You want him back?" Amos sent her a piercing look. Lisa nodded miserably.

"Then go after him, girl. That's what you need to do. It won't be hard to find out where he's gone: I'll have somebody at the office get right on it."

Lisa thought about this for a moment, then slowly shook her head. "No, I refuse to go running after him like some lovesick teenager. He's the one who started the whole thing—let him be the one to apologize!"

Amos sighed. "It's your decision, granddaughter, but I think you're making a mistake. However, if that's the way you want it, so be it. Only, I don't think you ought to count on him running back here like a mongrel dog with its tail between its legs. If I'm any judge of men, he won't do it."

Amos, as usual, was right. Lisa waited for almost a month, hoping every day that Sam would appear on the doorstep, properly penitent, or at the very least call. As weeks passed—weeks when she did nothing but hang around the house waiting for the phone to ring—she stopped caring whether he was properly penitent. All he had to do was get in touch, and she'd take his apology as read. But he didn't. Finally, toward the end of January, Lisa was gradually brought to the realization that if she wanted Sam she would have to go to him. Swallowing her pride took some doing, but she finally managed it. Then she went to Amos and asked him if he could have someone discover where Sam and Jay had gone. Amos, it seemed, had anticipated her request by some days. He had the answer almost as soon as the question was out of her mouth. Jay was back in school, he said; Sam was in Montana, living out at some ranch he was in the process of buying.

"The Circle C," Lisa said, remembering.

Amos, looking at her compassionately, nodded. "It's just outside of Anaconda. Your best bet would be to fly to Butte and then rent a car. I'll call the airport and have a plane readied. When did you want to go?"

Lisa's every instinct urged her to say "now." Now that she had decided to go to Sam, she was dying to see him. She couldn't wait. How would he look, she wondered, when she appeared? What would he say? She imagined him sweeping her into his arms and kissing her, and her knees went weak at the idea.

"Tomorrow morning," she said, knowing that it would take time to pack. If all went well, she might not be coming back. She should take enough for at least a week. In that length of time, Amos could have the rest of her things packed and sent on to her.

"I'll make the arrangements," Amos said, and Lisa smiled gratefully at him, then turned to leave the room, eager to get started on her packing.

Amos's voice halted her with her hand on the doorknob. "If you think you'll need moral support, I'll be glad to come with you," he offered gruffly.

Lisa, knowing that he disliked flying and that his arthritis had been acting up again, was touched to the heart. She turned to look at him. He was regarding her anxiously.

"It would probably work out better if I went alone," she said softly. "But, Amos—thank you."

He nodded at her jerkily. Lisa blew him a quick kiss and left the room.

It was nearly four the following afternoon when the small jet belonging to one of Amos's many companies landed in Butte.

"Do you want us to wait, Mrs. Collins?" the pilot asked, coming back to speak with her after the plane had rolled to a stop outside the terminal.

Lisa shook her head. "No, thanks. That won't be necessary."

The pilot nodded. "Okay. We'll be taking off again as soon as we've chowed down. Have a pleasant stay," he added as the door opened and the steward let down the steps.

"Thank you," Lisa replied, smiling sunnily at him, and allowed herself to be assisted off the plane.

She hired a cab to take her the rest of the way, a distance of about fifty miles. There was no point in renting a car, she thought, and then having to worry about returning it. Settling back in the rather grubby rear seat, she looked out the window at the passing scenery. Excitedly, she realized that she was getting her first glimpse of the state that would be her new home.

Her first impression was that it was very cold. Snow lay everywhere, covering the ground in deep swirls that looked like vanilla icing. The wind blew steadily, shifting across the surface of the snow, bending the branches of the tall pines that were sprinkled thickly across the landscape, whistling in through gaps around the cab's windows. The sky was dark gray, heavy with clouds. More snow had been forecast for later in the day, the driver told her. Might even be a blizzard. They got a lot of those, this time of year. Tall mountain peaks rose all around to disappear into the clouds. Looking at them, Lisa remembered that Anaconda was located in the middle of the Rocky Mountains. The sheer majesty of the land had her marveling. It had a dark, frozen kind of grandeur, and she found it beautiful.

The Circle C was located some distance from the main highway, down a little two-lane road that seemed to get narrower and narrower the farther they went. At last the driver pulled off onto what seemed to be a dirt driveway. Covered with deep drifts of snow, as it was, it was hard to be certain.

"House is about a half-mile up that way," the driver said laconically, pointing. "If you want to get up there, you'll have to walk. Car can't go no further. Take my advice, and I'll take you back to town."

Lisa looked from the driver's seamed face to the snow-covered land. Half a mile didn't sound like much, but on foot, in such deep snow, as cold as it was? It would be hard going. But she hadn't come all this way to turn back now. If walking was the only way to get to Sam, then walk she would.

"Are you sure it's only half a mile?" she queried, wanting to be absolutely certain that she wasn't going to be left stranded in the middle of nowhere if she got out of the car.

"Yup," the man answered. "Can't miss it—just follow the driveway. Don't know why he hasn't shoveled out. Most folks do."

"Then I'll walk," Lisa decided. "How much do I owe you?"

He told her, and she paid him. Then he lifted her suitcase out of the trunk and set it down in the snow, which came halfway up its sides.

"If I were you, young lady, I'd leave this here bag right where it is. Let your friend up there come fetch it later. He's a big healthy feller—I've seen him once or twice in town. I'm sure he'll be glad to get it for you."

Lisa nodded, thanking the man for his trouble, and decided to take his advice about the suitcase. She didn't really have much choice: there was no way she could lug that heavy piece of luggage up a half a mile of snow-covered driveway.

The driver sat and watched her until she crested a hill and was out of sight. Lisa, plodding through the snow, which came almost to her knees, felt reassured by his stolid presence. When at last she heard him put the cab into gear and drive slowly away, she felt almost bereft.

It was bitterly cold, as she had noted before, maybe ten degrees below zero. Lisa was dressed in skin-tight jeans, a red turtleneck lambswool sweater, a pair of high-heeled cowboy boots, and a thigh-length, charcoal gray persian lamb coat with a deep hood. Except for the coat, which was toasty warm, it was not exactly ideal gear for a half-mile hike in such weather. But when she had donned it that morning, her only intent had been to impress Sam with how at home she looked on his ranch. And blue jeans, she had decided, were just what was needed.

She saw the house from some distance. It was a long, low, white clapboard structure. At least, it used to be white. The paint had peeled and weathered until it was more of a dirty gray. A barn and various outbuildings stood some little distance from the house. Lisa, looking at the ranch that would be her home for perhaps the rest of her life, felt a little taken aback at its shabbiness. But then she thought of Sam and her spirits revived. After all, the house could be fixed up—it would be fun. And if she had to, to have

Sam, she would live in a hole in the ground and like it.

By the time she reached the edge of the yard, her face was stiff with cold and her eyes were watering from the wind. Her feet were twin blocks of ice, and her legs, with only the jeans to protect them, had gone numb. Her hands, thrust deep in the pockets of her coat, were faintly blue at the tips.

There was a light on in the house. Lisa stared at it, thinking of the warmth that must lie inside—with Sam. If her legs hadn't been so frozen, she would have run to it, and him.

Even as she looked at the house, the front door opened and a man's tall body was silhouetted against the light streaming out from behind it.

"Sam!" she tried to call out joyfully, but what emerged was more in the nature of a strangled croak. No matter. He was here, and as soon as he recognized her he would come striding out into the snow and sweep her up into his arms.

She was right—at least to a point. He did come striding out into the snow to meet her. But when he got close enough that she could see him properly, she had no difficulty interpreting what was stamped all over that lean, hard face: it was annoyance, pure and simple.

"What the hell are you doing here?" he bit out, his eyes distinctly hostile as they met hers. Then, seeing how her teeth chattered, his face altered slightly. "Damn fool woman," he muttered, peering sharply into her cold-pinched face. "Don't you have any sense at all? Where did you walk from, the end of the driveway? What if you had gotten lost, somehow missed the house? You could have frozen to death in a couple of hours, as cold as it is tonight! Since I didn't know you were coming, I certainly wouldn't have looked for you!"

"Sam..." Lisa began, mumbling through lips that were stiff with cold. He uttered a terse profanity and picked her up in his arms. As she felt herself being lifted high against his muscular chest, which was protected from the elements only by the thickness of a flannel shirt, she snuggled closer, her arms sliding around his neck. This was more like the greeting she had been expecting!

He carried her through the yard, up the rickety steps, and into the house, kicking the door shut behind them. Lisa was aware of a blessed sensation of warmth and light as he carried her down an uncarpeted hallway, past several opened doors, to the kitchen at the rear of the house. In a lightning-fast glance from the safety of Sam's shoulder, she saw that the kitchen looked even shabbier than the outside of the house. Grubby red-and-white linoleum squares covered the floor, clashing hideously with the green-painted cabinets. Rusty-looking metal that had once been white formed the countertop surrounding the single, stained sink. An old white gas stove and refrigerator were pushed against the wall at right angles to each other. A fluorescent light glaringly illuminated every shortcoming.

"Not quite up to your standards, I know, but better than freezing to death," Sam said, not missing the fleeting expression of surprise that widened Lisa's eyes. He plopped her down with scant ceremony into a vinyl kitchen chair that he had drawn up with his foot to a wood-burning stove. Lisa realized that this was the source of the delicious heat.

"It's very—nice," Lisa said lamely, then wished she had just not replied when Sam's mouth tightened.

"Sam..." she began, hurriedly trying to retrieve her position, but he brusquely interrupted her.

"Get those wet boots off—and the jeans, too, they're soaked to the knee."

After issuing that curt order, Sam swung on his heel and left the room. When he returned minutes later, Lisa had managed to shed her coat and tug off one wet boot. Seeing her progress—or lack of it—he gave a disgusted grunt, dropping to one knee on the floor in front of her and pulling off her remaining boot. Then he reached up for the zip of her jeans, his actions as impersonal as if he were preparing to peel an onion.

"Stand up."

Lisa obediently stood, her toes curling against the cold linoleum as he slid her jeans down over her hips and told her to step out. It was as he was doing the same to her pantyhose—which he accorded one half-fascinated and half-scornful look—that Lisa registered what was different about him.

"Your cast!" She gasped, staring down at the jean-clad leg that looked to be as good as new.

He finished peeling off her pantyhose and stood up, towering over her, seemingly oblivious to the fact that she was clad only in a sweater and a pair of silky white bikini panties, her long legs left bare.

"They took it off last week," he said indifferently, turning to scoop from the kitchen table some items of clothing that he had brought back into the room with him earlier. "Here, put these on. They don't have designer labels, but at least they'll keep you warm."

"That's unfair and you know it." Lisa took the garments—which were a pair of athletic socks and the bottom half of a set of men's longjohns—from him. She suspected that he had selected such unglamorous things for the sole purpose of annoying her. Well, she would wear them and be glad to do it. And show him a thing or two in the process!

"Is it?" He turned away and busied himself at the stove as she stepped into the longjohns, then sat to pull on the socks. By the time Lisa was dressed, he was pouring some sort of liquid from a battered-looking aluminum sauce pan into two mugs.

"Hot chocolate?" He turned, proffering one of the mugs. Lisa took it, cradling the warmth gratefully, sipping at the rich sweetness. She was still seated in front of the wood-burning stove; he stood a few feet away, looking down at her broodingly.

"Now," he said briskly after she had drunk about half of her chocolate. "Suppose you tell me what the hell you're doing here."

Lisa cast him a sideways glance. Clearly, he did not intend to make this easy for her.

"You don't sound as if you're very glad to see me," she murmured provocatively.

"I'm not."

The blunt words took Lisa aback. She stared at him, affronted. Her lips tightened. So he was going to demand every ounce of his pound of flesh, was he?

"I didn't mean what I said to you that night," she said, her eyes meeting his with a coaxing smile in their green depths. "I lost my temper—as I know you did. I'm sorry, Sam. Will you forgive me?"

Once the words were out, she breathed easier. That hadn't been so bad....

"Of course," he said, as she had known he would.

A brilliant smile curved her lips; she set her half-empty mug on the floor and jumped up, practically throwing herself into his arms, her own arms closing around his neck as she hugged him ecstatically.

"Whoa, there." He set down his mug on the table and reached up to untangle her arms from about his neck, holding her a little away from him.

Lisa looked up at him, her puzzled gaze revealing her confusion. "What's wrong?"

His mouth twisted wryly as he looked down at her. His hands were tight around her forearms.

"I think you may have jumped the gun a little bit here. All I said was that I accepted your apology."

"So?"

"So that's all I meant."

Lisa began to get some inkling of what he was trying to say. She stiffened, her eyes beginning to spark.

"You swine, you're really going to rub my nose in it, aren't you?" she snapped. "What do you want, to see me beg? All right, I'm begging. Are you satisfied?"

"No."

Lisa practically stamped her foot as she glared at him. "What else do you want? I've gone as far as I'm going to go. If you want to marry me..."

"I don't."

"What?" Lisa stared at him, incredulous. She couldn't believe her ears.

"It wouldn't work."

"What!" She practically shrieked the word at him.

"You heard me." His face was implacable. "It wouldn't work. And if you weren't such a spoiled little brat, always used to grabbing for what you want without thinking about the cost, you'd know it. Oh, you'd enjoy being my wife—for about six months. Then you'd start wanting things I can't give you, start wishing for Granddaddy's mansion and servants and clothes and fancy cars, start feeling bored stuck out here on a rundown ranch in the middle of nowhere,

with no shops and no restaurants and no parties—
and you'd realize you'd made a mistake."

"I would not!" Lisa protested vehemently, staring
at him. He meant what he was saying, she could tell.
He wasn't just trying to give her a hard time. A cold
little fear snaked up her spine. "Sam, I would not!"

"You would." He was inexorable. His fingers were
still clenched tightly around her forearms, and those
blue eyes seemed to bore into hers. "Be honest with
yourself for once in your life, Lisa, and admit it. This
just isn't your scene."

"It is!" she cried, but he ignored her, continuing
with the words that were stabbing her to the heart.

"I saw your face when I carried you in here. You
were appalled. And you're right. This isn't much—
but it's my home. You would have to live here—and
you wouldn't like it."

"I would!"

"For God's sake, Lisa, use your head for once!" His
patience was fraying about the edges, she could tell.
"If you married me, you'd be a rancher's wife—and
not a rich one. You'd have to cook all the meals—and
from what I've sampled, you're one of the world's
worst cooks—"

"I could learn!"

"... And clean the house, and wash the dishes—
there's not even a dishwasher, and somehow I can't
picture you up to your elbows in suds."

"You could buy a dishwasher, couldn't you?" He
was being so unreasonable, she couldn't believe it.
She knew that they could work all these things out, if
he would just give them a chance.

"Maybe—in a year or so. Right now, all my money
is tied up in land—and stock."

"I have money...." As soon as she said it, she knew

she'd made a mistake. His eyes narrowed, and his mouth tightened into a hard, straight line.

"That's what you had in mind, wasn't it?" he asked, his voice deceptively cool. "To use your money to buy yourself the luxuries you wouldn't be able to afford as my wife. Well, as I believe I told you once before, no way. My wife lives on what I can give her."

"All right," Lisa said desperately. "I wouldn't mind, honestly, Sam. If you would only give me a chance...."

"No."

"But I love you!" Lisa practically wailed.

"You love what I do to your body," he said brutally. "That's all there is between us, baby: good sex!"

"That's not true and you know it!"

"It is true. When you get a little more experience, you'll realize it."

"I love you...."

"You think you love me," he corrected.

"I want to marry you!" Lisa glared at him.

He met her look with an odd little glitter in his eyes. "Well, now, that's too bad," he drawled after a moment. "Because I don't want to marry you!"

Heartbreak and outrage combined to make Lisa fighting mad. She gave an infuriated little cry and reached for the nearest object, which happened to be his discarded mug. Her fingers clenched around the smooth round shape, and she hurled it at his head. The remnants of the hot chocolate sprayed out over the room. Sam ducked, and the mug whistled harmlessly past him to shatter against the far wall. Furiously she reached for something else to throw, but he was too quick for her. Even as her fingers closed over a saucer that was left on the table apparently from his supper, he was beside her, catching her hands in his, pulling her away from the table to stand in the middle of the floor while he kept a tight grip on her wrists.

"Temper tantrums won't make me change my mind, Lisa," he said quietly, his eyes burning down into hers.

Lisa glared up at him, helpless to inflict any damage on him with her hands imprisoned so tightly in his.

"Let me go!" she demanded, temper, hurt pride, and pain at his rejection making her quiver from head to toe.

"Not until you calm down," he said, watching her as if she were a specimen under a microscope.

"I'm calm. Now let me go!"

Slowly he released his grip on her wrists, keeping an eagle eye on her in case she decided suddenly to reach for another weapon. They studied each other in silence for a long moment; Lisa's breasts were heaving and her cheeks were flushed with the force of her emotions, but Sam looked maddeningly unruffled. And maddeningly attractive. If she hadn't been so furious with him that she could cheerfully have buried a knife in his ribs, she would have wanted to throw herself into his arms!

"Sam..." She simply was not going to allow him to pitch her out of his life in this insane fashion. There had to be a way to make him see sense. If she could just keep her temper, and find a way to sneak past his guard...

"How did you get here?" he asked abruptly.

Taken off balance, Lisa had to think for a moment before she answered.

"I hired a cab from Butte. Oh, Sam, my suitcase is still down at the end of your driveway. Could you...?"

"I suppose you flew into Butte on one of Amos's

convenient little private jets?" There was the barest suggestion of a sneer in his voice.

"Yes, I did," Lisa admitted defiantly. "Sam, about my suitcase . . ."

"You won't need it. I'm taking you back to Butte tonight. In the morning, you can get on your ritzy little airplane and fly away."

"You can't take me back to Butte!" Her cry was instinctive. Her last hope of changing his mind involved staying the night. "Your driveway's not shoveled," she added lamely, unable to think of a stronger clincher.

His look showed his contempt. "I have a Land Rover," he said dryly. "So that won't even slow us down. Put your clothes back on while I go get it out."

Even before he had finished speaking he was turning away, heading out the kitchen and down through that narrow hallway toward the door. Lisa trailed unhappily behind him, trying to think of some way to delay what she was rapidly coming to realize was the inevitable. Then, as he pulled open the door, a slow smile spread across her face. All was not yet lost, she thought smugly.

"It's snowing," she pointed out, as Sam just stood there staring out at the billowing curtain of white. Sam cast her a hard look over his shoulder, then reluctantly turned away from the door, closing it again. As determined as he was to get rid of her, he knew it would be insane to try to drive fifty miles in that.

"So you leave in the morning," he said coldly, brushing past her as she still stood in the hall. Lisa didn't answer, but she smiled.

A little later Sam put on a pair of snowshoes and a fleece-lined parka and trudged down to the end of the driveway and back to fetch her suitcase. While he was gone, Lisa rinsed the pan he had used for making hot chocolate and the one cup that was still in one piece. Then she swept up the pieces of the other and wiped the mess from the kitchen floor. Feeling very virtuous, she decided to take a quick tour of the house.

It consisted of the kitchen, a living room, a dining room, three smallish bedrooms, and a single bath. Every bit of it was in at least as bad a shape as the kitchen. Lisa shook her head over the rundown state of the place and considered Sam's words briefly. Could she stand living in a place like this for the rest of her life? She looked at the paint peeling from the walls, the grubby hardwood and linoleum floors, the stained bathroom fixtures, and made up her mind: absolutely. A house was just four walls and a roof, after all. Love was what turned it into a home. And she was prepared to love this derelict of a place, because Sam did; and, no matter what he said to the contrary, she loved Sam.

By the time Sam returned with her suitcase, Lisa had already decided that with a little paint and some scrubbing up, the house really wouldn't be so impossible after all. Fixing it up would be fun.... But she very sensibly kept her plans from Sam—for the time being, at least.

He ignored her for the rest of the evening, poring over some papers at the kitchen table without looking up even once. Lisa, seated across from him with a stack of *Field and Stream* magazines that he had handed her with a mocking look, eyed his bent head with some acerbity and asked herself if this infuriating male was really worth all the trouble she was going through to get him. Her eyes slid over the wavy black hair, down to the harsh planes of his dark face, to his massive shoulders and wide chest, and a familiar little flare of excitement ignited inside her. Oh, yes, he was, she decided.

At last he looked up and informed her that it was time they went to bed. Lisa couldn't help the little spark of hope that lit her eyes at that. If he saw it, he pretended not to. Instead he led her to the small bedroom where he had dropped her case, and with a gesture indicated that it was all hers. She had already discovered, during her exploration of the house, that he slept in the larger bedroom just across the hall. So he intended to hold out to the bitter end, did he? she thought with grim determination. She would just have to see what she could do about *that*.

Sam allowed her to use the bathroom first, and she hurriedly showered and brushed her teeth before tying a silky green robe around her waist and quitting the bathroom. She wanted to give him plenty of time to fall asleep....

She heard the shower running and the toilet flush. Then the bathroom door opened and his bare feet padded down the hall to his bedroom. His door shut behind him with a sharp click. With a quiver of indignation, Lisa realized that he didn't even intend to bid her good night!

Still, her mild annoyance didn't stop her from setting her plan into motion. She put on a beautiful turquoise nightgown that was made almost entirely of lace and left very little to the imagination, brushed her hair until it felt like silk, dabbed perfume liberally on all her pulse points, and even applied a touch of makeup (not that he would be able to see it in the dark, but it was always good to be prepared—he might flick on the bedside lamp). When she was finally ready, she sat on the end of her bed and waited. If this was going to work, she had to catch him at his most vulnerable: after he had gone to sleep.

When at last she judged that enough time had lapsed, she stood up and crept from her bedroom, carefully closing the door behind her so that it didn't make a sound. As she snuck across the hall, she thought about how it would be: She would crawl into his bed, snuggling down beside him, and let him discover she was there. Lusty animal that he was, she knew that if she got that close, when he was unprepared, he would be unable to resist. And while he was making love to her, she was sure she could get him to promise her anything....

She stood outside his door, her ear pressed against the cheap wood, straining to hear any sound that would tell her if he was asleep or awake. Ah, yes: she thought she detected the deep, untroubled sound of his breathing. Her hand reached for the knob, turned it—it wouldn't turn. Something must be wrong with it, she thought, pushing against the door in irritation. The door didn't budge, either. She pushed harder, rattling the knob faintly as she tried to get in. From the other side of the door, she thought she heard a new sound. Then she was sure of it: Sam was laughing! Suddenly the whole thing became clear: he'd locked his bedroom door!

"You bastard!" she stormed at him, kicking the door in frustration. She heard that hateful laugh again. It infuriated her.

"Good night, Lisa," he called mockingly through the panel, and as she flounced back to her bedroom she heard him laugh again.

XVIII

FOUR months later, Sam was finally forced to admit to himself that he had made a mistake. Instead of dying, as he had imagined it would, his love for Lisa just kept getting stronger until he was starting to feel that it was eating him alive. He had lost weight over the past months, he knew. Even Jay, newly home from school, had commented on his haggard appearance with the brutal candor so characteristic of the young. The truth was, he hadn't been eating properly because he simply hadn't been hungry; and he hadn't been sleeping, because every time he closed his eyes her image rose to haunt him like a taunting ghost. He saw the silver-gilt hair, the green eyes, the exquisite modeling of her face as if she stood before him. He imagined kissing those rosy lips, caressing those perfect breasts and creamy thighs, possessing her, until he was nearly driven crazy with desire. She had gotten under his skin, and, like a particularly resistant parasite, none of the methods he had tried for eradicating her had worked. He was simply going to have to learn to live with the knowledge that he loved her, like it or not.

And he most definitely didn't like it—at least, not at first. Over the years he had learned to cherish his independence, and he didn't relish giving it up for a flighty young woman of twenty-five, be she ever so gorgeous. The plain and simple truth was that he was scared. Lisa had hit the nail on the head with that one, he reflected wryly. He was scared to let himself love her the way he was aching to love her, scared that she would stay with him only a short time and then flit off in search of greener pastures, leaving him to try to put together the shattered pieces of his life.

He tried to figure out when she had first started getting such a grip on his emotions, and decided that it went all the way back to the very beginning. Bruised and dirty, injured and helplessly dependent on him for succor, she had started to twine herself around his heart. He had wanted her from the first moment he had laid eyes on her; that night in her tent, when he had possessed her beautiful, sexy body for the first time, her lovemaking had taken his breath away. To be strictly honest—and it was time and past that he was strictly honest with himself, he thought—her taking matters into her own hands as she had done had only speeded up the process by a few days. He would have taken her sooner or later, and he had known it from the beginning. It had just been easier for him to let her think she had initiated the whole thing.

But he had told himself that it was all sex between them. No tenderness, or, God forbid, love, but simply a male and a female body generating an extraordinary chemistry. And he had really believed that was all it was. Until that day when he had taken her shooting out in the harsh African scrubland, and she had turned in his arms and kissed him so sweetly....He had wanted her then more than he had ever wanted a woman in his life. And he had taken her, loving the feel of her, the touch and taste and smell of her. Her lips and tongue and hands on him had driven him wild. He had emerged from their encounter shaken to the core—and what had he done? What had he said? Had he thanked her for the most beautiful experience of his life? Hell, no! He had insulted her, deliberately, with malice aforethought, then taken her body again, cruelly, in as degrading a manner as he knew how, simply to prove to her and to himself that she meant nothing to him. Looking back on that now, Sam winced.

When she had told him that she loved him, it had seemed like a miracle. She had touched a cord in him that he had not even known existed, satisfied a craving that he had never realized he felt. In all his life, no woman had really loved him. Oh, there had been lots of sex, lots of women and lots of bodies. But there had always been a price, a payoff of some kind. No woman had ever offered him the generous, unselfish tenderness that Lisa had been ready to give him, and for nothing. And he, stupid, stubborn fool that he was, had thrown it all away.

Lisa had accused him once of being a coward, and she wasn't far wrong. She scared the pants off him. Which was almost funny, when he thought about it. He, who had faced enemy bullets and bombs and bayonets without flinching, was afraid of what couldn't have been more than 120 pounds of female flesh. Because he loved her. And that was what he had to force himself to face.

He didn't want just to sleep with her, although he reflected with an inward grin that that was certainly a nice bonus. He wanted to care for her, to protect her, to smile at her and have her smile back, to have her laugh and cry in his arms, even to be the object of her ridiculous temper tantrums. He would rather

329

have Lisa hurling cups at him than anyone else kissing him. Which showed just how far gone he was. There was no help for it, he decided resignedly: he would have to marry her. If she would have him, after all he had said and done.

As for the money—well, he had to admit that it stuck in his craw a little bit. He had always believed that it was a man's responsibility to provide for his woman, to furnish her food and shelter and clothing and all the dozens of small luxuries so dear to female hearts. He wanted to do that for Lisa. In fact, he was surprised at the strength of the urge he felt to provide for her. And if she had been an ordinary woman, a secretary, say, or a store clerk, or even a reporter living on a reporter's salary, he could have done so—quite nicely. He had made, and would continue to make, plenty to support a wife, in comfort if not in luxury. But Lisa... His mouth twisted wryly. She was used to big houses and servants, to jewels and furs and designer clothes, to ladies' luncheons and fancy evening parties. He couldn't give her that. But he had told her that, more than once, and she had insisted that it didn't matter. And now Sam had to believe her, had to take her at her word. He wanted her far too much to do anything else. And he thought—he hoped—she wanted him too. Enough to gamble on him, to take a chance.

After he had made up his mind to that, Sam's mood lightened considerably. He didn't anticipate having any real problems persuading Lisa to marry him. All he had to do was to get her into bed and the hot little witch would promise him anything. And he would apologize, he told himself sternly. He owed her that.

Before he could go fetch her home, however, there were a few things that needed to be done. With

Jay home from school and the men he had hired to help tend his fledgling cattle herd available, there was no reason why the house couldn't be gotten into some kind of order as well. He set two of the men to painting it, and brought others out from town to work on the plumbing and wiring. He even ordered new kitchen appliances, right down to a dishwasher. Then he and Jay spent every night for a week stripping and sanding and restaining the hardwood floors, and when that was done painting the interior walls. Nothing fancy, just good plain white paint. If he knew women, Lisa would want to do the fancy stuff herself.

Jay, when informed why these elaborate preparations were taking place, fell on the work with a will. He had never understood why the two of them had broken up in the first place, he said. Anybody could see that Lisa would make a great wife, even if she couldn't do things like cook. And then, to Sam's amusement, his son had proceeded to give him detailed instructions on how to go about proposing marriage to a woman. Rolling around on the floor behind a couch just didn't make it, Jay told him sternly.

Despite the almost overwhelming preoccupation with Lisa, Sam found time to make a few inquiries into the fate of the men who had accompanied him on that ill-starred mission to Rhodesia. When he finally got Frank Leads on the phone—at his daughter's house in Florida—Sam was conscious of a deep sense of relief. As the leader, he had been responsible for the safety of his men, and to his own mind he had failed them miserably. Although exactly what he could have done to avert the shambles the mission had been reduced to he didn't know. But he couldn't help thinking that if he had not been so caught up with Lisa, things might have turned out differently. Very differently.

Sam could tell from Frank's voice that his old friend was as relieved to hear his voice as he was to hear Frank's. They laughed and joked, each recounting his experiences in getting out of Rhodesia—although Sam's carefully edited version was by far the more exciting of the two, as Frank and the rest of the survivors managed to catch the scheduled airplane out. Then the talk turned serious. Five men had died over there, the four killed by the initial blast and young Mike Harley. And at least one—either of the survivors or of the dead—had betrayed them. At this point it was impossible to positively identify the traitor, although Frank, like Sam, had his suspicions. In any case, it no longer mattered. Again like Sam, Frank had decided that he was getting too old to lay his life on the line for every crazy despot with a fistful of money. He had retired as of the day he had set foot back in the States, he told Sam, and was in the process of setting up a little business taking tourists out on boats to fish. When Sam confessed, almost sheepishly, to his own plans to marry Lisa—if she would have him—Frank guffawed and twitted him loudly for some minutes before growing serious and wishing him the best. Sam returned those wishes, then both men grew embarrassed by their lapse into sentimentality. The conversation ended quickly. But afterward Sam felt better than he had for a long time.

It was the middle of June before Sam finally felt that everything at the ranch was as ready as it was going to get. There was nothing left to do but go fetch Lisa. Sitting in his seat in a plane bound for Washington, D.C., Sam felt as nervous as a young kid getting ready to ask a girl out for the first time.

Which was stupid, at his age, he knew, but—what if she wouldn't have him?

It was hot as hell when he walked out of National Airport in Washington toward the rental car that awaited him. Must have been ninety in the shade. The sun shone over everything, reflecting hotly off the pavement and the shiny tops of the cars as they pulled in and out of the airport. People bustled about everywhere, always in a hurry. He had never liked Washington: it was too crowded and noisy and dirty.

By the time he had fought his way out of the city's congested traffic and set the cream-colored LeMans on the road for Annapolis, Sam was burning up. Of course, the damned air-conditioner was on the blink. He shed the lightweight tan sportscoat in which he had traveled, thanking God that his pale blue sports shirt was short-sleeved, and wished vainly for a pair of cut-off jeans instead of the navy-blue slacks he was wearing. But with the windows rolled down so that the breeze generated by the car's movement circulated through the interior, it wasn't too bad. With a faint grin, he decided that he would survive it.

His first setback came at the house. Mary Dobson, giving him a long, disapproving look that he couldn't account for, informed him that Mrs. Collins no longer lived there: she had taken an apartment in Baltimore. Sam was floored by this announcement, at least temporarily. Then he realized that he would just have to drive on to Baltimore, which was only about twenty-five miles away. To his surprise, Mary flatly refused to give him the address. He would have to wait and talk to Mr. Bennet, who was in the city and wouldn't be back until later that evening, she said, before practically closing the door in his face.

Sam had been about to bang on it again, demanding the information he wanted, when he spied Henry Dobson around at the side. Getting Lisa's address out of Henry took only a few minutes, but something in the man's attitude started Sam thinking. He had seemed almost as disapproving as his wife.

The sun was going down in a blaze of orange fire when Sam finally located the street on which Lisa now lived. It surprised him, because it was nothing fancy. Just Victorian-era brick houses that had apparently been converted into apartments with neat little yards and a few tall shade trees lining either side of the street—not Lisa's kind of neighborhood at all. Maybe Henry had given him the wrong address. Frowning, Sam parked the car and walked up to a three-story house with Victorian-style porch painted a cheerful shade of yellow running around the front, and gables spouting from the roof. According to Henry, Lisa lived on the very top floor.

On the porch, just outside the ornate walnut door, were three small mailboxes set into the wall. The third one bore the label L. COLLINS. Lisa did live here, after all; Henry hadn't made a mistake. Sam had started to knock on the door, not seeing a security intercom or anything, when a young couple came out and smilingly held it open for him, not even questioning what he wanted. Frowning, Sam walked inside. What the hell was Amos thinking of, to let Lisa live in a place like this? he wondered irritably as he climbed the old-fashioned staircase. It wasn't safe. He could have been anybody—rapist, murderer, anybody—and here he was, inside the house. What was going on?

As Sam reached the third-floor landing and stood outside the door that was all that separated him from Lisa, such useless speculation fled in the face of his returning nervousness. Would she be glad to see him? What would she say?

Taking a deep breath, he knocked on the door, noting that there wasn't even such an elemental precaution as a peephole. Good God . . . But at least she would be totally surprised.

Then the door opened. Sam found himself looking into the slanting green eyes that had been haunting his dreams for months. They widened at the sight of him; she was surprised, all right, no doubt about that. She didn't say anything for a moment, then her brows snapped together and she frowned. Sam drank in every nuance of her expression like a marooned man coming across water in a desert.

"What are you doing here?" she demanded, not looking at all pleased to see him.

Well, he had half-expected that. Sam smiled wheedlingly at her, leaning against the doorjamb with one arm curving over his head.

"I bought a dishwasher," he said huskily, and then his eyes traveled down from her face to her throat to her soft, sexy body—and he suddenly felt like he had been kicked in the gut. Her stomach pushed out against the soft white fabric of her sleeveless smock like she had swallowed a basketball. She had to be at least six months' pregnant!

"Christ!" he said after a moment, staring at her burgeoning belly. He couldn't take his eyes off it; he shook his head, hoping to clear it, thinking that maybe, just maybe, he was hallucinating. But no, the bulge didn't disappear.

"Christ!" he said again, his eyes coming up to meet hers in horrified question.

Her mouth tightened. "Go away!" she ordered, starting to close the door.

This galvanized Sam into action. He put his foot in the rapidly diminishing space, then shouldered his way inside. Lisa, helpless in the face of his greater strength, stood holding the edge of the door, glaring at him.

"Get out of my apartment!"

Sam shook his head. "No way!"

"Get out!"

"Don't be stupid, Lisa," he said, regaining control of his tongue at last. "You must see we've got to talk. You're pregnant!"

"Really? I hadn't noticed!"

Sam merely looked at her. After the stunning blow of coming here and finding her in such a state, her sarcasm bounced off him like water off a duck's back.

"Why didn't you tell me?" he asked finally, staring at her.

"Because it was none of your damned business!" she snapped, her face white except for two flags of angry color in her cheeks.

"None of my business! That's my baby!"

"Is it?" She smiled tauntingly at him.

"You know it is." He felt not the slightest doubt about that.

Lisa looked at him, her eyes challenging. When he met her stare with rocklike determination, her eyes flickered.

"So what?" she said finally, no longer even bothering to deny that he was the father.

"So what?" Sam was momentarily flabbergasted. "So I had a right to be told, that's what! Christ, you must have been pregnant when you came out to the ranch! Why the hell didn't you say so? I . . ."

"I didn't know," she muttered resentfully. "I didn't find out until two weeks later."

Sam shut his eyes, taking a deep breath. When he

opened them again, he had mentally settled everything to his own satisfaction. If anything, this unexpected development just made everything that much easier.

"For God's sake, shut the door," he said, turning away from her and moving on into the small living room. Like the rest of the building, it was not luxurious, but it was comfortably furnished in light, airy tones of yellow and green and white.

"I want you to leave!" she said imperiously, glaring after him.

"Well, that's too bad, because I'm not leaving, and you can't throw me out." He seated himself in a chintz-covered armchair as he spoke. "Shut the door, Lisa."

She hesitated for a moment, then shut the door. Her mouth was set mutinously and her eyes were shooting sparks when she came to stand in the middle of the room, fixing him with a darkling look.

"I have nothing to say to you, Sam," she said frigidly.

"When is it due?" He gestured at her stomach, totally ignoring her words.

"The end of September," Lisa answered, reluctant to provide him with even that much information.

Sam thought back rapidly. "Then it must have happened that night in your room...." His voice trailed off as he remembered giving her the ring, and what had come after. Lisa blushed. Sam, seeing her embarrassment, felt his heart turn over. What she must have gone through, discovering that she was expecting his child after he had sent her away so callously! He deserved to be shot for that, he thought. But he hadn't known.... If only she'd told him, he would have eased her worry at once.

"Honey, I'm sorry, sorrier than I can tell you, that

you had to go through all this by yourself," he said in a gentle tone, standing up and moving to take her carefully into his arms. She was rigid as his arms slid around her. "I'll do my best to make it up to you. We'll get married right away, and . . ."

"No!" She pushed away from him, thrusting against his chest with a strength that surprised him.

Sam stared down at her. "What do you mean, no?" he questioned carefully, still retaining his grip on her upper arms.

"I mean no! N-o! Negative! I don't want to marry you!"

"You're going to have my baby," he pointed out, as if she had somehow overlooked that fact.

"That doesn't mean I have to marry you!"

"Oh, yes, it does!" Sam was fast beginning to lose his patience.

"No, it doesn't!"

Sam counted to ten carefully before he said anything. He had to remind himself that she was pregnant, and that women, when pregnant, tended to be a trifle unreasonable.

"Honey, I realize you're angry with me. And I'll even admit that you have cause. And I'll apologize again, if you like. But whether you're angry or not, it doesn't change the fact that that baby needs a father—and you need a husband. You did divorce Collins, didn't you?" he added in a sharper tone.

"The divorce was final three months ago." She was pulling away from him as she spoke, and he released his grip on her arms, letting her go.

"Then there's nothing to stop us from getting married," he said, as if that settled everything.

She planted her hands on her hips, staring up at him defiantly. Sam found himself fascinated by the picture she presented. Pregnant, with her belly sticking out to there, she was lovelier than ever. Her silver-gilt hair had grown longer, and she had swept it up in a ponytail that made her look about seventeen, if one disregarded her stomach. Her skin was flawless, a rich cream color with roses in her cheeks and lips. Her eyes were a clear sparkling emerald, very bright as she glared at him. The white cotton smock she wore was ruffled around the sleeves and hem and had embroidered flowers around the square neck. Her long, slender legs were clad in blue jeans, and her feet were bare. She was the very essence of femininity, and he was shaken by the emotions that tore through him as he looked at her, standing there challenging him while she was big with his child. She was his woman, he thought fiercely, and it was time to put a stop to all this nonsense to the contrary.

"We're getting married as soon as I can arrange it," he said with finality, his eyes taking on a hard gleam as they dared her to contradict him.

She didn't even hesitate. "Oh, no, we're not," she retorted. "Try to get it through your head, Sam: I no longer take orders from you. I intend to do what's best for me, and the baby, and that doesn't include marrying you! And if that leaves you with a guilty conscience, then I'm sorry!"

Sam's mouth compressed. He eyed her, not liking the determined set to her jaw or the green glitter of her eyes. Clearly, she was determined to make him pay in blood before she relented. He couldn't believe that her defiance was any more serious than that. Dammit, she was a woman, wasn't she? A woman pregnant with his child! She needed him—and she was going to get him, if he had to drag her to the altar by her hair. But he would try reason first. After all, she had every right to be angry, and he was willing to do anything he could to make amends—at least, to a point.

"Shouldn't you be sitting down?" he asked, completely changing the subject as it occurred to him that she had been on her feet ever since he had entered her apartment.

"I'm not ill, I'm pregnant," she answered evenly. "A perfectly natural state. And I think you should remember that I've gotten this far without your solicitude, so there's no need for you to start acting like an anxious father-to-be at this juncture. Too little and too late, Sam." Her tone as she finished was faintly mocking.

"Sit down." This time it was an order.

Looking up at him, Lisa recognized the steely-eyed man who had ruthlessly bent her to his will out in the Rhodesian bush. Only this time they weren't in Rhodesia—and she would be damned if she would meekly obey! She didn't deign to answer, just folded her arms over her breasts and eyed him with her head tilted slightly to one side as she remained on her feet. For a moment, as his eyes flickered, she thought he might mean physically to enforce his command. Then his mouth softened, even smiled at her a tad ruefully.

"Lisa, honey, if I'd known you were pregnant I would have come right away," he said in as gentle a voice as she had yet heard from him. He made as if to come toward her, enfold her in his arms.

She held him off with an upraised hand. "You don't understand, do you?" The words were cool, the expression in her eyes remote. "I never doubted that you would come back—and offer to marry me—if you knew I was pregnant. But I don't want to get married for a reason like that. It's not a very sound basis for a lifelong commitment. I've lived through one bad marriage, and so have you. I'm not going to make another mistake like that."

"I came here today to ask you to marry me," he said, regarding her steadily. He stood perhaps five feet away, his arms folded over his broad chest, his rough black hair tumbling in a heat-induced wave over the bronzed skin of his forehead.

Despite herself, Lisa was conscious of a faint, niggling urge to throw herself into his arms, to be sheltered and protected, to be loved. Then she reminded herself that he didn't love her—at least, not enough to marry her in the teeth of all the potential problems her money and their disparate social positions might bring. Not enough to marry her at all—without her pregnancy to force his hand.

"I hadn't the faintest notion that you were pregnant until you opened the door, Lisa," he continued when she didn't answer. "But I came back for you anyway. Because I realized that I love you. Baby or no baby, I want you for my wife."

Lisa stared at him. She was tempted—oh, so tempted!—to take him at his word. To marry him. It was what she wanted, had wanted all along. But if he didn't really want her—if he was just marrying her because of the baby—she wouldn't be able to stand it. She had had her heart broken twice already, first by Jeff, then by Jennifer. She was afraid that a third time would wound her past bearing. And she had trusted Sam once, loved him unreservedly, offered herself to him without any holding back. And he had sent her away. It seemed almost unbelievable that now, when she was expecting his child, after months without a word, he had turned up out of the blue, asking her to marry him.

"Has Amos been in touch with you?" she asked, trying but not quite succeeding in keeping the suspicion that had suddenly occurred to her out of her voice.

He eyed her. "No," he said. "I haven't heard from Amos in months."

"How did you know where I lived?"

"I stopped by the house—I thought you were still living there. Henry Dobson gave me your address. I don't even think Amos was there. If he had been, I'm sure he would have had a few things to say to me." A wry smile twisted his mouth. "What does he think about this," he nodded at her belly, "by the way?"

"Oh, he's horrified," she said with a grimace. "Although he's trying his best to hide it. To his way of thinking, 'nice girls' don't get themselves in situations like this. At first, he naturally assumed that you and I would be getting married, so that made it a little better. Then when I told him that we weren't, I was afraid for a moment that he would pass out. He wanted to go to the Circle C to drag you back here and make you marry me, whether you wanted to or not. But I told him that if he interfered in this, I'd never forgive him. And he saw that I meant it. Since then he's been very good about the whole thing—I think." The last two words were muttered under her breath as she eyed Sam speculatively. It was just too much of a coincidence that he had turned up like this... wanting to marry her. She could not shake the feeling that he must have known about the baby.

"I swear I haven't talked to Amos," Sam said. His blue eyes met hers without any hint of evasion.

Maybe he was telling the truth, Lisa thought, suddenly wanting fiercely to believe it. Then her common sense reasserted itself.

"Marry me, Lisa," Sam repeated quietly.

He was still standing some five feet away, his arms

crossed over his chest, the setting sun sending orange-gold rays through the big picture window behind him to paint a bright aureole around his dark head. His face was shadowed in contrast, but Lisa felt the intensity of his gaze on her. Once again she had to fight the urge to cross the small space that separated them and throw herself into his arms. But no—there was too much at stake, for the child that was even now twisting inside her as well as for herself. She couldn't afford to make a mistake again. This time, before she committed herself to love, she had to be sure.

"I told you, Sam, no." Her arms came up to hug her stomach, and she wet her lips with the tip of her tongue. His eyes followed every movement she made. "At least—I have to think about it. This child will be better off without any father at all than with a father who resents him, or with parents who are constantly at each other's throats. Before, when it was just you and me, it didn't matter so much. If it didn't work out, we could have gotten a divorce, and we would have been the only ones hurt. Now—now everything is so much more complicated. I would find it hard to divorce the father of my child."

"There wouldn't be a divorce. I love you, Lisa."

She smiled, almost bitterly. "Do you, Sam? You said that before—and then you left. What about the money? I'm still rich, Sam, and you're not. When is that going to start bothering you again?"

He turned away from her to take a quick, angry turn about the room. Finally he stopped by the darkening window and turned to face her, his hands behind his back gripping the carved-oak sill.

"During the last few months, I've come to realize that it doesn't matter," he said, the words quiet. "The money's yours. I won't touch it—but you can use it, if you want. To buy clothes and personal things for yourself—and the baby."

"That's quite a switch."

She was mocking him, her head tilted to one side. In the deepening gloom, she was a faint pale blur with her ivory skin and silver-gilt hair. Her eyes and the expression on her face were hidden from him by the shadows.

"I've had plenty of time to think about it. And I came to the conclusion that you're what's important— you and what we have together. Nothing else matters, compared to that."

At his words, Lisa felt a little flame begin to flicker and grow inside her, melting the block of ice that her heart seemed to have been encased in since Sam had thrown her off the ranch—and she had found out about the baby. He sounded almost humble, as if he was pleading with her to give him a chance. Not at all like the arrogant, authoritative soldier she had come to know. He sounded sincere—and, she thought, maybe he was. At this moment. But what would it be like when they had been married six months, a year, five years? Would the money prove an impossible stumbling block between them? Before, she had been willing to take that chance. Now, she had to be sure—because of the baby.

"Well?" His tone told her clearly that he was getting impatient with her continuing silent regard. It also told her that he expected only one answer.

"I have to think about this, Sam. It's not something I can decide right now, on the spur of the moment. You'll have to give me time."

"Goddamm it!" The oath ripped out of his mouth, cutting through the gloom like a knife.

Lisa's head came up, and she regarded him warily as he turned with quick, efficient movements to draw

the drapes across the now-darkened window and
flick on the pair of china lamps flanking the sofa.
When the room was bathed in a soft, golden pool of
light, he crossed to her, putting his hands on her
upper arms and holding her when she would have
pulled away. She felt the touch of his long, strong
fingers gripping her bare skin all the way down to
her toes. It had been months since she had felt
anything sexual, months since she had even allowed
herself to think of her body as anything except the
vessel carrying her child, and the sudden rush of
desire from nothing more than the touch of his
hands startled her like an electric shock. She tried to
draw away, but he held her, not hurting, but
inescapable.

"How long are you planning to keep up this nonsense?" His words were clipped. The deep blaze in
his eyes told her that he was suddenly very angry.

"As long as it takes for me to be sure—and it's not
nonsense."

His anger ripped away the veil that had shrouded
her own over the last, miserable months. Her eyes
met his defiantly, a clash of blazing emeralds and
sapphires. Most women—indeed, most men—Lisa
thought as she stared up into the fiercely carved face
intent on bending her to his will, would have been
frightened if Sam had turned such a glare on them.
She was not—she knew him too well, and the stakes
were too high.

"And that's your last word on the subject?"

From the whitening of the deep grooves at the
sides of his mouth, she could tell that he was keeping
a tight rein on his temper. His hands on her arms
had tightened just a little, so that she felt his fingers
digging into her flesh. Still, she felt no pain. Instead,
she was conscious of an odd feeling surging through

her veins. A feeling almost of exhilaration, as if her blood had been frozen for centuries and was just now beginning to melt. In love or in anger, Lisa realized, Sam made her come alive.

"Until I've had time to think about it, yes."

His hands tightened even more, then they released her, dropping to his sides abruptly as he swung away. Lisa gaped after him as he strode toward the door.

"You're not leaving?" The words were surprised out of her.

"Yes, I am. Isn't that what you wanted?" His voice was tight, angry. His stride didn't slacken until he had the door open. Then he turned back to face her.

Lisa blinked at him. Knowing Sam, she hadn't expected him to concede so rapidly, at least not without one heck of a fight.

"Well, isn't it?" he demanded.

"Yes." There wasn't much else she could say.

"Right." The single word was clipped. "I'll be in touch."

Then he swung on his heel and walked through the door, pulling it shut behind him. Lisa was left gaping after him, her thoughts in such turmoil that it was some minutes before she remembered to cross the room and lock the door.

XIX

H E was waiting for her when she left work the next day, his car parked illegally in front of the building that housed the magazine's offices, himself dressed casually in jeans and a crew-neck yellow T-shirt. He was leaning against the closed car door, his arms, bronzed and hair-roughened, crossed over his chest, the afternoon sun glinting off his wavy black hair. The snug-fitting jeans showed off his narrow hips and long legs, while the soft cotton of the T-shirt emphasized the powerful muscles of his upper arms and shoulders. When he saw her walking toward him, he straightened away from the car, his arms dropping to his sides, and smiled. His mouth curved up lopsidedly, making deep gashes appear in his tanned cheeks; those blue eyes watched her with an expression that should have been outlawed for the effect it had on her. Lisa eyed him warily. With her heart doing flipflops the way it was at the mere sight of him, it would be all too easy to give in and agree to marry him without more ado. And she still wasn't sure whether that was the best thing to do. For any of the three of them.

"What are you doing here?" she demanded as she got close enough, hoping that her severe tone would

347

disguise the way her heart had leaped at the sight of him.

His curious, twisted smile deepened. "I thought I'd take you out to dinner," he said, as if it was the most natural thing in the world for him to be waiting for her. "Okay?"

He was impossibly handsome, standing there watching her with those blue eyes while he held open the passenger-side for her. Lisa noticed several of the women with whom she worked giving him interested looks as they walked past on the way to the parking lot, then looking at her with a combination of speculation and envy. Tomorrow she would be in for countless curious questions. . . .

"I have my car," she said, wavering. Suddenly she knew that she really wanted to go with him, wanted to be with him. She had missed him more than she had let herself admit over the last months; now she felt like a flower left too long in the sun that at last senses the promise of rain.

"No problem. I'll bring you back here afterward and you can pick it up. Or I can drive you to work in the morning."

She looked at him sharply. "If I go to dinner with you, you won't be spending the night, Sam."

He grinned at her. "What a suspicious mind you have! All I meant was that I'd be glad to stop by your apartment in the morning and pick you up. Nothing to get excited about."

"I prefer to come back for my car."

"Anything you say. Are you going to get in or not? I'm starting to feel pretty silly, standing here holding the car door open while you eye me like I'm a cross between Jack the Ripper and Bruno Hauptmann."

Lisa had to chuckle at that. And, chuckling, she got into the car.

"How did you know where I work?" she asked as he slid behind the steering wheel and switched on the ignition. The motor turned over, and then he was expertly maneuvering them out into the streaming traffic.

"Amos," he said briefly, not taking his eyes off the road.

"Amos?" All her instincts were suddenly on the alert. So, despite his protestations the night before, he had seen Amos. She should have known. . . .

"You can forget what you're thinking." He threw her a quick glance before his attention was once again claimed by the traffic. "I saw Amos this morning. For the first time since Jay and I left Annapolis. And he was mighty pleased to see me, I must say. Said it was about time I showed up."

"I bet." Lisa could just imagine the scene. If Sam had told Amos that he had come back to marry her, Amos must have practically fallen on the younger man's neck.

"He also told me that you were recently promoted to assistant editor of the magazine you're working for. What's it called, *Baltimore Alive*?" Lisa nodded. "And that you got the job entirely on your own, without anyone at the magazine even knowing that you're related to him. Why?"

Lisa shrugged. "I guess I got tired of hanging on to Amos's coattails. Always, all my life, I wondered if the things I did—getting good grades in school, getting into Bryn Mawr, even Jeff asking me to marry him—were because I was Amos's granddaughter. The only job I ever had except this one I got through him. I started to wonder what I could do by myself, without anyone to help me. So I decided to find out. I actually read the want ads in the newspaper like hundreds of other people do every day, typed up a resumé, and went out looking for a job. And I got one. Because they like the way I write. Not because of Amos."

He looked over at her and smiled suddenly. "Very admirable. So Lisa Bennet Collins, with all her money and social connections a carefully guarded secret, is now an ordinary working girl—beg pardon, woman. How do you like it?"

She met his eyes steadily, unsmiling. There was even a hint of defiance in the green depths. "Very much." And it was true. For the first time in her life, she felt that she, as a person, had value. It was a good feeling—but she didn't really want to talk about it. Not even to Sam. Not now, while the feeling was so new. "Where are you headed, anyway?" she asked, changing the subject as she glanced out the window to find that they were in a line of traffic getting ready to pull onto the packed freeway.

Sam momentarily looked surprised, as if he had been driving without thinking much about it. "I don't really know, to tell you the truth. What do you feel like eating? Amos suggested a seafood restaurant that he said you loved, but I've forgotten the name of it."

"The Blue Crab," Lisa supplied automatically, not really liking the idea of the two of them plotting against her—and that's certainly what it sounded like!—behind her back. She lifted her chin. "I feel like pizza."

"Pizza?" Sam couldn't have sounded more taken aback if she'd said "marigolds." He took his eyes from the cars lined up in front of them to glance down at her figure, still slender except for the bulge at her middle, which even the pale blue maternity suit did not quite disguise. "Are you sure that's good for you—in your condition?"

Lisa returned his look with a trace of irritation. "For goodness' sake, Sam, I'm in perfect health, and pizza is a perfectly healthy food. But if it makes you feel any better, I'll drink a glass of milk instead of a Coke. Okay?"

"Okay."

His smile was meant to be disarming. Lisa knew that, but it worked nonetheless. She had to smile back, hating to admit even to herself that she liked his concern for her. He had already proved that he could be a good father with Jay. It seemed that he was just as ready to be a good father to the coming baby—and a good husband to her. If she could only be sure he loved her enough not to be deterred by the obstacles that stood between them...

"This is all new to me, honey, so you'll have to bear with me," he added with a trace of a grin as he followed Lisa's directions to pull out of the line of traffic and head back toward the pizza parlor that was a scant two blocks from her apartment. "It's been seventeen years since Jay was born, and I was out on maneuvers most of the time Beth was carrying him. But I do remember that she was sick a lot and had to spend a lot of time in bed. Have you been sick?" The overly casual tone of the question did little to mask his concern.

Lisa shook her head. "Only the first three months—and only a little. Since then I've felt fine. I was that way with Jennifer, too." Lisa could think of her daughter now with more love than pain, and she realized that she owed much of her inner healing to Sam. He had been good for her in lots of ways....

"I should have been with you," she heard him mutter under his breath. As she looked over at him she saw that a frown darkened his features, etching harsh lines around his mouth and between his eyebrows.

"If you hadn't been so stupid about the money, you would have been," Lisa pointed out with more truth than tact.

He winced. "I would have been, wouldn't I?" he acknowledged slowly; then, turning to look at her, he added in an urgent tone, "Lisa..."

But she still wasn't quite ready for the discussion that tone of voice promised. She had to work out what was best for herself and the baby by herself, without allowing Sam's undeniable powers of persuasion—and the love she felt for him—to sway her. She was determined to make this decision with her mind, not her heart. For once.

The brightly painted facade of the pizza parlor on the next corner saved her. "Pull in here," she directed. And the topic was shelved. For the present.

Once inside, they ordered pizza with beer for Sam and milk for Lisa, then played video games as they waited for it. Lisa felt more like a teenager on a date than an unmarried mother-to-be with a divorce and the tragedy of a dead child behind her, and she loved it. As she played Pac Man and Donkey Kong, she giggled like a sixteen-year-old. Sam, who had had the benefit of Jay's expert tuition, was much better than Lisa, and he demolished her with a single-minded intensity that she secretly found hilarious. Like her, he seemed to have reverted to his teenage years, or younger. Did men ever grow up? she wondered with amusement as he let out a whoop, which caused nearly everyone in the restaurant to look around, after beating her for the third time in a row at computer Ping-Pong.

When the pizza came, they retired to their table, Sam flushed with victory and Lisa flushed with trying to suppress an almost-irresistible tide of giggles. For a while, as they munched, Sam entertained her with tall tales (no way did she believe all that stuff!) about his exploits as a soldier and with stories of his early years as a rebellious teenager in a town that worshipped conformity. Then he listened with unflagging interest as she talked about her job and the interview with a local disc jockey she was trying to arrange.

"So when did you move into the apartment?" he asked, picking up a prized corner piece of the pizza and taking a large bite.

"About two weeks after I found out I was pregnant." The words were slightly muffled as Lisa fought with strings of cheese that seemed determined not to abandon the bite she had in her mouth.

"Why?"

The genuine puzzlement in the single word made her answer more thoughtful than it would have been. If she and Sam were to have a chance, a real chance, of making a marriage work, then he had to understand her as she was trying to understand him. So far, their relationship had been more fire and passion than simple friendship, but Lisa had a feeling that friendship was the stronger glue when it came to holding two people together for twenty or thirty years.

"I thought it was time I lived on my own," she answered, meeting his eyes steadily. "It occurred to me that I'd never really been alone. I lived with Amos until I got married, and then I lived with Jeff until I went to Rhodesia. And then I lived with you."

"But why that particular apartment? In that area of town? It doesn't strike me as exactly your kind of place."

"But then you really don't have any idea what my kind of place is, do you, Sam?" The words were gentle for all their astringency. "You just took it for granted that I couldn't be happy anywhere that wasn't the very last word in luxury! After I came home from your ranch, I even began to wonder if you might be right—if perhaps I was so spoiled that I couldn't do without a big house and servants and expensive clothes and nice cars! So I decided to find out. For the last few months I've been totally self-supporting, living on money I earn from a job I work hard at, and I like it! I like knowing that I'm not the useless little social butterfly that you and Jeff and Amos made me feel!"

There was a moment's silence. Sam met her eyes, and slowly put down the slice of pizza he held in one hand.

"If I made you feel like that, then I'm sorry," he said quietly. "I never thought you were useless, Lisa. Just accustomed to more luxuries than I could give you. I didn't want you to have to do without anything you wanted, just because you had married me."

"But what you never understood was that it was you I wanted." Lisa's voice was so low Sam had to strain to hear. The single, glass-encased candle in the center of the table lent a rosy glow to her pale skin, and her eyes gleamed brightly with reflected candlelight as they met his. "I've never been short of money, or anything that money could buy. And what I learned from that is that money isn't important. People are, Sam. People, and relationships."

"If you feel that way, then marry me. I love you—and you love me. With that going for us, we should be able to handle anything."

Lisa smiled, an almost-sad curve to the sweet line of her lips. "But how long would it be before the thought of all that money in a bank account in my name started to bother you? How long would it be before you started to wonder if I regretted not living the kind of life you seem to think I need? How long would it be before we started fighting over it? How long would it be before you started hating me?"

"Lisa..." His voice was hoarse.

Lisa shook her head. "Don't say anything right now, Sam. Just think about it. And for your sake as well as mine and the baby's, be honest. Please."

She stood up abruptly, leaving Sam to pay the bill as she hurried out of the restaurant before the tears that threatened to erupt could disgrace her completely. By the time Sam joined her, steering her to his car, she had them under control, but the look he bent on her was heavy with concern.

"All right?" he asked her when he had put her into the passenger seat and gotten in beside her.

Lisa nodded, not trusting herself to speak. Sam looked at her, parted his lips as if to say something, then apparently thought better of it. Without a word, he drove her back to her apartment.

"My car..." were the only words Lisa uttered as she saw where they were.

"I'll bring it by for you later. Don't worry about it," he said brusquely, coming around to open her door for her. Lisa was already on the pavement before he reached her.

"There's no need..." *to walk me up,* she started to say, but the derisive look he shot her made her abandon the words as a waste of time. He walked silently behind her up the steps, and then as they reached her apartment took her key from her hand and opened the door.

"Wait here." Before she knew what he was about he was inside, turning on the lights, checking quickly through the rooms before returning to where she had moved to stand just inside the door.

"I hardly think that was necessary. I've been living here for months without any trouble."

"Don't you want me to earn my Boy Scout badge?" He smiled at her, then caught her chin in his hand and tilted her face up to his. "Good night, Lisa," he murmured. Then he bent his head to press a hard, fast kiss on her soft lips. Before she could respond as her every instinct urged her to, he straightened to look down at her.

"I want *you* to think about *this*," he said softly. "If you don't marry me, how long will it be before you hate yourself for not having given us a chance? How long before our child hates you for depriving him or her of a father?"

She stared up at him, shaken. He smiled down at her, pressed another quick kiss to her lips, and released her.

"Lock the door behind me," he ordered. Then, as she continued to stare after him, he left. And she was alone.

XX

THE roses were delivered while she was at lunch the next day. When she got back to the small cubbyhole that served as her office, there they were, a dozen bloodred blooms in a crystal vase, filling the small space with their heady fragrance. Lisa stopped dead in her doorway when she saw them, nearly causing Emily Pfeiffer, the magazine's other assistant editor, who had just lunched with her and then followed her to her office to continue their conversation on an upcoming story, to bump into her.

"Wow!" Emily said, peering over Lisa's shoulder at the blooms. The awed syllable brought Lisa back to her senses. She moved toward the roses, smiling despite herself. Sam! Even before she opened the white embossed card nestled among the green foliage she knew that. The simple message brought a suspicious fog to her eyes. "I love you," it said. "Marry me."

"I suppose those are from the hunk who met you after work last night?" Emily's half-envious voice brought Lisa's attention back to her. She blinked surreptitiously, hoping the other woman wouldn't notice the film of moisture. Then she smiled without answering.

"Boy, some people have all the luck," Emily continued, apparently not needing an answer to draw the correct conclusion. "What I wouldn't give to have a sexy specimen like that after me." Then she looked down at her own short, slightly-too-plump body and reached up to touch her wire-rimmed glasses ruefully. "Not much chance, huh? Unless he has a fetish for fat thighs?"

The teasing hopefulness in her voice made Lisa laugh.

"Don't be silly, Em," she said in as nearly normal a tone as she could manage. "You know you do very well for yourself, and your thighs are not fat. Now, if you're quite through fishing for compliments and trying to steal my male friends, why don't you come in so that we can get to work?"

Emily came in and sat down in the chair opposite Lisa's desk, while Lisa settled in the chair behind the desk, making a conscious effort not to look at the roses with their flagrant message of love. Emily, however, had no such inhibition.

"He doesn't have a friend, does he?" she inquired hopefully in the middle of a conversation about various ways to cover the opening of a local mall. Lisa merely frowned severely in answer, and continued with what she had been saying. With a last, mournful look at the roses, Emily allowed the subject to drop.

As Lisa had half-expected, Sam was waiting for her that evening when she left work. He was leaning against the passenger door of her car—which, as promised, she had found parked outside her apartment that morning. When he saw her walking toward him, he grinned, straightening away from the car and watching her walk with a warm appreciation that went a long way toward making her forget that

the green-and-gold-striped dress she was wearing
was from a maternity store and that her middle bore
more resemblance to a basketball than to the slender
wand described so often in popular fiction.

"Introduce me!" a throaty voice whispered just
behind her. Lisa turned to see Emily regarding Sam
with mock-dazzled eyes.

"Not on your life," Lisa was surprised to hear
herself reply.

When Emily chuckled, Lisa grinned back, then
went to join Sam. Watching him as he opened the
door for her—the passenger door, she noted with
amused resignation; apparently his male-chauvinist
tendencies hadn't subsided sufficiently to allow her
to drive while he was in the car—she could see why
he reduced Emily to envious drools. He towered
over the pale, slender, and not-so-slender men streaming through the parking lot in their three-piece suits;
the breadth of his shoulders and chest and the
muscles clearly visible in his arms beneath the short-
sleeved red T-shirt he wore bespoke a man of action,
not a pencil pusher. The strength of his thighs in the
white duck slacks, the narrow virility of his hips—all
were the stuff women's fantasies were made of. Add
to that a bronzed face with uncompromisingly male
features, a shock of wavy black hair, a grin that
flashed charm along with white teeth whenever he
cared to use it, and those blue eyes—Lisa nearly
drooled herself.

"Emily was right—you are a hunk," she told him
with a grin as he bore her off to the Blue Crab.

Sam glanced over at her with some surprise. "Who's
Emily?" he asked suspiciously.

Lisa laughed, and told him.

"So you think I'm a hunk, too, do you?" he drawled

when she had finished. "I'm not sure I like that. You should want me for my mind, not my body."

"But you have such a nice body," Lisa teased.

He looked over at her, that familiar lopsided grin tilting his mouth. "So marry me, and you get exclusive rights."

Lisa looked at him. His tone was light, playful, but the expression in his eyes told her that he was serious. She was tempted. . . .

"Watch where you're driving," she said severely. And the subject was allowed to drop. For the moment.

When the roses arrived the next day, bearing the same message, Lisa was surprised. Since the first bouquet took up most of the extra space on her desk, she put this second dozen—as bloodred and fragrant as the first—on top of the file cabinet. And endured the good-natured teasing from her office mates that was the inevitable result of having two bunches of flowers delivered to her office in two days.

"They're beautiful—but please, no more roses," Lisa told Sam that night. She hadn't even been surprised to find him waiting for her. Having him take her to dinner seemed the most natural thing in the world; and the brief good-night kiss that was all he allowed her seemed natural, too—except that it left her wanting more.

The next day it was carnations, pink and spicy, accompanied by the same message that had come with the roses. Lisa stared at them, aghast, before finding them a spot on the windowsill. And that night she remonstrated with Sam. But he made her no promises, merely grinned an aggravating grin.

As she had half-expected, the next day brought more flowers. As did the next, and the next, and the next. Baskets of delphiniums, bowls of irises, pitchers of daisies. All with the same message. Her office reeked of perfume; it was full to overflowing with gorgeous blossoms. She gave them to the secretaries, to her fellow editors, to anyone who would take them—much to the hilarity of the entire office staff. But still they kept coming. Lisa was furious, amused, and touched in turn. That a man such as Sam was capable of such a gesture—she would never have believed it if the incontrovertible proof did not fill her eyes and her nostrils every minute of every working day.

"Please stop, Sam," she wailed one night about a week later. As had become his habit, he had met her after work and taken her to dinner—at a fast-food place this time, because they were going on to see a movie. "I'm drowning in flowers; the whole office is drowning in flowers! What do you think you're doing?"

He looked at her meditatively while munching on a french fry. "Don't you know?" She shook her head. "I'm courting you, my darling Lisa," he said with a grin. And turned his attention to his meal despite her best efforts to continue the conversation.

After two weeks, the arrival of the flowers was a commonplace part of her day. Every desk in the building was decorated with them. Lisa threw out faded blossoms only to have their place taken by new ones. Then, over hot dogs at a baseball game, Sam told her that something had come up and he had to return to the Circle C for a while.

"How long will you be gone?" Lisa asked, conscious of a sudden feeling of emptiness in the pit of her stomach. The half of the hot dog she had eaten suddenly felt like a pound of lead inside her.

"A week—maybe two. I wouldn't go if it wasn't necessary." He looked at her, and lifted his hand to wipe a trace of mustard from her lower lip. "Lisa—come with me."

Lisa returned his look, her eyes touching on every plane and angle of that harshly carved face. Slowly she shook her head.

"I'm—not ready. I need more time, Sam."

He drew in a harsh breath. "I can't stay here forever," he said in a low, tight voice. "You're going to have to make up your mind one way or the other. I'll want your answer when I come back. And I'm warning you, if you say no, I won't ask again. So think hard while I'm gone, Lisa."

She blinked at him. The charming, lighthearted companion who had laughed with her and teased her over the past two weeks had been replaced by a man who was suddenly as hard and unyielding as granite. He meant what he said, she had no doubt. Before she could reply, he was on his feet, taking her arm and practically lifting her from the unyielding wooden bleacher. On the drive home he spoke not a word. And at the door to her apartment, he left her without even the meager good-night kiss she had come to crave.

With Sam gone, each day seemed at least a week long. She even missed the daily arrival of the flowers. On her regular visit to her obstetrician for her routine prenatal check, she found herself wishing vainly that Sam was with her, ready to share in the growing excitement of their coming child. In bed at night, she longed for him; her dreams were filled with the height and breadth of him, his smile, his eyes; when she woke in the morning, her pillow would be damp where she had cried for him the night before. At work, she had to put a good face on the inevitable remarks that accompanied the cessation of the flowers—and the absence of Sam waiting for her each night, which it seemed every female on the magazine's staff noticed. In short, she missed him more than she had ever dreamed possible. But still—still, she could not make up her mind to marry him. If she was this devastated by his absence after only two weeks, what would it be like if she married him—allowed herself once again to love him without reserve—and it didn't work out? She was very much afraid that she would die of grief—or allow it to destroy her.

Amos came to see her, as he had every week since she had moved into the apartment—except, now that she thought about it, when Sam had been with her. He tried to be casual, tried his best not to mention Sam, but Lisa wasn't having any of that.

"Did you call Sam? Before he came, I mean. Did you tell him about the baby?" Her eyes and voice were accusing.

Amos, seated on her couch with a glass of iced tea in his hand, looked up at her with something resembling alarm. "No, of course not," he said. But Lisa was not convinced.

"Amos, I'm on the verge of making the biggest decision of my life. And I need all the facts. Please, if you told Sam about the baby before he came to see me, tell me. I need to know. It's very important to me, Amos."

"I didn't call him, granddaughter. I'll admit, I thought about it; I wanted to. But you told me to keep out of it, and I decided that you were enough of an adult to make your own decision about this. I give you my word of honor that I didn't tell Eastman that you were expecting his child. As far as I know, he knew nothing about it until he saw for himself."

Lisa was silent. Her grandfather's voice carried the ring of truth. Not that he wouldn't lie to her, she knew, if he thought it was for her own good, but this time she tended to believe him. Maybe because she wanted to, she thought with an inward grimace.

"He wants to marry you." It was a statement, not a question. Nevertheless, Lisa nodded. Amos snorted impatiently.

"Then for God's sake, girl, what are you shilly-shallying about? Six months ago you were crazy to have him! He's the father of that baby you're carrying, and whether you like it or not that means something. And, though he's not the man I would have picked for you, he's a good man. He cares about you. He'll keep you safe. I won't be around forever, Lisa, and I'd feel better knowing that you were married to him. He strikes me as the kind of man who looks after his own—you and that boy of his and the baby."

Lisa looked at him sharply. Never before had she heard him mention his possible demise. Could he be ill, and not telling her? But he looked as robust as ever, sitting there in his immaculate gray suit with the white shirt and tasteful silk tie and matching pocket square that made up his inevitable Sunday uniform. And something about the expression in his eyes told her that he'd been playing on her sympathies.

"Amos, you old fraud, you'll live to be a hundred, so don't try that on me. If—and I say *if*—I decide to marry Sam, it won't be to ease your worry on your deathbed! Now come on, if you're going to take me to church, we'd better go. We're going to be late as it is."

The next few days passed even more slowly than the first week of Sam's absence had. It was torture not knowing exactly when he would be back. He didn't call, which surprised Lisa until she figured out that he was giving her a chance to see how much she missed him. She could have called him—getting his number from the directory service in Montana would have been ridiculously easy—but she didn't. To take the initiative and call him would have seemed too much like an admission of some kind.

Finally, exactly twelve days, four hours, and sixteen minutes after Sam had told her goodbye, Lisa decided that a burst of activity was what she needed to work off the blues that threatened to engulf her. She would paint the bathroom ceiling, as she had been meaning to do ever since she'd moved into the apartment. The previous tenant had apparently had a thing for hot pink, and that was the color of the ceiling. Lisa meant to change it to a cool, unnauseating white.

She had been up on the ladder for almost an hour when a knock sounded on the door. Probably the girl who lived downstairs, wanting to chat, Lisa surmised as she climbed down off the ladder and stretched her cramped back. The girl was very nice, as was her young husband, but Lisa wasn't in the mood for idle conversation. Her back hurt, she was tired, and she missed Sam. In her book, that added up to nothing short of misery.

Still, she pasted a smile on her lips as she opened the door. It widened with incredulous delight as she saw who stood there, an answering smile curving his lips and a bouquet of red roses in one hand.

"Not more flowers," she said, groaning automatically, when what she really wanted to do was throw herself in his arms and cling and cling.

"I thought you might have missed them," he explained, thrusting them at her as he walked in without waiting for an invitation.

Lisa closed the door behind him and moved toward the kitchen, where she hoped to find at least one container that had not been pressed into flower duty at the office. Sam followed her, lounging against the arched door that led from the hallway to the small kitchen, his arms crossed over his chest as he watched her search through the cabinets.

"Did you?" he asked softly.

Lisa, having located a plastic pitcher and begun to fill it with water, looked at him over her shoulder. "Did I what?"

"Miss the flowers. And me."

"The flowers, no. I was beginning to feel like I was working in a funeral parlor. You—what do you think?"

She set the roses in the pitcher and put the make-shift flower arrangement on a side counter. Then she turned to face him, fighting like mad to quell the urge to fling herself at him and press kisses all over that bronzed face. Dressed in jeans and a ridiculous Hawaiian-print shirt, he was so handsome he took her breath. Ruefully, she thought of her own paint-spattered jeans and the ancient, once-white shirt that had belonged to Jeff. In the glamor department, he won hands down, she conceded, and had to grin to herself. She'd never thought that she'd live to see the day when the male in her life was more beautiful than she!

"I think you did. I know I missed you. I came back two days sooner than I should have because I couldn't stand to stay away any longer."

Lisa stared at him, mesmerized, as he straightened away from the door and came toward her. Then she no longer had to fight the impulse to throw herself at him because he was taking her in his arms and holding her close against his hard muscles, his arms tight around her but gentle, as if he was mindful of the baby, his mouth seeking hers. . . . She met those warm lips eagerly, kissing him with a passion that was almost shocking when she remembered, later, that she was pregnant, her arms twining around his neck, her fingers tangling in the thick softness of his hair.

"You missed me," he said with satisfaction when finally he had to let her come up for air.

Lisa couldn't have said anything to refute that smug statement even if she'd wanted to. Her impassioned response to his kiss had answered for her.

"Lisa..." he began in a throaty, thickened voice.

She thought, Uh-oh, here it comes. The moment of decision. She had been dreading it, waiting for it, hoping for it, for days. Yet still she wasn't sure what answer to give. At least, she told herself she wasn't.

"What on earth have you been doing?" he said in a totally different tone, pushing her a little away from him and lifting his hand to touch the bridge of her nose. When he drew back his finger, it was streaked with white paint.

"Oh. Painting." Lisa rubbed self-consciously at her nose. Though she refused to admit it even to herself, she felt just the tiniest bit disappointed that he had not gone ahead and pressed her for her decision. He had been distracted by a little bit of white paint.... Despite herself, Lisa felt more than a trifle piqued.

"Painting what?"

She disengaged herself from his arms, struggling to overcome a rising spiral of indignation. Did he want to marry her or didn't he? she wondered acerbically. Because if he did, he sure didn't seem in any hurry to demand her answer!

"The bathroom ceiling."

"Show me."

The words were clipped, but Lisa was too caught up in her own feelings to notice. As far as she was concerned, the bathroom ceiling was pretty low on her list of immediate priorities. She wanted to be wooed, dammit—and, yes, won! She did not want to stand around discussing the activities of her day.

"It's in the bathroom."

If there was sarcasm in her voice—and there was—it didn't stop Sam from following her down the hall to the bathroom. He stopped in the doorway, frowning, while she walked on inside and gestured at the ceiling, which was now about one-quarter white.

"See?"

His lips tightened. "Oh, I see, all right," he said, his eyes surveying the paint can and brush balanced precariously on the top rung of the ladder. "I see you're not safe to be left alone! You little idiot, don't you know better than to go climbing around on ladders in your condition?"

The anger in his tone nettled her. She put her hands on her hips and glared back at him.

"You're not my keeper, Sam Eastman!" she flared. "If I want to paint my ceiling—in my *condition*—I will! And don't call me an idiot!"

"You need a keeper," he retorted grimly, totally ignoring her ending salvo. "And if you don't have enough sense to stay off ladders while you're expecting a baby—*my* baby—then I'll see to it that you get one!"

"Oh, you will, will you?"

Lisa's green eyes flashed sparks at him. With speckles of white paint dotting her nose and cheeks like freckles and more streaks of white decorating her ponytailed hair, she looked like the little girl on one of the popular hamburger commercials—except for her rounded stomach, which was unmistakable even in the overlarge man's shirt she wore. Sam glared at her. Lisa glared back, then swung around and with a defiant flourish scooped up the still-wet paintbrush and started to ascend the ladder.

"If I want to paint my ceiling—with *my* baby—I will, so there!"

She reached the top of the ladder as she spoke, and stretched up to take a defiant swipe at the ceiling. Before she could repeat it, or look around to measure his reaction, his hands were on her waist, lifting her down from her perch as if she weighed no more than a little child.

"Put me down!"

As soon as her feet touched the floor, she hit out at him with the handiest weapon—which happened to be the paintbrush. It caught him full in the face. Lisa stared, aghast, as the bronzed features were overlaid with a thick, dripping coat of white—and then as his eyes opened, twin spheres of cobalt blue regarding her with mingled anger and disbelief from amid that oozing mask, she giggled. And giggled again.

He glared at her. Then his lips twitched. Seconds later that twitch turned into a full-scale grin.

"Bitch," he said with curious satisfaction.

Lisa didn't have long to wonder at his tone. He bent his head toward her despite her shrieking protests, capturing her mouth with his and stealing her breath with a hot, hard kiss that managed to share the coating of paint very effectively.

"Isn't there a saying about he who laughs last?" Sam murmured, grinning down into her white-smeared face after he released her. His arms were still locked loosely around her waist.

Lisa laughed back at him, her hands—one still holding the paintbrush—coming up to rub ineffectively at her cheeks. He looked so funny with paint covering his nose and cheeks and running down his chin, and so handsome despite it, with his black hair in wild disorder and his blue eyes twinkling at her, and so dear that her heart turned over in her breast. Suddenly she knew that her decision was made—had been made, probably, since he had first shown up in her apartment wanting to take care of her and the baby. For better or worse, she was going to take one more chance. On Sam. On love.

Paintbrush and all, she reached up to twine her arms around his neck and tell him so.

Epilogue

Sam sat in a chair in Lisa's hospital room, watching her as she lay sleeping, feeling utterly drained. It was eight o'clock on the morning of September 14. A Wednesday. Lisa had given birth by cesarian section to a little girl, Katherine Elizabeth, during the night. Standing helpless outside the operating-room door while they had cut his child from the unconscious body of the woman he loved had been the worst experience of his life. He had prayed endlessly, bargaining with God, willing to sell his soul to the devil if it could be arranged, if in so doing it would save Lisa's life. During the two months since their marriage, they had been happy, almost unbelievably so. Lisa had taken to life on the Circle C like a spaniel to water, decorating the house, getting a room ready for the baby, doing her best to cook a fair portion of their meals, being a friend as well as a stepmother to Jay and a wife to Sam. Such happiness had been too good to last. Sam had known it all along—feared it. And last night he had feared that the time had come to pay the piper. With Lisa's life. It had seemed like a miracle when the doctor had come out with the little girl in his arms and told him that Lisa would be all right. For the first time since he was twenty-three years old, he had felt tears run down his cheeks.

He had hardly spared the infant a glance, although he supposed that he would be interested enough in her now that Lisa was out of danger. During the last weeks, he had visited her obstetrician with her, taken part in childbirth-education classes, planned to be with her throughout the birth of their baby. But last night had been so unexpected, so horrible, that he hadn't quite recovered from the shock. She had started hemorrhaging at the ranch.... Even now he could see the blood that had soaked through the blanket he had wrapped around her for the mad drive to the hospital. Small wonder that he hadn't felt an upsurge of fatherly affection for the wrinkled mite who had caused her such pain, and himself such fright. But he would, he promised himself, he would.... He had not slept at all the night before, in fact had not slept in more than twenty-four hours. Suddenly he was conscious of feeling dead tired. His eyes felt like they had lead weights attached to the lids. If he could close them, just for a second ...

When Lisa awoke, the first thing she saw was Sam sprawled in what looked to be a very uncomfortable upright chair, his head lolling back against its vinyl upholstery, his arms trailing limply to the floor on either side of him. He was sound asleep; a faint snore issued periodically from between his parted lips. Lisa smiled at the long form and hard face softened now as he slept. She had only hazy memories of what had taken place the previous afternoon and night, but she could recall him constantly at her side until the doctors had put her to sleep. He had been a tower of strength for her throughout the ordeal, rushing her to the hospital while masking his fear so as not to increase hers, carrying her into the emergency entrance, holding her hand while wave after wave of burning pain had tortured her body. . . .

Their baby: she had not yet seen their baby, did not even know if it was a boy or a girl. In a sudden fever of impatience, she sat up, wincing at the soreness of her abdomen, and pushed the nurses' call button by the bed. A white-clad nurse appeared almost instantly.

"I want to see my baby," Lisa said, speaking softly so as not to wake Sam. The nurse followed the direction of her glance, and smiled.

"I always think it's harder on the father," she said with a twinkle, and went out. When she came back, she was carrying a squirming infant in her arms.

"My baby!" Lisa said, enraptured, holding out her arms to take the precious bundle. "Is it a boy, or . . . ?"

"Mrs. Eastman, meet Katherine Elizabeth Eastman. Your husband gave us the name you picked out while you were asleep."

"A girl," Lisa whispered as the woman placed the blanket-wrapped bundle in her arms.

"Call me when you want me," the nurse said, smiling at Lisa's absorbed expression as she inspected her tiny daughter. Then she went out.

Lisa stared down at her child, enraptured by the crinkly little face topped by a crown of dark hair. She unwrapped the blanket swaddling the child, inspecting its tiny, bowed legs and waving arms, counting its little fingers and toes. The little girl kicked and wriggled, but she kept her eyes shut and she didn't cry.

"What do you think?" The voice was Sam's.

Lisa looked up to find him straightening in the

chair, watching her with an almost diffident expression on his dark face. Lisa smiled blindingly at him.

"I think she's beautiful," she said sincerely.

"She must take after you, then." His smile was warm.

Lisa grinned at him. "No, as a matter of fact, I think she looks more like you. See?"

Lisa lifted their daughter so that he could see the spiky black hair covering the tiny skull. Sam leaned closer, looking fascinatedly at his daughter.

"I don't think I've ever seen anything that small." He sounded awed.

Lisa laughed, and eased herself a little higher against the pillows, cradling the child against her breast.

"She'll grow."

"Yes." Sam cleared his throat, his eyes suddenly intent as they met hers. "I love you, Lisa."

Lisa smiled at him. But before she could return the compliment, as she had every intention of doing, the tiny scrap in her arms let out a little mewling cry. Lisa looked down, surprised to see that the child's eyes were open at last as she chewed hungrily on one miniscule fist. To Lisa's amazement, they were blue. Not the baby blue of nearly all infants, which in many cases changes with time, but a striking cobalt blue as deep and arresting as that of the man who had fathered her.

As Lisa stared down at that tiny face, which she guessed would in time become a feminized version of Sam's, she was shaken by the enormity of the emotion that surged through her. Never in her life had she felt anything like the strength of the love that swept her. She looked from Katherine Elizabeth's slightly unfocused blue eyes to the very focused ones of the man she loved, and smiled tenderly.

"I love you, too," she said to Sam, meaning it from the depths of her soul. Then she looked back at her daughter. "Both of you."